THE RIVALS OF SHERLOCK HOLMES

THE GREATEST DETECTIVE STORIES: 1837-1914

EDITED BY

GRAEME DAVIS

PEGASUS CRIME

NEW YORK LONDON

THE RIVALS OF SHERLOCK HOLMES

Pegasus Crime is an imprint of
Pegasus Books Ltd.
148 W 37th Street, 13th Floor
New York, NY 10018

Compilation copyright © 2019 by Graeme Davis

Introduction © 2019 by Graeme Davis

"The Origins of Sherlock Holmes" copyright © 2019 by Leslie S. Klinger

First Pegasus Books cloth edition June 2019

Interior design by Maria Fernandez

Library of Congress Cataloging-in-Publication Data is available.

ISBN: 978-1-64313-071-2

10 9 8 7 6 5 4 3 2 1

Printed in the United States of America
Distributed by W. W. Norton & Company

Dedicated to my wife, Jamie Paige Davis,
the best partner in crime—or detection—anyone could desire.
I love you.

CONTENTS

THE ORIGINS OF
SHERLOCK HOLMES[*]

by Leslie S. Klinger

Why did the twenty-seven-year-old Arthur Conan Doyle decide to write detective stories? What were the inspirations for the stories, the literary sources that Doyle drew upon? Understanding the context in which Doyle wrote, the authors and books that he knew and was inspired by, could lead to a greater understanding of why Sherlock Holmes became the Great Detective and why the tales of Holmes's adventures forever changed the course of literature.

Conan Doyle himself is—as perhaps is true of all writers—a less-than-reliable guide in connection with these questions. His autobiography, *Memories and Adventures*, offers some insights. "During these first ten years I was a rapid reader," he recalled. "My tastes were boylike enough, for Mayne Reid was my favourite author, and his 'Scalp Hunters' my favourite book."[†] He sold the first story he mentions writing, "The Mystery of Sasassa Valley," in 1879.[‡] Another early story recalled by Conan Doyle was "My Friend the Murderer" written in 1882.[§] He also recalled fondly "J. Habakuk Jephson's Statement" that he sold in 1884 to *Cornhill Magazine*. Some of these included supernatural or pseudo-supernatural

---

[*] A slightly modified version of this essay appears in the Winter 2018 issue of the *Baker Street Journal*.

[†] At thirteen. Thomas Mayne Reid (1818–1883) was a Scottish-Irish-American writer of dozens of adventure tales, usually set in exotic locations; his books were popular with children in the second half of the nineteenth century, and Theodore Roosevelt credited him as an influence on his interests.

[‡] It appeared anonymously in *Chambers's Journal*, No. 819 (6 Sep. 1879), pp. 568–572.

[§] It first appeared in the September 1882 issue of *London Society*, signed "A. Conan Doyle."

elements; none were detective stories. In 1886, however, about a year after his marriage, Conan Doyle decided, "I was capable of something fresher and crisper and more workmanlike. Gaboriau had rather attracted me by the neat dovetailing of his plots, and Poe's masterful detective, M. Dupin, had from boyhood been one of my heroes. But could I bring an addition of my own?"[*]

Famously, Conan Doyle credits his inspiration to write of Holmes to his "old teacher Joe Bell, of his eagle face, of his curious ways, of his eerie trick of spotting details. If he were a detective he would surely reduce this fascinating but unorganized business to something nearer to an exact science. I would try if I could get this effect."[†] But this can hardly be the whole picture. To understand the context of Conan Doyle's decision, we must first understand the existing body of "mystery" or crime fiction.

Dorothy L. Sayers, in her masterful introduction to *The Omnibus of Crime*, written in 1929, dates the earliest mystery writing to antiquity. The first four stories in that important anthology appeared in the Jewish Apocrypha, Herodotus, and the *Æneid*.[‡] There are other early examples of detective fiction. For example, E. T. A. Hoffmann's novella, *Mademoiselle de Scudéri*, a tale of detection of a serial killer, was published in 1819, and William Evans Burton's "The Secret Cell," featuring an unnamed police detective, was published in *The Gentleman's Magazine*, a short-lived American publication, in 1837. There is no basis, however, for thinking that Conan Doyle knew these stories or paid any real attention to them.

Crime writing, as contrasted with the writing of crime fiction, was of course already widespread by the second half of the nineteenth century. The earliest crime writing was probably "execution" sermons, accounts of the careers of heinous criminals recounted from the pulpit for the benefit of congregations hungry to learn more about the sins that they were exhorted to avoid. It appears that truthful accounts were often supplemented by sermonizers who had limited access to criminal records and historical documents, and in some cases, shocking as it may seem, well-intentioned preachers invented appropriate life stories for the benefit of their flocks. A similar dissemination of stories of crime and punishment occurred in both England and America in the form of broadsheets, penny-priced tabloids consisting of a single printed sheet of history and testimony of notorious criminals, complete with colorful illustrations, often sold to enormous audiences

---

[*] Arthur Conan Doyle, *Memories and Adventures*, London: Hodder and Stoughton, p. 74.

[†] Conan Doyle, p. 75.

[‡] These were, respectively, *The History of Bel* and *The History of Susanna, The Story of Hercules and Cacus*, and *The Story of Rhampsinitus*.

of public executions. *The Newgate Calendar,* a chapbook first published in 1773 by the officials of Newgate Prison and later by other opportunistic publishers, contained garishly illustrated accounts of historical and contemporary criminals. *The New Newgate Calendar* was published in 1826 in a four-volume set, and ultra-cheap editions began to appear in the 1860s. So popular was the *Calendar* that it was said to have been as likely to be found in English homes as the Bible.

A significant factor in the growth of crime fiction was the advent of the idea of official police. Previously, the prevention of crime and the apprehension of criminals were matters left to the general populace. For example, in William Godwin's *Things as They Are; or The Adventures of Caleb Williams* (1794), a novel of an obsessive pursuit of an innocent man, no officials take the suspect into custody, merely a "lover of justice" and his servants. Similarly, in *Frankenstein, or The Modern Prometheus* (1818), when Justine Moritz and, later, Victor Frankenstein are incarcerated and examined for various crimes, no law enforcement officials are mentioned other than prosecutors or judicial officers.

In the first half of the nineteenth century, organized governmentally-sponsored policing was implemented throughout most of the English-speaking world, and with the rise of the official police came the detective. Short for "detective-police," a phrase appearing in *Chambers's Journal* in 1843, the detective force was a special branch of the police. *Chambers's* described them as "intelligent men," who attired themselves in the dress of ordinary men.

As the public began to interact with professional criminal investigators, books about these fascinating figures appeared. The first great writer of tales of criminal detection was the Frenchman Eugène Vidocq (1775–1857), whose memoirs—some of dubious historicity—and works of admitted fiction found a ready audience. Vidocq, a reformed criminal, was appointed in 1813 to be the first head of the Sûreté Nationale, the outgrowth of an informal detective force created by Vidocq and adopted by Napoleon as a supplement to the police. His memoirs, which first appeared in 1828, recounted his adventures in the detection and capture of criminals, often involving disguises and wild flights. Later books told of his criminal career, and sensational novels published under his name (probably written by others) capitalized on his reputation as a bold detective. Vidocq's impoverished and criminal early life is likely the model for the character of Jean Valjean, the heroic victim of Victor Hugo's *Les Misérables* (1862). The story begins in 1815, and much of its plot tells of the pursuit of Valjean by Javert, a police inspector. While there were such police in France at that date, Hugo's novel reflects in no small part the popular reaction to the growth of official police forces later in the century.

While Vidocq's stories captivated the public, they were not billed as original tales of detective fiction. Although others had written of sleuthing,* the first great purveyor of fictional stories about a detective was Edgar Allan Poe (1809–1849), whose Chevalier C. Auguste Dupin set the standard for a generation to come. The cerebral Dupin first appeared in Poe's short story "The Murders in the Rue Morgue" (1841). At the same time, Poe introduced another staple of detective fiction, the partner and chronicler (nameless in Poe's tales) who is less intelligent than the detective but serves as a sounding board for the detective's brilliant deductions. In each of the three Dupin stories—the other two are "The Mystery of Marie Rogêt" (1842) and "The Purloined Letter" (1844)—the detective outwits the police and shows them to be ineffective crime-fighters and problem-solvers. Yet Poe apparently lost interest in the notion, and his detective "series" ended with the third Dupin tale.

By his own admission, Conan Doyle was deeply influenced by Poe's stories. Despite Holmes's scoffing that Dupin was "inferior,"† there are clear resemblances. Dupin is a private individual who works with the official police yet is critical of their methods, a careful observer of minute traces of evidence, a meticulous examiner of logical chains of action, and a heavy smoker (smoking a meerschaum pipe, ironically identified with Holmes, though the latter likely never smoked one); he does his best reasoning in his closed-up apartment in an atmosphere of tobacco. His adventures are chronicled by a Watson-like character, though John Watson is certainly to be credited as a vastly more likeable and therefore credible narrator.

It is harder to see the influence on Conan Doyle of the work of Émile Gaboriau, the French writer who drew heavily on Vidocq as his model for the detective known as Monsieur Lecoq. First appearing in *L'Affaire Lerouge* (1866), Lecoq was a minor police detective who rose to fame in six cases published between 1866 and 1880. Lecoq does follow evidence logically, such as deducing whether a bed has been slept in or observing when a clock was wound, but these are not central elements of his methods. Although Holmes describes Lecoq as a "miserable bungler," Gaboriau's works were immensely popular, and it may well be that the most important influence that Gaboriau had on Conan Doyle was the realization

---

* For example, Edward Bulwer-Lytton wrote the underappreciated multi-genre novel *Pelham*, first published in 1828, in the last quarter of which the eponymous protagonist takes up sleuthing to solve a murder.

† In *A Study in Scarlet*, after Watson remarks Holmes reminds him of Dupin, Holmes replies, "'No doubt you think that you are complimenting me in comparing me to Dupin. . . . Now, in my opinion, Dupin was a very inferior fellow. That trick of his of breaking in on his friends' thoughts with an apropos remark after a quarter of an hour's silence is really very showy and superficial. He had some analytical genius, no doubt; but he was by no means such a phenomenon as Poe appeared to imagine.'"

that he could make a good living from his writing. Fergus Hume, the English author of the best-selling detective novel of *The Mystery of a Hansom Cab* (1886),* explained that Gaboriau's financial success inspired his own work.

In England, criminals and detectives appeared from time to time in Charles Dickens's tales as well. While not widely regarded as an author of detective fiction, Dickens created Inspector Bucket, the first significant detective in English literature. When Bucket appeared in *Bleak House* (1852–1853), he became the prototype of the official representative of the police department: honest, diligent, stolid, and confident, albeit not very colorful, dramatic, or exciting. Wilkie Collins, author of two of the greatest nineteenth-century novels of suspense—*The Woman in White* (1860) and *The Moonstone* (1868)—created a similar character, Sergeant Cuff, in *The Moonstone*. Cuff is known as the finest police detective in England, who solves his cases with perseverance and energy, rather than genius. Sadly, after *The Moonstone*, he is not heard from again. In each case, however, the detective is too late to help any of the affected persons, and while Bucket and Cuff may have been known to Conan Doyle and reshaped into the policemen of the Canon, there are no real resemblances between anyone in the works of Dickens or Collins and Sherlock Holmes.

Another important but often-overlooked part of the stream of detective fiction is the dime novel, or penny dreadful as it was known in England. These serials started in the 1830s in England, originally as a cheaper alternative to mainstream fictional part-works, such as those by Charles Dickens (which cost a shilling a part) for working class adults. By the 1850s, the serial stories were aimed exclusively at teenagers.† Although many of the stories were reprints or rewrites of Gothic thrillers, some stories were possibly historical urban legends such as Sweeney Todd and Spring-Heeled Jack or had lurid titles like *The Boy Detective; or, The Crimes of London* (1866) and *The Dance of Death; or, The Hangman's Plot. A Thrilling Romance of Two Cities* (1866, by "Detective Brownlow and Monsieur Tuevoleur, Sergeant of the French Police") or a series like *Lives of the Most Notorious Highwaymen, Footpads and Murderers* (1836–1837). Highwaymen were popular protagonists. *Black Bess or the Knight of the Road*, outlining the largely imaginary exploits of real-life highwayman Dick Turpin, continued for 254 episodes. Did Conan Doyle partake of these readily available entertainments as a young man? He never said.

---

* The book sold over 500,000 copies worldwide.

† Early popular American titles include *The Old Sleuth, Butts the Boy Detective*, and, of course, countless Sexton Blake and Nick Carter stories.

The 1860s, when Conan Doyle was a child, was a decade that witnessed the birth of the detective novel. There is much debate about which title deserves the crown as the first, but worthy candidates include *The Trail of the Serpent* (1860) by Mary Elizabeth Braddon, *The Notting Hill Mystery* (1862) by Charles Felix,* and *The Dead Letter* (1864) by Metta Victoria Fuller Victor (as "Seeley Regester"), the first American crime novel.†

Although well known later in her career as a prolific author of "sensation" fiction, Mary Elizabeth Braddon (1835–1915) also wrote an important crime novel, *The Trail of the Serpent*. Originally titled *Three Times Dead; or, The Secret of the Heath*,‡ it focuses on Jabez North (Ephraim East in the original verison), a criminal who changes his identity three times, and Mr. Peters (Waters in the original), an unrelenting, mute police-detective. Peters bears little resemblance to Sherlock Holmes. For example, although he makes astute observations about the "clean soles" of a man's body found in a field, he fails to observe either the identifying tattoo on the arm of the corpse or the absence of a telltale scar on his forehead and accepts the corpse as evidence that the criminal he sought was dead. Only years later when he rediscovers the criminal (the body was that of his unknown twin brother) does he mention the clean soles and the absence of the scar. The story, like so many sensational novels before it, is filled with coincidences that ultimately bring about the clever villain's capture. If Conan Doyle knew the book—the popularity of Braddon's later work might have brought it to his attention—it surely represented the very kind of "detective" writing he had in mind to avoid.

The Notting Hill Mystery is a remarkable work, an assemblage of crime scene reports, maps, depositions, and commentary by the detective, an insurance investigator. Julian Symons hailed it as an important forerunner of twentieth-century "police procedurals," with a style very different from its sensational forerunners.§ However, the only deduction based on observation is made by a police officer, not the investigator, and the deduction is a minor one, relating

---

* The story was first published in eight parts in 1862–1863 in *Once a Week Magazine*. It was published as a single volume in 1865 by Saunders, Otley & Co. Although the author's true identity was not revealed during his lifetime, Charles Warren Adams (1853–1903), the publisher of the magazine who wrote several other pseudonymous works that appeared in the magazine, is the likeliest candidate.

† The book first appeared in 1866, published in New York by Beadle & Co. It is doubtful that it had much circulation in England.

‡ The book was published under this title in 1860, revised and shortened as *The Trail of the Serpent* in 1861, serialized in the revised form in 1864, and thereafter published in numerous editions. Braddon, writing in 1893, expressed doubt that a single copy of the original book had been sold. The revised edition did quite well, however, as Braddon's reputation grew.

§ Julian Symons, *Bloody Murder*, New York, Viking, 1981, p. 52.

to the side of the bed on which a piece of paper was dropped. (The observation suggests that the paper was planted rather than dropped by the victim.) The means of murder—sympathetic commands via mesmerism—is so outlandish and dependent on near-mystical ideas as to make clear that no source of Conan Doyle's inspirations can be found here.

Similarly, *The Dead Letter* is devoid of Holmesian traces. Although Mr. Burton, the chief professional detective (the protagonist also does his own detecting), claims to be deeply versed in investigative techniques, the reader sees none. Indeed, the principal discoveries, of the whereabouts of key witnesses and the killer himself, are provided through the psychic talents of Burton's daughter. Although the murder is much less outré than that of *The Notting Hill Mystery*, the solution to the crime is provided by the confession of the hired killer, not deductive reasoning or a chain of evidence. Especially in light of its relative obscurity, it is not likely that Conan Doyle would have read it when he began his reading in the new genre.

Of course, there were also plentiful short-story writers plowing the fields of crime fiction. Dozens of books appeared between the time of Vidocq's memoirs and the 1890s that purported to be memoirs or reminiscences of police detectives. One of the earliest in English was *Richmond; or, Scenes in the Life of a Bow Street Officer, Drawn up from His Private Memoranda*, published anonymously in 1827, purported to be true tales of criminal detection (though now thought to be largely fictional). Another was *Recollections of a Police-Officer* by "Waters," first published in New York in 1852 under the title *Recollections of a Policeman* as by Thomas Waters, and in London in 1856.* Others of this period include Warren Warner's *Experiences of a Barrister* (1852), Gustavas Sharp's *The Confessions of an Attorney* (1852),† James Holbrook's *Ten Years among the Mail Bags: or, Notes from the Diary of a Special Agent of the Post-Office Department* (1855), Charles Martel's *Detective's Notebook* and *Diary of an Ex-Detective* (both 1860), Henry

---

*   Ellery Queen, *Queen's Quorum*, Boston: Little, Brown and Company, 1951, p. 14, thought the London edition was "probably pirated, the text lifted from 'Chambers's Edinburgh Journal' and 'some of our American Magazines.'"

†   Warren Warner and Gustavas Sharp were both pseudonyms of Samuel Warren, a barrister with Edinburgh medical training. He also wrote *Passages from the Diary of a Late Physician* (1832) and *Leaves from the Diary of a Law Clerk* (1857). Andrew Lycett asserts that Conan Doyle was familiar with his work. (*Conan Doyle: The Man Who Created Sherlock Holmes*, p. 110). The *Barrister* book featured a pair of attorneys named Ferret and Sharpe, while the *Attorney* book is written in the first person by Mr. Sharp, whose partner is Mr. Flint. These are names that Doyle made fun of: "I still possess the leaf of a notebook with various alternative names [for Sherlock Holmes]," he wrote in *Memories and Adventures*. "One rebelled against the elementary art which give some inkling of character in the name, and creates Mr. Sharps or Mr. Ferrets." (p. 75) This jest certainly suggests that he was familiar with Warren's work.

R. Addison's *Diary of a Judge: Being Trials of Life Drawn from the Note-book of a Recently Deceased Judge* (1860), Andrew Forrester's *Revelations of a Private Detective* (1863), William Russell's *Autobiography of a London Detective* (1864), and James M'Govan's *Brought to Bay or Experiences of a City Detective* (1878).* It is certain that the great bulk of the material contained in these books was fictional. Others were more straightforwardly writing fiction. Robert Louis Stevenson, whom Conan Doyle greatly admired and who later praised the Holmes stories as "the class of literature that I like when I have the toothache,"† published *New Arabian Nights* in 1882, a collection of his stories which includes "The Suicide Club," three connected mysteries. In 1886, Dick Donovan (the pen name of Joyce Emerson Preston Muddock) began his tremendous output of more than 300 detective and mystery stories, purporting to be accounts of his own adventures.‡

Of course, there were also many writers producing crime fiction outside of England, including the Australian author Mary Fortune, who wrote over 500 police procedural short stories between 1865 and 1908, and Anna Katharine Green, whose *The Leavenworth Case* (1878) is hailed as the first full-fledged American detective novel. While Fortune worked in virtual anonymity, Green was a great success. Green's output included thirteen stories about New York police detective Ebenezer Gryce (including *The Leavenworth Case*, though Gryce's work is not instrumental in catching the killer there), the last appearing in 1917. Green created several other memorable detectives as well: Amelia Butterworth, a spinster and probable model for Christie's Miss Marple, and Violet Strange, a debutante who becomes a professional detective to pay for her sister's debut.

That others were making serious attempts to write high quality "crime fiction" may have impressed the young Arthur Conan Doyle, but it was far from his chosen field. It must be remembered that he did not return to Sherlock Holmes after selling *A Study in Scarlet*; instead, devoting himself to the historical novel *Micah Clarke*. *The Sign of the Four* was an interruption of his serious work on the great historical novel *The White Company*, and even while the first six of *The*

---

* The last was by William C. Honeyman (1845–1919), a Scottish violinist and orchestra leader, who wrote a long series of fictional reminiscences of a "city detective" as well as a number of books on the violin. It is certainly tempting to think that Conan Doyle was familiar with the man or his work.

† Robert Louis Stevenson, letter to Conan Doyle, 5 April 1893.

‡ Muddock probably eventually met Conan Doyle, for Muddock's daughter Dorothy married Herbert Greenhough Smith, Conan Doyle's editor at *The Strand*, in 1900 (though the wedding took place in the first quarter of the year, while Conan Doyle was in South Africa). However, Muddock mentions none of Dorothy, Herbert, or Conan Doyle in his 1907 autobiography *Pages from an Adventurous Life*, and Doyle does not mention Muddock in his autobiography.

Adventures of Sherlock Holmes were appearing, he published *Beyond the City*, a tale of suburban life, and dove into his long historical novel *The Refugees*. Conan Doyle finished writing the last of *The Memoirs* tales in early 1893 and put Holmes aside—for good, or so he planned.[*]

Willard Wright, the author of the enormously successful Philo Vance mysteries that appeared in the 1920s and 1930s, famously spent two years of convalescence reading widely in crime fiction before setting out to make his fortune as a popular writer.[†] Conan Doyle did not. In his ode to beloved books, *Through the Magic Door*—based on essays he wrote in 1894, shortly after the success of Sherlock Holmes—he mentions only two of the authors discussed here, Poe and Stevenson. In neither case does he mention their stories of detection. Conan Doyle's eye was on what he believed to be greater prizes: He sought to be known for his historical fiction and his literary work. Crime fiction was only one of many possible paths to the financial success he sought, with the aim of providing himself the freedom to write books that mattered (in his estimation). Every bit of evidence suggests he read narrowly, if at all, in the genre when he was young and had little interest in crafting crime fiction.[‡] Only the serendipitous thought of his old teacher Joseph Bell appears to have led him to the path to becoming the greatest writer of detective tales ever to put pen to paper.

---

[*]   One wonders whether Doyle ever discussed crime fiction with his friend Israel Zangwill, who published his mystery novel *The Big Bow Mystery* (generally regarded as the first "locked-room" mystery) in 1892, just as Conan Doyle was concluding the first Holmes tales. That they discussed art and writing is apparent from Doyle's June 1894 "Before My Bookcase" essay in which he mentions that Zangwill admonished him that "mere horror was not art."

[†]   Wright also edited *The Great Detective Stories: A Chronological Anthology*, New York: Charles Scribner's Sons, 1927, and provided an extensive and learned introduction.

[‡]   Later in his career, Conan Doyle amassed a substantial collection of "true crime" writing, much of it acquired in 1911 from the collection of W. S. Gilbert. The collection is discussed in detail by Walter Klinefelter, in his essay "The Conan Doyle Crime Library," reprinted in Klinefelter's *Origins of Sherlock Holmes* (1983). Klinefelter observes that of the eighty items catalogued, only six books have publication dates before 1911 and *could* have been used as source material. However, Klinefelter concludes, "[I]f Conan Doyle did draw on them for anything prior to the stories of the 'Case-Book,' it could not have been of any great moment." Margalit Fox, in her excellent *Conan Doyle for the Defense* (New York: Random House, 2018), states: "Long an avid reader of detective fiction, Conan Doyle was also deeply interested in true crime." (p. 144) While it is evident from his writings after the turn of the century that the latter part of this statement is true, sadly there is no evidence of the former part, except his expressed admiration of Poe and Gaboriau.

INTRODUCTION

by Graeme Davis

Coal-smoke and fog wreathe the city, dampening the clop and rattle of hansom cabs in the street. A cry rings out; a body has been discovered. The family is distraught; the police are baffled. Only one detective can solve the case and bring the killer to justice: a brilliant thinker, a master of science, an eccentric genius, a detective named . . .

C Auguste Dupin, Martin Hewitt, Professor Augustus S. F. X. Van Dusen, Doctor John Thorndyke, Lady Molly Robertson-Kirk, Professor Craig Kennedy, Max Carrados, or one of many other detectives in the mystery story's first golden age.

Today, the figure of Sherlock Holmes towers over detective fiction like a colossus—but it was not always so. Edgar Allan Poe's French detective Dupin, the hero of "The Murders in the Rue Morgue," anticipated Holmes's deductive reasoning by more than forty years with his "tales of ratiocination." In *A Study in Scarlet,* the first of Holmes's adventures, Doyle acknowledged his debt to Poe—and to Émile Gaboriau, whose thief-turned-detective Monsieur Lecoq debuted in France twenty years earlier.

Although detective fiction did not emerge as a genre in the English language until the mid-nineteenth century, its roots run deep. The Old Testament story of Susanna and the Elders is regarded by some as an ancestor of the detective story, with Daniel as the detective. The story of "The Three Apples" in *The Thousand and One Nights* faces its protagonist, the vizier Ja'far, with a murder to solve, although he does little in the way of actual detection. Song Dynasty China (960–1279) saw the birth of *gong'an* ("legal fiction"), a genre of plays and puppet shows featuring a magistrate or other government official. By the succeeding

Yuan Dynasty (1271–1368), the form had expanded into novels: the adventures of some celebrated *gong'an* detectives, such as Judge Bao and Judge Dee, may still be found in print today.

In Europe, the novel emerged as a literary form in the eighteenth century, and fictional genres began to develop as readers found they liked one type of story or another. Stories involving crimes and feats of analysis began to appear across Europe from the middle of the century, and E. T. A. Hoffman's novella *Mademoiselle de Scudéri*, widely regarded as the first true detective story in European literature, was published in 1819.

While Poe's "The Murders in the Rue Morgue" is often hailed as the first detective story in English, it is not without antecedents. Published in 1793, William Godwin's three-volume novel *Things as They Are; or, The Adventures of Caleb Williams* shows how the legal system of the day could fail; its protagonist solves a murder, but detection takes a back seat to political and social commentary as he is framed by the aristocratic culprit and forced to live on the run. "The Secret Cell," by Poe's publisher William Evans Burton—with which this collection begins—appeared in the September 1837 issue of *The Gentleman's Magazine,* of which Poe became an editor two years later. By the time "The Murders in the Rue Morgue" was published, Burton had fired Poe and the two were bitter enemies. Even if he had been inspired by Burton's story, Poe would not have admitted it—and in any case, Burton's detective was a policeman rather than an amateur genius, and was remarkable only for his dogged persistence and familiarity with London's underworld.

If "Rue Morgue" was the first true detective story in English, the title of the first full-length detective novel is more hotly contested. Two books by Wilkie Collins—*The Woman in White* (1859) and *The Moonstone* (1868)—are often given that honor, with the latter showing many of the features that came to identify the genre: a locked-room murder in an English country house; bungling local detectives outmatched by a brilliant amateur detective; a large cast of suspects and a plethora of red herrings; and a final twist before the truth is revealed. Others point to Mary Elizabeth Braddon's *The Trail of the Serpent* (1861) or *Aurora Floyd* (1862), and others still to *The Notting Hill Mystery* (1862–3) by the pseudonymous "Charles Felix." Then there is *The Ticket-of-Leave Man* (1863), a melodrama translated from a French original, *Léonard* by Édouard Brisbarre and Eugène Nus, by dramatist Tom Taylor—best known today for *Our American Cousin,* the play Abraham Lincoln was watching when he was assassinated.

The debate about the first detective novel may never be settled, but what is certain—and certainly more interesting—is to note just how popular detective fiction had become by the early 1860s, both with the reading public and with writers from widely differing backgrounds. In the words of a contemporary music-hall song, there was a lot of it about.

This burst of detective fiction coincided neatly with the boyhood of Arthur Conan Doyle. While he publicly acknowledged the contributions of Poe and Gaboriau in the creation of Sherlock Holmes, he can hardly have failed to read, and be influenced by, other works in the developing genre of detective fiction.

Between 1887 and 1927, Doyle wrote four novels and fifty-six short stories featuring Holmes, and the success of the great detective brought both imitators and competitors. Doyle killed Holmes in "The Final Problem" (1893), beginning a nine-year hiatus in which many other fictional detectives tried to fill his shoes. The first—appearing in *The Strand* just three months later—was Martin Hewitt, another master of deduction; others followed, and in 1898, Doyle's brother-in-law E. W. Hornung published the first adventures of A. J. Raffles, the gentleman thief.

Holmes's return in *The Hound of the Baskervilles* only seemed to intensify the reading public's thirst, and no fictional detective was entirely free of his influence. There was Professor Augustus S. F. X. Van Dusen, "The Thinking Machine;" Doctor John Evelyn Thorndyke, a prototypical forensic scientist; Professor Craig Kennedy, scientist and gadgeteer; and Duckworth Drew of the Foreign Office, who combined the qualities of Sherlock Holmes and James Bond.

As the early years of detective fiction gave way to two separate golden ages—of hard-boiled tales in America and intricately-plotted, so-called "cosy" murders in Britain—the legacy of Sherlock Holmes, with his fierce devotion to science and logic, gave way to street smarts on the one hand and social insight on the other—but even though these new sub-genres went their own ways, their detectives still required the intelligence and clear-sightedness that characterized the earliest works of detective fiction: the trademarks of Sherlock Holmes, and of all the detectives featured in these pages.

THE SECRET CELL

by William Evans Burton

1837

While Edgar Allan Poe is often credited with the creation of the first fictional detective in the person of C. Auguste Dupin—one of whose adventures can be found later in this volume—he is not unchallenged in this claim. "The Secret Cell" was published four years before Dupin's debut in "The Murders in the Rue Morgue," and it is even possible that Burton's tale inspired Poe to pen a detective story in the first place.

Born in London, Burton tried to establish a monthly magazine before drifting into the theater. At the age of thirty he left an unsuccessful marriage, abandoning his wife and son to make a new life in the United States, working as an actor and manager in New York, Philadelphia, and Baltimore.

In 1837 he founded *Burton's Gentleman's Magazine* in Philadelphia, publishing "The Secret Cell" in the September issue, and in 1839 he employed Poe as an editor. The two did not get along: Burton disliked the harshness of Poe's literary reviews, and he may have written a particularly negative review of Poe's "The Narrative of Arthur Gordon Pym of Nantucket." Burton tried to sell the magazine without telling Poe, who responded by planning to launch a competing publication of his own. Burton fired Poe in 1840 and sold the magazine, using the money to renovate his theater—he had never entirely given up the stage—before returning to work as a writer and editor.

While a police officer rather than a private detective, Burton's hero L— is skilled in the art of disguise and enjoys the company of an admiring narrator, as Holmes does. Instead of the Baker Street Irregulars, he has a resourceful wife with a talent for eliciting information, and instead of Lestrade, he can call upon the services of a friendly magistrate and a number of subordinate officers. He needs all of these resources—and a modicum of luck—when the search for a missing person leads to the discovery of a large and disturbing criminal enterprise.

> I'll know no more—the heart is torn
> By views of woe we cannot heal;
> Long shall I see these things forlorn,
> And oft again their griefs shall feel,
> As each upon the mind shall steal;
> That wan projector's mystic style,
> That lumpish idiot leering by,
> That peevish idler's ceaseless wile,
> And that poor maiden's half-form'd smile.
> While straggling for the full-drawn sigh!
>
> — *Crabbe.*

About eight years ago, I was the humble means of unravelling a curious piece of villainy that occurred in one of the suburbs of London; it is well worth recording, in exemplification of that portion of "Life" which is constantly passing in the holes and corners of the Great Metropolis. My tale, although romantic enough to be a fiction, is excessively common-place in some of the details—it is a jumble of real life; a conspiracy, an abduction, a nunnery, and a lunatic asylum, are mixed up with constables, hackney-coaches, and an old washerwoman. I regret also that my heroine is not only without a lover, but is absolutely free from the influence of the passions, and is not persecuted on account of her transcendent beauty.

Mrs. Lobenstein was the widow of a German coachman, who had accompanied a noble family from the continent of Europe; and, anticipating a lengthened stay, he had prevailed upon his wife to bring over their only child, a daughter, and settle down in the rooms apportioned to his use, over the stable, in one of the fashionable mews at the west end of London. But Mr. Lobenstein had scarcely embraced his family, ere he was driven off, post haste, to the other world, leaving his destitute relict[*], with a very young daughter, to buffet her way along the rugged path of life.

With a little assistance from the nobleman in whose employ her husband had for some time been settled, Mrs. Lobenstein was enabled to earn a respectable livelihood, and filled the honorable situation of laundress to many families of gentility, besides divers[†] stray bachelors, dandies, and men about town. The little girl grew to be an assistance, instead of a drag, to her mother; and the widow found that her path was not entirely desolate, nor "choked with the brambles of despair."

In the sixth year of her bereavement, Mrs. Lobenstein, who presided over the destinies of my linen, called at my rooms, in company with a lady of equal width, breadth, and depth. Mrs. L. was of the genuine Hanseatic[‡] build—of the real Bremen beam—when in her presence, you felt the overwhelming nature of her pretensions to be considered a woman of some weight in the world, and standing in society. On the occasion of the visit in question, her friend was equally adipose, and it would have puzzled a conjurer to have turned the party into a tallowy[§] trio. Mrs. L. begged leave to recommend her friend as her successor in the lavatorial[¶] line—for her own part, she was independent of work, thank heaven! and meant to retire from the worry of trade.

I congratulated her on the successful termination of her flourish with the wash tubs.

"Oh, *I* have not made the money, bless you! I might have scrubbed my fingers to the bones before I could have done more than earn my daily bread, and get, maybe, a black silk gown or so for Sundays. No, no! my Mary has done more with her quiet, meeting-day face in one year, than either the late Mr. Lobenstein or myself could compass in our lives."

Mary Lobenstein, an artless, merry, blue-eyed girl of seventeen had attracted the attention of a bed-ridden lady whose linen she was in the habit of carrying home; and in compliance with the importunities of the old lady, she agreed to reside in her house as the invalid's sole and especial attendant. The old lady, luckily, was almost friendless; an hypocritical hyena of a niece, who expected,

---

[*] His penniless widow.

[†] Various

[‡] The Hanseatic League was an alliance of merchant guilds from northern Europe, principally Germany, which dominated Baltic trade in the Middle Ages. German towns like Bremen and Hamburg are still proud of their membership in the League.

[§] Tallow is beef or mutton fat.

[¶] Washing, in this instance. Literally translated from the original Latin, "lavatory" means "washroom."

and had been promised, the reversion of her fortune, would occasionally give an inquiry relative to the state of her aunt's health; but so miserably did she conceal her joy at the approach of the old lady's dissolution, that the party in question perceived her selfish and mercenary nature, and disgusted at her evident security of purpose, called in an attorney, and executed an entirely new will. There was no other relative to select—Mary Lobenstein had been kind and attentive; and, more from revenge than good nature, the old lady bequeathed the whole of her property to the lucky little girl, excepting a trifling annuity to the old maid, her niece, who also held the chance of possession in case of Mary's death.

When this will was read by the man of law, who brought it forth in due season after the old lady's demise, Mary's wonder and delight almost equaled the rage and despair of the hyena of a niece, whom we shall beg leave to designate by the name of Elizabeth Bishop. She raved and swore the deadliest revenge against the innocent Mary, who one minute trembled at the denunciations of the thin and yellow spinster, and in the next chuckled and danced at the suddenness of her unexpected good fortune.

Mr. Wilson, the lawyer, desired the disinherited to leave the premises to the legal owner, and stayed by Miss Mary Lobenstein and her fat mama till they were in full and undisturbed possession. The "good luck," as Mrs. L. called it, had fallen so suddenly upon them, that a very heavy wash was left unfinished, to attend to the important business; and the complaints of the naked and destitute customers alone aroused the lucky laundress to a sense of her situation. The right and privilege of the routine of customers were sold to another fat lady, and Mrs. Lobenstein called upon me, among the rest of her friends, to solicit the continuance of my washing for her stout successor.

A year passed away. I was lying in bed one wintry morning, and shivering with dread at the idea of poking my uncased legs into the cold air of the room, when my landlady disturbed my cogitations by knocking loudly at the room door, and requesting my instant appearance in the parlor, where "a fat lady in tears" wished my presence. The existence of the obese Mrs. Lobenstein had almost slipped my memory; and I was somewhat startled at seeing that lady, dressed in a gaudy colored silk gown, and velvet hat and feathers, in violent hysterics upon my crimson silk ottoman, that groaned beneath its burden. The attentions of my landlady and her domestic soon restored my *ci-devant** laundress to a state of comparative composure, when the distressed lady informed me that her daughter,

---

*   French: "from before," "former."

her only child, had been missing for several days, and that, notwithstanding the utmost exertions of herself, her lawyer, and her friends, she had been unable to obtain the smallest intelligence respecting her beloved Mary. She had been to the police offices, had advertised in the newspapers, had personally inquired of all her friends or acquaintance, yet every exertion had resulted in disappointment.

"Every body pities me, but no one suggests a means of finding my darling, and I am almost distracted. She left me one evening—it was quite early—to carry a small present to the chandlers'-shop woman, who was so kind to us when I was left a destitute widow. My dear girl had but three streets to go, and ran out without a cloak or shawl; she made her gift to the poor woman, and instantly set out to return home. She never reached home—and, woe is me, I fear she never will. The magistrates at the police office said that she had eloped with some sweetheart; my Mary loved no one but her mother—and my heart tells me that my child could not willingly abandon her widowed parent for any new affection that might have entered her young breast. She had no followers—we were never for one hour apart, and I knew every thought of her innocent mind. One gentleman—he said he was a parson—called on me this morning, to administer consolation; yet he hinted that my poor girl had probably committed self-destruction—that the light of grace had suddenly burst upon her soul, and the sudden knowledge of her sinful state had been too much for her to bear, and, in desperation, she had hurried from the world. Alas! if my poor Mary is indeed no more, it was not by her own act that she appeared in haste before her Maker—God loved the little girl that he had made so good; the light of heavenly happiness glistened in her bright and pretty eyes; and she was too fond of this world's beauties, and the delights of life showered by the Almighty upon His children, to think of repaying Him by gloom and suicide! No, no! Upon her bended knees, morning and night, she prayed to her Father in Heaven, that His will might be done; her religion, like her life, was simple, but pure. She was not of the creed professed by him who thought to cheer a parent's broken heart by speaking of a daughter's shameful death."

The plain, but earnest eloquence of the poor lady excited my warmest sympathy. She had called on me for advice; but I resolved to give her my personal assistance, and exert all my faculties in the clearance of this mystery. She denied the probability of any one being concerned in kidnapping, or conveying away her daughter—for, as she simply expressed herself, "she was too insignificant to have created an enemy of such importance."

I had a friend in the police department—a man who suffered not his intimacy with the villainy of the world to dull the humanities of nature. At the period of my tale, he was but little known, and the claims of a large family pressed hard upon him; yet his enemies have been unable to affix a stain upon his busy life. He has since attained a height of reputation that must ensure a sufficient income; he is established as the head of the private police of London—a body of men possessing rare and wonderful attainments. To this man I went; and, in a few words, excited his sympathy for the heart-stricken mother, and obtained a promise of his valuable assistance.

"The mother is rich," said I, "and if successful in your search, I can warrant you a larger reward than the sum total of your last year's earnings."

"A powerful inducement, I confess," replied L—, "but my professional pride is roused; it is a case deserving attention from its apparent inexplicability—to say nothing of the mother's misery, and that is something to a father and a son."

I mentioned every particular connected with the affair, and as he declined visiting Mrs. Lobenstein's house, invited her to a conference with the officer at my lodgings, where he was made acquainted with many a curious item that seemed to have no connexion with the subject we were in consultation upon. But this minute curiosity pleased the mother, and she went on her way rejoicing, for she was satisfied in her own mind that the officer would discover the fate of her child. Strange to say, although L— declared that he possessed not the slightest clue, this feeling on the part of the mother daily became stronger; a presentiment of the officer's success became the leading feature of her life; and she waited for many days with a placid face and a contented mind. The prophetic fancies of her maternal heart were confirmed; and L— eventually restored the pretty Mary to her mother's arms.

About ten days after the consultation, he called on me, and reported progress—requiring my presence at the police office for the purpose of making the affidavit necessary for the procuration of a search warrant.

"I have been hard at work," said he, "and if I have not found out where the young lady is concealed, I have at least made a singular discovery. My own inquiries in the mother's neighbourhood were not attended with any success; I therefore sent my wife, a shrewd woman, and well adapted for the business. She went without a shawl or bonnet, as if she had but stepped out from an adjacent house, into the baker's, the grocer's, the chandler's, and the beer shop; and while making her trifling purchases, she asked in a careless gossiping way, if any intelligence of Miss Lobenstein had been obtained? Every body was willing to talk of such a remarkable circumstance; and my wife listened patiently to many different versions of the story but without obtaining any useful intelligence. One day, the last attempt that I had determined she should make, she observed that a huckster˙ woman, who was standing in a baker's shop when the question was discussed, betrayed a violence of speech against the bereaved parent, and seemed to rejoice in her misfortunes. The womanly feeling of the rest of the gossips put down her inhuman chucklings, but my wife, with considerable tact, I must say, joined the huckster in her vituperation, rightly judging that there must be some peculiar reason for disliking a lady who seems generally esteemed, and who was then suffering under an affliction the most distressing to a female heart. The huckster invited my wife to walk down the street with her.

"'I say—are you one of Joe's gang?' whispered the huckster.

"'Yes,' said my wife.

"'I thought so, when I seed you grinning at the fat old Dutchey's† trouble. Did Joe come down with the rhino‡ pretty well to you about this business?'

"'Not to me,' said my wife, at a venture.

"'Nor to me, neither, the shabby varmint. Where was your post?'

"This question rather bothered my wife, but she answered, 'I swore not to tell.'

"'Oh, stuff! they've got the girl, and it's all over now, in course; though Sal Brown who giv'd Joe the information about the girl, says that five pounds won't stop her mouth, when there's a hundred offered for the information—so we thought of splitting§ upon Joe, and touching the rhino, if you knows any more nor we do, and can make your share of the work, you may join our party, and come in for your whacks.'¶

"'Well, I know a good deal, if I liked to tell it—what do you know?'

"'Why, I knows that four of us were employed to watch when Miss Lobenstein went out in the evening without her mother, and to let Joe know directly; and I know that we did watch for six months and more; and when Sal Brown *did* let him know, that the girl was missing that same night, and ha'n't been heard on since.'

"'But do you know where she is?' said my wife in a whisper.

"'Well, I can't say that I do. My stall is at the corner near the mother's house; and Sal Brown was walking past, up and down the street, a-following her

---

˙ A hawker or peddler. The word had yet to acquire its current negative connotations.

† It was common at that time to mistake a German (Deutsch) person for Dutch.

‡ A slang term for money.

§ Snitching.

¶ Your share.

profession. She's of opinion that the girl has been sent over the herring pond* to some place abroad; but my idea is that she ha'n't far off, for Joe hasn't been away many hours together, I know.'"

"My wife declared that she was acquainted with every particular, and would join them in forcing Joe to be more liberal in his disbursements, or give him up to justice, and claim the reward. She regretted that she was compelled to go to Hornsey to her mother for the next few days, but agreed to call at the huckster's stall immediately on her return.

"There was one point more that my wife wished to obtain. 'I saw the girl alone one night when it was quite dark, but Joe was not to be found when I went after him. Where did Sal Brown meet with him, when she told of the girl?'

"'Why, at the Blue Lion beer-shop, to be sure,' said the other.

"I was waiting in the neighborhood, well disguised. I received my wife's valuable information, and in a few minutes was sitting in the tap room of the Blue Lion, an humble public house of inferior pretension. I was dressed in a shooting jacket, breeches, and gaiters, with a shot belt and powder horn slung round me. A huge pair of red whiskers circled my face, and a dark red shock of hair peeped from the sides of my broad-rimmed hat. I waited in the dull room, stinking of beer and tobacco, till the house closed for the night, but heard nothing of my Joe, although I listened attentively to the conversation of the incomers, a strange, uncouth set, entirely composed of the lower order of laborers, and seemingly unacquainted with each other.

"The whole of the next day, I lounged about the sanded tap room, and smoked my pipe, and drank my beer in silent gloominess. The landlord asked me a few questions, but when his curiosity was satisfied, he left me to myself. I pretended to be a runaway gamekeeper, hiding from my master's anger for selling his game without permission. The story satisfied the host, but I saw nothing of any stranger, nor did I hear any of the old faces called by the name I wished to hear. One of the visitors was an ill-looking thick-set fellow, and kept up a continual whispering with the landlord—I made sure† that he was my man, when, to my great regret I heard him hailed by the name of George.

"I was standing inside the bar, chattering with the landlord, and settling for my pipes and my beer, when a good-looking, fresh-coloured, smiling-faced young fellow, danced into the bar, and was immediately saluted by the host, 'Hollo, JOE, where have you been these two days?'

---

* The sea.

† I was certain.

"'Heavy business on hand, my buck—occupies all my time, but pays well. So give us a mug of your best, and d— the expense.'

"I had no doubt but this was my man. I entered into conversation with him, in my assumed manner, and my knowledge of the Somersetshire dialect materially assisted my disguise. Joe was evidently a sharp-witted fellow, who knew exactly what he was about. All my endeavors to draw him into talking of his own avocations completely failed; he would laugh, drink, and chatter, but not a word relative to the business that occupied his time could I induce him to utter.

"'Who's going to the hop* in St. John street?' said the lively Joe. 'I mean to have eighteen-penny worth of shake-a-leg there to-night, and have it directly too, for I must be back at my place at daybreak.'

"This was enough for me. I walked with Joe to the vicinity of the dancing-rooms, when, pleading a prior engagement, I quitted him, and returned home. My disguise was soon completely altered; my red wig and whiskers, drab hat and shooting dress were exchanged for a suit of black, with a small French cloak of dark cloth, and plain black hat. Thus attired, I watched the entrance of the humble ball-room, fearing that my man might leave it at an early period, for I knew not how far he had to journey to his place in the country, where he was compelled to be by the break of day.

"I walked the pavement of St. John Street for six long hours, and was obliged to make myself known to the watchman to prevent his interference, for he doubted the honesty of my intentions. Just before the dawn of day, my friend Joe, who seemed determined to have enough dancing for his money, appeared in the street with a lady on each arm. I had to keep him in sight till he had escorted the damsels to their domiciles; when, buttoning up his coat, and pressing his hat down over his brows, he walked forward with a determined pace. I followed him at a convenient distance. I felt that he was in my power—that I was on the point of tracing the mystery of the girl's disappearance, and ascertaining the place of her detention.

"Joe walked rapidly towards Shoreditch Church. I was within a hundred feet of him, when the early Cambridge coach dashed down the Kingsland Road. Joe seized the guard's hold at the side of the back boot, placed his feet upon the hind spring, and in one moment was on the top of the coach, and trundling away from me at the rate of twelve miles an hour.

---

* Dance, as in 1950s America.

"I was beaten. It was impossible for me to overtake the coach. I thought of hiring a hack,* but the rapid progress of the stage defied all idea of overtaking it. I returned dispirited to my home.

"My courage rose with the conception of fresh schemes. In the course of the day, I called on a friend, a stage coachman, and telling him some of the particulars of my object, asked him to introduce me to the driver of the Cambridge coach. I met him on his return to town the next day, and, by the help of my friend, overcame his repugnance to talk with strangers respecting the affairs of his passengers. I learnt, at last, that Joe never travelled more than half a dozen miles, but Elliott, the coachman, was unable to say who he was, or where he went to. My plan was soon arranged, and Elliott was bribed to assist me.

"The next morning by daybreak, I was sitting on the top of the Cambridge coach, well wrapped up in a large white top coat, with a shawl tied over my mouth. I got on the coach at the inn yard, and as we neared the church, looked out anxiously for my friend Joe; but he was not to be seen, nor could I discern anything of him for six or seven miles along the road. The first stage was performed, and while the horses were being changed, Elliott, the coachman, pointed out a strange ill-looking man, in a close light waist coat with white sleeves, white breeches, yarn stockings, and high-low shoes.† 'That fellow,' said Elliott, 'is always in company with the man you have been inquiring about. I have seen them frequently together come from over that style;‡ he is now waiting for Joe, I'll bet a pound.'

"I alighted, and bargained with the landlord of the small road-side inn for the use of the front bedroom, up stairs. I took my post, and as the stage departed, began my watch. Joe did not appear till late in the afternoon—his friend eagerly seized him by the arm, and began to relate something with great anxiety of look and energy of action. They moved off over the style. I glided out of the house, and followed them. A footpath wound through an extensive meadow, and the men were rapidly nearing the farthest end. I hastened my pace, and gained the centre of the field, ere they were aware of my approach. I observed a telegraphic signal pass between them, and they instantly stopped their expedition, and turning back upon their path, sauntered slowly towards me. I kept on; we met—their eyes were searchingly bent upon me, but I maintained an easy gait and undisturbed countenance, and continued my walk for some minutes after they were past. As I climbed the farthest

* Horse.

† Meaning uncertain. Perhaps an ankle-height boot with a low heel, or possibly high at the back with a low instep.

‡ Spelled "stile" now.

style, I observed them watching me from the other end of the field. I saw no more of Joe or his friend for the rest of that day and the whole of the next.

"I was much annoyed at my disappointment, and resolved not to be again out-witted. Every possible inquiry that could be made without exciting the curiosity of the neighbourhood, was instituted, but I was unable to obtain the smallest information, either of the abducted lady or of Joe's individuality. His friend was known as a vagabond of the first class—a discharged ostler,* with a character that marked him ready for the perpetration of every crime.

"I was hunting in the dark. I had nothing but surmises to go upon, excepting the declaration of the huckster, that a man named Joe was the means of Miss Lobenstein's absence, but I was not sure that I was in pursuit of that identical Joe. The mystery attending the object of my suspicion gave an appearance of probability to my supposition, but it seemed as if I was not to proceed beyond the limits of uncertainty. I resolved, after waiting till the evening of the next day, to return to the inn-room of the Blue Lion, and the impenetrability of my gamekeeper's disguise.

"Tying my rough coat up in my shawl, I clapped the bundle under my arm, and walked quietly along the road. As I passed through some twists on the side walk, a post-chaise† was coming through the adjoining toll-gate. A scuffle, accompanied with high oaths, in the interior of the chaise, attracted my attention; a hand was dashed through the carriage-window, and cries for help were loudly vociferated. I ran towards the chaise; and ordered the postillion‡ to stop; a coarse voice desired him to drive on; the command was repeated with violent imprecations, and the horses, severely lashed, bounded rapidly away. I was sufficiently near to catch hold of the back of the springs as the vehicle moved; the motion was violent, but I kept my grasp. The back board of the chaise, where the footman should stand, had been covered with a double row of iron spikes, to prevent the intrusion of idle boys; but, determined not to lose sight of the ruffians who were thus violating the peace of the realm, I pressed my bundle hard upon the spikes, and jumping nimbly up, found myself in a firm and pleasant seat.

"The carriage rolled speedily along. I determined, at the very first halting place, to summon assistance, and desire an explanation of the outcries and demands for help. If, as there seemed but little doubt, some act of lawless violence was being

---

* Stableman.

† A fast, four-wheeled carriage, similar to a stagecoach.

‡ A coachman who rides one of the horses rather than sitting on the coach itself. More commonly spelled "postilion."

perpetrated, I resolved to arrest the principals upon the spot. While cogitating on the probabilities of the result, I received a tremendous cut across the face, from the thong of a heavy leather whip, jerked with considerable violence from the window of the post-chaise. A second well-directed blow drove me from my seat, and I fell into the road, severely lacerated, and almost blind.

"I rolled upon the dusty ground, and writhed in excessive agony. A thick wale* crossed each cheek, and one of my eyes had been terrifically hit. It was yet early night, and the public nature of the road soon afforded me assistance. A young man passed me, driving a gig† towards London; I hailed him, and requested his services. A slight detail of the cause in which I had received my injuries, induced him to turn round and receive me in the vacant seat. The promise of half a guinea‡ tempted him to drive rapidly after the chaise, and in a few minutes we heard the sound of wheels. The young man cheered his horse to greater progress, but we were unable to pass the vehicle in advance, and it was not till we both drew up to the door of the roadside inn, where I had previously stopped, that we discovered that we had been in pursuit of a mail-coach instead of a post-chaise.

"The waiter declared that 'nothin' of a four-veel natur, 'cept a vaggin and a nearse§ had passed within the previous half hour. Placing my gig friend over some brandy and water, I sought the recesses of the kitchen, that I might procure some cooling liquid to bathe my face with. While busily employed at the yard pump, the sound of voices from an adjoining stable arrested my attention. The dim light of a lantern fell upon the figure of the ostler whom I had seen in company with mysterious Joe. I advanced lightly, in hopes of hearing the conversation. When I reached the door, I was startled by the sudden approach of some one from the other side of the yard, and compelled to hide behind the door. A stable helper popped his head into the building, and said—

"'See here, Billee, vot I found sticking on the spikes of the chay¶ you've left in the lane.'

"My luckless bundle was produced, and speedily untied. Directly Billy, for so was the suspicious ostler named, saw my rough, white, great coat, he exclaimed, with considerable energy—

---

* Welt.

† A light, two-wheeled carriage.

‡ Ten shillings and six pence. Worth £57.23 (US $76.79) in 2018, according to online sources.

§ A wagon and a hearse. Burton is using phonetic spelling to convey the character's accent.

¶ Chaise.

"'I'm blessed if ve haint been looked arter. I seed this 'ere toggery* a-valking a'ter Joe and me in the meadow yonder. Ve thought it suspectable, so ve mizzled[†] back. And I'm jiggered if the owner vornt sitting behind our conweyance, ven Joe hit him a vollop[‡] or two vith your vip to knock him off. Tommy, my tulip, I'll go back vi' you to-night, and veil a vhile till the vind changes.'

"It was evident then, that Joe was connected with the abduction of the day—another convincing proof that he was the active agent in Miss Lobenstiein's affair. With respect to my friend the ostler, I determined to try the effects of a little coercion, but concluded that it would be better to let him reach some distance from his usual haunts, to prevent alarming his comate[§] Joe.

"In about an hour the post-chaise was driven to the door; and the ostler, much the worse for his potations, was placed within the body of the vehicle. I was soon after them, in company with the young man in the gig, and we kept the chaise in sight till it had entered the still and deserted streets of the city. It was nearly midnight; the drunken ostler desired the scarcely sober postillion to put him out at the door of a tavern. I walked up to the astonished couple and, arresting them on a charge of felony, slipped a pair of small but powerful spring handcuffs over the ostler's wrists. I conducted him, helpless and amazed, to an adjacent watch-house; and mentioning my name and office, desired his safe custody till I could demand his body. The postillion, who was guarded by my gig friend, became much alarmed; and volunteered any information that I might desire. He confessed that he had been employed that afternoon, by one Joseph Mills, to carry a lunatic priest to the Franciscan Monastery at Enfield Chase, from whence it was asserted that he had made his escape. The existence of a religious establishment in that neighborhood was entirely unknown to me, and I questioned the postillion respecting the number of its inmates, and the name of the superior, but he professed to know nothing beyond the locality of the building, and declared that he had never been inside the yard gate. He admitted that Joseph Mills had employed him several times upon the same business; and that, rather more than a fortnight ago, Billy, the ostler, had desired him to bring up a post-chaise from his master's yard at a minute's notice, and that a young lady was lifted, in a senseless state, into the chaise, and driven down to the building at Enfield as rapidly as the horses could be made to go.

---

* Clothing.

† Doubled back.

‡ Wallop.

§ Confederate.

"I took down his directions respecting the house, and at daybreak this morning I reconnoitered the front and back of the building. If I am any judge, that house is not devoted to monastic purposes alone; but you will see it to-morrow, I trust; for I wish you to accompany me as early in the morning as we can start, after procuring the warrants for a general search into the secrets of this most mysterious monastery."

It was nearly noon the next day before we were enabled to complete our necessary arrangements. L—, Mr. Wilson, the attorney, Mr. R—, a police magistrate of some distinction, and the reader's humble servant, stepped into a private carriage, while a police officer, well armed, sat with the driver. The magistrate had been interested in the details necessary for the procuration of the warrant, and had invited himself to the development of the mystery. An hour's ride brought us to the entrance of a green lane that wound its mazy length between hedges of prickly holly and withered hawthorn trees. After traversing this lane for nearly two miles, we turned again to the left, by L—'s direction, and entered a narrow pass between a high brick wall and a huge bank, surmounted by a row of high and gloomy trees. The wall formed the boundary of the monastery grounds, and, at a certain place, where an ascent in the narrow road favored the purpose, we were desired by L— to mount the roof of the coach, and, by looking over the wall, to inspect the back front* of the building. Massive bars of iron were fastened across every window of the house; in some places, the frames and glass were entirely removed, and the gratings were fixed in the naked brick work; or the apertures were fitted with thick boarding, excepting a small place at the top for the admission of the smallest possible quantity of light and air. The windows of a range of out-houses, which extended down one side of the extensive yard, were also securely barred; and a small square stone building stood in the middle of the garden, which immediately adjoined the yard. Two sides of this singular construction were visible from our coach top, yet neither door nor window were to be discerned.

One of our party pointed out a pale and wild-looking face glaring at us from one of the grated windows of the house. "Let us away," said L—, "we are observed; and a farther gratification of our curiosity may prevent a successful issue to my scheme."

"This looks more like a prison than a monastery or convent," said the magistrate.

"I fear that we shall find it worse than either," replied L—.

---

* Confusingly, at the time, "front" could mean something like "face" rather than the side on which the main door was situated.

In a few minutes the carriage stopped at the gate of the building, the front of which exhibited but few points for the attachment of suspicion. The windows were shaded by blinds and curtains, but free from gratings or bars. The palings that enclosed a small fore court, were of massive oak, and being mounted on a dwarf wall, effectually prevented the intrusion of uninvited guests. The gates were securely closed, but the handle of a small bell invited attention, and a lusty pull by the driver gave notice of our presence.

L——, who had quitted the vehicle by the off door,* requested the magistrate to keep out of sight, and with his brother officer, retired behind the coach. Our course of proceeding had been well arranged; when the door of the house was opened, I put my head from the carriage window, and requested to see the superior of the convent. The attendant, a short, ill-looking fellow in a fustian coat and gaiters, desired to know my business with him. "It is of great secrecy and importance," I replied; "I cannot leave the carriage, because I have somebody here that requires my strictest attention. Give your master this card, and he will know exactly who I am, and what I require."

Our scheme succeeded. The fellow left his post, and, unfastening the paling gate, advanced to the edge of the footpath, and put his hand in at the window of the carriage for my card. L—— and the officer glided from their concealment, and secured possession of the outer gate and the door of the house, before the fellow had time to give the alarm. The driver, who had pretended to busy himself with the horses, immediately opened the carriage door; and in a few seconds, the whole of our party was mustered in the entrance hall. The man who had answered the bell, when he recovered his surprise, rushed to the door, and attempted to force his way to the interior of the house. The police officer stopped him, and an angry altercation ensued—he placed his finger in his mouth, and gave a loud and lengthy whistle. L——, who was busily engaged in searching for the fastenings of an iron screen, that crossed the width of the hall, observed the noise, and turning round to his mate, said quietly, "If he's troublesome, Tommy, *give him a pair of gloves.*"† In two minutes, the fellow was sitting helpless on the ground, securely hand-cuffed.

"Confound him," said L——, "he must have come out through this grating; there is no other entrance to the hall, and yet I cannot discover the door-way; and I am afraid that his signal has made it worse, for I heard the click of spring work directly after he gave his whistle."

---

* The door on the side of the coach facing away from the house.

† Handcuffs.

"This grating is a common appendage to a convent or religious house," said Mr. Wilson. "Perhaps we are giving ourselves unnecessary trouble—let us ring the bell again, and we may obtain admission without the use of force."

The officer and the magistrate exchanged a smile. The latter went to the man who had opened the door, and said, in a low tone of voice, "We must get into the house, my man; show us how we can pass this grating, and I will give you five guineas.* If you refuse, I shall commit you to jail, whether your connexion with this establishment deserves it or no. I am a magistrate, and these, my officers, are acting under my direction."

The man spoke not; but, raising his manacled hands to his mouth, gave another whistle of peculiar shrillness and modulation.

The hall in which we were detained, was of great height and extent. Beyond the iron screen, a heavy partition of wood work cut off the lower end, and a door of heavy oak opened from the room thus formed into the body of the hall. An open, but grated window, was immediately above the door, and extended almost from one end of the partition to the other. L—, observing this, climbed up the iron screen with the agility of the cat, and had scarcely attained the top, ere we observed him level a pistol towards some object in the enclosure, and exclaim, with a loud voice, "Move one step, and I'll drive a couple of bullets through your skull."

"What do you require?" exclaimed a tremulous voice from within.

"Send your friend there, Joe Mills, to open the door of the grating. If *you* move hand or foot, I'll pull trigger, and your blood be upon your own head."

L— afterwards informed me, that upon climbing the screen, he discerned a gentleman in black in close consultation with a group of men. They were standing at the farther end of the enclosure against a window, the light of which enabled him to pick out the superior, and to discern the physiognomy of his old acquaintance Joe.

"Come, come, Joe, make haste," said L—, "my fingers are cramped, and I may fire in mistake."

The threat was effectual in its operation. The man was afraid to move, and the door of the enclosure was opened by his direction. Joe walked trippingly across the hall, and, touching a spring in one of the iron rails, removed the fastenings from a portion of the screen, and admitted our party.

"How do you do, Mr. Mills?" said L—; "how are our friends at the Blue Lion? You must excuse me if I put you to a little inconvenience, but you are so volatile

---

* Five pounds and five shillings. Worth £572.25 (US $767.94) in 2018, according to online sources.

that we can't make sure of finding you when we want you, unless we take the requisite precaution. Tommy, tackle him to his friend, and by way of greater security, fasten them to the grating—but don't waste the gloves, for we have several more to fit."

"Gentlemen," said the man in black, advancing to the door of the enclosure, "what is the reason of this violence? Why is the sanctity of this holy establishment thus defiled? Who are you, and what seek you here?"

"I am a magistrate, sir, and these men are officers of justice armed with proper authority to search this house for the person of Mary Lobenstein, and we charge you with her unlawful detention. Give her to our care, and you may save yourself much trouble."

"I know nothing of the person you mean, nor are we subject to the supervision of your laws. This house is devoted to religious purposes—it is the abode of penitents who have abjured the world and all its vanities. We are under the protection of the Legate of His Holiness the Pope, and the laws of England do not forbid our existence. Foreigners only dwell with in these walls, and I cannot allow the interference of any party unauthorised by the head of the church."

"I shall not stop," said the magistrate, "to expose the errors of your statement; I am furnished with sufficient power to demand a right of search in any house in the kingdom. Independent of ascertaining the safety of the individual with whose abduction you are charged, it is my duty to inquire into the nature of an establishment assuming the right to capture the subjects of the king of this realm, and detain them in a place having all the appointments of a common prison, yet disowning the surveillance of the English laws. Mr. L—, you will proceed in your search, and if any one attempts to oppose you, he must take the consequences."

The countenance of the man in black betrayed the uneasiness he felt; the attendants, six in number, who, with our friend Mills, had formed the council whose deliberations were disturbed by the sight of L—'s pistol, were ranged beneath the window that looked into the yard, and waited the commands of the chief. This man, whose name we afterwards ascertained was Farrell, exchanged a look of cunning with his minions, and, with apparent resignation, replied,

"Well, sir, it is useless for me to contend with the authority you possess; Mr. Nares, throw open the yard door, and, do you and your men attend the gentlemen round the circuit of the cells."

The person addressed, unbolted the fastenings of a huge door that opened into the yard, and bowed to our party as if waiting their precedence. Mr. Wilson being nearest the door, went first, and Nares, with a bend of his head, motioned two of his party to follow. As they passed him, he gave them a knowing wink, and said, "Take the gentlemen to the stone house first." The magistrate was about to pass into the yard, when L— seized him by the collar of his coat, and violently pulling him back into the room, closed the door, and jerked the principal bolt into its socket.

"Excuse my rudeness, sir, but you will soon perceive that it was necessary. Your plan, Mr. Nares, is a very good plan, but will scarcely answer your purpose. We do not intend placing ourselves at the mercy of your men in any of your stone houses, or cells with barred windows. You have the keys of the establishment at your girdle—go round with us yourself, and let those five or six fellows remain here instead of dancing at our heels. Come, come, sir, we are not to be trifled with; no hesitation, or I shall possess myself of your keys, and leave you securely affixed to your friend Mills."

Nares grinned defiance, but made no reply; Farrell, whose pale face exhibited his dismay, took courage from the dogged bearing of his official, and stuttered not, "Mr. Nares, I desire that you will not give up your keys." The hint was sufficient. Nares and his fellows, who were all furnished with bludgeons, raised their weapons in an altitude of attack, and a general fight was inevitable. The closing of the yard door had cut off one of our friends, but it also excluded two of the enemy. Still the odds were fearfully against us, not only in point of numbers, which rated five to four, but our antagonists were all of them armed, while the magistrate and I were totally unprovided with the means of defence.

Hostilities commenced by one of the men striking me a violent blow upon the fleshy part of the left shoulder, that sent me staggering to the other side of the room. Two of the ruffians simultaneously faced the police officer, as if to attack him; he received the blow of the nearest, upon his mace or staff of office, and before the fellow had time to lift his guard, returned him a smashing rap upon the fingers of his right hand, compelling him to drop his cudgel, and run howling into the corner of the room. The officer then turned his attention to the fellow who had assaulted me, and who was flourishing his stick with the intent of repeating the blow—but receiving a severe crack across his shins from the officer's mace, he was unable to keep his legs, and dropped upon the floor. I immediately wrested the bludgeon from his grasp, and left him *hors de combat.* The officer, while assisting me, received a knock-down blow from the fellow who had hesitated joining in the first attack, but, cat like, had been watching his opportunity for a

***

* French: "out of action."

pounce. I gave him in return a violent thump upon his head, and drove his hat over his eyes—then, rushing in upon him, I pinioned his arms, and held him till the officer rose and assisted me to secure him. While placing the handcuffs upon him, I was favored with a succession of kicks from the gentleman with the crippled hand.

L—, having drawn a pistol from his pocket, advanced to Nares and desired him to deliver up the keys; the ruffian answered him by striking a heavy blow on L—'s ear that immediately produced blood. The officer, exhibiting the utmost self-possession under these irritating circumstances, did not fire the pistol at his adversary, but dashed the weapon into his face, and inflicted a painful wound. Nares was a man of bull-dog courage. He seized the pistol, and struggled fearfully for its possession. His gigantic frame and strength overpowered his antagonist; the pistol was discharged in the scuffle, luckily without wounding anyone—and the ruffian, holding the conquered L— upon the ground, was twisting his cravat for the purpose of choking him, when, having satisfactorily arranged our men, we arrived to the rescue, and prevented the scoundrel from executing his villainous intention. But Nares, although defeated by numbers, evinced a determination to die game—it was with the utmost difficulty that we were enabled to secure his arms, and while slipping the handcuffs over his wrists, he continued to leave the marks of his teeth upon the fingers of the policeman.

While this furious *mêlée* was going on, the magistrate had been unceremoniously collared by the master of the house, and thrust forth into that part of the hall which adjoined the iron screen. But his worship did not reverence this ungentlemanly proceeding, and turned valiantly upon his assailer. Both of them were unprovided with weapons, and a furious bout of fisty-cuffs ensued, wherein his worship was considerably worsted. Mills and the porter, who had been fastened by the policeman to the railing of the screen, encouraged Farrell by their cheers. The magistrate was severely punished, and roared for help; Farrell, dreading collision with the conquerors of his party, left his man, and started off, through the open door of the grating; he ran down the lane with a speed that defied pursuit. The driver and the magistrate both endeavored to overtake him, but they soon lost sight of the nimble rogue, and returned discomforted to the house.

During the scuffle, the two men, who, with Mr. Wilson, were shut out by the promptitude of L—, clamored loudly at the door for re-admission. The attorney, as he afterwards confessed, was much alarmed at the position in which he found himself—cut off from all communication with his friends, and left at the mercy of two ill-looking scoundrels, in a strange place, and surrounded by a range of grated prisons, while a number of cadaverous, maniac looking faces glared at him from between the bars.

Upon mustering our party, we were all more or less wounded. The magistrate was outrageous in his denunciations of vengeance upon all the parties concerned; his discolored eye and torn apparel, besides the bruises about his person, had inflamed his temper, and he declared that it was his firm determination to offer a large reward for the apprehension of the chief ruffian, Farrell. L— was much hurt, and for some time appeared unable to stand alone—his ear bled profusely, and relieved his head, which had been seriously affected by Nares's attempt at strangulation. The other officer had received a severe thumping, and his bitten hand gave him much pain. My left arm was almost useless, and many bloody marks exhibited the effects of the fellow's kicks upon my shins. Nevertheless, we had fought a good fight, and had achieved a perilous victory.

The magistrate threw up the window sash, and addressed the men in the yard from between the iron gratings. "Harkee, you sirs, we have thrashed your fellows, and have them here in custody. If you attempt resistance, we shall serve you exactly in the same manner. But if either of you feel inclined to assist us in the discharge of our duty, and will freely answer every question, and render all the help in his power, you shall not only be forgiven for any part you may have taken in scenes of past violence, short of murder, but shall be well rewarded into the bargain."

One of the men, and I must say that he was the most ill-looking of the whole lot, immediately stepped forward, and offered to turn "King's evidence," if the magistrate would swear to keep his promise. The other fellow growled his contempt of "the sneak what would snitch," and darted rapidly down the yard. As we never saw him again, it is supposed that he got into the garden, and found some means of escaping over the walls.

The yard door was opened, and the lawyer and the informer were admitted. The latter personage told us that his wife was the matron of the establishment, and, with her sister, would be found up stairs. The keys were taken from Nares, and we began our search. Mr. Wilson desired the man to conduct us to Mary Lobenstein's room, but he positively denied the knowledge of any such person. His wife, a coarse, pock-marked, snub-nosed woman, with a loud, masculine voice, also declared that no female answering to that name had ever been within the house. L— remarked that no credit was to be attached to their assertions, and ordered them to lead the way to the search.

It would occupy too much space to describe minutely the nature of the persons and events that we encountered in our rounds. Suffice it to say, we soon discovered that the suspicions of the police officer and the magistrate barely reached the truth. Farrell's establishment had no connexion with any religious house, nor could we discover either monk, friar, nun, or novice in any of the cells. But the name was a good cloak for the villainous usages practised in the house, as it disarmed suspicion, and prevented the interference of the police. The house, in reality, was a private mad-house, but subject to the foulest abuses; wives who were tired of their husbands, and vice versa—reprobate sons, wishing to *dispose* of fathers—or villains who wanted to remove their rivals, either in love or wealth, could secure safe lodgings for the obnoxious personages in Farrell's Farm, as it was named by the knowing few. Farrell could always obtain a certificate of the lunacy of the person to be removed; Nares had been bred to the pestle and the mortar; and as the act* then stood, an apothecary's signature was sufficient authority for immuring a suspected person. Incurables, of the worst description, were received by Farrell, and boarded at the lowest rate. He generally contracted for a sum down, guaranteeing that their friends should never again be troubled by them—and, as the informer said, "He gave them little enough to eat, and if they did not die, it wasn't his fault."

The house was also appropriated to other purposes of secrecy and crime. Ladies in a delicate situation were accommodated with private rooms for their *accouchement*†, and the children effectually provided for. Fugitives from justice were sure of concealment, if they could obtain admission to the farm. In short, Farrell's doors, although closed to the world and the eye of the law, were open to all who could afford to pay, or be paid for—from the titled seducer and his victim, whose ruin was effected in the elegant suite of rooms fronting the lane—to the outcast bedlamite,‡ the refuse of the poor-house, and the asylum, who was condemned to a slow, but certain death in the secret cells of this horrible abode.

It would fill a volume to recount the history of the sufferers whom we released from their almost hopeless imprisonment—a volume of crime, of suffering, and of sorrow.

After a painful and fruitless search through all the various rooms, cells, and hiding places of that singular house, we were compelled to acknowledge that the assertions of the under-keeper and his wife were but too correct. Mary Lobenstein

---

* The Acts of Parliament governing lunacy and madhouses were not significantly reformed until 1845, and permitted many abuses.

† French: "childbirth."

‡ Bethlem (sic) Royal Hospital, nicknamed Bedlam, was one of London's earliest and most notorious madhouses.

was not among the number of the *detenues** at the Farm, nor could we discover the slightest trace of her. Still L— clung to the hope that, in the confusion necessarily attending our first search, we had passed over some secret cell or dungeon in which the poor girl was immured. The square stone building in the centre of the garden afforded some ground for this surmise—we were unable to open the small iron-banded door that was fixed in the side of this apparently solid structure. The under-keeper declared that the key was always in the possession of Farrell, his principal; and that no one ever entered the place but Nares and his master. He was not aware that any person was ever confined in it; a spring of water bubbled up within the building, and he believed that Farrel used it as a wine cellar only. He had seen wine carried in and out of the place. Indeed, the whole appearance of the building corroborated the man's statement—there was no window, air hole, or aperture of any description, excepting the small door before mentioned; and the contracted[†] site of the place itself prevented the possibility of its containing a hiding hole for a human being, if a well or spring occupied the area, as the keeper affirmed.

Resigning this last hope of finding the poor girl, we gave our assistance to the magistrate in removing the prisoners, and placing the unfortunates whom we had released in temporary but appropriate abodes. In this service, the under-keeper and his wife proved valuable auxiliaries, in pointing out the incurable mad folks, and those who, in his opinion, had been unjustly detained. The prisoners were placed in our carriage, and conveyed to London, under the superintendance of L— himself, who promised to return during the evening with additional assistance. The policeman was despatched to Enfield for several carriages and post-chaises. Some of the most desperate and confirmed maniacs were sent to the lunatic asylum, with the magistrate's order for their admittance, and two or three of the sick and sorrowing were removed to the Middlesex hospital.

I assisted the lawyer and the magistrate in taking the depositions of several of the sufferers who appeared sane enough to warrant the truth of their stories. As night approached, I prepared for a departure, and Mr. Wilson resolved to accompany me; we received the addresses of several persons from various inmates of the Farm, who requested us to let their families know of the place of their detention. As we drove down the lane, we met L—, and a posse of police officers, who were to accompany the magistrate in his night sojourn at the house, and assist him in the removal of the rest of the inmates in the morning.

---

* French: "detainees."

† Cramped.

During the evening, I called, with a heavy heart, upon Mrs. Lobenstein, and communicated the melancholy remit of our scheme. I related minutely the particulars of our transaction—she listened quietly to my story, and occasionally interrupted me, when describing the zeal of the officer L——, by invoking the blessings of heaven upon his head. When she learnt the unsuccessful issue of our search, she remained silent for a minute only—when, with a confident tone, and a cheerful voice, she said—"My daughter Mary is in that stone house. The workings of the fingers of Providence are too evident in the wonderful train of circumstances that led to the discovery of Farrell and his infamous mansion. My child is there, but you have not been able to penetrate the secret of her cell. I will go with you in the morning, if you can spare another day to assist a bereaved mother."

I declared my readiness to accompany her, but endeavored to impress upon her mind the inutility of farther search. She relied securely upon the faith of her divine impression, as she termed it, and declared that God would never suffer so good a man as L— to be disappointed in his wonderful exertions; the keenness of a mother's eye, the instinct of a mother's love would help him in the completion of his sacred trust. It was impossible to argue with her; and I agreed to be with her at an early hour.

I slept but little during the night, for my bruised shins and battered shoulder pained me considerably, and the strange excitement of the day's events materially assisted to heighten both my corporeal and mental fever. When I arose in the morning, I felt so badly, that nothing but the earnest and confident tone of the poor childless widow induced me to undertake the annoyance of the trip—I could not bear to disappoint her. I found the carriage ready at the door—a couple of mechanics, with sledge hammers, crow bars, and huge bunches of skeleton keys, occupied the front seat, and having placed myself beside Mrs. Lobenstein upon the other seat, the horses trotted briskly along the street. During our ride she informed me that a lawyer had called upon her from Elizabeth Bishop, the disappointed spinster, who, it will be recollected, had lost her expected fortune by the intervention of the gentle Mary Lobenstein. The man stated that Miss Bishop had heard of the disappearance of the inheritor of her aunt's estate, and had desired him to give notice that if proof was not forthcoming of Miss Lobenstein's existence, she should take possession of the property, agreeably to the provision existing in the will. "I am sure," said the mother, "that woman is at the bottom of this affair—she has concerted the abduction of my daughter to obtain possession of the estate—but I trust in God that she will be disappointed in her foul design. A fearful whisper comes across my heart that those who would rob a mother of a child for gold, would not object to rob that child of her existence; but my trust is in the Most High, who tempers the wind to the shorn lamb, and will not consent to the spoliation of the widow and the fatherless."

The probability of the poor girl's murder had been suggested by L— at the termination of our unsuccessful search, and had occupied a serious portion of my thoughts during the wakeful moments of the past night. Expecting nothing from the mother's repetition of the search, I determined to consult L— upon the feasibility of offering rewards to the villains Mills and Nares for a revelation of the truth, and if we failed in eliciting any intelligence, to institute a rigorous examination of the garden and the yard, and discover, if possible, the remains of the murdered girl.

The magistrate received Mrs. Lobenstein with tenderness and respect, and sanctioned her desire to penetrate into the mystery of the square stone house. L— had nothing new to disclose, excepting that, in one of the rooms several articles of female apparel had been discovered, and he suggested that Mrs. L. should inspect them, as, perhaps, something that belonged to her daughter might be among them. The mother remarked that her daughter left home without a bonnet or a shawl, and it was scarcely likely that her body-clothes would be in the room: she, therefore, thought it useless to waste time in going up stairs, but requested the locksmith to accompany her to the stone house in the garden. It was impossible to help sympathising with Mrs. Lobenstein in her anxiety; the magistrate deferred his return to Loudon, where his presence was absolutely necessary to preside at the examination of Messrs. Nares, Mills, and Co., and the warm-hearted L— wiped the moisture from his eyes as he followed the mother across the yard, and heard her encourage the workmen to commence the necessary proceedings for the release of her darling child. The lock of the stone house was picked—the door was thrown wide open—and the maternal voice was heard in loud citation, but the dull echo of the stone room was the only reply—there was no living creature within the place.

We found the interior of the building to correspond with the description given by the under-keeper. The walls were hollowed into binns,* which were filled with wine bottles, packed in sawdust; a circular well, bricked up a little above the level of the floor, filled the centre of the room; the water rose to within a foot of the ground—an old pulley and bucket, rotten from desuetude,† clogged up one side of

---

* An archaic spelling.

† Disuse.

the doorway, and two or three wine barrels filled up the remaining vacancy of space. It was impossible that a human being could be concealed in any part of the building.

Mrs. Lobenstein sighed, and her countenance told of her dismay; but the flame of hope had warmed her heart into a heat that was not to be immediately cooled. "Gentlemen," said she, "accompany me once more round the cells and secret places—let me be satisfied with my own eyes that a thorough search has been made, and it will remove my doubts that you have overlooked some obscure nook wherein the wretches have concealed my little girl." The range of chambers was again traversed, but without success, and the widow was compelled to admit that every possible place had been looked into, and that a farther sojourn in the house was entirely useless. The old lady sat down upon the last stair of the second flight, and with a grievous expression of countenance, looked into our several faces as we stood around her, as if she was searching for that consolation it was not in our power to bestow. Tears rolled down her cheeks, and mighty sobs told of the anguish of her heart. I was endeavoring to rouse her to exertion, as the only means of breaking the force of her grief, when my attention was drawn to the loud yelping of a dog, a small cocker spaniel, that had accompanied us in the carriage from Mrs. Lobenstein's house, and in prowling round the building, had been accidentally shut up in one of the rooms. "Poor Dash!" said the widow, "I must not lose you; my dear Mary was fond of you, and I ought to be careful of her favorite." I took the hint, and walking down the gallery, opened the door of the room from whence the barking proceeded. It was the apartment that contained the articles of wearing apparel, which Mrs. L. had visited in her round, without discovering any token of her daughter. But the animal's superior instinct enabled him to detect the presence of a pair of shoes that had graced the feet of the little Mary when she quitted her mother's house, on the day of her abduction. Immediately the door was opened, the faithful creature gathered up the shoes in his mouth, and ran to his mistress, and dropped them at her feet, inviting her attention by a loud and sagacious bark. The old lady knew the shoes in a moment—"Yes, they are my girl's—I bought them myself for my darling—she has been here—has been murdered—and the body of my child is now mouldering in the grave." A violent fit of hysterics ensued, and I consigned her to the care of the wife and sister of the under-keeper, who had not been allowed to leave the house.

I deemed the finding of the shoes to be of sufficient importance to recall the magistrate, who was in the carriage at the door, and about to start for London. He immediately alighted, and inquired into the particulars of the affair. Directly it was proved that Mary Lobenstein had been in the house, L— rushed up stairs, and dragged the keeper into the presence of the magistrate, who sternly asked the man why he had deceived him in declaring that the girl had never been there. The fellow was evidently alarmed, and protested vehemently that he knew no female of the name of Lobenstein—and the only clue he could give to the mystery of the shoes was, that a young girl answering our description of Mary, had been brought into the house at night time about a fortnight ago, but she was represented as an insane prostitute, of the name of Hill, who had been annoying some married gentlemen by riotous conduct at their houses—and it was said at first that she was to remain at the Farm for life—but that she had suddenly been removed by Nares, but where, he could not say. L— shook his head ominously when he heard this statement, and it was evident to us all that the mother's suspicions were right, and that a deed of blood had been recently perpetrated. The best means of ascertaining the place of burial was consulted on, and we adjourned to the garden to search for any appearance of freshly disturbed ground, or other evidence that might lead to a discovery of her remains. When we had crossed the yard, and were about entering the garden gate, L— suggested the propriety of fetching the little dog, whose excellent nose had afforded the only clue we had been able to obtain. I went back for the animal, but he refused to leave his mistress, and it was not without some danger of a bite, that I succeeded in catching him by the neck, and carrying him out of the room. I put him on his feet when we were past the garden gate, and endeavored to excite him to sprightliness by running along the walk, and whistling to him to follow, but he sneaked after me with a drooping tail and a bowed head, as if he felt his share of the general grief.

We walked round the garden without discovering any signs that warranted farther search. We had traversed every path in the garden, excepting a narrow, transverse one, that led from the gate to a range of green and hot houses that lined the farthest wall. We were on the point of leaving the place, satisfied that it was not in our power to remove the veil of mystery that shrouded the girl's disappearance, when the dog, who had strayed into the entrance of the narrow path, gave extraordinary signs of liveliness and emotion—his tail wagged furiously—his ears were thrown forward—and a short but earnest yaffle broke into a continuous bark as he turned rapidly from one side of the path to another, and finally ran down toward the green house with his nose bent to the ground.

"He scents her," said L—; "there is still a chance." Our party, consisting of the magistrate, L— and two other officers, the under-keeper, the locksmiths, and myself, followed the dog down the narrow path into the centre of a piece of ground containing three or four cucumber beds, covered with sliding glass frames. The spaniel, after searching round the bed, jumped upon the centre frame, and howled piteously. It was evident that he had lost the scent. L— pointed out to our notice that the sliding lid was fastened to the frame by a large padlock—this extraordinary security increased our suspicions—he seized a crow bar from one of the smiths, and the lock was soon removed. The top of the frame was pulled up, and the dog jumped into the tan that filled the bed, and commenced scratching with all his might. L— thrust the bar into the yielding soil, and at the depth of a foot, the iron struck a solid substance. This intimation electrified us—we waited not for tools—our hands were dug into the bed, and the tan and black mould were dragged from the frame with an eagerness that soon emptied it, and exhibited the boarding of a large trap door, divided into two parts, but securely locked together. While the smiths essayed their skill upon the lock, the magistrate stood by with lifted hands and head uncovered—a tear was in the good man's eye—and he breathed short from the excess of his anxiety. Every one was visibly excited, and the loud and cheerful bark of the dog was hailed as an omen of success. L—'s impatience could not brook delay. He seized the sledge hammer of the smiths, and with a blow that might have knocked in the side of a house, demolished the lock and bolt, and the doors jumped apart in the recoil from the blow. They were raised—a black and yawning vault was below— and a small flight of wooden steps, green and mouldy, from the effects of the earth's dampness, led to the gloomy depths of the cavern.

The little dog dashed bravely down the stairway, and L—, requesting us to stand from between him and the light, picked his way down the narrow, slimy steps. One of the smiths followed, and the rest of us hung our heads anxiously over the edge of the vault's mouth, watching our friends as they receded in the distant gloom. A pause ensued; the dog was heard barking, and an indistinct muttering between L— and the smith ascended to the surface of the earth. I shouted to them, and was frightened at the reverberation of my voice. Our anxiety became painful in the extreme—the magistrate called to L—, but obtained no answer; and we were on the point of descending in a body, when the officer appeared at the foot of the stairs. "We have found her," said he—we gave a simultaneous shout. "But she is dead," was the appalling finish of his speech, as he emerged from the mouth of the vault.

The smith, with the lifeless body of Mary Lobenstein swung over his shoulder, was assisted up the stairs. The corse* of the little girl was placed on one of the garden settees,† and, with heavy hearts and gloomy faces, we carried

---

* Corpse (archaic).

† Benches.

the melancholy burden into the house. The mother had not recovered from the shock which the anticipation of her daughter's death had given to her feelings; she was lying senseless upon the bed where she had been placed by the keeper's wife. We laid the body of her daughter in an adjoining room, and directed the woman to perform the last sad duties to the senseless clay while we awaited the parent's restoration. The magistrate returned to London; the smiths were packing up their tools preparatory to departure, and I was musing in melancholy mood over the events of the day, when the forbidding face of the keeper's wife peeped in at the half-opened door, and we were beckoned from the room.

"Please your honor, I never seed a dead body look like that there corpse of the little girl up stairs. I've seed a many corpses in my time, but there's something unnatural about that there one, not like a dead body ought to be."

"What do you mean?"

"Why, though her feet and hands are cold, her jaw ain't dropped, and her eyes ain't open—and there's a limberness in her limbs that I don't like. I really believe she's only swounded."*

L— and I hurried up stairs, and the smiths, with their baskets of tools dangling at their backs, followed us into the room. I anxiously searched for any pulsation at the heart and the wrists of poor Mary, whose appearance certainly corroborated the woman's surmise, but the total absence of all visible signs of life denied us the encouragement of the flattering hope. One of the smiths took from his basket a tool of bright, fine-tempered steel; he held it for a few seconds against Mary's half-closed mouth, and upon withdrawing it, said, with a loud and energetic voice, "She is alive! Her breath has damped the surface of the steel!"

The man was right. Proper remedies were applied to the daughter and to her parent, and L— had the gratification of placing the lost Mary within her mother's arms.

Miss Lobenstein's explanation afforded but little additional information. When she was brought to the Farm by the villain Mills and his friend Billy the ostler, she was informed that it was to be the residence of her future life. She was subjected to the treatment of a maniac, her questions remained unanswered, and her supplications for permission to send to her mother were answered with a sneer. About three nights ago, she was ordered from her room, her shoes were taken off that she might noiselessly traverse the passages, and she was removed to the secret cell in the garden; some biscuits and a jug of water were placed beside her, and she

---

* Swooned.

had remained in undisturbed solitude till the instinct of her favorite dog led to her discovery, shortly after she had fainted from exhaustion and terror. There is little doubt but that the ruffians were alarmed at the watchings and appearances of the indefatigable L—, and withdrew their victim to the securest hiding-place. I had the curiosity, in company with some of the officers, to descend into the Secret Cell; it had originally been dug out for the foundation of an intended house; the walls and partitions were solidly built, but the bankruptcy of the projector prevented any farther progress. When Farrell and his gang took possession of the place, it was deemed easier to cover the rafters of the cellar with boards and earth, than to fill it up—in time, the existence of the hole became forgotten, save by those most interested in its concealment. Farrell contrived the mode of entrance through the glass frame of the forcing bed, and when the adjacent green-houses were constructed, an artificial flue or vent was introduced to the depths of the cell, and supplied it with a sufficiency of air.

Mrs. Lobenstein refused to prosecute the spinster Bishop, the malignancy of whose temper preyed upon her own heart, and speedily consigned her unlamented to the grave. The true particulars of this strange affair were never given to the public, although I believe that its occurrence mainly contributed to affect an alteration in the English laws respecting private mad houses and other receptacles for lunatics.

The magistracy of the county knew that they were to blame in permitting the existence of such a den as Farrell's Farm, and exerted themselves to quash proceedings against the fellows Mills and Nares, and their coadjutors.* A few months' imprisonment was the only punishment awarded them, and that was in return for the assault upon the head of the police; but in Billy, the ostler, was recognized an old offender—various unpunished offences rose against him, and he was condemned to "seven penn'orth"† aboard the hulks at Chatham.‡ The greatest rogue escaped the arm of justice for a time; but L— has since assured me he has every reason to believe that Farrell was, under a feigned name, executed in Somersetshire for horse stealing.

The Farm was converted into a Poor House for some of the adjacent parishes; L— received his reward, and when I left England, our heroine Mary was the blooming mother of a numerous family.

---

* Colleagues.

† Literally seven pennies' worth: underworld slang for a seven-month sentence.

‡ Decommissioned ships used as floating prisons.

THE MYSTERY OF MARIE ROGÊT

by Edgar Allan Poe

1842

Poe's "The Murders in the Rue Morgue," published in 1841, is widely credited with having founded the modern detective genre. His protagonist, C. Auguste Dupin, may have been inspired by Eugène François Vidocq, a former criminal who founded France's famous *Sûreté Nationale,* as well as what is thought to be the world's first private detective agency. Poe's inspiration for the following story is drawn from life: in July of 1841, the body of Mary Rogers was found floating in the Hudson River in Hoboken, New Jersey. Her murder remains unsolved; several conflicting theories were proposed at the time, and the case was much debated in the press.

Using the character of Dupin, Poe conducts a thorough critical analysis of the evidence, the press reports, the various witnesses, and some relevant science, and although he does not name the murderer, he indicates a clear line of inquiry which might have led to the case being solved. As it was, however, interest in Mary Rogers waned when another murder case stole the headlines nine weeks later.

Published forty-five years before *A Study in Scarlet*, "The Mystery of Marie Rogêt" shows many of the hallmarks of a Sherlock Holmes story. Dupin's "ratiocination" anticipates the deductive reasoning of Holmes. His unnamed associate provides an audience for the great detective and commentary for the readers, in much the same way as Watson did. The unnamed Prefect of Police, G—, who brings Dupin this case and those in the other stories, plays the role of Lestrade in "The Adventure of the Six Napoleons," "The Boscombe Valley Mystery," and other stories.

Doyle wrote fifty-six short stories and four novels starring Holmes; Poe only wrote three short stories featuring Dupin. Had Poe written more Dupin tales, Holmes's place in literature and popular culture might not have been so secure.

Es giebt eine Reihe idealischer Begebenheiten, die der Wirklichkeit parallel lauft. Selten fallen sie zusammen. Menschen und zufalle modifieiren gewohulich die idealische Begebenheit, so dass sie unvollkommen erscheint, und ihre Folgen gleichfalls unvollkommen sind. So bei der Reformation; statt des Protestantismus kam das Lutherthum hervor.

("There are ideal series of events which run parallel with the real ones. They rarely coincide. Men and circumstances generally modify the ideal train of events, so that it seems imperfect, and its consequences are equally imperfect. Thus with the Reformation; instead of Protestantism came Lutheranism.")

—Novalis,[*] *Moral Ansichten* ("Moral Views").

Thisere are few persons, even among the calmest thinkers, who have not occasionally been startled into a vague yet thrilling half-credence in the supernatural, by coincidences of so seemingly marvelous a character that, as mere coincidences, the intellect has been unable to receive them. Such sentiments—for the half-credences of which I speak have never the full force of thought—such sentiments are seldom thoroughly stifled, unless by reference to the doctrine of chance, or, as it is technically termed, the Calculus of Probabilities. Now this Calculus is, in its essence, purely mathematical; and thus we have the anomaly of the most rigidly exact in science applied to the shadow and spirituality of the most intangible in speculation.

The extraordinary details which I am now called upon to make public will be found to form, as regards sequence of time, the primary branch of a series of scarcely intelligible coincidences, whose secondary or concluding branch will be recognized by all readers in the late murder of Mary Cecilia Rogers, at New York.

---

[*] Pseudonym of German Romantic poet, mystic and philosopher Georg Philipp Friedrich von Hardenburg (1772-1801). A friend of the philosopher Schlegel, von Hardenburg's works influenced Hermann Hesse, Martin Heidegger, Wagner, Borges—and, evidently, Poe.

When, in an article entitled "The Murders in the Rue Morgue," I endeavored, about a year ago, to depict some very remarkable features in the mental character of my friend, the Chevalier C. Auguste Dupin, it did not occur to me that I should ever resume the subject. This depicting of character constituted my design; and this design was thoroughly fulfilled in the wild train of circumstances brought to instance Dupin's idiosyncrasy. I might have adduced other examples, but I should have proven no more. Late events, however, in their surprising development, have startled me into some further details, which will carry with them the air of extorted confession. Hearing what I have lately heard, it would be, indeed, strange, should I remain silent in regard to what I both heard and saw so long ago.

Upon the winding up of the tragedy involved in the deaths of Madame L'Espanaye and her daughter,* the Chevalier dismissed the affair at once from his attention, and relapsed into his old habits of moody reverie. Prone, at all times, to abstraction, I readily fell in with his humor; and, continuing to occupy our chambers in the Faubourg Saint-Germain, we gave the Future to the winds, and slumbered tranquilly in the Present, weaving the dull world around us into dreams.

But these dreams were not altogether uninterrupted. It may readily be supposed that the part played by my friend, in the drama at the Rue Morgue, had not failed of its impression upon the fancies of the Parisian police. With its emissaries, the name of Dupin had grown into a household word. The simple character of those inductions by which he had disentangled the mystery never having been explained even to the Prefect, or to any other individual than myself, of course it is not surprising that the affair was regarded as little less than miraculous, or that the Chevalier's analytical abilities acquired for him the credit of intuition. His frankness would have led him to disabuse every inquirer of such prejudice; but his indolent humor forbade all farther agitation of a topic whose interest to himself had long ceased. It thus happened that he found himself the cynosure of the political eyes; and the cases were not few in which attempt was made to engage his services at the Prefecture. One of the most remarkable instances was that of the murder of a young girl named Marie Rogêt.

This event occurred about two years after the atrocity in the Rue Morgue. Marie, whose Christian and family name will at once arrest attention from their resemblance to those of the unfortunate "cigar-girl," was the only daughter of the widow Estelle Rogêt. The father had died during the child's infancy, and from the period of his death, until within eighteen months before the assassination which

---

* i.e. the case of "The Murders in the Rue Morgue."

forms the subject of our narrative, the mother and daughter had dwelt together in the Rue Pavée-Saint-Andrée; Madame there keeping a *pension,* * assisted by Marie. Affairs went on thus, until the latter had attained her twenty-second year, when her great beauty attracted the notice of a perfumer, who occupied one of the shops in the basement of the Palais Royal, and whose custom lay chiefly among the desperate adventurers infesting that neighborhood. Monsieur Le Blanc was not unaware of the advantages to be derived from the attendance of the fair Marie in his perfumery; and his liberal proposals were accepted eagerly by the girl, although with somewhat more of hesitation by Madame.

The anticipations of the shopkeeper were realized, and his rooms soon became notorious through the charms of the sprightly *grisette.* † She had been in his employ about a year, when her admirers were thrown into confusion by her sudden disappearance from the shop. Monsieur Le Blanc was unable to account for her absence and Madame Rogêt was distracted with anxiety and terror. The public papers immediately took up the theme, and the police were upon the point of making serious investigations, when, one fine morning, after the lapse of a week, Marie, in good health, but with a somewhat saddened air, made her reappearance at her usual counter in the perfumery. All inquiry, except that of a private character, was, of course, immediately hushed. Monsieur Le Blanc professed total ignorance, as before. Marie, with Madame, replied to all questions, that the last week had been spent at the house of a relation in the country. Thus the affair died away, and was generally forgotten; for the girl, ostensibly to relieve herself from the impertinence of curiosity, soon bade a final *adieu* to the perfumer, and sought the shelter of her mother's residence in the Rue Pavée-Saint-Andrée.

It was about five months after this return home, that her friends were alarmed by her sudden disappearance for the second time. Three days elapsed and nothing was heard of her. On the fourth her corpse was found floating in the Seine, near the shore which is opposite the Quartier of the Rue Saint-Andrée, and at a point not very far distant from the secluded neighborhood of the Barrière du Roule.

The atrocity of this murder (for it was at once evident that murder had been committed), the youth and beauty of the victim, and, above all, her previous notoriety, conspired to produce intense excitement in the minds of the sensitive

---

* A kind of guest-house or boarding-house, common in continental European countries.

† A young working woman, often of flirtatious temperament. The term would have been familiar to American readers when this story was published; the 1830 poem "Our Yankee Girls" by Oliver Wendell Holmes Sr. (father of the famous jurist and, alongside Longfellow, John Greenleaf Whittier, and others, one of the popular "Fireside Poets") includes the words "the gay *grisette,* whose fingers touch love's thousand chords so well."

Parisians. I can call to mind no similar occurrence producing so general and so intense an effect. For several weeks, in the discussion of this one absorbing theme, even the momentous political topics of the day were forgotten. The Prefect made unusual exertions and the powers of the whole Parisian police were, of course, tasked to the utmost extent.

Upon the first discovery of the corpse, it was not supposed that the murderer would be able to elude, for more than a very brief period, the inquisition which was immediately set on foot. It was not until the expiration of a week that it was deemed necessary to offer a reward; and even then this reward was limited to a thousand francs. In the meantime the investigation proceeded with vigor, if not always with judgment, and numerous individuals were examined to no purpose; while, owing to the continual absence of all clew* to the mystery, the popular excitement greatly increased. At the end of the tenth day it was thought advisable to double the sum originally proposed; and, at length, the second week having elapsed without leading to any discoveries and the prejudice which always exists in Paris against the Police having given vent to itself in several serious *émeutes*,† the Prefect took it upon himself to offer the sum of twenty thousand francs "for the conviction of the assassin," or, if more than one should prove to have been implicated, "for the conviction of any one of the assassins." In the proclamation setting forth this reward, a full pardon was promised to any accomplice who should come forward in evidence against his fellows; and to the whole was appended, wherever it appeared, the private placard of a committee of citizens, offering ten thousand francs, in addition to the amount proposed by the Prefecture. The entire reward thus stood at no less than thirty thousand francs, which will be regarded as an extraordinary sum when we consider the humble condition of the girl, and the great frequency, in large cities, of such atrocities as the one described.

No one doubted now that the mystery of this murder would be immediately brought to light. But although, in one or two instances, arrests were made which promised elucidation, yet nothing was elicited which could implicate the parties suspected; and they were discharged forthwith. Strange as it may appear, the third week from the discovery of the body had passed, and passed without any light being thrown upon the subject, before even a rumor of the events which had so agitated the public mind reached the ears of Dupin and myself. Engaged in

---

* Poe uses an archaic spelling here. "Clew" means a spool of yarn, and refers to the yarn with which Ariadne supplied Theseus in the myth of the Labyrinth. "Clue" became a separate word, with its modern meaning, in the late 16th century.

† French: riots.

researches which had absorbed our whole attention, it had been nearly a month since either of us had gone abroad, or received a visitor, or more than glanced at the leading political articles in one of the daily papers. The first intelligence of the murder was brought us by G—*, in person. He called upon us early in the afternoon of the thirteenth of July, 18—, and remained with us until late in the night. He had been piqued by the failure of all his endeavors to ferret out the assassins. His reputation—so he said with a peculiarly Parisian air—was at stake. Even his honor was concerned. The eyes of the public were upon him; and there was really no sacrifice which he would not be willing to make for the development of the mystery. He concluded a somewhat droll speech with a compliment upon what he was pleased to term the tact of Dupin, and made him a direct and certainly a liberal proposition, the precise nature of which I do not feel myself at liberty to disclose, but which has no bearing upon the proper subject of my narrative.

The compliment my friend rebutted as best he could, but the proposition he accepted at once, although its advantages were altogether provisional. This point being settled, the Prefect broke forth at once into explanations of his own views, interspersing them with long comments upon the evidence; of which latter we were not yet in possession. He discoursed much, and, beyond doubt, learnedly; while I hazarded an occasional suggestion as the night wore drowsily away. Dupin, sitting steadily in his accustomed armchair, was the embodiment of respectful attention. He wore spectacles during the whole interview; and an occasional signal glance beneath their green glasses sufficed to convince me that he slept not the less soundly, because silently, throughout the seven or eight leaden-footed hours which immediately preceded the departure of the Prefect.

In the morning, I procured, at the Prefecture, a full report of all the evidence elicited, and, at the various newspaper offices, a copy of every paper in which, from first to last, had been published any decisive information in regard to this sad affair. Freed from all that was positively disproved, this mass of information stood thus:

Marie Rogêt left the residence of her mother, in the Rue Pavée-Saint-Andrée, about nine o'clock in the morning of Sunday, June the twenty-second, 18—. In going out, she gave notice to a Monsieur Jacques St. Eustache, and to him only, of her intention to spend the day with an aunt, who resided in the Rue des Drômes. The Rue des Drômes is a short and narrow, but populous, thoroughfare, not far

---

* The Prefect of Police. As in "The Murders in the Rue Morgue" and "The Purloined Letter," he is identified only by his initial. From 1836 to 1848, the period in which all three of these stories were published, this office was held by Gabriel Delessert, who may be the model for Poe's "G—."

from the banks of the river, and at a distance of some two miles, in the most direct course possible, from the *pension* of Madame Rogêt. St. Eustache was the accepted suitor of Marie, and lodged, as well as took his meals, at the *pension*. He was to have gone for his betrothed at dusk, and to have escorted her home. In the afternoon, however, it came on to rain heavily; and, supposing that she would remain all night at her aunt's, (as she had done under similar circumstances before) he did not think it necessary to keep his promise. As night drew on, Madame Rogêt (who was an infirm old lady, seventy years of age) was heard to express a fear "that she should never see Marie again;" but this observation attracted little attention at the time.

On Monday it was ascertained that the girl had not gone to the Rue des Drômes; and when the day elapsed without tidings of her, a tardy search was instituted at several points in the city and its environs. It was not, however, until the fourth day from the period of disappearance that anything satisfactory was ascertained respecting her. On this day (Wednesday, the twenty-fifth of June) a Monsieur Beauvais, who, with a friend, had been making inquiries for Marie near the Barrière du Roule, on the shore of the Seine which is opposite the Rue Pavée-Saint-Andrée, was informed that a corpse had just been towed ashore by some fishermen, who had found it floating in the river. Upon seeing the body, Beauvais, after some hesitation, identified it as that of the perfumery-girl. His friend recognized it more promptly.

The face was suffused with dark blood, some of which issued from the mouth. No foam was seen, as in the case of the merely drowned. There was no discoloration in the cellular tissue. About the throat were bruises and impressions of fingers. The arms were bent over on the chest and were rigid. The right hand was clenched; the left partially open. On the left wrist were two circular excoriations, apparently the effect of ropes, or of a rope in more than one volution. A part of the right wrist, also, was much chafed, as well as the back throughout its extent, but more especially at the shoulder-blades. In bringing the body to the shore the fishermen had attached to it a rope, but none of the excoriations had been effected by this. The flesh of the neck was much swollen. There were no cuts apparent, or bruises which appeared the effect of blows. A piece of lace was found tied so tightly around the neck as to be hidden from sight. It was completely buried in the flesh, and was fastened by a knot which lay just under the left ear. This alone would have sufficed to produce death. The medical testimony spoke confidently of the virtuous character of the deceased. She had been subjected, it said, to brutal violence. The corpse was in such condition when found, that there could have been no difficulty in its recognition by friends.

The dress was much torn and otherwise disordered. In the outer garment, a slip, about a foot wide, had been torn upward from the bottom hem to the waist, but not torn off. It was wound three times around the waist, and secured by a sort of hitch in the back. The dress immediately beneath the frock was of fine muslin; and from this a slip eighteen inches wide had been torn entirely out—torn very evenly and with great care. It was found around her neck, fitting loosely, and secured with a hard knot. Over this muslin slip and the slip of lace the strings of a bonnet were attached, the bonnet being appended. The knot by which the strings of the bonnet were fastened was not a lady's, but a slip or sailor's knot.

After the recognition of the corpse, it was not, as usual, taken to the Morgue, (this formality being superfluous), but hastily interred not far from the spot at which it was brought ashore. Through the exertions of Beauvais the matter was industriously hushed up, as far as possible; and several days had elapsed before any public emotion resulted. A weekly paper, however, at length took up the theme; the corpse was disinterred, and a re-examination instituted; but nothing was elicited beyond what has been already noted. The clothes, however, were now submitted to the mother and friends of the deceased and fully identified as those worn by the girl upon leaving home.

Meantime, the excitement increased hourly. Several individuals were arrested and discharged. St. Eustache fell especially under suspicion; and he failed, at first, to give an intelligible account of his whereabouts during the Sunday on which Marie left home. Subsequently, however, he submitted to Monsieur G—, affidavits, accounting satisfactorily for every hour of the day in question. As time passed and no discovery ensued, a thousand contradictory rumors were circulated, and journalists busied themselves in suggestions. Among these, the one which attracted the most notice, was the idea that Marie Rogêt still lived—that the corpse found in the Seine was that of some other unfortunate. It will be proper that I submit to the reader some passages which embody the suggestion alluded to. These passages are literal translations from *L'Etoile*, a paper conducted, in general, with much ability.

"Mademoiselle Rogêt left her mother's house on Sunday morning, June the twenty-second, 18—, with the ostensible purpose of going to see her aunt, or some other connection, in the Rue des Drômes. From that hour, nobody is proved to have seen her. There is no trace or tidings of her at all. . . . There has no person, whatever, come forward, so far, who saw her at all, on that day, after she left her mother's door. . . . Now, though we have no evidence that Marie Rogêt was in the land of the living after nine o'clock on Sunday, June the twenty-second, we have proof that, up to that hour, she was alive. On Wednesday noon, at twelve, a female body was discovered afloat on the shore of the Barrière de Roule. This was, even if we presume that Marie Rogêt was thrown into the river within three hours after she left her mother's house, only three days from the time she left her home—three days to an hour. But it is folly to suppose that the murder, if murder was committed on her body, could have been consummated soon enough to have enabled her murderers to throw the body into the river before midnight. Those who are guilty of such horrid crimes, choose darkness rather the light. . . . Thus we see that if the body found in the river was that of Marie Rogêt, it could only have been in the water two and a half days, or three at the outside. All experience has shown that drowned bodies, or bodies thrown into the water immediately after death by violence, require from six to ten days for decomposition to take place to bring them to the top of the water. Even where a cannon is fired over a corpse, and it rises before at least five or six days' immersion, it sinks again, if let alone. Now, we ask, what was there in this case to cause a departure from the ordinary course of nature? . . . If the body had been kept in its mangled state on shore until Tuesday night, some trace would be found on shore of the murderers. It is a doubtful point, also, whether the body would be so soon afloat, even were it thrown in after having been dead two days. And, furthermore, it is exceedingly improbable that any villains who had committed such a murder as is here supposed, would have thrown the body in without weight to sink it, when such a precaution could have so easily been taken."

The editor here proceeds to argue that the body must have been in the water "not three days merely, but, at least, five times three days," because it was so far decomposed that Beauvais had great difficulty in recognizing it. This latter point, however, was fully disproved. I continue the translation:

"What, then, are the facts on which M. Beauvais says that he has no doubt the body was that of Marie Rogêt? He ripped up the gown sleeve, and says he found marks which satisfied him of the identity.

The public generally supposed those marks to have consisted of some description of scars. He rubbed the arm and found hair upon it—something as indefinite, we think, as can readily be imagined—as little conclusive as finding an arm in the sleeve. M. Beauvais did not return that night, but sent word to Madame Rogêt, at seven o'clock, on Wednesday evening, that an investigation was still in progress respecting her daughter. If we allow that Madame Rogêt, from her age and grief, could not go over (which is allowing a great deal), there certainly must have been some one who would have thought it worth while to go over and attend the investigation, if they thought the body was that of Marie. Nobody went over. There was nothing said or heard about the matter in the Rue Pavée-Saint-Andrée, that reached even the occupants of the same building. M. St. Eustache, the lover and intended husband of Marie, who boarded in her mother's house, deposes that he did not hear of the discovery of the body of his intended until the next morning, when M. Beauvais came into his chamber and told him of it. For an item of news like this, it strikes us it was very coolly received."

In this way the journal endeavored to create the impression of an apathy on the part of the relatives of Marie, inconsistent with the supposition that these relatives believed the corpse to be hers. Its insinuations amount to this: that Marie, with the connivance of her friends, had absented herself from the city for reasons involving a charge against her chastity; and that these friends, upon the discovery of a corpse in the Seine, somewhat resembling that of the girl, had availed themselves of the opportunity to impress the public with the belief of her death. But *L'Etoile* was again over-hasty. It was distinctly proved that no apathy, such as was imagined, existed; that the old lady was exceedingly feeble and so agitated as to be unable to attend to any duty; that St. Eustache, so far from receiving the news coolly, was distracted with grief, and bore himself so frantically, that M. Beauvais prevailed upon a friend and relative to take charge of him, and prevent his attending the examination at the disinterment. Moreover, although it was stated by *L'Etoile*, that the corpse was re-interred at the public expense—that an advantageous offer of private sepulture was absolutely declined by the family—and that no member of the family attended the ceremonial;—although, I say, all this was asserted by *L'Etoile* in furtherance of the impression it designed to convey—yet all this was satisfactorily disproved. In a subsequent number of the paper an attempt was made to throw suspicion upon Beauvais himself. The editor says:

"Now, then, a change comes over the matter. We are told that on one occasion, while a Madame B— was at Madame Rogêt's house, M. Beauvais, who was going out, told her that a *gendarme* was expected there, and she, Madame B., must not say anything to the *gendarme* until he returned, but let the matter be for him. . . . In the present posture of affairs, M. Beauvais appears to have the whole matter locked up in his head. A single step cannot be taken without M. Beauvais; for, go which way you will, you run against him. . . . For some reason, he determined that nobody shall have anything to do with the proceedings but himself, and he has elbowed the male relatives out of the way, according to their representations, in a very singular manner. He seems to have been very much averse to permitting the relatives to see the body."

By the following fact some color was given to the suspicion thus thrown upon Beauvais. A visitor at his office, a few days prior to the girl's disappearance, and during the absence of its occupant, had observed a rose in the key-hole of the door, and the name "Marie" inscribed upon a slate which hung near at hand.

The general impression, so far as we were enabled to glean it from the newspapers, seemed to be, that Marie had been the victim of a gang of desperadoes—that by these she had been borne across the river, maltreated and murdered. *Le Commerciel*, however, a print of extensive influence, was earnest in combating this popular idea. I quote a passage or two from its columns:

"We are persuaded that pursuit has hitherto been on a false scent, so far as it has been directed to the Barrière du Roule. It is impossible that a person so well known to thousands as this young woman was, should have passed three blocks without some one having seen her; and any one who saw her would have remembered it, for she interested all who knew her. It was when the streets were full of people, when she went out. . . . It is impossible that she could have gone to the Barrière du Roule, or to the Rue des Drômes, without being recognized by a dozen persons; yet no one has come forward who saw her outside her mother's door, and there is no evidence, except the testimony concerning her expressed intentions, that she did go out at all. Her gown was torn, bound round her, and tied; and by that the body was carried as a bundle. If the murder had been committed at the Barrière du Roule, there would have been no necessity for any such arrangement. The fact that the body was found floating near the Barrière, is no proof as to where it was thrown into the water. . . . A piece of one of the unfortunate girl's petticoats, two feet long and one foot wide, was torn out and tied under her chin around the back of her head, probably to prevent screams. This was done by fellows who had no pocket-handkerchief."

A day or two before the Prefect called upon us, however, some important information reached the police, which seemed to overthrow, at least, the chief portion of Le Commerciel's argument. Two small boys, sons of a Madame Deluc, while roaming among the woods near the Barrière du Roule, chanced to penetrate a close thicket, within which were three or four large stones, forming a kind of seat with a back and footstool. On the upper stone lay a white petticoat; on the second a silk scarf. A parasol, gloves, and a pocket-handkerchief were also here found. The handkerchief bore the name "Marie Rogêt." Fragments of dress were discovered on the brambles around. The earth was trampled, the bushes were broken, and there was every evidence of a struggle. Between the thicket and the river the fences were found taken down and the ground bore evidence of some heavy burthen having been dragged along it.

A weekly paper, Le Soleil, had the following comments upon this discovery—comments which merely echoed the sentiment of the whole Parisian press:

"The things had all evidently been there at least three or four weeks; they were all mildewed down hard with the action of the rain and stuck together from mildew. The grass had grown around and over some of them. The silk on the parasol was strong, but the threads of it were run together within. The upper part, where it had been doubled and folded, was all mildewed and rotten, and tore on its being opened. . . . The pieces of her frock torn out by the bushes were about three inches wide and six inches long. One part was the hem of the frock, and it had been mended; the other piece was part of the skirt, not the hem. They looked like strips torn off, and were on the thorn bush, about a foot from the ground. . . . There can be no doubt, therefore, that the spot of this appalling outrage has been discovered."

Consequent upon this discovery, new evidence appeared. Madame Deluc testified that she keeps a roadside inn not far from the bank of the river, opposite the Barrière du Roule. The neighborhood is secluded—particularly so. It is the usual Sunday resort of blackguards from the city, who cross the river in boats. About three o'clock, in the afternoon of the Sunday in question, a young girl arrived at the inn, accompanied by a young man of dark complexion. The two remained here for some time. On their departure they took the road to some thick woods in the vicinity. Madame Deluc's attention was called to the dress worn by the girl, on account of its resemblance to one worn by a deceased relative. A scarf was particularly noticed. Soon after the departure of the couple, a gang of miscreants made their appearance, behaved boisterously, ate and drank without making payment, followed in the route of the young man and girl, returned to the inn about dusk, and re-crossed the river as if in great haste.

It was soon after dark, upon this same evening, that Madame Deluc, as well as her eldest son, heard the screams of a female in the vicinity of the inn. The screams were violent but brief. Madame D. recognized not only the scarf which was found in the thicket, but the dress which was discovered upon the corpse. An omnibus driver, Valence, now also testified that he saw Marie Rogêt cross a ferry on the Seine, on the Sunday in question, in company with a young man of dark complexion. He, Valence, knew Marie, and could not be mistaken in her identity. The articles found in the thicket were fully identified by the relatives of Marie.

The items of evidence and information thus collected by myself, from the newspapers, at the suggestion of Dupin, embraced only one more point—but this was a point of seemingly vast consequence. It appears that, immediately after the discovery of the clothes as above described, the lifeless, or nearly lifeless body of St. Eustache, Marie's betrothed, was found in the vicinity of what all now supposed the scene of the outrage. A phial labelled "laudanum," and emptied, was found near him. His breath gave evidence of the poison. He died without speaking. Upon his person was found a letter, briefly stating his love for Marie, with his design of self-destruction.

"I need scarcely tell you," said Dupin, as he finished the perusal of my notes, "that this is a far more intricate case than that of the Rue Morgue; from which it differs in one important respect. This is an ordinary, although an atrocious, instance of crime. There is nothing peculiarly *outré** about it. You will observe that, for this reason, the mystery has been considered easy, when, for this reason,

---

* French: bizarre.

it should have been considered difficult, of solution. Thus; at first, it was thought unnecessary to offer a reward. The myrmidons of G— were able at once to comprehend how and why such an atrocity might have been committed. They could picture to their imaginations a mode—many modes; and a motive—many motives; and because it was not impossible that either of these numerous modes and motives could have been the actual one, they have taken it for granted that one of them must. But the ease with which these variable fancies were entertained, and the very plausibility which each assumed, should have been understood as indicative rather of the difficulties than of the facilities which must attend elucidation. I have, before, observed that it is by prominences above the plane of the ordinary that reason feels her way, if at all, in her search for the true, and that the proper question, in cases such as this, is not so much 'what has occurred?' as 'what has occurred that has never occurred before?' In the investigations at the house of Madame L'Espanaye, the agents of G— were discouraged and confounded by that very unusualness which, to a properly regulated intellect, would have afforded the surest omen of success; while this same intellect might have been plunged in despair at the ordinary character of all that met the eye in the case of the perfumery-girl, and yet told of nothing but easy triumph to the functionaries of the Prefecture.

"In the case of Madame L'Espanaye and her daughter there was, even at the beginning of our investigation, no doubt that murder had been committed. The idea of suicide was excluded at once. Here, too, we are freed, at the commencement, from all supposition of self-murder. The body found at the Barrière du Roule was found under such circumstances as to leave us no room for embarrassment upon this important point. But it has been suggested that the corpse discovered is not that of the Marie Rogêt for the conviction of whose assassin, or assassins, the reward is offered, and respecting whom, solely, our agreement has been arranged with the Prefect. We both know this gentleman well. It will not do to trust him too far. If, dating our inquiries from the body found, and thence tracing a murderer, we yet discover this body to be that of some other individual than Marie; or, if starting from the living Marie, we find her, yet find her unassassinated—in either case we lose our labor; since it is Monsieur G— with whom we have to deal. For our own purpose, therefore, if not for the purpose of justice, it is indispensable that our first step should be the determination of the identity of the corpse with the Marie Rogêt who is missing.

"With the public the arguments of *L'Etoile* have had weight; and that the journal itself is convinced of their importance would appear from the manner in which it commences one of its essays upon the subject—'Several of the morning papers of the day,' it says, 'speak of the conclusive article in Monday's *Etoile*.' To me, this article appears conclusive of little beyond the zeal of its inditer. We should bear in mind that, in general, it is the object of our newspapers rather to create a sensation—to make a point—than to further the cause of truth. The latter end is only pursued when it seems coincident with the former. The print which merely falls in with ordinary opinion (however well founded this opinion may be) earns for itself no credit with the mob. The mass of the people regards as profound only him who suggests pungent contradictions of the general idea. In ratiocination, not less than in literature, it is the epigram which is the most immediately and the most universally appreciated. In both, it is of the lowest order of merit.

"What I mean to say is, that it is the mingled epigram and *melodrame* of the idea, that Marie Rogêt still lives, rather than any true plausibility in this idea, which have suggested it to *L'Etoile*, and secured it a favorable reception with the public. Let us examine the heads of this journal's argument, endeavoring to avoid the incoherence with which it is originally set forth.

"The first aim of the writer is to show, from the brevity of the interval between Marie's disappearance and the finding of the floating corpse, that this corpse cannot be that of Marie. The reduction of this interval to its smallest possible dimension becomes thus, at once, an object with the reasoner. In the rash pursuit of this object, he rushes into mere assumption at the outset. 'It is folly to suppose,' he says, 'that the murder, if murder was committed on her body, could have been consummated soon enough to have enabled her murderers to throw the body into the river before midnight.' We demand at once, and very naturally, why? Why is it folly to suppose that the murder was committed within five minutes after the girl's quitting her mother's house? Why is it folly to suppose that the murder was committed at any given period of the day? There have been assassinations at all hours. But, had the murder taken place at any moment between nine o'clock in the morning of Sunday and a quarter before midnight, there would still have been time enough 'to throw the body into the river before midnight.' This assumption, then, amounts precisely to this—that the murder was not committed on Sunday at all—and, if we allow *L'Etoile* to assume this, we may permit it any liberties whatever. The paragraph beginning 'It is folly to suppose that the murder, etc.,' however it appears as printed in *L'Etoile*, may be imagined to have existed actually thus in the brain of its inditer—'It is folly to suppose that the murder, if murder was committed on the body, could have been committed soon enough to have enabled her murderers to throw the body into the river before midnight; it is folly, we say, to suppose all this, and to suppose at the same time, (as we are resolved to suppose), that the body was not thrown in until after midnight'—a sentence sufficiently inconsequential in itself, but not so utterly preposterous as the one printed.

"Were it my purpose," continued Dupin, "merely to make out a case against this passage of *L'Etoile*'s argument, I might safely leave it where it is. It is not, however, with *L'Etoile* that we have to do, but with the truth. The sentence in question has but one meaning, as it stands; and this meaning I have fairly stated; but it is material that we go behind the mere words for an idea which these words have obviously intended and failed to convey. It was the design of the journalist to say that, at whatever period of the day or night of Sunday this murder was committed, it was improbable that the assassins would have ventured to bear the corpse to the river before midnight. And herein lies, really, the assumption of which I complain. It is assumed that the murder was committed at such a position, and under such circum-stances, that the bearing it to the river became necessary. Now, the assassination might have taken place upon the river's brink, or on the river itself; and, thus, the throwing the corpse in the water might have been resorted to at any period of the day or night, as the most obvious and most immediate mode of disposal. You will understand that I suggest nothing here as probable, or as coincident with my own opinion. My design, so far, has no reference to the facts of the case. I wish merely to caution you against the whole tone of *L'Etoile*'s suggestion, by calling your attention to its *ex-parte** character at the outset.

"Having prescribed thus a limit to suit its own preconceived notions; having assumed that, if this were the body of Marie, it could have been in the water but a very brief time; the journal goes on to say:

'All experience has shown that drowned bodies, or bodies thrown into the water immediately after death by violence, require from six to ten days for sufficient decomposition to take place to bring them to the top of the water. Even when a cannon is fired over a corpse, and it rises before at least five or six days' immersion, it sinks again if let alone.'

"These assertions have been tacitly received by every paper in Paris, with the exception of *Le Moniteur*. This latter print endeavors to combat that portion of the paragraph which has reference to 'drowned bodies' only, by citing some five

---

*   Latin: one-sided.

or six instances in which the bodies of individuals known to be drowned were found floating after the lapse of less time than is insisted upon by *L'Etoile*. But there is something excessively unphilosophical in the attempt on the part of *Le Moniteur* to rebut the general assertion of *L'Etoile*, by a citation of particular instances militating against that assertion. Had it been possible to adduce fifty, instead of five examples, of bodies found floating at the end of two or three days, these fifty examples could still have been properly regarded only as exceptions to *L'Etoile*'s rule, until such time as the rule itself should be confuted. Admitting the rule, (and this *Le Moniteur* does not deny, insisting merely upon its exceptions), the argument of *L'Etoile* is suffered to remain in full force; for this argument does not pretend to involve more than a question of the probability of the body having risen to the surface in less than three days; and this probability will be in favor of *L'Etoile*'s position until the instances so childishly adduced shall be sufficient in number to establish an antagonistical rule.

"You will see at once that all argument upon this head should be urged, if at all, against the rule itself; and for this end we must examine the rationale of the rule. Now the human body, in general, is neither much lighter nor much heavier than the water of the Seine; that is to say, the specific gravity of the human body, in its natural condition, is about equal to the bulk of fresh water which it displaces. The bodies of fat and fleshy persons, with small bones, and of women generally, are lighter than those of the lean and large-boned, and of men; and the specific gravity of the water of a river is somewhat influenced by the presence of the tide from sea. But, leaving this tide out of question, it may be said that very few human bodies will sink at all, even in fresh water, of their own accord. Almost any one, falling into a river, will be enabled to float, if he suffer the specific gravity of the water fairly to be adduced in comparison with his own—that is to say, if he suffer his whole person to be immersed, with as little exception as possible. The proper position for one who cannot swim is the upright position of the walker on land, with the head thrown fully back, and immersed; the mouth and nostrils alone remaining above the surface. Thus circumstanced, we shall find that we float without difficulty and without exertion. It is evident, however, that the gravities of the body, and of the bulk of water displaced, are very nicely balanced, and that a trifle will cause either to preponderate. An arm, for instance, uplifted from the water, and thus deprived of its support, is an additional weight sufficient to immerse the whole head, while the accidental aid of the smallest piece of timber will enable us to elevate the head so as to look about. Now, in the struggles of one unused to swimming, the arms are invariably thrown upward, while an attempt is made to keep the head in its usual perpendicular position. The result is the immersion of the mouth and nostrils, and the inception, during efforts to breathe while beneath the surface, of water into the lungs. Much is also received into the stomach, and the whole body becomes heavier by the difference between the weight of the air originally distending these cavities, and that of the fluid which now fills them. This difference is sufficient to cause the body to sink, as a general rule; but is insufficient in the cases of individuals with small bones and an abnormal quantity of flaccid or fatty matter. Such individuals float even after drowning.

"The corpse, being supposed at the bottom of the river, will there remain until, by some means, its specific gravity again becomes less than that of the bulk of water which it displaces. This effect is brought about by decomposition, or otherwise. The result of decomposition is the generation of gas, distending the cellular tissues and all the cavities, and giving the puffed appearance which is so horrible. When this distension has so far progressed that the bulk of the corpse is materially increased without a corresponding increase of mass or weight, its specific gravity becomes less than that of the water displaced, and it forthwith makes its appearance at the surface. But decomposition is modified by innumerable circumstances—is hastened or retarded by innumerable agencies; for example, by the heat or cold of the season, by the mineral impregnation or purity of the water, by its depth or shallowness, by its currency or stagnation, by the temperament of the body, by its infection or freedom from disease before death. Thus it is evident that we can assign no period, with anything like accuracy, at which the corpse shall rise through decomposition. Under certain conditions this result would be brought about within an hour; under others, it might not take place at all. There are chemical infusions by which the animal frame can be preserved forever from corruption; the bi-chloride of mercury is one. But, apart from decomposition, there may be, and very usually is, a generation of gas within the stomach, from the acetous fermentation of vegetable matter (or within other cavities from other causes) sufficient to induce a distension which will bring the body to the surface. The effect produced by the firing of a cannon is that of simple vibration. This may either loosen the corpse from the soft mud or ooze in which it is imbedded, thus permitting it to rise when other agencies have already prepared it for so doing; or it may overcome the tenacity of some putrescent portions of the cellular tissue; allowing the cavities to distend under the influence of the gas.

"Having thus before us the whole philosophy of this subject, we can easily test by it the assertions of *L'Etoile*. 'All experience shows,' says this paper, 'that drowned bodies, or bodies thrown into the water immediately after death by violence, require from six to ten days for sufficient decomposition to take place to bring them to the top of the water. Even when a cannon is fired over a corpse, and it rises before at least five or six days' immersion, it sinks again if let alone.'

"The whole of this paragraph must now appear a tissue of inconsequence and incoherence. All experience does not show that 'drowned bodies' require from six to ten days for sufficient decomposition to take place to bring them to the surface. Both science and experience show that the period of their rising is, and necessarily must be, indeterminate. If, moreover, a body has risen to the surface through firing of cannon, it will not 'sink again if let alone,' until decomposition has so far progressed as to permit the escape of the generated gas. But I wish to call your attention to the distinction which is made between 'drowned bodies,' and 'bodies thrown into the water immediately after death by violence.' Although the writer admits the distinction, he yet includes them all in the same category. I have shown how it is that the body of a drowning man becomes specifically heavier than its bulk of water, and that he would not sink at all, except for the struggle by which he elevates his arms above the surface, and his gasps for breath while beneath the surface—gasps which supply by water the place of the original air in the lungs. But these struggles and these gasps would not occur in the body 'thrown into the water immediately after death by violence.' Thus, in the latter instance, the body, as a general rule, would not sink at all—a fact of which L'Etoile is evidently ignorant. When decomposition had proceeded to a very great extent—when the flesh had in a great measure left the bones—then, indeed, but not till then, should we lose sight of the corpse.

"And now what are we to make of the argument that the body found could not be that of Marie Rogêt, because, three days only having elapsed, this body was found floating? If drowned, being a woman, she might never have sunk; or having sunk, might have reappeared in twenty-four hours or less. But no one supposes her to have been drowned; and, dying before being thrown into the river, she might have been found floating at any period afterwards whatever.

"'But,' says L'Etoile, 'if the body had been kept in its mangled state on shore until Tuesday night, some trace would be found on shore of the murderers.' Here it is at first difficult to perceive the intention of the reasoner. He means to anticipate what he imagines would be an objection to his theory—viz: that the body was kept on shore two days, suffering rapid decomposition—more rapid than if immersed in water. He supposes that, had this been the case, it might have appeared at the surface on the Wednesday, and thinks that only under such circumstances it could have so appeared. He is accordingly in haste to show that it was not kept on shore; for, if so, 'some trace would be found on shore of the murderers.' I presume you smile at the *sequitur.* You cannot be made to see how the mere duration of the corpse on the shore could operate to multiply traces of the assassins. Nor can I.

"'And furthermore it is exceedingly improbable,' continues our journal, 'that any villains who had committed such a murder as is here supposed would have thrown the body in without weight to sink it, when such a precaution could have so easily been taken.' Observe, here, the laughable confusion of thought! No one—not even *L'Etoile*—disputes the murder committed on the body found. The marks of violence are too obvious. It is our reasoner's object merely to show that this body is not Marie's. He wishes to prove that Marie is not assassinated—not that the corpse was not. Yet his observation proves only the latter point. Here is a corpse without weight attached. Murderers, casting it in, would not have failed to attach a weight. Therefore it was not thrown in by murderers. This is all which is proved, if anything is. The question of identity is not even approached, and *L'Etoile* has been at great pains merely to gainsay now what it has admitted only a moment before. 'We are perfectly convinced,' it says, 'that the body found was that of a murdered female.'

"Nor is this the sole instance, even in this division of his subject, where our reasoner unwittingly reasons against himself. His evident object, I have already said, is to reduce, as much as possible, the interval between Marie's disappearance and the finding of the corpse. Yet we find him urging the point that no person saw the girl from the moment of her leaving her mother's house. 'We have no evidence,' he says, 'that Marie Rogêt was in the land of the living after nine o'clock on Sunday, June the twenty-second.' As his argument is obviously an *ex-parte* one, he should, at least, have left this matter out of sight; for, had any one been known to see Marie, say on Monday, or on Tuesday, the interval in question would have been much reduced, and, by his own ratiocination, the probability much diminished of the corpse being that of the *grisette.* It is, nevertheless, amusing to observe that *L'Etoile* insists upon its point in the full belief of its furthering its general argument.

"Re-peruse now that portion of this argument which has reference to the identification of the corpse by Beauvais. In regard to the hair upon the arm, *L'Etoile* has been obviously disingenuous. M. Beauvais, not being an idiot, could never have urged, in identification of the corpse, simply hair upon its arm. No arm is without hair. The generality of the expression of *L'Etoile* is a mere perversion of the witness's phraseology. He must have spoken of some peculiarity in this hair. It must have been a peculiarity of color, of quantity, of length, or of situation.

"'Her foot,' says the journal, 'was small—so are thousands of feet. Her garter is no proof whatever—nor is her shoe—for shoes and garters are sold in packages. The same may be said of the flowers in her hat. One thing upon which M. Beauvais strongly insists is, that the clasp on the garter found had been set back to take it in. This amounts to nothing; for most women find it proper to take a pair of garters home and fit them to the size of the limbs they are to encircle, rather than to try them in the store where they purchase.' Here it is difficult to suppose the reasoner in earnest. Had M. Beauvais, in his search for the body of Marie, discovered a corpse corresponding in general size and appearance to the missing girl, he would have been warranted (without reference to the question of habiliment at all) in forming an opinion that his search had been successful. If, in addition to the point of general size and contour, he had found upon the arm a peculiar hairy appearance which he had observed upon the living Marie, his opinion might have been justly strengthened; and the increase of positiveness might well have been in the ratio of the peculiarity, or unusualness, of the hairy mark. If, the feet of Marie being small, those of the corpse were also small, the increase of probability that the body was that of Marie would not be an increase in a ratio merely arithmetical, but in one highly geometrical, or accumulative. Add to all this shoes such as she had been known to wear upon the day of her disappearance, and, although these shoes may be 'sold in packages,' you so far augment the probability as to verge upon the certain. What, of itself, would be no evidence of identity, becomes through its corroborative position, proof most sure. Give us, then, flowers in the hat corresponding to those worn by the missing girl, and we seek for nothing farther. If only one flower, we seek for nothing farther—what then if two or three, or more? Each successive one is multiple evidence—proof not added to proof, but multiplied by hundreds or thousands. Let us now discover, upon the deceased, garters such as the living used, and it is almost folly to proceed. But these garters are found to be tightened, by the setting back of a clasp, in just such a manner as her own had been tightened by Marie, shortly previous to her leaving home. It is now madness or hypocrisy to doubt. What *L'Etoile* says in respect to this abbreviation of the garters being an unusual occurrence, shows nothing beyond its own pertinacity in error. The elastic nature of the clasp-garter is self-demonstration of the unusualness of the abbreviation. What is made to adjust itself, must of necessity require foreign adjustment but rarely. It must have been by an accident, in its strictest sense, that these garters of Marie needed the tightening described. They alone would have amply established her identity. But it is not that the corpse was found to have the garters of the missing girl, or found to have her shoes, or her bonnet, or the flowers of her bonnet, or her feet, or a peculiar mark upon the arm, or her general size and appearance—it is that the corpse had each, and all collectively. Could it be proved that the editor of *L'Etoile* really entertained a doubt, under the circumstances, there would be no need, in his case, of a commission *de lunatico inquirendo.** He has thought it sagacious to echo the small talk of the lawyers, who, for the most part, content themselves with echoing the rectangular precepts of the courts. I would here observe that very much of what is rejected as evidence by a court is the best of evidence to the intellect. For the court, guiding itself by the general principles of evidence—the recognized and booked principles—is averse from swerving at particular instances. And this steadfast adherence to principle, with rigorous disregard of the conflicting exception, is a sure mode of attaining the maximum of attainable truth, in any long sequence of time. The practice, in mass, is therefore philosophical; but it is not the less certain that it engenders vast individual error.

"In respect to the insinuations levelled at Beauvais, you will be willing to dismiss them in a breath. You have already fathomed the true character of this good gentleman. He is a busy-body, with much of romance and little of wit. Any one so constituted will readily so conduct himself, upon occasion of real excitement, as to render himself liable to suspicion on the part of the over acute, or the ill-disposed. M. Beauvais (as it appears from your notes) had some personal interviews with the editor of *L'Etoile*, and offended him by venturing an opinion that the corpse, notwithstanding the theory of the editor, was, in sober fact, that of Marie. 'He persists,' says the paper, 'in asserting the corpse to be that of Marie, but cannot give a circumstance, in addition to those which we have commented upon, to make others believe.' Now, without re-adverting to the fact that stronger evidence 'to make others believe,' could never have been adduced, it may be remarked that a man may very well be understood to believe, in a case of this kind, without the ability to advance a single reason for the belief of a second party. Nothing is more vague than impressions of individual identity. Each man recognizes his neighbor, yet there are few instances in which any one is prepared to give a reason for his recognition. The editor of *L'Etoile* had no right to be offended at M. Beauvais' unreasoning belief.

---

* Latin: "inquiry into lunacy." A 19th-century legal term for a sanity hearing.

"The suspicious circumstances which invest him, will be found to tally much better with my hypothesis of romantic busy-bodyism than with the reasoner's suggestion of guilt. Once adopting the more charitable interpretation, we shall find no difficulty in comprehending the rose in the key-hole; the 'Marie' upon the slate; the 'elbowing the male relatives out of the way;' the 'aversion to permitting them to see the body;' the caution given to Madame B——, that she must hold no conversation with the *gendarme* until his (Beauvais') return; and, lastly, his apparent determination 'that nobody should have anything to do with the proceedings except himself.' It seems to me unquestionable that Beauvais was a suitor of Marie's; that she coquetted with him; and that he was ambitious of being thought to enjoy her fullest intimacy and confidence. I shall say nothing more upon this point; and, as the evidence fully rebuts the assertion of *L'Etoile*, touching the matter of apathy on the part of the mother and other relatives—an apathy inconsistent with the supposition of their believing the corpse to be that of the perfumery-girl—we shall now proceed as if the question of identity were settled to our perfect satisfaction."

"And what," I here demanded, "do you think of the opinions of *Le Commerciel*?"

"That, in spirit, they are far more worthy of attention than any which have been promulgated upon the subject. The deductions from the premises are philosophical and acute; but the premises, in two instances, at least, are founded in imperfect observation. *Le Commerciel* wishes to intimate that Marie was seized by some gang of low ruffians not far from her mother's door. 'It is impossible,' it urges, 'that a person so well known to thousands as this young woman was, should have passed three blocks without some one having seen her.' This is the idea of a man long resident in Paris—a public man—and one whose walks to and fro in the city have been mostly limited to the vicinity of the public offices. He is aware that he seldom passes so far as a dozen blocks from his own bureau, without being recognized and accosted. And, knowing the extent of his personal acquaintance with others, and of others with him, he compares his notoriety with that of the perfumery-girl, finds no great difference between them, and reaches at once the conclusion that she, in her walks, would be equally liable to recognition with himself in his. This could only be the case were her walks of the same unvarying, methodical character, and within the same species of limited region as are his own. He passes to and fro, at regular intervals, within a confined periphery, abounding in individuals who are led to observation of his person through interest in the kindred nature of his occupation with their own. But the walks of Marie may, in general, be supposed discursive. In this particular instance, it will be understood as most probable that she proceeded upon a route of more than average diversity from her accustomed ones. The parallel which we imagine to have existed in the mind of *Le Commerciel* would only be sustained in the event of the two individuals traversing the whole city. In this case, granting the personal acquaintances to be equal, the chances would be also equal that an equal number of personal *rencontres* would be made. For my own part, I should hold it not only as possible, but as very far more than probable, that Marie might have proceeded, at any given period, by any one of the many routes between her own residence and that of her aunt, without meeting a single individual whom she knew, or by whom she was known. In viewing this question in its full and proper light, we must hold steadily in mind the great disproportion between the personal acquaintances of even the most noted individual in Paris, and the entire population of Paris itself.

"But whatever force there may still appear to be in the suggestion of *Le Commerciel* will be much diminished when we take into consideration the hour at which the girl went abroad. 'It was when the streets were full of people,' says *Le Commerciel*, 'that she went out.' But not so. It was at nine o'clock in the morning. Now at nine o'clock of every morning in the week, with the exception of Sunday, the streets of the city are, it is true, thronged with people. At nine on Sunday, the populace are chiefly within doors preparing for church. No observing person can have failed to notice the peculiarly deserted air of the town, from about eight until ten on the morning of every Sabbath. Between ten and eleven the streets are thronged, but not at so early a period as that designated.

"There is another point at which there seems a deficiency of observation on the part of *Le Commerciel*. 'A piece,' it says, 'of one of the unfortunate girl's petticoats, two feet long, and one foot wide, was torn out and tied under her chin, and around the back of her head, probably to prevent screams. This was done, by fellows who had no pocket-handkerchiefs.' Whether this idea is or is not well founded, we will endeavor to see hereafter; but by 'fellows who have no pocket-handkerchiefs' the editor intends the lowest class of ruffians. These, however, are the very description of people who will always be found to have handkerchiefs even when destitute of shirts. You must have had occasion to observe how absolutely indispensable, of late years, to the thorough blackguard, has become the pocket-handkerchief."

"And what are we to think," I asked, "of the article in *Le Soleil*?"

"That it is a vast pity its inditer was not born a parrot—in which case he would have been the most illustrious parrot of his race. He has merely repeated the individual items of the already published opinion; collecting them, with a laudable industry, from this paper and from that. 'The things had all evidently been there,' he says, 'at least, three or four weeks, and there can be no doubt that the spot of this appalling outrage has been discovered.' The facts here restated by *Le Soleil* are very far indeed from removing my own doubts upon this subject, and we will examine them more particularly hereafter in connection with another division of the theme.

"At present we must occupy ourselves with other investigations. You cannot fail to have remarked the extreme laxity of the examination of the corpse. To be sure, the question of identity was readily determined, or should have been; but there were other points to be ascertained. Had the body been in any respect despoiled? Had the deceased any articles of jewelry about her person upon leaving home? If so, had she any when found? These are important questions utterly untouched by the evidence; and there are others of equal moment, which have met with no attention. We must endeavor to satisfy ourselves by personal inquiry. The case of St. Eustache must be re-examined. I have no suspicion of this person; but let us proceed methodically. We will ascertain beyond a doubt the validity of the affidavits in regard to his whereabouts on the Sunday. Affidavits of this character are readily made matter of mystification. Should there be nothing wrong here, however, we will dismiss St. Eustache from our investigations. His suicide, how-ever corroborative of suspicion, were there found to be deceit in the affidavits, is, without such deceit, in no respect an unaccountable circumstance, or one which need cause us to deflect from the line of ordinary analysis.

"In that which I now propose, we will discard the interior points of this tragedy and concentrate our attention upon its outskirts. Not the least usual error in investigations such as this is the limiting of inquiry to the immediate, with total disregard of the collateral or circumstantial events. It is the malpractice of the courts to confine evidence and discussion to the bounds of apparent relevancy. Yet experience has shown, and a true philosophy will always show, that a vast, perhaps the larger portion of truth, arises from the seemingly irrelevant. It is through the spirit of this principle, if not precisely through its letter, that modern science has resolved to calculate upon the unforeseen. But perhaps you do not comprehend me. The history of human knowledge has so uninterruptedly shown that to collateral, or incidental, or accidental events we are indebted for the most numerous and most valuable discoveries, that it has at length become necessary, in any prospective view of improvement, to make not only large, but the largest allowances for inventions that shall arise by chance, and quite out of the range of ordinary expectation. It is no longer philosophical to base, upon what has been, a vision of what is to be. Accident is admitted as a portion of the substructure. We make chance a matter of absolute calculation. We subject the unlooked for and unimagined, to the mathematical formulae of the schools.

"I repeat that it is no more than fact that the larger portion of all truth has sprung from the collateral; and it is but in accordance with the spirit of the principle involved in this fact, that I would divert inquiry, in the present case, from the trodden and hitherto unfruitful ground of the event itself to the contemporary circumstances which surround it. While you ascertain the validity of the affidavits, I will examine the newspapers more generally than you have as yet done. So far, we have only reconnoitred the field of investigation; but it will be strange indeed if a comprehensive survey, such as I propose, of the public prints will not afford us some minute points which shall establish a direction for inquiry."

In pursuance of Dupin's suggestion, I made scrupulous examination of the affair of the affidavits. The result was a firm conviction of their validity, and of the consequent innocence of St. Eustache. In the meantime my friend occupied himself, with what seemed to me a minuteness altogether objectless, in a scrutiny of the various newspaper files. At the end of a week he placed before me the following extracts:

"About three years and a half ago, a disturbance very similar to the present was caused by the disappearance of this same Marie Rogêt from the *parfumerie* of Monsieur Le Blanc in the Palais Royal. At the end of a week, however, she re-appeared at her customary *comptoir*, as well as ever, with the exception of a slight paleness not altogether usual. It was given out by Monsieur Le Blanc and her mother that she had merely been on a visit to some friend in the country; and the affair was speedily hushed up. We presume that the present absence is a freak of the same nature, and that, at the expiration of a week, or, perhaps, of a month, we shall have her among us again."—*Evening Paper*, Monday June 23.

"An evening journal of yesterday, refers to a former mysterious disappearance of Mademoiselle Rogêt. It is well known that, during the week of her absence from Le Blanc's *parfumerie*, she was in the company of a young naval officer much noted for his debaucheries. A quarrel, it is supposed, providentially led to her return home. We have the name of the Lothario in question, who is at present stationed in Paris, but for obvious reasons forbear to make it public."—*Le Mercurie*, Tuesday Morning, June 24.

"An outrage of the most atrocious character was perpetrated near this city the day before yesterday. A gentleman, with his wife and daughter, engaged, about dusk, the services of six young men, who were idly rowing a boat to and fro near the banks of the Seine, to convey him across the river. Upon reaching the opposite shore, the three passengers stepped out, and had proceeded so far as to be beyond the view of the boat, when the daughter discovered that she had left in it her parasol. She returned for it, was seized by the gang, carried out into the stream, gagged, brutally treated, and finally taken to the shore at a point not far from that at which she had originally entered the boat with her parents. The villains have escaped for the time, but the police are upon their trail, and some of them will soon be taken."—*Morning Paper*, June 25.

"We have received one or two communications, the object of which is to fasten the crime of the late atrocity upon Mennais*; but as this gentleman has been fully exonerated by a legal inquiry, and as the arguments of our several correspondents appear to be more zealous than profound, we do not think it advisable to make them public."—*Morning Paper*, June 28.

"We have received several forcibly written communications, apparently from various sources, and which go far to render it a matter of certainty that the unfortunate Marie Rogêt has become a victim of one of the numerous bands of blackguards which infest the vicinity of the city upon Sunday. Our own opinion is decidedly in favor of this supposition. We shall endeavor to make room for some of these arguments hereafter."—*Evening Paper*, Tuesday, June 31.

"On Monday, one of the bargemen connected with the revenue service saw an empty boat floating down the Seine. Sails were lying in the bottom of the boat. The bargeman towed it under the barge office. The next morning it was taken from thence, without the knowledge of any of the officers. The rudder is now at the barge office."—*Le Diligence*, Thursday, June 26.

Upon reading these various extracts, they not only seemed to me irrelevant, but I could perceive no mode in which any one of them could be brought to bear upon the matter in hand. I waited for some explanation from Dupin.

"It is not my present design," he said, "to dwell upon the first and second of those extracts. I have copied them chiefly to show you the extreme remissness

---

* Original footnote: "Mennais was one of the parties originally suspected and arrested, but discharged through total lack of evidence."

of the police, who, as far as I can understand from the Prefect, have not troubled themselves, in any respect, with an examination of the naval officer alluded to. Yet it is mere folly to say that between the first and second disappearance of Marie there is no supposable connection. Let us admit the first elopement to have resulted in a quarrel between the lovers, and the return home of the betrayed. We are now prepared to view a second elopement (if we know that an elopement has again taken place) as indicating a renewal of the betrayer's advances, rather than as the result of new proposals by a second individual—we are prepared to regard it as a 'making up' of the old *amour*, rather than as the commencement of a new one. The chances are ten to one that he who had once eloped with Marie would again propose an elopement, rather than that she to whom proposals of elopement had been made by one individual, should have them made to her by another. And here let me call your attention to the fact that the time elapsing between the first ascertained and the second supposed elopement is a few months more than the general period of the cruises of our men-of-war. Had the lover been interrupted in his first villainy by the necessity of departure to sea, and had he seized the first moment of his return to renew the base designs not yet altogether accomplished—or not yet altogether accomplished by him? Of all these things we know nothing.

"You will say, however, that, in the second instance, there was no elopement as imagined. Certainly not—but are we prepared to say that there was not the frustrated design? Beyond St. Eustache, and perhaps Beauvais, we find no recognized, no open, no honorable suitors of Marie. Of none other is there anything said. Who, then, is the secret lover, of whom the relatives (at least most of them) know nothing, but whom Marie meets upon the morning of Sunday, and who is so deeply in her confidence, that she hesitates not to remain with him until the shades of the evening descend, amid the solitary groves of the Barrière du Roule? Who is that secret lover, I ask, of whom, at least, most of the relatives know nothing? And what means the singular prophecy of Madame Rogêt on the morning of Marie's departure?—'I fear that I shall never see Marie again.'

"But if we cannot imagine Madame Rogêt privy to the design of elopement, may we not at least suppose this design entertained by the girl? Upon quitting home, she gave it to be understood that she was about to visit her aunt in the Rue des Drômes and St. Eustache was requested to call for her at dark. Now, at first glance, this fact strongly militates against my suggestion;—but let us reflect. That she did meet some companion, and proceed with him across the river, reaching the Barrière du Roule at so late an hour as three o'clock in the afternoon, is known. But, in consenting so to accompany this individual (for whatever purpose—to her mother known or unknown), she must have thought of her expressed intention when leaving home, and of the surprise and suspicion aroused in the bosom of her affianced suitor, St. Eustache, when, calling for her, at the hour appointed, in the Rue des Drômes, he should find that she had not been there, and when, moreover, upon returning to the *pension* with this alarming intelligence, he should become aware of her continued absence from home. She must have thought of these things, I say. She must have foreseen the chagrin of St. Eustache, the suspicion of all. She could not have thought of returning to brave this suspicion; but the suspicion becomes a point of trivial importance to her, if we suppose her not intending to return.

"We may imagine her thinking thus—'I am to meet a certain person for the purpose of elopement, or for certain other purposes known only to myself. It is necessary that there be no chance of interruption—there must be sufficient time given us to elude pursuit—I will give it to be understood that I shall visit and spend the day with my aunt at the Rue des Drômes—I will tell St. Eustache not to call for me until dark—in this way, my absence from home for the longest possible period, without causing suspicion or anxiety, will be accounted for, and I shall gain more time than in any other manner. If I bid St. Eustache call for me at dark, he will be sure not to call before; but, if I wholly neglect to bid him call, my time for escape will be diminished, since it will be expected that I return the earlier, and my absence will the sooner excite anxiety. Now, if it were my design to return at all—if I had in contemplation merely a stroll with the individual in question—it would not be my policy to bid St. Eustache call; for, calling, he will be sure to ascertain that I have played him false—a fact of which I might keep him forever in ignorance, by leaving home without notifying him of my intention, by returning before dark, and by then stating that I had been to visit my aunt in the Rue des Drômes. But, as it is my design never to return—or not for some weeks—or not until certain concealments are effected—the gaining of time is the only point about which I need give myself any concern.'

"You have observed, in your notes, that the most general opinion in relation to this sad affair is, and was from the first, that the girl had been the victim of a gang of blackguards. Now, the popular opinion, under certain conditions, is not to be disregarded. When arising of itself—when manifesting itself in a strictly spontaneous manner—we should look upon it as analogous with that intuition which is the idiosyncrasy of the individual man of genius. In ninety-nine cases from the hundred I would abide by its decision. But it is important that we find no palpable traces of suggestion. The opinion must be rigorously the public's own; and the distinction is often exceedingly difficult to perceive and to maintain. In the present instance, it appears to me that this 'public opinion' in respect to a gang, has been superinduced by the collateral event which is detailed in the third of my extracts. All Paris is excited by the discovered corpse of Marie, a girl young, beautiful and notorious. This corpse is found, bearing marks of violence and floating in the river. But it is now made known that, at the very period, or about the very period, in which it is supposed that the girl was assassinated, an outrage similar in nature to that endured by the deceased, although less in extent, was perpetuated, by a gang of young ruffians, upon the person of a second young female. Is it wonderful that the one known atrocity should influence the popular judgment in regard to the other unknown? This judgment awaited direction, and the known outrage seemed so opportunely to afford it! Marie, too, was found in the river; and upon this very river was this known outrage committed. The connection of the two events had about it so much of the palpable that the true wonder would have been a failure of the populace to appreciate and to seize it. But, in fact, the one atrocity, known to be so committed, is, if anything, evidence that the other, committed at a time nearly coincident, was not so committed. It would have been a miracle indeed, if, while a gang of ruffians were perpetrating, at a given locality, a most unheard-of wrong, there should have been another similar gang, in a similar locality, in the same city, under the same circumstances, with the same means and appliances, engaged in a wrong of precisely the same aspect, at precisely the same period of time! Yet in what, if not in this marvellous train of coincidence, does the accidentally suggested opinion of the populace call upon us to believe?

"Before proceeding farther, let us consider the supposed scene of the assassination, in the thicket at the Barrière du Roule. This thicket, although dense, was in the close vicinity of a public road. Within were three or four large stones, forming a kind of seat with a back and footstool. On the upper stone was discovered a white petticoat; on the second, a silk scarf. A parasol, gloves, and a pocket-handkerchief, were also here found. The handkerchief bore the name 'Marie Rogêt.' Fragments of dress were seen on the branches around. The earth was trampled, the bushes were broken, and there was every evidence of a violent struggle.

"Notwithstanding the acclamation with which the discovery of this thicket was received by the press, and the unanimity with which it was supposed to indicate the precise scene of the outrage, it must be admitted that there was some very good reason for doubt. That it was the scene, I may or I may not believe—but there was excellent reason for doubt. Had the true scene been, as *Le Commerciel* suggested, in the neighborhood of the Rue Pavée-Saint-Andrée, the perpetrators of the crime, supposing them still resident in Paris, would naturally have been stricken with terror at the public attention thus acutely directed into the proper channel; and, in certain classes of minds, there would have arisen, at once, a sense of the necessity of some exertion to re-divert this attention. And thus, the thicket of the Barrière du Roule having been already suspected, the idea of placing the articles where they were found, might have been naturally entertained. There is no real evidence, although *Le Soleil* so supposes, that the articles discovered had been more than a very few days in the thicket; while there is much circumstantial proof that they could not have remained there, without attracting attention, during the twenty days elapsing between the fatal Sunday and the afternoon upon which they were found by the boys. 'They were all mildewed down hard,' says *Le Soleil*, adopting the opinions of its predecessors, 'with the action of the rain, and stuck together from mildew. The grass had grown around and over some of them. The silk of the parasol was strong, but the threads of it were run together within. The upper part, where it had been doubled and folded, was all mildewed and rotten, and tore on being opened.' In respect to the grass having 'grown around and over some of them,' it is obvious that the fact could only have been ascertained from the words, and thus from the recollections, of two small boys; for these boys removed the articles and took them home before they had been seen by a third party. But the grass will grow, especially in warm and damp weather (such as was that of the period of the murder), as much as two or three inches in a single day. A parasol lying upon a newly turfed ground, might, in a single week, be entirely concealed from sight by the upspringing grass. And touching that mildew upon which the editor of *Le Soleil* so pertinaciously insists, that he employs the word no less than three times in the brief paragraph just quoted, is he really unaware of the nature of this mildew? Is he to be told that it is one of the many classes of fungus, of which the most ordinary feature is its upspringing and decadence within twenty-four hours?

"Thus we see, at a glance, that what has been most triumphantly adduced in support of the idea that the articles had been 'for at least three or four weeks' in the thicket, is most absurdly null as regards any evidence of that fact. On the other hand, it is exceedingly difficult to believe that these articles could have remained in the thicket specified for a longer period than a single week—for a longer period than from one Sunday to the next. Those who know anything of the vicinity of Paris know the extreme difficulty of finding seclusion, unless at a great distance from its suburbs. Such a thing as an unexplored or even an unfrequently visited recess, amid its woods or groves, is not for a moment to be imagined. Let any one who, being at heart a lover of nature, is yet chained by duty to the dust and heat of this great metropolis—let any such one attempt, even during the week-days, to slake his thirst for solitude amid the scenes of natural loveliness which immediately surround us. At every second step, he will find the growing charm dispelled by the voice and personal intrusion of some ruffian or party of carousing blackguards. He will seek privacy amid the densest foliage, all in vain. Here are the very nooks where the unwashed most abound—here are the temples most desecrate. With sickness of the heart the wanderer will flee back to the polluted Paris, as to a less odious, because less incongruous, sink of pollution. But if the vicinity of the city is so beset during the working days of the week, how much more so on the Sabbath! It is now especially that, released from the claims of labor, or deprived of the customary opportunities of crime, the town blackguard seeks the precincts of the town, not through love of the rural, which in his heart he despises, but by way of escape from the restraints and convention-alities of society. He desires less the fresh air and the green trees, than the utter license of the country. Here, at the roadside inn, or beneath the foliage of the woods, he indulges, unchecked by any eye except those of his boon companions, in all the mad excess of a counterfeit hilarity—the joint offspring of liberty and of rum. I say nothing more than what must be obvious to every dispassionate observer, when I repeat that the circumstance of the articles in question having remained undiscovered, for a longer period than from one Sunday to another, in any thicket in the immediate neighborhood of Paris, is to be looked upon as little less than miraculous.

"But there are not wanting other grounds for the suspicion that the articles were placed in the thicket with the view of diverting attention from the real scene of the outrage. And, first, let me direct your notice to the date of the discovery of the articles. Collate this with the date of the fifth extract made by myself from the newspapers. You will find that the discovery followed, almost immediately, the urgent communications sent to the evening paper. These communications, although various and apparently from various sources, tended all to the same point—viz; the directing of attention to a gang as the perpetrators of the outrage, and to the neighborhood of the Barrière du Roule as its scene. Now here, of course, the sus-picion is not that, in consequence of these communications, or of the public attention by them directed, the articles were found by the boys; but the suspicion might and may well have been, that the articles were not before found by the boys, for the reason that the articles had not before been in the thicket; having been deposited there only at so late a period as at the date, or shortly prior to the date of the communications by the guilty authors of these communications themselves.

"This thicket was a singular—an exceedingly singular one. It was unusually dense. Within its naturally walled enclosure were three extraordinary stones, forming a seat with a back and footstool. And this thicket, so full of a natural art, was in the immediate vicinity, within a few rods*, of the dwelling of Madame Deluc, whose boys were in the habit of closely examining the shrubberies about them in search of the bark of the sassafras. Would it be a rash wager—a wager of one thousand to one—that a day never passed over the heads of these boys without finding at least one of them ensconced in the umbrageous hall, and enthroned upon its natural throne? Those who would hesitate at such a wager have either never been boys themselves, or have forgotten the boyish nature. I repeat—it is exceedingly hard to comprehend how the articles could have remained in this thicket undiscovered for a longer period than one or two days; and that thus there is good ground for suspicion, in spite of the dogmatic ignorance of *Le Soleil*, that they were, at a comparatively late date, deposited where found.

"But there are still other and stronger reasons for believing them so deposited, than any which I have as yet urged. And, now, let me beg your notice to the highly artificial arrangement of the articles. On the upper stone lay a white petticoat; on the second, a silk scarf; scattered around were a parasol, gloves, and a pocket-handkerchief bearing the name 'Marie Rogêt.' Here is just such an arrangement as would naturally be made by a not over-acute person wishing to dispose the articles naturally. But it is by no means a really natural arrangement. I should rather have looked to see the things all lying on the ground and trampled under foot. In the narrow limits of that bower it would have been scarcely possible that the petticoat and scarf should have retained a position upon the stones, when subjected to the brushing to and fro of many struggling persons. 'There was evidence,' it is said, 'of a struggle; and the earth was trampled, the bushes were broken,'—but the petticoat and the scarf are found deposited as if upon shelves. 'The pieces of the frock torn out by the bushes were about three inches wide and six inches long. One part was the hem of the frock and it had been mended. They looked like strips torn off.' Here, inadvertently, *Le Soleil* has employed an exceedingly suspicious phrase. The pieces, as described, do indeed 'look like strips torn off;' but purposely and by hand. It is

---

* A rod is a unit of distance equal to five and one-half yards, now largely obsolete.

one of the rarest of accidents that a piece is 'torn off,' from any garment such as is now in question, by the agency of a thorn. From the very nature of such fabrics, a thorn or nail becoming entangled in them, tears them rectangularly—divides them into two longitudinal rents, at right angles with each other, and meeting at an apex where the thorn enters—but it is scarcely possible to conceive the piece 'torn off.' I never so knew it, nor did you. To tear a piece off from such fabric, two distinct forces, in different directions, will be, in almost every case, required. If there be two edges to the fabric—if, for example, it be a pocket-handkerchief, and it is desired to tear from it a slip, then, and then only, will the one force serve the purpose. But in the present case the question is of a dress, presenting but one edge. To tear a piece from the interior, where no edge is presented, could only be effected by a miracle through the agency of thorns, and no one thorn could accomplish it. But, even where an edge is presented, two thorns will be necessary, operating, the one in two distinct directions, and the other in one. And this in the supposition that the edge is unhemmed. If hemmed, the matter is nearly out of the question. We thus see the numerous and great obstacles in the way of pieces being 'torn off' through the simple agency of 'thorns;' yet we are required to believe not only that one piece but that many have been so torn. 'And one part,' too, 'was the hem of the frock!' Another piece was 'part of the skirt, not the hem,'—that is to say, was torn completely out through the agency of thorns, from the uncaged interior of the dress! These, I say, are things which one may well be pardoned for disbelieving; yet, taken collectedly, they form, perhaps, less of reasonable ground for suspicion than the one startling circumstance of the articles having been left in this thicket at all by any murderers who had enough precaution to think of removing the corpse. You will not have apprehended me rightly, however, if you suppose it my design to deny this thicket as the scene of the outrage. There might have been a wrong here, or, more possibly, an accident at Madame Deluc's. But, in fact, this is a point of minor importance. We are not engaged in an attempt to discover the scene, but to produce the perpetrators of the murder. What I have adduced, notwithstanding the minuteness with which I have adduced it, has been with the view, first, to show the folly of the positive and headlong assertions of *Le Soleil*, but secondly and chiefly, to bring you, by the most natural route, to a further contemplation of the doubt whether this assassination has, or has not been, the work of a gang.

"We will resume this question by mere allusion to the revolting details of the surgeon examined at the inquest. It is only necessary to say that his published inferences, in regard to the number of ruffians, have been properly ridiculed as unjust and totally baseless, by all the reputable anatomists of Paris. Not that the matter might not have been as inferred, but that there was no ground for the inference. Was there not much for another?

"Let us reflect now upon 'the traces of a struggle;' and let me ask what these traces have been supposed to demonstrate. A gang. But do they not rather demonstrate the absence of a gang? What struggle could have taken place—what struggle so violent and so enduring as to have left its 'traces' in all directions—between a weak and defenceless girl and the gang of ruffians imagined? The silent grasp of a few rough arms and all would have been over. The victim must have been absolutely passive at their will. You will here bear in mind that the arguments urged against the thicket as the scene are applicable, in chief part, only against it as the scene of an outrage committed by more than a single individual. If we imagine but one violator, we can conceive, and thus only conceive, the struggle of so violent and so obstinate a nature as to have left the 'traces' apparent.

"And again. I have already mentioned the suspicion to be excited by the fact that the articles in question were suffered to remain at all in the thicket where discovered. It seems almost impossible that these evidences of guilt should have been accidentally left where found. There was sufficient presence of mind (it is supposed) to remove the corpse; and yet a more positive evidence than the corpse itself (whose features might have been quickly obliterated by decay) is allowed to lie conspicuously in the scene of the outrage—I allude to the handkerchief with the name of the deceased. If this was accident, it was not the accident of a gang. We can imagine it only the accident of an individual. Let us see. An individual has committed the murder. He is alone with the ghost of the departed. He is appalled by what lies motionless before him. The fury of his passion is over, and there is abundant room in his heart for the natural awe of the deed. His is none of that confidence which the presence of numbers inevitably inspires. He is alone with the dead. He trembles and is bewildered. Yet there is a necessity for disposing of the corpse. He bears it to the river, but leaves behind him the other evidences of guilt; for it is difficult, if not impossible, to carry all the burthen at once, and it will be easy to return for what is left. But in his toilsome journey to the water his fears redouble within him. The sounds of life encompass his path. A dozen times he hears or fancies the step of an observer. Even the very lights from the city bewilder him. Yet, in time and by long and frequent pauses of deep agony, he reaches the river's brink, and disposes of his ghastly charge—perhaps through the medium of a boat. But now what treasure does the world hold—what threat of vengeance could it hold out—which would have power to urge the return of that lonely murderer over that toilsome and perilous path, to the thicket and its blood chilling recollections? He returns not, let the consequences be what they may. He could not return if he would. His sole thought is immediate escape. He turns his back forever upon those dreadful shrubberies and flees as from the wrath to come.

"But how with a gang? Their number would have inspired them with confidence; if, indeed confidence is ever wanting in the breast of the arrant blackguard; and of arrant blackguards alone are the supposed gangs ever constituted. Their number, I say, would have prevented the bewildering and unreasoning terror which I have imagined to paralyze the single man. Could we suppose an oversight in one, or two, or three, this oversight would have been remedied by a fourth. They would have left nothing behind them; for their number would have enabled them to carry all at once. There would have been no need of return.

"Consider now the circumstance that in the outer garment of the corpse when found, 'a slip, about a foot wide had been torn upward from the bottom hem to the waist wound three times round the waist, and secured by a sort of hitch in the back.' This was done with the obvious design of affording a handle by which to carry the body. But would any number of men have dreamed of resorting to such an expedient? To three or four, the limbs of the corpse would have afforded not only a sufficient, but the best possible hold. The device is that of a single individual; and this brings us to the fact that 'between the thicket and the river, the rails of the fences were found taken down, and the ground bore evident traces of some heavy burthen having been dragged along it!' But would a number of men have put themselves to the superfluous trouble of taking down a fence, for the purpose of dragging through it a corpse which they might have lifted over any fence in an instant? Would a number of men have so dragged a corpse at all as to have left evident traces of the dragging?

"And here we must refer to an observation of *Le Commerciel*; an observation upon which I have already, in some measure, commented. 'A piece,' says this journal, 'of one of the unfortunate girl's petticoats was torn out and tied under her chin, and around the back of her head, probably to prevent screams. This was done by fellows who had no pocket-handkerchiefs.'

"I have before suggested that a genuine blackguard is never without a pocket-handkerchief. But it is not to this fact that I now especially advert. That it was not through want of a handkerchief, for the purpose imagined by *Le Commerciel*, that this bandage was employed, is rendered apparent by the handkerchief left in the thicket; and that the object was not 'to prevent screams' appears, also, from the bandage having been employed in preference to what would so much better have answered the purpose. But the language of the evidence speaks of the strip in question as 'found around the neck, fitting loosely, and secured with a hard knot.' These words are sufficiently vague, but differ materially from those of *Le Commerciel*. The slip was eighteen inches wide, and therefore, although of muslin, would form a strong band when folded or rumpled longitudinally. And thus rumpled it was discovered. My inference is this. The solitary murderer, having borne the corpse for some distance, (whether from the thicket or elsewhere) by means of the bandage hitched around its middle, found the weight, in this mode of procedure, too much for his strength. He resolved to drag the burthen—the evidence goes to show that it was dragged. With this object in view, it became necessary to attach something like a rope to one of the extremities. It could be best attached about the neck, where the head would prevent its slipping off. And, now, the murderer bethought him, unquestionably, of the bandage about the loins. He would have used this, but for its volution about the corpse, the hitch which embarrassed it, and the reflection that it had not been 'torn off' from the garment. It was easier to tear a new slip from the petticoat. He tore it, made it fast about the neck, and so dragged his victim to the brink of the river. That this 'bandage,' only attainable with trouble and delay, and but imperfectly answering its purpose—that this bandage was employed at all, demonstrates that the necessity for its employment sprang from circumstances arising at a period when the handkerchief was no longer attainable—that is to say, arising, as we have imagined, after quitting the thicket, (if the thicket it was), and on the road between the thicket and the river.

"But the evidence, you will say, of Madame Deluc points especially to the presence of a gang in the vicinity of the thicket, at or about the epoch of the murder. This I grant. I doubt if there were not a dozen gangs, such as described by Madame Deluc, in and about the vicinity of the Barrière du Roule at or about the period of this tragedy. But the gang which has drawn upon itself the pointed animadversion, although the somewhat tardy and very suspicious evidence of Madame Deluc, is the only gang which is represented by that honest and scrupulous old lady as having eaten her cakes and swallowed her brandy, without putting themselves to the trouble of making her payment. *Et hinc illae irae?**

"But what is the precise evidence of Madame Deluc? 'A gang of miscreants made their appearance, behaved boisterously, ate and drank without making payment, followed in the route of the young man and girl, returned to the inn about dusk, and re-crossed the river as if in great haste.'

---

*   Latin: "and at this they are angry?"

"Now this 'great haste' very possibly seemed greater haste in the eyes of Madame Deluc, since she dwelt lingeringly and lamentingly upon her violated cakes and ale—cakes and ale for which she might still have entertained a faint hope of compensation. Why, otherwise, since it was about dusk, should she make a point of the haste? It is no cause for wonder, surely, that even a gang of blackguards should make haste to get home, when a wide river is to be crossed in small boats, when storm impends, and when night approaches.

"I say approaches; for the night had not yet arrived. It was only about dusk that the indecent haste of these 'miscreants' offended the sober eyes of Madame Deluc. But we are told that it was upon this very evening that Madame Deluc, as well as her eldest son, 'heard the screams of a female in the vicinity of the inn.' And in what words does Madame Deluc designate the period of the evening at which these screams were heard? 'It was soon after dark,' she says. But 'soon after dark,' is, at least, dark; and 'about dusk' is as certainly daylight. Thus it is abundantly clear that the gang quitted the Barrière du Roule prior to the screams overheard (?) by Madame Deluc. And although, in all the many reports of the evidence, the relative expressions in question are distinctly and invariably employed just as I have employed them in this conversation with yourself, no notice whatever of the gross discrepancy has, as yet, been taken by any of the public journals, or by any of the myrmidons of police.

"I shall add but one to the arguments against a gang; but this one has, to my own understanding at least, a weight altogether irresistible. Under the circumstances of large reward offered, and full pardon to any king's evidence,* it is not to be imagined, for a moment, that some member of a gang of low ruffians, or of any body of men, would not long ago have betrayed his accomplices. Each one of a gang so placed, is not so much greedy of reward, or anxious for escape, as fearful of betrayal. He betrays eagerly and early that he may not himself be betrayed. That the secret has not been divulged, is the very best of proof that it is, in fact, a secret. The horrors of this dark deed are known only to one, or two, living human beings, and to God.

"Let us sum up now the meagre, yet certain, fruits of our long analysis. We have attained the idea either of a fatal accident under the roof of Madame Deluc, or of a murder perpetrated, in the thicket at the Barrière du Roule, by a lover, or at least by an intimate and secret associate of the deceased. This associate is of swarthy complexion. This complexion, the 'hitch' in the bandage, and the 'sailor's

---

* A British legal term for a deal to provide evidence in exchange for immunity from prosecution.

knot' with which the bonnet-ribbon is tied, point to a seaman. His companionship with the deceased—a gay, but not an abject young girl—designates him as above the grade of the common sailor. Here the well-written and urgent communications to the journals are much in the way of corroboration. The circumstance of the first elopement, as mentioned by *Le Mercurie*, tends to blend the idea of this seaman with that of the 'naval officer' who is first known to have led the unfortunate into crime.

"And here, most fitly, comes the consideration of the continued absence of him of the dark complexion. Let me pause to observe that the complexion of this man is dark and swarthy; it was no common swarthiness which constituted the sole point of remembrance, both as regards Valence and Madame Deluc. But why is this man absent? Was he murdered by the gang? If so, why are there only traces of the assassinated girl? The scene of the two outrages will naturally be supposed identical. And where is his corpse? The assassins would most probably have disposed of both in the same way. But it may be said that this man lives, and is deterred from making himself known, through dread of being charged with the murder. This consideration might be supposed to operate upon him now—at this late period—since it has been given in evidence that he was seen with Marie, but it would have had no force at the period of the deed. The first impulse of an innocent man would have been to announce the outrage, and to aid in identifying the ruffians. This policy would have suggested. He had been seen with the girl. He had crossed the river with her in an open ferry-boat. The denouncing of the assassins would have appeared, even to an idiot, the surest and sole means of relieving himself from suspicion. We cannot suppose him, on the night of the fatal Sunday, both innocent himself and incognizant of an outrage committed. Yet only under such circumstances is it possible to imagine that he would have failed, if alive, in the denouncement of the assassins.

"And what means are ours, of attaining the truth? We shall find these means multiplying and gathering distinctness as we proceed. Let us sift to the bottom this affair of the first elopement. Let us know the full history of 'the officer,' with his present circumstances, and his whereabouts at the precise period of the murder. Let us carefully compare with each other the various communications sent to the evening paper, in which the object was to inculpate a gang. This done, let us compare these communications, both as regards style and MS.,* with those sent to the morning paper, at a previous period, and insisting so vehemently upon the guilt of

---

* Manuscript (abbreviation).

Mennais. And, all this done, let us again compare these various communications with the known MSS. of the officer. Let us endeavor to ascertain, by repeated questionings of Madame Deluc and her boys, as well as of the omnibus driver, Valence, something more of the personal appearance and bearing of the 'man of dark complexion.' Queries, skilfully directed, will not fail to elicit, from some of these parties, information on this particular point (or upon others)—information which the parties themselves may not even be aware of possessing. And let us now trace the boat picked up by the bargeman on the morning of Monday the twenty-third of June, and which was removed from the barge-office, without the cognizance of the officer in attendance, and without the rudder, at some period prior to the discovery of the corpse. With a proper caution and perseverance we shall infallibly trace this boat; for not only can the bargeman who picked it up identify it, but the rudder is at hand. The rudder of a sail-boat would not have been abandoned, without inquiry, by one altogether at ease in heart. And here let me pause to insinuate a question. There was no advertisement of the picking up of this boat. It was silently taken to the barge-office, and as silently removed. But its owner or employer—how happened he, at so early a period as Tuesday morning, to be informed, without the agency of advertisement, of the locality of the boat taken up on Monday, unless we imagine some connection with the navy—some personal permanent connection leading to cognizance of its minute interests—its petty local news?

"In speaking of the lonely assassin dragging his burden to the shore, I have already suggested the probability of his availing himself of a boat. Now we are to understand that Marie Rogêt was precipitated from a boat. This would naturally have been the case. The corpse could not have been trusted to the shallow waters of the shore. The peculiar marks on the back and shoulders of the victim tell of the bottom ribs of a boat. That the body was found without weight is also corroborative of the idea. If thrown from the shore a weight would have been attached. We can only account for its absence by supposing the murderer to have neglected the precaution of supplying himself with it before pushing off. In the act of consigning the corpse to the water, he would unquestionably have noticed his oversight; but then no remedy would have been at hand. Any risk would have been preferred to a return to that accursed shore. Having rid himself of his ghastly charge, the murderer would have hastened to the city. There, at some obscure wharf, he would have leaped on land. But the boat—would he have secured it? He would have been in too great haste for such things as securing a boat. Moreover, in fastening it to the wharf, he would have felt as if securing evidence against himself. His natural thought would have been to cast from him, as far as possible, all that had held connection with his crime. He would not only have fled from the wharf, but he would not have permitted the boat to remain. Assuredly he would have cast it adrift. Let us pursue our fancies. In the morning, the wretch is stricken with unutterable horror at finding that the boat has been picked up and detained at a locality which he is in the daily habit of frequenting—at a locality, perhaps, which his duty compels him to frequent. The next night, without daring to ask for the rudder, he removes it. Now where is that rudderless boat? Let it be one of our first purposes to discover. With the first glimpse we obtain of it, the dawn of our success shall begin. This boat shall guide us, with a rapidity which will surprise even ourselves, to him who employed it in the midnight of the fatal Sabbath. Corroboration will rise upon corroboration, and the murderer will be traced."

[For reasons which we shall not specify, but which to many readers will appear obvious, we have taken the liberty of here omitting, from the MSS. placed in our hands, such portion as details the following up of the apparently slight clew obtained by Dupin. We feel it advisable only to state, in brief, that the result desired was brought to pass; and that the Prefect fulfilled punctually, although with reluctance, the terms of his compact with the Chevalier. Mr. Poe's article concludes with the following words.—Eds.]

It will be understood that I speak of coincidences and no more. What I have said above upon this topic must suffice. In my own heart there dwells no faith in præter-nature.[†] That Nature and its God are two, no man who thinks will deny. That the latter, creating the former, can, at will, control or modify it, is also unquestionable. I say "at will;" for the question is of will, and not, as the insanity of logic has assumed, of power. It is not that the Deity cannot modify his laws, but that we insult him in imagining a possible necessity for modification. In their origin these laws were fashioned to embrace all contingencies which could lie in the Future. With God all is Now.

I repeat, then, that I speak of these things only as of coincidences. And further; in what I relate it will be seen that between the fate of the unhappy Mary Cecilia Rogers, so far as that fate is known, and the fate of one Marie Rogêt up

---

* This footnote is a part of Poe's original, connecting the Dupin narrative with the narrator's thoughts on the real-life murder by invoking, in fiction, the editors of the periodical in which the story was first published.

† i.e. the preternatural.

to a certain epoch in her history, there has existed a parallel in the contemplation of whose wonderful exactitude the reason becomes embarrassed. I say all this will be seen. But let it not for a moment be supposed that, in proceeding with the sad narrative of Marie from the epoch just mentioned, and in tracing to its *dénouement* the mystery which enshrouded her, it is my covert design to hint at an extension of the parallel, or even to suggest that the measures adopted in Paris for the discovery of the assassin of a *grisette*, or measures founded in any similar ratiocination, would produce any similar result.

For, in respect to the latter branch of the supposition, it should be considered that the most trifling variation in the facts of the two cases might give rise to the most important miscalculations, by diverting thoroughly the two courses of events; very much as, in arithmetic, an error which, in its own individuality, may be inappreciable, produces, at length, by dint of multiplication at all points of the process, a result enormously at variance with truth. And, in regard to the former branch, we must not fail to hold in view that the very Calculus of Probabilities to which I have referred, forbids all idea of the extension of the parallel—forbids it with a positiveness strong and decided, just in proportion as this parallel has already been long-drawn and exact. This is one of those anomalous propositions which, seemingly appealing to thought altogether apart from the mathematical, is yet one which only the mathematician can fully entertain. Nothing, for example, is more difficult than to convince the merely general reader that the fact of sixes having been thrown twice in succession by a player at dice is sufficient cause for betting the largest odds that sixes will not be thrown in the third attempt. A suggestion to this effect is usually rejected by the intellect at once. It does not appear that the two throws which have been completed, and which lie now absolutely in the Past, can have influence upon the throw which exists only in the Future. The chance for throwing sixes seems to be precisely as it was at any ordinary time—that is to say, subject only to the influence of the various other throws which may be made by the dice. And this is a reflection which appears so exceedingly obvious that attempts to controvert it are received more frequently with a derisive smile than with anything like respectful attention. The error here involved—a gross error redolent of mischief—I cannot pretend to expose within the limits assigned me at present; and with the philosophical it needs no exposure. It may be sufficient here to say that it forms one of an infinite series of mistakes which arise in the path of Reason through her propensity for seeking truth in detail.

THE DETECTIVE POLICE

by Charles Dickens

1850

If Poe's Dupin prefigured Sherlock Holmes, the "Detective Police" of Charles Dickens might be seen as the ancestors of Inspector Lestrade.

While Dickens is not known for his detective stories, the Detective Police featured in three stories—one a collection of three "anecdotes"—that were published in his magazine *Household Words* in 1850 and 1851. These are tales of solid and patient police work rather than brilliant deduction; their protagonists are professional officers rather than gentlemen sleuths, and their successes rely on a thorough knowledge of their "patch" and its criminal population—as well as the occasional good idea and stroke of luck.

The stories are presented as fact, and there seems no doubt that they were drawn from life. Inspector Wield, who appears in this story and its sequel, "Three Detective Anecdotes," is almost certainly based on Inspector Charles Frederick Field of the Metropolitan Police—in fact, he appears under his own name in the third, and so far as is known, final Detective Police story, "On Duty with Inspector Field." Field is commonly regarded as the model for Inspector Bucket in *Bleak House*; public speculation on this point forced Dickens to respond in the *Times*, though he was careful neither to confirm nor deny the rumors.

Through the stories of these detectives, Dickens provides many insights into London's underworld, including many pieces of slang that, well-known in his day, have lapsed into obscurity. Explanatory footnotes have been provided where necessary.

W e are not by any means devout believers in the old Bow Street Police.* To say the truth, we think there was a vast amount of humbug about those worthies. Apart from many of them being men of very indifferent character, and far too much in the habit of consorting with thieves and the like, they never lost a public occasion of jobbing and trading in mystery and making the most of themselves. Continually puffed besides by incompetent magistrates anxious to conceal their own deficiencies, and hand-in-glove with the penny-a-liners of that time, they became a sort of superstition. Although as a Preventive Police they were utterly ineffective, and as a Detective Police were very loose and uncertain in their operations, they remain with some people a superstition to the present day.

On the other hand, the Detective Force organised since the establishment of the existing Police, is so well chosen and trained, proceeds so systematically and quietly, does its business in such a workmanlike manner, and is always so calmly and steadily engaged in the service of the public, that the public really do not know enough of it, to know a tithe of its usefulness. Impressed with this conviction, and interested in the men themselves, we represented to the authorities at Scotland Yard, that we should be glad, if there were no official objection, to have some talk with the Detectives. A most obliging and ready permission being given, a certain evening was appointed with a certain Inspector for a social conference between ourselves and the Detectives, at the *Household Words* Office in Wellington Street, Strand, London. In consequence of which appointment the party "came off," which we are about to describe. And we beg to repeat that, avoiding such topics as it might for obvious reasons be injurious to the public, or disagreeable to respectable individuals, to touch upon in print, our description is as exact as we can make it.

The reader will have the goodness to imagine the Sanctum Sanctorum of *Household Words*. Anything that best suits the reader's fancy, will best represent that magnificent chamber. We merely stipulate for a round table in the middle, with some glasses and cigars arranged upon it; and the editorial sofa elegantly hemmed in between that stately piece of furniture and the wall.

It is a sultry evening at dusk. The stones of Wellington Street are hot and gritty, and the watermen and hackney-coachmen at the Theatre opposite,† are

---

* Founded in 1749, the Bow Street Runners were London's first police force. They were amalgamated with the Metropolitan Police in 1839, and a new "Detective Branch" was formed in 1842.

† Probably the Lyceum.

much flushed and aggravated. Carriages are constantly setting down the people who have come to Fairy-Land;* and there is a mighty shouting and bellowing every now and then, deafening us for the moment, through the open windows.

Just at dusk, Inspectors Wield† and Stalker are announced; but we do not undertake to warrant the orthography of any of the names here mentioned. Inspector Wield presents Inspector Stalker. Inspector Wield is a middle-aged man of a portly presence, with a large, moist, knowing eye, a husky voice, and a habit of emphasising his conversation by the aid of a corpulent fore-finger, which is constantly in juxtaposition with his eyes or nose. Inspector Stalker is a shrewd, hard-headed Scotchman—in appearance not at all unlike a very acute, thoroughly-trained schoolmaster, from the Normal Establishment at Glasgow. Inspector Wield one might have known, perhaps, for what he is—Inspector Stalker, never.

The ceremonies of reception over, Inspectors Wield and Stalker observe that they have brought some sergeants with them. The sergeants are presented—five in number, Sergeant Dornton, Sergeant Witchem, Sergeant Mith, Sergeant Fendall, and Sergeant Straw. We have the whole Detective Force from Scotland Yard, with one exception. They sit down in a semi-circle (the two Inspectors at the two ends) at a little distance from the round table, facing the editorial sofa. Every man of them, in a glance, immediately takes an inventory of the furniture and an accurate sketch of the editorial presence. The Editor feels that any gentleman in company could take him up, if need should be, without the smallest hesitation, twenty years hence.

The whole party are in plain clothes. Sergeant Dornton about fifty years of age, with a ruddy face and a high sunburnt forehead, has the air of one who has been a Sergeant in the army—he might have sat to Wilkie for the Soldier in the *Reading of the Will*.‡ He is famous for steadily pursuing the inductive process, and, from small beginnings, working on from clue to clue until he bags his man. Sergeant Witchem, shorter and thicker-set, and marked with the small-pox, has something of a reserved and thoughtful air, as if he were engaged in deep arithmetical calculations. He is renowned for his acquaintance with the Swell Mob.§

---

* The "fairy extravaganzas" of British dramatist James Robinson Planché and others were popular at the time. The genre began in Paris in the early 19th century, and combined dance, drama, and acrobatics with extravagant costumes and special effects.

† Probably Inspector Charles Frederick Field.

‡ An 1811 painting by Scottish artist Sir David Wilkie.

§ Young, male thieves and pickpockets who imitated "swells" (society gentlemen) in their dress and manners, to throw their victims off guard.

Sergeant Mith, a smooth-faced man with a fresh bright complexion, and a strange air of simplicity, is a dab* at housebreakers. Sergeant Fendall, a light-haired, well-spoken, polite person, is a prodigious hand at pursuing private inquiries of a delicate nature. Straw, a little wiry Sergeant of meek demeanour and strong sense, would knock at a door and ask a series of questions in any mild character you choose to prescribe to him, from a charity-boy upwards, and seem as innocent as an infant. They are, one and all, respectable-looking men; of perfectly good deportment and unusual intelligence; with nothing lounging or slinking in their manners; with an air of keen observation and quick perception when addressed; and generally presenting in their faces, traces more or less marked of habitually leading lives of strong mental excitement. They have all good eyes; and they all can, and they all do, look full at whomsoever they speak to.

We light the cigars, and hand round the glasses (which are very temperately used indeed), and the conversation begins by a modest amateur reference on the Editorial part to the swell mob. Inspector Wield immediately removes his cigar from his lips, waves his right hand, and says, "Regarding the swell mob, sir, I can't do better than call upon Sergeant Witchem. Because the reason why? I'll tell you. Sergeant Witchem is better acquainted with the swell mob than any officer in London."

Our heart leaping up when we beheld this rainbow in the sky, we turn to Sergeant Witchem, who very concisely, and in well-chosen language, goes into the subject forthwith. Meantime, the whole of his brother officers are closely interested in attending to what he says, and observing its effect. Presently they begin to strike in, one or two together, when an opportunity offers, and the conversation becomes general. But these brother officers only come in to the assistance of each other—not to the contradiction—and a more amicable brotherhood there could not be. From the swell mob, we diverge to the kindred topics of cracksmen†, fences, public-house dancers, area-sneaks, designing young people who go out "gonophing,"‡ and other "schools." It is observable throughout these revelations, that Inspector Stalker, the Scotchman, is always exact and statistical, and that when any question of figures arises, everybody as by one consent pauses, and looks to him.

When we have exhausted the various schools of Art—during which discussion the whole body have remained profoundly attentive, except when some

---

* An expert. The more usual expression is "a dab hand."

† A burglar or safecracker.

‡ A "gonoph" was a pickpocket or thief in the underworld slang of that time.

unusual noise at the Theatre over the way has induced some gentleman to glance inquiringly towards the window in that direction, behind his next neighbour's back—we burrow for information on such points as the following. Whether there really are any highway robberies in London, or whether some circumstances not convenient to be mentioned by the aggrieved party, usually precede the robberies complained of, under that head, which quite change their character? Certainly the latter, almost always. Whether in the case of robberies in houses, where servants are necessarily exposed to doubt, innocence under suspicion ever becomes so like guilt in appearance, that a good officer need be cautious how he judges it? Undoubtedly. Nothing is so common or deceptive as such appearances at first. Whether in a place of public amusement, a thief knows an officer, and an officer knows a thief—supposing them, beforehand, strangers to each other—because each recognises in the other, under all disguise, an inattention to what is going on, and a purpose that is not the purpose of being entertained? Yes. That's the way exactly. Whether it is reasonable or ridiculous to trust to the alleged experiences of thieves as narrated by themselves, in prisons, or penitentiaries, or anywhere? In general, nothing more absurd. Lying is their habit and their trade; and they would rather lie—even if they hadn't an interest in it, and didn't want to make themselves agreeable—than tell the truth.

From these topics, we glide into a review of the most celebrated and horrible of the great crimes that have been committed within the last fifteen or twenty years. The men engaged in the discovery of almost all of them, and in the pursuit or apprehension of the murderers, are here, down to the very last instance. One of our guests gave chase to and boarded the emigrant ship, in which the murderess last hanged in London was supposed to have embarked. We learn from him that his errand was not announced to the passengers, who may have no idea of it to this hour. That he went below, with the captain, lamp in hand—it being dark, and the whole steerage abed and sea-sick—and engaged the Mrs. Manning who was on board, in a conversation about her luggage, until she was, with no small pains, induced to raise her head, and turn her face towards the light. Satisfied that she was not the object of his search, he quietly re-embarked in the Government steamer along-side, and steamed home again with the intelligence.

When we have exhausted these subjects, too, which occupy a considerable time in the discussion, two or three leave their chairs, whisper to Sergeant Witchem, and resume their seats. Sergeant Witchem, leaning forward a little, and placing a hand on each of his legs, then modestly speaks as follows:

"My brother-officers wish me to relate a little account of my taking Tally-ho Thompson. A man oughtn't to tell what he has done himself; but still, as nobody was with me, and, consequently, as nobody but myself can tell it, I'll do it in the best way I can, if it should meet your approval."

We assure Sergeant Witchem that he will oblige us very much, and we all compose ourselves to listen with great interest and attention.

"Tally-ho Thompson," says Sergeant Witchem, after merely wetting his lips with his brandy-and-water, "Tally-ho Thompson was a famous horse-stealer, couper,* and magsman.† Thompson, in conjunction with a pal that occasionally worked with him, gammoned‡ a countryman out of a good round sum of money, under pretence of getting him a situation—the regular old dodge—and was afterwards in the 'Hue and Cry'§ for a horse—a horse that he stole down in Hertfordshire. I had to look after Thompson, and I applied myself, of course, in the first instance, to discovering where he was. Now, Thompson's wife lived, along with a little daughter, at Chelsea. Knowing that Thompson was somewhere in the country, I watched the house—especially at post-time in the morning—thinking Thompson was pretty likely to write to her. Sure enough, one morning the postman comes up, and delivers a letter at Mrs. Thompson's door. Little girl opens the door, and takes it in. We're not always sure of postmen, though the people at the post-offices are always very obliging. A postman may help us, or he may not,—just as it happens. However, I go across the road, and I say to the postman, after he has left the letter, 'Good morning! how are you?' 'How are you?' says he. 'You've just delivered a letter for Mrs. Thompson.' 'Yes, I have.' 'You didn't happen to remark what the post-mark was, perhaps?' 'No,' says he, 'I didn't.' 'Come,' says I, 'I'll be plain with you. I'm in a small way of business, and I have given Thompson credit, and I can't afford to lose what he owes me. I know he's got money, and I know he's in the country, and if you could tell me what the post-mark was, I should be very much obliged to you, and you'd do a service to a tradesman in a small way of business that can't afford a loss.' 'Well,' he said, 'I do assure you that I did not observe what the post-mark was; all I know is, that there was money in the letter—I should say a sovereign.' This was enough for me, because of course I knew that Thompson having sent his wife money,

---

*   Meaning unknown. Possibly derived from the French *couper,* "to cut."

†   Confidence trickster.

‡   Conned. "Gammon!" was a common rebuttal of the time, meaning "nonsense!"

§   A chase after an accused thief or other criminal.

it was probable she'd write to Thompson, by return of post, to acknowledge the receipt. So I said 'Thankee' to the postman, and I kept on the watch. In the afternoon I saw the little girl come out. Of course I followed her. She went into a stationer's shop, and I needn't say to you that I looked in at the window. She bought some writing-paper and envelopes, and a pen. I think to myself, 'That'll do!'—watch her home again—and don't go away, you may be sure, knowing that Mrs. Thompson was writing her letter to Tally-ho, and that the letter would be posted presently. In about an hour or so, out came the little girl again, with the letter in her hand. I went up, and said something to the child, whatever it might have been; but I couldn't see the direction of the letter, because she held it with the seal upwards.* However, I observed that on the back of the letter there was what we call a kiss—a drop of wax by the side of the seal—and again, you understand, that was enough for me. I saw her post the letter, waited till she was gone, then went into the shop, and asked to see the Master. When he came out, I told him, 'Now, I'm an Officer in the Detective Force; there's a letter with a kiss been posted here just now, for a man that I'm in search of; and what I have to ask of you, is, that you will let me look at the direction of that letter.' He was very civil—took a lot of letters from the box in the window—shook 'em out on the counter with the faces downwards—and there among 'em was the identical letter with the kiss. It was directed, Mr. Thomas Pigeon, Post Office, B—, to be left till called for. Down I went to B— (a hundred and twenty miles or so) that night. Early next morning I went to the Post Office; saw the gentleman in charge of that department; told him who I was; and that my object was to see, and track, the party that should come for the letter for Mr. Thomas Pigeon. He was very polite, and said, 'You shall have every assistance we can give you; you can wait inside the office; and we'll take care to let you know when anybody comes for the letter.' Well, I waited there three days, and began to think that nobody ever would come. At last the clerk whispered to me, 'Here! Detective! Somebody's come for the letter!' 'Keep him a minute,' said I, and I ran round to the outside of the office. There I saw a young chap with the appearance of an Ostler,† holding a horse by the bridle—stretching the bridle across the pavement, while he waited at the Post Office Window for the letter. I began to pat the horse, and that; and I said to the boy, 'Why, this is Mr. Jones's Mare!' 'No. It an't.' 'No?' said I. 'She's very like Mr. Jones's Mare!' 'She an't Mr. Jones's Mare, anyhow,' says he. 'It's Mr. So

---

* i.e. the wax seal, normally applied to the back of a letter.

† A kind of groom, employed by an inn to look after guests' horses.

and So's, of the Warwick Arms.' And up he jumped, and off he went—letter and all. I got a cab, followed on the box, and was so quick after him that I came into the stable-yard of the Warwick Arms, by one gate, just as he came in by another. I went into the bar, where there was a young woman serving, and called for a glass of brandy-and-water. He came in directly, and handed her the letter. She casually looked at it, without saying anything, and stuck it up behind the glass over the chimney-piece. What was to be done next?

"I turned it over in my mind while I drank my brandy-and-water (looking pretty sharp at the letter the while), but I couldn't see my way out of it at all. I tried to get lodgings in the house, but there had been a horse-fair, or something of that sort, and it was full. I was obliged to put up somewhere else, but I came backwards and forwards to the bar for a couple of days, and there was the letter always behind the glass. At last I thought I'd write a letter to Mr. Pigeon myself, and see what that would do. So I wrote one, and posted it, but I purposely addressed it, Mr. John Pigeon, instead of Mr. Thomas Pigeon, to see what that would do. In the morning (a very wet morning it was) I watched the postman down the street, and cut into the bar, just before he reached the Warwick Arms. In he came presently with my letter. "Is there a Mr. John Pigeon staying here?" "No!—stop a bit though," says the barmaid; and she took down the letter behind the glass. "No," says she, "it's Thomas, and he is not staying here. Would you do me a favour, and post this for me, as it is so wet?" The postman said Yes; she folded it in another envelope, directed it, and gave it him. He put it in his hat, and away he went.

"I had no difficulty in finding out the direction of that letter. It was addressed Mr. Thomas Pigeon, Post Office, R—, Northamptonshire, to be left till called for. Off I started directly for R—; I said the same at the Post Office there, as I had said at B—; and again I waited three days before anybody came. At last another chap on horseback came. 'Any letters for Mr. Thomas Pigeon?' 'Where do you come from?' 'New Inn, near R—.' He got the letter, and away he went at a canter.

"I made my inquiries about the New Inn, near R—, and hearing it was a solitary sort of house, a little in the horse line, about a couple of miles from the station, I thought I'd go and have a look at it. I found it what it had been described, and sauntered in, to look about me. The landlady was in the bar, and I was trying to get into conversation with her; asked her how business was, and spoke about the wet weather, and so on; when I saw, through an open door, three men sitting by the fire in a sort of parlour, or kitchen; and one of those men, according to the description I had of him, was Tally-ho Thompson!

"I went and sat down among 'em, and tried to make things agreeable; but they were very shy—wouldn't talk at all—looked at me, and at one another, in a way quite the reverse of sociable. I reckoned 'em up, and finding that they were all three bigger men than me, and considering that their looks were ugly—that it was a lonely place—railroad station two miles off—and night coming on—thought I couldn't do better than have a drop of brandy-and-water to keep my courage up. So I called for my brandy-and-water; and as I was sitting drinking it by the fire, Thompson got up and went out.

"Now the difficulty of it was, that I wasn't sure it was Thompson, because I had never set eyes on him before; and what I had wanted was to be quite certain of him. However, there was nothing for it now, but to follow, and put a bold face upon it. I found him talking, outside in the yard, with the landlady. It turned out afterwards that he was wanted by a Northampton officer for something else, and that, knowing that officer to be pock-marked (as I am myself), he mistook me for him. As I have observed, I found him talking to the landlady, outside. I put my hand upon his shoulder—this way—and said, 'Tally-ho Thompson, it's no use. I know you. I'm an officer from London, and I take you into custody for felony!' 'That be d—d!' says Tally-ho Thompson.

"We went back into the house, and the two friends began to cut up rough, and their looks didn't please me at all, I assure you. 'Let the man go. What are you going to do with him?' 'I'll tell you what I'm going to do with him. I'm going to take him to London to-night, as sure as I'm alive. I'm not alone here, whatever you may think. You mind your own business, and keep yourselves to yourselves. It'll be better for you, for I know you both very well.' I'd never seen or heard of 'em in all my life, but my bouncing cowed 'em a bit, and they kept off, while Thompson was making ready to go. I thought to myself, however, that they might be coming after me on the dark road, to rescue Thompson; so I said to the landlady, 'What men have you got in the house, Missis?' 'We haven't got no men here,' she says, sulkily. 'You have got an ostler, I suppose?' 'Yes, we've got an ostler.' 'Let me see him.' Presently he came, and a shaggy-headed young fellow he was. 'Now attend to me, young man,' says I; 'I'm a Detective Officer from London. This man's name is Thompson. I have taken him into custody for felony. I am going to take him to the railroad station. I call upon you in the Queen's name to assist me; and mind you, my friend, you'll get yourself into more trouble than you know of, if you don't!' You never saw a person open his eyes so wide. 'Now, Thompson, come along!' says I. But when I took out the handcuffs, Thompson cries, 'No! None of that! I won't stand *them*! I'll go along with you quiet, but I won't bear none of that!' 'Tally-ho

Thompson,' I said, 'I'm willing to behave as a man to you, if you are willing to behave as a man to me. Give me your word that you'll come peaceably along, and I don't want to handcuff you.' 'I will,' says Thompson, 'but I'll have a glass of brandy first.' 'I don't care if I've another,' said I. 'We'll have two more, Missis,' said the friends, 'and confound you, Constable, you'll give your man a drop, won't you?' I was agreeable to that, so we had it all round, and then my man and I took Tally-ho Thompson safe to the railroad, and I carried him to London that night. He was afterwards acquitted, on account of a defect in the evidence; and I understand he always praises me up to the skies, and says I'm one of the best of men."

This story coming to a termination amidst general applause, Inspector Wield, after a little grave smoking, fixes his eye on his host, and thus delivers himself:

"It wasn't a bad plant* that of mine, on Fikey, the man accused of forging the Sou'-Western Railway debentures†—it was only t'other day—because the reason why? I'll tell you.

"I had information that Fikey and his brother kept a factory over yonder there,"—indicating any region on the Surrey side of the river‡—"where he bought second-hand carriages; so after I'd tried in vain to get hold of him by other means, I wrote him a letter in an assumed name, saying that I'd got a horse and shay§ to dispose of, and would drive down next day that he might view the lot, and make an offer—very reasonable it was, I said—a reg'lar bargain. Straw and me then went off to a friend of mine that's in the livery and job business, and hired a turn-out¶ for the day, a precious smart turn-out it was—quite a slap-up thing! Down we drove, accordingly, with a friend (who's not in the Force himself); and leaving my friend in the shay near a public-house, to take care of the horse, we went to the factory, which was some little way off. In the factory, there was a number of strong fellows at work, and after reckoning 'em up, it was clear to me that it wouldn't do to try it on there. They were too many for us. We must get our man out of doors. 'Mr. Fikey at home?' 'No, he ain't.' 'Expected home soon?' 'Why, no, not soon.' 'Ah! Is his brother here?' 'I'm his brother.' 'Oh! well, this is an ill-conwenience, this is. I wrote him a letter yesterday, saying I'd got a little turn-out to dispose of, and I've took the trouble to bring the turn-out down

---

* In Victorian underworld slang, a "plant" was a victim. Wield uses the word to cast the criminal Fikey as the victim of Wield's own deception.

† A kind of bond secured against a company's assets.

‡ The south bank of the Thames, as it flows through London.

§ A light, two-wheeled, open carriage. "Shay" is a corruption of the French *chaise*.

¶ An outfit.

a' purpose, and now he ain't in the way.' 'No, he ain't in the way. You couldn't make it convenient to call again, could you?' 'Why, no, I couldn't. I want to sell; that's the fact; and I can't put it off. Could you find him anywheres?' At first he said No, he couldn't, and then he wasn't sure about it, and then he'd go and try. So at last he went up-stairs, where there was a sort of loft, and presently down comes my man himself in his shirt-sleeves.

"'Well,' he says, 'this seems to be rayther a pressing matter of yours.' 'Yes,' I says, 'it *is* rayther a pressing matter, and you'll find it a bargain—dirt cheap.' 'I ain't in partickler want of a bargain just now,' he says, 'but where is it?' 'Why,' I says, 'the turn-out's just outside. Come and look at it.' He hasn't any suspicions, and away we go. And the first thing that happens is, that the horse runs away with my friend (who knows no more of driving than a child) when he takes a little trot along the road to show his paces. You never saw such a game in your life!

"When the bolt is over, and the turn-out has come to a standstill again, Fikey walks round and round it as grave as a judge—me too. 'There, sir!' I says. 'There's a neat thing!' 'It ain't a bad style of thing,' he says. 'I believe you,' says I. 'And there's a horse!'—for I saw him looking at it. 'Rising eight!' I says, rubbing his fore-legs. (Bless you, there ain't a man in the world knows less of horses than I do, but I'd heard my friend at the Livery Stables say he was eight year old, so I says, as knowing as possible, 'Rising eight.') 'Rising eight, is he?' says he. 'Rising eight,' says I. 'Well,' he says, 'what do you want for it?' 'Why, the first and last figure for the whole concern is five-and-twenty pound!' 'That's very cheap!' he says, looking at me. 'Ain't it?' I says. 'I told you it was a bargain! Now, without any higgling and haggling about it, what I want is to sell, and that's my price. Further, I'll make it easy to you, and take half the money down, and you can do a bit of stiff* for the balance.'

"'Well,' he says again, 'that's very cheap.' 'I believe you,' says I; 'get in and try it, and you'll buy it. Come! take a trial!'

"Ecod,† he gets in, and we get in, and we drive along the road, to show him to one of the railway clerks that was hid in the public-house window to identify him. But the clerk was bothered, and didn't know whether it was him, or wasn't—because the reason why? I'll tell you,—on account of his having shaved his whiskers. 'It's a clever little horse,' he says, 'and trots well; and the shay runs light.' 'Not a doubt about it,' I says. 'And now, Mr. Fikey, I may as well make it all

---

* Give a bill or I.O.U.

† By God. An alternative form of "egad."

right, without wasting any more of your time. The fact is, I'm Inspector Wield, and you're my prisoner.' 'You don't mean that?' he says. 'I do, indeed.' 'Then burn my body,' says Fikey, 'if this ain't too bad!'

"Perhaps you never saw a man so knocked over with surprise. 'I hope you'll let me have my coat?' he says. 'By all means.' 'Well, then, let's drive to the factory.' 'Why, not exactly that, I think,' said I; 'I've been there, once before, to-day. Suppose we send for it.' He saw it was no go, so he sent for it, and put it on, and we drove him up to London, comfortable."

This reminiscence is in the height of its success, when a general proposal is made to the fresh-complexioned, smooth-faced officer, with the strange air of simplicity, to tell the "Butcher's Story."

The fresh-complexioned, smooth-faced officer, with the strange air of simplicity, began with a rustic smile, and in a soft, wheedling tone of voice, to relate the Butcher's Story, thus:

"It's just about six years ago, now, since information was given at Scotland Yard of there being extensive robberies of lawns* and silks going on, at some wholesale houses in the City.† Directions were given for the business being looked into; and Straw, and Fendall, and me, we were all in it."

"When you received your instructions," said we, "you went away, and held a sort of Cabinet Council together!"

The smooth-faced officer coaxingly replied, "Ye-es. Just so. We turned it over among ourselves a good deal. It appeared, when we went into it, that the goods were sold by the receivers extraordinarily cheap—much cheaper than they could have been if they had been honestly come by. The receivers were in the trade, and kept capital shops—establishments of the first respectability—one of 'em at the West End, one down in Westminster. After a lot of watching and inquiry, and this and that among ourselves, we found that the job was managed, and the purchases of the stolen goods made, at a little public-house near Smithfield, down by Saint Bartholomew's; where the Warehouse Porters, who were the thieves, took 'em for that purpose, don't you see? and made appointments to meet the people that went between themselves and the receivers. This public-house was principally used by journeymen butchers from the country, out of place, and in want of situations; so, what did we do, but—ha, ha, ha!—we agreed that I should be dressed up like a butcher myself, and go and live there!"

---

* Linen.

† London's central financial and business district.

Never, surely, was a faculty of observation better brought to bear upon a purpose, than that which picked out this officer for the part. Nothing in all creation could have suited him better. Even while he spoke, he became a greasy, sleepy, shy, good-natured, chuckle-headed, unsuspicious, and confiding young butcher. His very hair seemed to have suet in it, as he made it smooth upon his head, and his fresh complexion to be lubricated by large quantities of animal food.

"—So I—ha, ha, ha!" (always with the confiding snigger of the foolish young butcher) "so I dressed myself in the regular way, made up a little bundle of clothes, and went to the public-house, and asked if I could have a lodging there? They says, 'yes, you can have a lodging here,' and I got a bedroom, and settled myself down in the tap.* There was a number of people about the place, and coming backwards and forwards to the house; and first one says, and then another says, 'Are you from the country, young man?' 'Yes,' I says, 'I am. I'm come out of Northamptonshire, and I'm quite lonely here, for I don't know London at all, and it's such a mighty big town.' 'It *is* a big town,' they says. 'Oh, it's a *very* big town!' I says. 'Really and truly I never was in such a town. It quite confuses of me!' and all that, you know.

"When some of the journeymen Butchers that used the house, found that I wanted a place, they says, 'Oh, we'll get you a place!' And they actually took me to a sight† of places, in Newgate Market, Newport Market, Clare, Carnaby—I don't know where all. But the wages was—ha, ha, ha!—was not sufficient, and I never could suit myself, don't you see? Some of the queer frequenters of the house were a little suspicious of me at first, and I was obliged to be very cautious indeed how I communicated with Straw or Fendall. Sometimes, when I went out, pretending to stop and look into the shop windows, and just casting my eye round, I used to see some of 'em following me; but, being perhaps better accustomed than they thought for, to that sort of thing, I used to lead 'em on as far as I thought necessary or convenient—sometimes a long way—and then turn sharp round, and meet 'em, and say, 'Oh, dear, how glad I am to come upon you so fortunate! This London's such a place, I'm blowed if I ain't lost again!' And then we'd go back all together, to the public-house, and—ha, ha, ha! and smoke our pipes, don't you see?

"They were very attentive to me, I am sure. It was a common thing, while I was living there, for some of 'em to take me out, and show me London. They showed me the Prisons—showed me Newgate—and when they showed me Newgate, I stops at the place where the Porters pitch their loads, and says, "Oh dear, is this

---

* The tap-room, or bar-room.

† A number.

where they hang the men? Oh Lor!"* "That!" they says, "what a simple cove he is! *That* ain't it!" And then, they pointed out which was it, and I says "Lor!" and they says, "Now you'll know it agen, won't you?" And I said I thought I should if I tried hard—and I assure you I kept a sharp look out for the City Police when we were out in this way, for if any of 'em had happened to know me, and had spoke to me, it would have been all up in a minute. However, by good luck such a thing never happened, and all went on quiet: though the difficulties I had in communicating with my brother officers were quite extraordinary.

"The stolen goods that were brought to the public-house by the Warehouse Porters, were always disposed of in a back parlour. For a long time, I never could get into this parlour, or see what was done there. As I sat smoking my pipe, like an innocent young chap, by the tap-room fire, I'd hear some of the parties to the robbery, as they came in and out, say softly to the landlord, 'Who's that? What does he do here?' 'Bless your soul,' says the landlord, 'he's only a'—ha, ha, ha!— 'he's only a green young fellow from the country, as is looking for a butcher's sitivation. Don't mind him!' So, in course of time, they were so convinced of my being green, and got to be so accustomed to me, that I was as free of the parlour as any of 'em, and I have seen as much as Seventy Pounds' Worth of fine lawn sold there, in one night, that was stolen from a warehouse in Friday Street. After the sale the buyers always stood treat—hot supper, or dinner, or what not—and they'd say on those occasions, 'Come on, Butcher! Put your best leg foremost, young 'un, and walk into it!' Which I used to do—and hear, at table, all manner of particulars that it was very important for us Detectives to know.

"This went on for ten weeks. I lived in the public-house all the time, and never was out of the Butcher's dress—except in bed. At last, when I had followed seven of the thieves, and set 'em to rights—that's an expression of ours, don't you see, by which I mean to say that I traced 'em, and found out where the robberies were done, and all about 'em—Straw, and Fendall, and I, gave one another the office, and at a time agreed upon, a descent was made upon the public-house, and the apprehensions effected. One of the first things the officers did, was to collar me—for the parties to the robbery weren't to suppose yet, that I was anything but a Butcher—on which the landlord cries out, 'Don't take him,' he says, 'whatever you do! He's only a poor young chap from the country, and butter wouldn't melt in his mouth!' However, they—ha, ha, ha!—they took me, and pretended to search my bedroom, where nothing was found but an old fiddle belonging to

---

* "Oh, Lord!"

the landlord, that had got there somehow or another. But, it entirely changed the landlord's opinion, for when it was produced, he says, 'My fiddle! The Butcher's a purloiner! I give him into custody for the robbery of a musical instrument!'

"The man that had stolen the goods in Friday Street was not taken yet. He had told me, in confidence, that he had his suspicions there was something wrong (on account of the City Police having captured one of the party), and that he was going to make himself scarce. I asked him, 'Where do you mean to go, Mr. Shepherdson?' 'Why, Butcher,' says he, 'the Setting Moon, in the Commercial Road, is a snug house, and I shall bang out there for a time. I shall call myself Simpson, which appears to me to be a modest sort of a name. Perhaps you'll give us a look in, Butcher?' 'Well,' says I, 'I think I will give you a call'—which I fully intended, don't you see, because, of course, he was to be taken! I went over to the Setting Moon next day, with a brother officer, and asked at the bar for Simpson. They pointed out his room, up-stairs. As we were going up, he looks down over the banister, and calls out, 'Halloa, Butcher! is that you?' 'Yes, it's me. How do you find yourself?' 'Bobbish,'' he says; 'but who's that with you?' 'It's only a young man, that's a friend of mine,' I says. 'Come along, then,' says he; 'any friend of the Butcher's is as welcome as the Butcher!' So, I made my friend acquainted with him, and we took him into custody.

"You have no idea, sir, what a sight it was, in Court, when they first knew that I wasn't a Butcher, after all! I wasn't produced at the first examination, when there was a remand; but I was at the second. And when I stepped into the box, in full police uniform, and the whole party saw how they had been done, actually a groan of horror and dismay proceeded from 'em in the dock!

"At the Old Bailey, when their trials came on, Mr. Clarkson was engaged for the defence, and he couldn't make out how it was, about the Butcher. He thought, all along, it was a real Butcher. When the counsel for the prosecution said, 'I will now call before you, gentlemen, the Police-officer,' meaning myself, Mr. Clarkson says, 'Why Police-officer? Why more Police-officers? I don't want Police. We have had a great deal too much of the Police. I want the Butcher!' However, sir, he had the Butcher and the Police-officer, both in one. Out of seven prisoners committed for trial, five were found guilty, and some of 'em were transported,[†] The respectable firm at the West End got a term of imprisonment; and that's the Butcher's Story!"

---

* Just fine.

† Sent to the penal colonies in Australia.

The story done, the chuckle-headed Butcher again resolved himself into the smooth-faced Detective. But, he was so extremely tickled by their having taken him about, when he was that Dragon in disguise, to show him London, that he could not help reverting to that point in his narrative; and gently repeating with the Butcher snigger, "'Oh, dear,' I says, 'is that where they hang the men? Oh, Lor!' '*That!*' says they. "What a simple cove he is!'"

It being now late, and the party very modest in their fear of being too diffuse,* there were some tokens of separation; when Sergeant Dornton, the soldierly-looking man, said, looking round him with a smile:

"Before we break up, sir, perhaps you might have some amusement in hearing of the Adventures of a Carpet Bag. They are very short; and, I think, curious."

We welcomed the Carpet Bag, as cordially as Mr. Shepherdson welcomed the false Butcher at the Setting Moon. Sergeant Dornton proceeded.

"In 1847, I was despatched to Chatham, in search of one Mesheck, a Jew. He had been carrying on, pretty heavily, in the bill-stealing way, getting acceptances from young men of good connexions (in the army chiefly), on pretence of discount, and bolting with the same.

"Mesheck was off, before I got to Chatham. All I could learn about him was, that he had gone, probably to London, and had with him—a Carpet Bag.

"I came back to town, by the last train from Blackwall, and made inquiries concerning a Jew passenger with—a Carpet Bag.

"The office was shut up, it being the last train. There were only two or three porters left. Looking after a Jew with a Carpet Bag, on the Blackwall Railway, which was then the high road to a great Military Depôt, was worse than looking after a needle in a hayrick. But it happened that one of these porters had carried, for a certain Jew, to a certain public-house, a certain—Carpet Bag.

"I went to the public-house, but the Jew had only left his luggage there for a few hours, and had called for it in a cab, and taken it away. I put such questions there, and to the porter, as I thought prudent, and got at this description of—the Carpet Bag.

"It was a bag which had, on one side of it, worked in worsted, a green parrot on a stand. A green parrot on a stand was the means by which to identify that—Carpet Bag.

"I traced Mesheck, by means of this green parrot on a stand, to Cheltenham, to Birmingham, to Liverpool, to the Atlantic Ocean. At Liverpool he was too

---

* Talkative

many for me.* He had gone to the United States, and I gave up all thoughts of Mesheck, and likewise of his—Carpet Bag.

"Many months afterwards—near a year afterwards—there was a bank in Ireland robbed of seven thousand pounds, by a person of the name of Doctor Dundey, who escaped to America; from which country some of the stolen notes came home. He was supposed to have bought a farm in New Jersey. Under proper management, that estate could be seized and sold, for the benefit of the parties he had defrauded. I was sent off to America for this purpose.

"I landed at Boston. I went on to New York. I found that he had lately changed New York paper money for New Jersey paper money,† and had banked cash in New Brunswick. To take this Doctor Dundey, it was necessary to entrap him into the State of New York, which required a deal of artifice and trouble. At one time, he couldn't be drawn into an appointment. At another time, he appointed to come to meet me, and a New York officer, on a pretext I made; and then his children had the measles. At last he came, *per* steamboat, and I took him, and lodged him in a New York prison called the Tombs;‡ which I dare say you know, sir?"

Editorial acknowledgment to that effect.

"I went to the Tombs, on the morning after his capture, to attend the examination before the magistrate. I was passing through the magistrate's private room, when, happening to look round me to take notice of the place, as we generally have a habit of doing, I clapped my eyes, in one corner, on a—Carpet Bag.

"What did I see upon that Carpet Bag, if you'll believe me, but a green parrot on a stand, as large as life!

"'That Carpet Bag, with the representation of a green parrot on a stand,' said I, 'belongs to an English Jew, named Aaron Mesheck, and to no other man, alive or dead!'

"I give you my word the New York Police Officers were doubled up with surprise.

"'How did you ever come to know that?' said they.

"'I think I ought to know that green parrot by this time,' said I; 'for I have had as pretty a dance after that bird, at home, as ever I had, in all my life!'"

"And was it Mesheck's?" we submissively inquired.

---

* "he defeated me."

† At that time, U.S. states and many banks issued their own paper money, in addition to Federal bills.

‡ The New York Halls of Justice and House of Detention, in Five Points, Manhattan.

"Was it, sir? Of course it was! He was in custody for another offence, in that very identical Tombs, at that very identical time. And, more than that! Some memoranda, relating to the fraud for which I had vainly endeavoured to take him, were found to be, at that moment, lying in that very same individual—Carpet Bag!"

Such are the curious coincidences and such is the peculiar ability, always sharpening and being improved by practice, and always adapting itself to every variety of circumstances, and opposing itself to every new device that perverted ingenuity can invent, for which this important social branch of the public service is remarkable! For ever on the watch, with their wits stretched to the utmost, these officers have, from day to day and year to year, to set themselves against every novelty of trickery and dexterity that the combined imaginations of all the lawless rascals in England can devise, and to keep pace with every such invention that comes out. In the Courts of Justice, the materials of thousands of such stories as we have narrated—often elevated into the marvellous and romantic, by the circumstances of the case—are dryly compressed into the set phrase, "in consequence of information I received, I did so and so." Suspicion was to be directed, by careful inference and deduction, upon the right person; the right person was to be taken, wherever he had gone, or whatever he was doing to avoid detection: he is taken; there he is at the bar; that is enough. From information I, the officer, received, I did it; and, according to the custom in these cases, I say no more.

These games of chess, played with live pieces, are played before small audiences, and are chronicled nowhere. The interest of the game supports the player. Its results are enough for justice. To compare great things with small, suppose Le Verrier or Adams[*] informing the public that from information he had received he had discovered a new planet; or Columbus informing the public of his day that from information he had received he had discovered a new continent; so the Detectives inform it that they have discovered a new fraud or an old offender, and the process is unknown.

Thus, at midnight, closed the proceedings of our curious and interesting party. But one other circumstance finally wound up the evening, after our Detective guests had left us. One of the sharpest among them, and the officer best acquainted with the Swell Mob, had his pocket picked, going home!

---

[*] Working separately, Le Verrier in France and Adams in England predicted the existence and position of Neptune mathematically.

THE TRAIL OF THE SERPENT

(EXTRACT)

by Mary Elizabeth Braddon

1861

Mary Elizabeth Braddon was born in London in 1835. Her parents separated when she was five years old, and her mother saw to her education. She dabbled with acting and actually supported herself and her mother for three years by playing minor roles on the London stage.

In 1860, she met the publisher John Maxwell. He was married with five children, but his wife was confined to an asylum. Mary moved in with him, acting as stepmother to his children until 1874, when Maxwell's wife died and the two were able to marry. They went on to have six children of their own.

Mary's first novel, *Three Times Dead; or, The Secret of the Heath,* was published the same year she met Maxwell. She went on to write more than eighty novels, many—including her best-known work, *Lady Audley's Secret* (1862)—in the popular "sensation fiction" style.

Sales of *Three Times Dead* were poor, and on Maxwell's advice a condensed and revised version was published in 1861 as *The Trail of the Serpent*. Hailed by some as the first British detective novel, *The Trail of the Serpent* shows its roots in sensation fiction. Its dense plot involves murder, insanity, suicide, impersonation, lust, blackmail, abandoned offspring, and a jailbreak as its villain schemes to gain control of an aristocratic fortune. The rightful heir, Richard Marwood, is framed for the murder of his uncle and pleads insanity to avoid the noose while his friends work to expose the true culprit: an orphaned schoolmaster named Jabez North.

The book's climax sees the mute detective Joseph Peters—an interesting character who would certainly anchor a series of titles in today's market—in Liverpool, along with Augustus Darley, a typical English "jolly good fellow" of the time, and Jim Stilson, a publican and former prizefighter known as the Left-handed Smasher. Jabez North—who has been masquerading as Raymond, Count de Marolles—plans to flee to America, and the three must pick up his trail.

T hree days after the above conversation, three gentlemen were assembled at breakfast in a small room in a tavern overlooking the quay at Liverpool. This triangular party consisted of the Smasher, in an elegant and simple morning costume, consisting of tight trousers of Stuart plaid, an orange-coloured necktie, a blue checked waistcoat, and shirt-sleeves. The Smasher looked upon a coat as an essentially outdoor garment, and would no more have invested himself in it to eat his breakfast than he would have partaken of that refreshment with his hat on, or an umbrella up. The two other gentlemen were Mr. Darley, and his chief, Mr. Peters, who had a little document in his pocket signed by a Lancashire magistrate, on which he set considerable value. They had come across to Liverpool as directed by the telegraph, and had there met with the Smasher, who had received letters for them from London with the details of the escape, and orders to be on the look-out for Peters and Gus. Since the arrival of these two, the trio had led a sufficiently idle and apparently purposeless life. They had engaged an apartment overlooking the quay, in the window of which they were seated for the best part of the day, playing the intellectual and exciting game of all-fours. There did not seem much in this to forward the cause of Richard Marwood. It is true that Mr. Peters was wont to vanish from the room every now and then, in order to speak to mysterious and grave-looking gentlemen, who commanded respect wherever they went, and before whom the most daring thief in Liverpool shrank as before Mr. Calcraft* himself. He held strange conferences with them in corners of the hostelry in which the trio had taken up their abode; he went out with them, and

---

* William Calcraft (1800–1879) was the official Executioner for the City of London and Middlesex at the time *The Trail of the Serpent* was published. He was one of the most prolific executioners in British history; in a forty-five-year career, he carried out an estimated 450 executions.

hovered about the quays and the shipping; he prowled about in the dusk of the evening, and meeting these gentlemen also prowling in the uncertain light, would sometimes salute them as friends and brothers, at other times be entirely unacquainted with them, and now and then interchange two or three hurried gestures with them, which the close observer would have perceived to mean a great deal. Beyond this, nothing had been done—and, in spite of all this, no tidings could be obtained of the Count de Marolles, except that no person answering to his description had left Liverpool either by land or water. Still, neither Mr. Peters's spirits nor patience failed him; and after every interview held upon the stairs or in the passage, after every excursion to the quays or the streets, he returned as briskly as on the first day, and reseated himself at the little table by the window, at which his colleagues—or rather his companions, for neither Mr. Darley nor the Smasher were of the smallest use to him—played, and took it in turns to ruin each other from morning till night. The real truth of the matter was, that, if anything, the detective's so-called assistants were decidedly in his way; but Augustus Darley, having distinguished himself in the escape from the asylum, considered himself an amateur Vidocque;* and the Smasher, from the moment of putting in his left, and unconsciously advancing the cause of Richard and justice by extinguishing the Count de Marolles, had panted to write his name, or rather make his mark, upon the scroll of fame, by arresting that gentleman in his own proper person, and without any extraneous aid whatever. It was rather hard for him, then, to have to resign the prospect of such a glorious adventure to a man of Mr. Peters's inches; but he was of a calm and amiable disposition, and would floor his adversary with as much good temper as he would eat his favourite dinner; so, with a growl of resignation, he abandoned the reins to the steady hands so used to hold them, and seated himself down to the consumption of innumerable clay pipes and glasses of bitter ale with Gus, who, being one of the most ancient of the order of the Cherokees, was an especial favourite with him.

On this third morning, however, there is a decided tone of weariness pervading the minds of both Gus and the Smasher. Three-handed all-fours, though a delicious and exciting game, will pall upon the inconstant mind, especially when your third player is perpetually summoned from the table to take part in a mysterious dialogue with a person or persons unknown, the result of which he declines to communicate to you. The view from the bow-window of the blue parlour in the White Lion, Liverpool, is no doubt as animated as it is beautiful;

---

* Eugène François Vidocq (1775–1857), founder of the French *Sûreté Nationale* and head of the first known private detective agency.

but Rasselas,* we know, got tired of some very pretty scenery, and there have been readers so inconstant as to grow weary of Dr. Johnson's book, and to go down peacefully to their graves unacquainted with the climax thereof. So it is scarcely perhaps to be wondered that the volatile Augustus thirsted for the waterworks of Blackfriars; while the Smasher, feeling himself to be blushing unseen, and wasting his stamina, if not his sweetness, on the desert air, pined for the familiar shades of Bow Street and Vinegar Yard, and the home-sounds of the rumbling and jingling of the wagons, and the unpolite language of the drivers thereof, on market mornings in the adjacent market. Pleasures and palaces are all very well in their way, as the song says; but there is just one little spot on earth which, whether it be a garret in Petticoat Lane or a mansion in Belgrave Square, is apt to be dearer to us than the best of them; and the Smasher languishes for the friendly touch of the ebony handles of the porter-engine, and the scent of the Welsh rarebits† of his youth. Perhaps I express myself in a more romantic manner on this subject, however, than I should do, for the remark of the Left-handed one, as he pours himself out a cup of tea from the top of the tea-pot—he despises the spout of that vessel as a modern innovation on ancient simplicity—is as simple as it is energetic. He merely observes that he is "jolly sick of this lot,"— this lot meaning Liverpool, the Count de Marolles, the White Lion, three-handed all-fours, and the detective police-force.

"There was nobody ill in Friar Street when I left," said Gus mournfully; "but there had been a run upon Pimperneckel's Universal Regenerator Pills: and if that don't make business a little brisker, nothing will."

"It's my opinion," observed the Smasher doggedly, "that this 'ere forrin cove has give us the slip out and out; and the sooner we gets back to London the better. I never was much of a hand at chasing wild geese, and"—he added, with rather a spiteful glance at the mild countenance of the detective—"I don't see neither that standin' and makin' signs to parties unbeknown at street-comers and stair-heads is the quickest way to catch them sort of birds; leastways it's not the opinion held by the gents belongin' to the Ring as I've had the honour to make acquaintance with."

"Suppose," said Mr. Peters, on his fingers.‡

"Oh!" muttered the Smasher, "blow them fingers of his. I can't understand 'em—there!" The left-handed Hercules knew that this was to attack the detective

---

* From Samuel Johnson's book *The History of Rasselas, Prince of Abissinia* (sic).

† A popular snack of the time, consisting of a cheese sauce poured over toasted bread.

‡ Mute, as previously noted, Peters is using sign language.

on his tenderest point. "Blest if I ever knows his p's from his v's, or his w's from his e's, let alone his vowels, and them would puzzle a conjuror."

Mr. Peters glanced at the prize-fighter more in sorrow than in anger, and taking out a greasy little pocket-book, and a greasier little pencil, considerably the worse for having been vehemently chewed in moments of preoccupation, he wrote upon a leaf of it thus—"Suppose we catch him to-day?"

"Ah, very true," said the Smasher sulkily, after he had examined the document in two or three different lights before he came upon its full bearings; "very true, indeed, suppose we do—and suppose we don't, on the other hand; and I know which is the likeliest. Suppose, Mr. Peters, we give up lookin' for a needle in a bundle of hay, which after a time gets tryin' to a lively disposition, and go back to our businesses. If you had a girl as didn't know British from best French a-servin' of your customers," he continued in an injured tone, "you'd be anxious to get home, and let your forrin counts go to the devil their own ways."

"Then go," Mr. Peters wrote, in large letters and no capitals.

"Oh, ah; yes, to be sure," replied the Smasher, who, I regret to say, felt painfully, in his absence from domestic pleasures, the want of somebody to quarrel with; "No, I thank you! Go the very day as you're going to catch him! Not if I'm in any manner aware of the circumstance. I'm obliged to you," he added, with satirical emphasis.

"Come, I say, old boy," interposed Gus, who had been quietly doing execution upon a plate of devilled kidneys during this little friendly altercation, "come, I say, no snarling, Smasher. Peters isn't going to contest the belt with you, you know."

"You needn't be a-diggin' at me because I ain't champion," said the ornament of the P.R.,* who was inclined to find a malicious meaning in every word uttered that morning; "you needn't come any of your sneers because I ain't got the belt any longer."

The Smasher had been Champion of England in his youth, but had retired upon his laurels for many years, and only occasionally emerged from private life in a public-house to take a round or two with some old opponent.

"I tell you what it is, Smasher—it's my opinion the air of Liverpool don't suit your constitution," said Gus. "We've promised to stand by Peters here, and to go by his word in everything, for the sake of the man we want to serve; and, however trying it may be to our patience doing nothing, which perhaps is about as much as we can do and make no mistakes, the first that gets tired and deserts the ship will be no friend to Richard Marwood."

---

* The "Prize Ring," London's illegal bare-knuckle fighting circuit.

"I'm a bad lot, Mr. Darley, and that's the truth," said the mollified Smasher; "but the fact is, I'm used to a turn with the gloves every morning before breakfast with the barman, and when I don't get it, I dare say I ain't the pleasantest company goin'. I should think they've got gloves in the house: would you mind taking off your coat and having a turn—friendly like?"

Gus assured the Smasher that nothing would please him better than that trifling diversion; and in five minutes they had pushed Mr. Peters and the breakfast-table into a corner, and were hard at it, Mr. Barley's knowledge of the art being all required to keep the slightest pace with the scientific movements of the agile though elderly Smasher.

Mr. Peters did not stay at the breakfast-table long, but after having drunk a huge breakfast cupful of very opaque and substantial-looking coffee at a draught, just as if it had been half a pint of beer, he slid quietly out of the room.

"It's my opinion," said the Smasher, as he stood, or rather lounged, upon his guard, and warded off the most elaborate combinations of Mr. Barley's fists with as much ease as he would have brushed aside so many flies—"it's my opinion that chap ain't up to his business."

"Isn't he?" replied Gus, as he threw down the gloves in despair, after having been half an hour in a violent perspiration, without having succeeded in so much as rumpling the Smasher's hair. "Isn't he?" he said, choosing the interrogative as the most expressive form of speech. "That man's got head enough to be prime minister, and carry the House along with every twist of his fingers."

"He must make his p's and b's a little plainer afore he'll get a bill through the Commons though," muttered the Left-handed one, who couldn't quite get over his feelings of injury against the detective for the utter darkness in which he had been kept for the last three days as to the other's plans.

The Smasher and Mr. Barley passed the morning in that remarkably intellectual and praiseworthy manner peculiar to gentlemen who, being thrown out of their usual occupation, are cast upon their own resources for amusement and employment. There was the daily paper to be looked at, to begin with; but after Gus had glanced at the leading article, a *rifacimento** of the *Times* leader of the day before, garnished with some local allusions, and highly spiced with satirical remarks *apropos* to our spirited contemporary the *Liverpool Aristides*; after the Smasher had looked at the racing fixtures for the coming week, and made rude observations on the editing of a journal which failed to describe the coming

---

* Italian: "reworking."

off of the event between Silver-polled Robert and the Chester Crusher—after, I say, the two gentlemen had each devoured his favourite page, the paper was an utter failure in the matter of excitement, and the window was the next best thing. Now to the peculiarly constituted mind of the Left-handed one, looking out of a window was in itself very slow work; and unless he was allowed to eject missiles of a trifling but annoying character—such as hot ashes out of his pipe, the last drop of his pint of beer, the dirty water out of the saucers belonging to the flower-pots on the window-sill, or lighted lucifer-matches—into the eyes of the unoffending passers-by, he didn't, to use his own forcible remark, "seem to see the fun of it." Harmless old gentlemen with umbrellas, mild elderly ladies with hand-baskets and brass-handled green silk parasols, and young ladies of from ten to twelve going to school in clean frocks, and on particularly good terms with themselves, the Smasher looked upon as his peculiar prey. To put his head out of the window and make tender and polite inquiries about their maternal parents; to go further still, and express an earnest wish to be informed of those parents' domestic arrangements, and whether they had been induced to part with a piece of machinery of some importance in the getting up of linen; to insinuate alarming suggestions of mad bulls in the next street, or a tiger just broke loose from the Zoological Gardens; to terrify the youthful scholar by asking him derisively whether he wouldn't "catch it when he got to school? Oh, no, not at all, neither!" and to draw his head away suddenly, and altogether disappear from public view; to act, in fact, after the manner of an accomplished clown in a Christmas pantomime, was the weak delight of his manly mind: and when prevented by Mr. Darley's friendly remonstrance from doing this, the Smasher abandoned the window altogether, and concentrated all the powers of his intellect on the pursuit of a lively young bluebottle,* which eluded his bandanna at every turn, and bumped itself violently against the window-panes at the very moment its pursuer was looking for it up the chimney.

Time and the hour made very long work of this particular morning, and several glasses of bitter had been called for, and numerous games of cribbage had been played by the two companions, when Mr. Darley, looking at his watch for not more than the twenty-second time in the last hour, announced with some satisfaction that it was half-past two o'clock, and that it was consequently very near dinner-time.

"Peters is a long time gone," suggested the Smasher.

---

* A kind of large housefly with an iridescent blue abdomen, common across Britain.

"Take my word for it," said Gus, "something has turned up; he has laid his hand upon De Marolles at last."

"I don't think it," replied his ally, obstinately refusing to believe in Mr. Peters's extra share of the divine afflatus; "and if he did come across him, how's he to detain him, I'd like to know? He couldn't go in with his left," he muttered derisively, "and split his head open upon the pavement to keep him quiet for a day or two."

At this very moment there came a tap at the door, and a youthful person in corduroy and a perspiration entered the room, with a very small and very dirty piece of paper twisted up into a bad imitation of a three-cornered note.

"Please, yon was to give me sixpence if I run all the way," remarked the youthful Mercury, "an' I 'ave: look at my forehead;" and, in proof of his fidelity, the messenger pointed to the water-drops which chased each other down his open brow and ran a dead heat to the end of his nose.

The scrawl ran thus—"The *Washington* sails at three for New York: be on the quay and see the passengers embark: don't notice me unless I notice you. Yours truly."

"It was just give me by a gent in a hurry wot was dumb, and wrote upon a piece of paper to tell me to run my legs off so as you should have it quick—thank you kindly, sir, and good afternoon," said the messenger, all in one breath, as he bowed his gratitude for the shilling Gus tossed him as he dismissed him.

"I said so," cried the young surgeon, as the Smasher applied himself to the note with quite as much, nay, perhaps more earnestness and solemnity than Chevalier Bunsen* might have assumed when he deciphered a half-erased and illegible inscription, in a language which for some two thousand years has been unknown to mortal man. "I said so; Peters is on the scent, and this man will be taken yet. Put on your hat, Smasher, and let's lose no time; it only wants a quarter to three, and I wouldn't be out of this for a great deal."

"I shouldn't much relish being out of the fun either," replied his companion; "and if it comes to blows, perhaps it's just as well I haven't had my dinner."

There were a good many people going by the *Washington*, and the deck of the small steamer which was to convey them on board the great ship, where she lay in graceful majesty down the noble Mersey river, was crowded with every species of luggage it was possible to imagine as appertaining to the widest varieties of the genus traveller. There was the maiden lady, with a small income from

---

* Ernest de Bunsen (1819–1903), an Anglo-German writer of speculative works in the field of comparative religion.

the three-per-cents, and a determination of blood to the tip of a sharp nose, going out to join a married brother in New York, and evidently intent upon importing a gigantic brass cage, containing a parrot in the last stage of bald-headedness—politely called moulting; and a limp and wandering-minded umbrella—weak in the ribs, aid further afflicted with a painfully sharp ferrule, which always appeared where it was not expected, and evidently hankered wildly after the bystanders' backbones—as favourable specimens of the progress of the fine arts in the mother country. There were several of those brilliant birds-of-passage popularly known as "travellers," whose heavy luggage consisted of a carpet-bag and walking-stick, and whose light ditto was composed of a pocket-book and a silver pencil-case of protean construction, which wag sometimes a pen, now and then a penknife, and very often a toothpick. These gentlemen came down to the steamer at the last moment, inspiring the minds of nervous passengers with supernatural and convulsive cheerfulness by the light and airy way in which they bade adieu to the comrades who had just looked round to see them start, and who made appointments with them for Christmas supper-parties, and booked bets with them for next year's Newmarket* first spring—as if such things as ship-wreck, peril by sea, heeling over *Royal Georges*,† lost *Presidents*,‡ with brilliant Irish comedians setting forth on their return to the land in which they had been so beloved and admired, never, never to reach the shore,§ were things that could not be. There were rosy-cheeked country lasses, going over to earn fabulous wages and marry impossibly rich husbands. There were the old people, who essayed this long journey on an element which they knew only by sight, in answer to the kind son's noble letter, inviting them to come and share the pleasant home his sturdy arm had won far away in the fertile West. There were stout Irish labourers armed with pickaxe and spade, as with the best sword wherewith to open the great oyster of the world in these latter degenerate days. There was the distinguished American family, with ever so many handsomely dressed, spoiled, affectionate children clustering round papa and mamma, and having their own way, after the manner of transatlantic youth. There were, in short, all the people who usually assemble when a good

---

* A famous race-course in the County of Suffolk.

† HMS *Royal George* heeled over and sank in August, 1782, with the loss of more than 600 lives.

‡ The SS *President*, the largest passenger ship in the world at the time, was lost at sea between New York and Liverpool in 1841.

§ Irish actor William Grattan Tyrone Power (1795–1841), an ancestor of the American actor, was among those lost aboard the SS *President*.

THE TRAIL OF THE SERPENT | 99

ship sets sail for the land of dear brother Jonathan;* but the Count de Marolles there was not.

No, decidedly, no Count de Marolles! There was a very quiet-looking Irish labourer, keeping quite aloof from the rest of his kind, who were sufficiently noisy and more than sufficiently forcible in the idiomatic portions of their conversation. There was this very quiet Irishman, leaning on his spade and pickaxe, and evidently bent on not going on board till the very last moment; and there was an elderly gentleman in a black coat, who looked rather like a Methodist parson, and who held a very small carpet-bag in his hand; but there was no Count de Marolles; and what's more, there was no Mr. Peters.

This latter circumstance made Augustus Darley very uneasy; but I regret to say that the Smasher wore, if anything, a look of triumph as the hands of the clocks about the quay pointed to three o'clock, and no Peters appeared.

"I knowed," he said, with effusion—"I knowed that cove wasn't up to his business. I wouldn't mind bettin' the goodwill of my little crib in London agen sixpenn'orth of coppers, that he's a-standin' at this very individual moment of time at a street-corner a mile off, makin' signs to one of the Liverpool police-officers."

The gentleman in the black coat standing before them turned round on hearing this remark, and smiled—smiled very very faintly; but he certainly did smile. The Smasher's blood, which was something like that of Lancaster, and distinguished for its tendency to mount, was up in a moment.

"I hope you find my conversation amusin', old gent," he said, with considerable asperity; "I came down here on purpose to put you in spirits, on account of bein' grieved to see you always a-lookin' as if you'd just come home from your own funeral, and the undertaker was a-dunnin' you for the burial-fees."

Gus trod heavily on his companion's foot as a friendly hint to him not to get up a demonstration; and addressing the gentleman, who appeared in no hurry to resent the Smasher's contemptuous animadversions, asked him when he thought the boat would start.

"Not for five or ten minutes, I dare say," he answered. "Look there; is that a coffin they're bringing this way? I'm rather short-sighted; be good enough to tell me if it is a coffin?"

The Smasher, who had the glance of an eagle, replied that it decidedly was a coffin; adding, with a growl, that he knowed somebody as might be in it, and no harm done to society.

---

* A personification of the states of New England, looking like a younger version of Uncle Sam. Now largely superseded by the national personification.

The elderly gentleman took not the slightest notice of this gratuitous piece of information on the part of the left-handed gladiator; but suddenly busied himself with his fingers in the neighbourhood of his limp white cravat.

"Why, I'm blest," cried the Smasher, "if the old baby ain't at Peters's game, a-talkin' to nobody upon his fingers!"

Nay, most distinguished professor of the noble art of self-defence, is not that assertion a little premature? Talking on his fingers, certainly—looking at nobody, certainly; but for all that, talking to somebody, and to a somebody who is looking at him; for, from the other side of the little crowd, the Irish labourer fixes his eyes intently on every movement of the grave elderly gentleman's fingers, as they run through four or five rapid words; and Gus Darley, perceiving this look, starts in amazement, for the eyes of the Irish labourer are the eyes of Mr. Peters of the detective police.

But neither the Smasher nor Gus is to notice Mr. Peters unless Mr. Peters notices them. It is so expressed in the note, which Mr. Darley has at that very moment in his waistcoat pocket. So Gus gives his companion a nudge, and directs his attention to the smock-frock and the slouched hat in which the detective has hidden himself, with a hurried injunction to him to keep quiet. We are human at the best; ay, even when we are celebrated for our genius in the muscular science, and our well-known blow of the left-handed postman's knock, or double auctioneer: and, if the sober truth must be told, the Smasher was sorry to recognize Mr. Peters in that borrowed garb. He didn't want the dumb detective to arrest the Count de Marolles. He had never read *Coriolanus*, neither had he seen *the* Roman, Mr. William Macready, in that character; but, for all that, the Smasher wanted to go home to the dear purlieus of Drury Lane, and say to his astonished admirers, "Alone I did it!" And lo, here were Mr. Peters and the elderly stranger both entered for the same event.

While gloomy and vengeful thoughts, therefore, troubled the manly breast of the Vinegar-Yard gladiator, four men approached, bearing on their shoulders the coffin which had so aroused the stranger's attention. They bore it on board the steamer, and a few moments after a gentlemanly and cheerful-looking man, of about forty, stepped across the narrow platform, and occupied himself with a crowd of packages, which stood in a heap, apart from the rest of the luggage on the crowded deck.

Again the elderly stranger's fingers were busy in the region of his cravat. The superficial observer would have merely thought him very fidgety about the limp bit of muslin; but this time the fingers of Mr. Peters telegraphed an answer.

"Gentlemen," said the stranger, addressing Mr. Darley and the Smasher in the most matter-of-fact manner, "you will be good enough to go on board that steamer with me? I am working with Mr. Peters in this affair. Remember, I am going to America by that vessel yonder, and you are my friends come with me to see me off. Now, gentlemen."

He has no time to say any more, for the bell rings; and the last stragglers, the people who will enjoy the latest available moment on *terra firma*, scramble on board; amongst them the Smasher, Gus, and the stranger, who stick very closely together.

The coffin has been placed in the centre of the vessel, on the top of a pile of chests, and its gloomy black outline is sharply defined against the clear blue autumn sky. Now there is a general feeling amongst the passengers that the presence of this coffin is a peculiar injury to them.

It is unpleasant, certainly. From the very moment of its appearance amongst them a change has come over the spirits of every one of the travellers. They try to keep away from it, but they try in vain; there is a dismal fascination in the defined and ghastly shape, which all the rough wrappers that can be thrown over it will not conceal. They find their eyes wandering to it, in preference even to watching receding Liverpool, whose steeples and tall chimneys are dipping down and down into the blue water, and will soon disappear altogether. They are interested in it in spite of themselves; they ask questions of one another; they ask questions of the engineer, and of the steward, and of the captain of the steamer, but can elicit nothing—except that lying in that coffin, so close to them, and yet so very very far away from them, there is an American gentleman of some distinction, who, having died suddenly in England, is being carried back to New York, to be buried amongst his friends in that city. The aggrieved passengers for the *Washington* think it very hard upon them that the American gentleman of distinction—they remember that he is a gentleman of distinction, and modify their tone accordingly—could not have been buried in England like a reasonable being. The British dominions were not good enough for *him*, they supposed. Other passengers, pushing the question still further, ask whether he couldn't have been taken home by some other vessel; nay, whether indeed he ought not to have had a ship all to himself, instead of harrowing the feelings and preying upon the spirits of first-class passengers. They look almost spitefully, as they make these remarks towards the shrouded coffin, which, to their great aggravation, is not entirely shrouded by the wrappers about it. One corner has been left uncovered, revealing the stout rough oak; for it is only a temporary coffin, and the gentleman of distinction will be put into something better befitting his rank when he arrives at his destination. It is to be observed, and it is observed by many, that the cheerful passenger in fashionable mourning, and with the last greatcoat which the inspiration of Saville Row has given to the London world thrown over his arm, hovers in a protecting manner about the coffin, and evinces a fidelity which, but for his perfectly cheerful countenance and self-possessed manner, would be really touching, towards the late American gentleman of distinction, whom he has for his only travelling companion.

Now, though a great many questions had been asked on all sides, one question especially, namely, whether *it*—people always dropped their voices when they pronounced that small pronoun—whether *it* would not be put in the hold as soon as they got on board the *Washington*, the answer to which question was an affirmative, and gave considerable satisfaction—except indeed to one moody old gentleman, who asked, "How about getting any little thing one happened to want on the journey out of the hold?" and was very properly snubbed for the suggestion, and told that passengers had no business to want things out of the hold on the voyage; and furthermore insulted by the liveliest of the lively travellers, who suggested, in an audible aside, that perhaps the old gentleman had only one clean shirt, and had put that at the bottom of his travelling chest,—now, though, I say, so many questions had been asked, no one had as yet presumed to address the cheerful-looking gentleman convoying the American of distinction home to his friends, though this very gentleman might, after all, be naturally supposed to know more than anybody else about the subject. He was smoking a cigar, and though he kept very close to the coffin, he was about the only person on board who did not look at it, but kept his gaze fixed on the fading town of Liverpool. The Smasher, Gus, and Mr. Peters's unknown ally stood very close to this gentleman, while the detective himself leant over the side of the vessel, near to, though a little apart from, the Irish labourers and rosy-cheeked country girls, who, as steerage passengers, very properly herded together, and did not attempt to contaminate by their presence the minds or the garments of those superior beings who were to occupy state-cabins six feet long by three feet wide, and to have green peas and new milk from the cow all the way out. Presently, the elderly gentleman of rather shabby-genteel but clerical appearance, who had so briefly introduced himself to Gus and the Smasher, made some remarks about the town of Liverpool to the cheerful friend of the late distinguished American.

The cheerful friend took his cigar out of his mouth, smiled, and said, "Yes; it's a thriving town, a small London, really—the metropolis in miniature."

"You know Liverpool very well?" asked the Smasher's companion.

"No, not very well; in point of fact, I know very little of England at all. My visit has been a brief one."

He is evidently an American from this remark, though there is very little of brother Jonathan in his manner.

"Your visit has been a brief one? Indeed. And it has had a very melancholy termination, I regret to perceive," said the persevering stranger, on whose every word the Smasher and Mr. Darley hung respectfully.

"A very melancholy termination," replied the gentleman, with the sweetest smile. "My poor friend had hoped to return to the bosom of his family, and delight them many an evening round the cheerful hearth by the recital of his adventures in, and impressions of, the mother country. You cannot imagine," he continued, speaking very slowly, and as he spoke, allowing his eyes to wander from the stranger to the Smasher, and from the Smasher to Gus, with a glance which, if anything, had the slightest shade of anxiety in it; "you cannot imagine the interest we on the other side of the Atlantic take in everything that occurs in the mother country. We may be great over there—we may be rich over there—we may be universally beloved and respected over there,—but I doubt—I really, after all, doubt," he said sentimentally, "whether we are truly happy. We sigh for the wings of a dove, or to speak practically, for our travelling expenses, that we may come over here and be at rest."

"And yet I conclude it was the especial wish of your late friend to be buried over there?" asked the stranger.

"It was—his dying wish."

"And the melancholy duty of complying with that wish devolved on you?" said the stranger, with a degree of puerile curiosity and frivolous interest in an affair entirely irrelevant to the matter in hand which bewildered Gus, and at which the Smasher palpably turned up his nose; muttering to himself at the same time that the forrin swell would have time to get to America while they was a-palaverin' and a-jawin' this 'ere humbug.

"Yes, it devolved on me," replied the cheerful gentleman, offering his cigar-case to the three friends, who declined the proffered weeds. "We were connections; his mother's half-sister married my second cousin—not very nearly connected certainly, but extremely attached to each other. It will be a melancholy satisfaction to his poor widow to see his ashes entombed upon his native shore, and the thought of that repays me threefold for anything I may suffer."

He looked altogether far too airy and charming a creature to suffer very much; but the stranger bowed gravely, and Gus, looking towards the prow of the vessel, perceived the earnest eyes of Mr. Peters attentively fixed on the little group.

As to the Smasher, he was so utterly disgusted with the stranger's manner of doing business, that he abandoned himself to his own thoughts and hummed a tune—the tune appertaining to what is generally called a comic song, being the last passages in the life of a humble and unfortunate member of the working classes as related by himself.

While talking to the cheerful gentleman on this very melancholy subject, the stranger from Liverpool happened to get quite close to the coffin, and, with an admirable freedom from prejudice which astonished the other passengers standing near, rested his hand carelessly on the stout oaken lid, just at that corner where the canvas left it exposed. It was a most speaking proof of the almost overstrained feeling of devotion possessed by the cheerful gentleman towards his late friend that this trifling action seemed to disturb him; his eyes wandered uneasily towards the stranger's black-gloved hand, and at last, when, in absence of mind, the stranger actually drew the heavy covering completely over this corner of the coffin, his uneasiness reached a climax, and drawing the dingy drapery hurriedly back, he rearranged it in its old fashion.

"Don't you wish the coffin to be entirely covered?" asked the stranger quietly.

"Yes—no; that is," said the cheerful gentleman, with some embarrassment in his tone, "that is—I—you see there is something of profanity in a stranger's hand approaching the remains of those we love."

"Suppose, then," said his interlocutor, "we take a turn about the deck? This neighbourhood must be very painful to you."

"On the contrary," replied the cheerful gentleman, "you will think me, I dare say, a very singular person, but I prefer remaining by him to the last. The coffin will be put in the hold as soon as we get on board the *Washington*; then my duty will have been accomplished and my mind will be at rest. You go to New York with us?" he asked.

"I shall have that pleasure," replied the stranger.

"And your friend—your sporting friend?" asked the gentleman, with a rather supercilious glance at the many-coloured raiment and mottled-soap complexion of the Smasher, who was still singing *sotto voce* the above-mentioned melody, with his arms folded on the rail of the bench on which he was seated, and his chin resting moodily on his coat-sleeves.

"No," replied the stranger; "my friends, I regret to say, leave me as soon as we get on board."

In a few minutes more they reached the side of the brave ship, which, from the Liverpool quay, had looked a white-winged speck not a bit too big for Queen Mab; but which was, oh, such a Leviathan of a vessel when you stood just under her, and had to go up her side by means of a ladder—which ladder seemed to be subject to shivering fits, and struck terror into the nervous lady and the bald-headed parrot.

All the passengers, except the cheerful gentleman with the coffin and the stranger—with Gus and the Smasher and Mr. Peters loitering in the background—seemed bent on getting up each before the other, and considerably increased the confusion by evincing this wish in a candid but not conciliating manner, showing a degree of ill-feeling which was much increased by the passengers that had not got on board looking daggers at the passengers that had got on board, and seemed settled quite comfortably high and dry upon the stately deck. At last, however, every one but the aforesaid group had ascended the ladder. Some stout sailors were preparing great ropes wherewith to haul up the coffin, and the cheerful gentleman was busily directing them, when the captain of the steamer said to the stranger from Liverpool, as he loitered at the bottom of the ladder, with Mr. Peters at his elbow,—"Now then, sir, if you're for the *Washington*, quick's the word. We're off as soon as ever they've got that job over," pointing to the coffin. The stranger from Liverpool, instead of complying with this very natural request, whispered a few words into the ear of the captain, who looked very grave on hearing them, and then, advancing to the cheerful gentleman, who was very anxious and very uneasy about the manner in which the coffin was to be hauled up the side of the vessel, he laid a heavy hand upon his shoulder, and said,—"I want the lid of that coffin taken off before those men haul it up."

Such a change came over the face of the cheerful gentleman as only comes over the face of a man who knows that he is playing a desperate game, and knows as surely that he has lost it. "My good sir," he said, "you're mad. Not for the Queen of England would I see that coffin-lid unscrewed."

"I don't think it will give us so much trouble as that," said the other quietly. "I very much doubt it's being screwed down at all. You were greatly alarmed just now, lest the person within should be smothered. You were terribly frightened when I drew the heavy canvas over those incisions in the oak," he added, pointing to the lid, in the corner of which two or three cracks were apparent to the close observer.

"Good Heavens! the man is mad!" cried the gentleman, whose manner had entirely lost its airiness. "The man is evidently a maniac! This is too dreadful! Is the sanctity of death to be profaned in this manner? Are we to cross the Atlantic in the company of a madman?"

"You are not to cross the Atlantic at all just yet," said the Liverpool stranger. "The man is not mad, I assure you, but he is one of the principal members of the Liverpool detective police-force, and is empowered to arrest a person who is supposed to be on board this boat. There is only one place in which that person can be concealed. Here is my warrant to arrest Jabez North, *alias* Raymond Marolles, *alias* the Count de Marolles. I know as certainly as that I myself stand here that he lies hidden in that coffin, and I desire that the lid may be removed. If I am mistaken, it can be immediately replaced, and I shall be ready to render you my most fervent apologies for having profaned the repose of the dead. Now, Peters!"

The dumb detective went to one end of the coffin, while his colleague stood at the other. The Liverpool officer was correct in his supposition. The lid was only secured by two or three long stout nails, and gave way in three minutes. The two detectives lifted it off the coffin—and there, hot, flushed, and panting, half-suffocated, with desperation in his wicked blue eyes, his teeth locked in furious rage at his utter powerlessness to escape from the grasp of his pursuers—there, run to earth at last, lay the accomplished Raymond, Count de Marolles!

They put the handcuffs on him before they lifted him out of the coffin, the Smasher assisting. Years after, when the Smasher grew to be an older and graver man, he used to tell to admiring and awe-stricken customers the story of this arrest. But it is to be observed that his memory on these occasions was wont to play him false, for he omitted to mention either the Liverpool detective or our good friend Mr. Peters as taking any part in the capture; but described the whole affair as conducted by himself alone, with an incalculable number of "I says," and "so then I thinks," and "well, what do I do next?" and other phrases of the same description.

The Count de Marolles, with tumbled hair, and a white face and blue lips, sitting handcuffed upon the bench of the steamer between the Liverpool detective and Mr. Peters, steaming back to Liverpool, was a sight not good to look upon. The cheerful gentleman sat with the Smasher and Mr. Darley, who had been told to keep an eye upon him, and who—the Smasher especially—kept both eyes upon him with a will.

Throughout the little voyage there were no words spoken but these from the Liverpool detective, as he first put the fetters on the white and slender wrists of his prisoner: "Monsieur de Marolles," he said, "you've tried this little game once before. This is the second occasion, I understand, on which you've done a sham die. I'd have you beware of the third time. According to superstitious people, it's generally fatal."

THE NOTTING HILL MYSTERY

(EXTRACT)

by "Charles Felix"

1862

The identity of "Charles Felix" is itself something of a mystery. It is generally thought that Charles Felix is a pseudonym used by Charles Warren Adams, a London lawyer who is known to have published under other *noms de plume*. "Felix" is a Latin word, which may be translated as "lucky" or "happy."

The Notting Hill Mystery appeared as a serial in *Once A Week* magazine between November 1862 and January 1863; it was republished in book form in 1865, one year after another mystery by "Charles Felix," *Velvet Lawn.*

Unusually for detective fiction, the story is told in epistolary form, consisting of recorded statements, letters, journal entries, and other documents bracketed by an introduction and a conclusion attributed to insurance investigator Ralph Henderson. This form has both advantages and disadvantages: on the one hand, it enables the writer to present readers with exactly the same evidence as the detective; on the other, the detective as a character is largely absent from the story.

The case concerns a Baron R**, whose wife died after drinking acid while apparently sleepwalking. Further suspicion is raised by the facts that the Baroness had recently inherited £25,000 following the deaths of a husband and wife who were prior heirs to the inheritance, and that the Baron had taken out no fewer than five life insurance policies on her, each for the maximum of £5,000. As a result of her death, he stood to gain £50,000:

an immense sum at the time, equivalent—according to online sources—to almost £6m (U.S. $8m) in today's terms.

As summed up in the detective's conclusion, the case involves poison, blackmail, and mesmerism, which was still taken seriously by the mainstream science of the day. While Henderson finds the Baron's behavior throughout to be highly suspicious, he is forced to admit that absolute certainty of his guilt is impossible to establish: he may have committed the perfect crime.

F irst then, for what may be called the preliminary portions of the evidence. With these we need here deal but very briefly. They consist almost entirely of letters furnished by the courtesy of a near relation of the late Mrs. Anderton, and read as follows:

Some six or seven and twenty years ago, the mother of Mrs. Anderton—Lady Boleton—after giving birth to twin daughters, under circumstances of a peculiarly exciting and agitating nature, died in child-bed. Both Sir Edward Boleton and herself appear to have been of a nervous temperament, and the effects of these combined influences is shown in the highly nervous and susceptible organisation of the orphan girls, and in a morbid sympathy of constitution, by which each appeared to suffer from any ailment of the other. This remarkable sympathy is very clearly shown in more than one of the letters I have submitted for your consideration, and I have numerous others in my possession which, should they be considered insufficient, will place the matter, irregular as it certainly is, beyond the reach of doubt. I must request you to bear it particularly and constantly in mind throughout the case.

Almost from the time of the mother's death, the children were placed in the care of a poor, but respectable woman, at Hastings. Here the younger, whose constitution appears to have been originally much stronger than that of her sister, seems to have improved rapidly in health, and in so doing to have mastered, in some degree, that morbid sympathy of temperament of which I have spoken, and which in the weaker organisation of her elder sister, still maintained its former ascendency. They were about six years old when, whether through the carelessness of the nurse or not, is immaterial to us now, the younger was lost during a pleasure excursion in the neighbourhood. Every inquiry was made, and it appeared pretty clear that she had fallen into the hands of a gang of gipsies, who at that time infested the country round, but no further trace of her was ever after discovered.

The elder sister, now left alone, seems to have been watched with redoubled solicitude. There is nothing, however, in the years immediately following Miss C. Boleton's disappearance having any direct bearing upon our case, and I have, therefore, confined my extracts from the correspondence entrusted to me, to two or three letters from a lady in whose charge she was placed at Hampstead, and one from an old friend of her mother, from which we gather the fact of her marriage. The latter is chiefly notable as pointing out the nervous and highly sensitive temperament of the young lady's husband, the late Mr. Anderton, to which I shall have occasion at a later period of the case, more particularly to direct your attention. The former give evidence of a very important fact; namely, that of the liability of Miss Boleton to attacks of illness equally unaccountable and unmanageable, bearing a perfect resemblance to those in which she suffered in her younger days sympathetically with the ailments of her sister; and, therefore, to be not improbably attributed to a similar cause.

Thus far for the preliminary portion of the evidence. The second division places before us (II.) certain peculiarities in the married life of Mrs. Anderton; its more especial object, however, being to elucidate the connection between the parties whose history we have hitherto been tracing, and the Baron R**, with whose proceedings we are properly concerned.

It appears then, that in all respects but one, the married life of Mr. and Mrs. Anderton was particularly happy. Notwithstanding their retired and often somewhat nomad life, and the limits necessarily imposed thereby to the formation of friendships, the evidence of their devoted attachment to each other is perfectly overwhelming. I have no less than thirty-seven letters from various quarters, all speaking more or less strongly upon this point, but I have thought it better to select from the mass a small but sufficient number, than to overload the case with unnecessary repetition. In one respect alone their happiness was incomplete. It was, as had been justly observed by Mrs. Ward, most unfortunate that the choice of Miss Boleton should have fallen upon a gentleman, who however eligible in every other respect, was, from his extreme constitutional nervousness, so peculiarly ill-adapted for union with a lady of such very similar organisation. The connection seems to have borne its natural fruit in the increased delicacy of both parties, their married life being spent in an almost continual search after health. Among the numerous experiments tried with this object, they at length appear to have had recourse to mesmerism, becoming finally patients of Baron R**, a well known professor of that and other kindred impositions.

Mrs. Anderton had not been long under his care when the remonstrances of several friends led to the cessation of the Baron's immediate manipulations, the mesmeric fluid being now conveyed to the patient through the intervention of a third party. Mademoiselle Rosalie, "the medium" thus employed, was a young person regularly retained by Baron R** for that purpose, and of her it is necessary here to say a few words.

She appears to have been about the age of Mrs. Anderton, though looking perhaps a little older than her years; slight in figure, with dark hair and eyes, and in all respects but one answering precisely to the description of that lady's lost sister. The single difference alluded to, that of wide and clumsy feet, is amply accounted for by the nature of her former avocation. She had been for several years a tight-rope dancer, &c., in the employ of a travelling-circus proprietor; who, by his own account, had purchased her for a trifling sum, of a gang of gipsies at Lewes, just at the very time when the younger Miss Boleton was stolen at Hastings by a gang whose course was tracked through Lewes to the westward. Of him she was again purchased by the Baron, who appears, even at the outset, to have exercised a singular power over her, the fascination of his glance falling on her whilst engaged upon the stage, having compelled her to stop short in the performance of her part. There can, I think, be little doubt that this girl Rosalie was in fact the lost sister of Mrs. Anderton, and of this we shall find that the Baron R** very shortly became cognisant.

It does not appear that on the first meeting of the sisters he had any idea of the relationship between them. He was, indeed, perfectly ignorant of the early history of both. The extraordinary sympathy therefore which immediately manifested itself between them was not improbably set down by him as a mere result of the mesmeric *rapport*, and it was not till he had been for some weeks in attendance on Mrs. Anderton that accident led him to divine its true origin. Nor, on the other hand, does this singular sympathy—a sympathy manifested in a precisely similar manner to that known to have existed years ago between the sisters—appear to have raised any suspicion of the truth in the mind of either Mrs. Anderton or her husband. From the former, indeed, all mention of her early life had been carefully kept till she had probably almost, if not entirely, forgotten the event, while the latter merely remembered it as a tale which had long since ceased to possess any present interest.

The two sisters were thus for several weeks in the closest contact, the effects of which may or may not have been heightened by the so-called mesmeric connection between them, before any suspicion of their relationship crossed the mind of any one. One evening, however,—and from certain peculiar circumstances we are enabled to fix the date precisely to the 13th of October, 1854,—the Baron appears beyond all doubt to have become cognisant of the fact. I must request your particular attention to the circumstances by which his discovery of it was attended.

On that evening the conversation appears to have very naturally turned upon a certain extraordinary case professed to be reported in a number of the "Zoist Mesmeric Magazine," published a few days before. The pretended case was that of a lady suffering from some internal disorder which forbade her to swallow any food, and receiving sustenance through mesmeric sympathy with the operator, who *ate for her.*" From this extraordinary tale the conversation turned naturally to other manifestations of constitutional sympathy, as an instance of which Mr. Anderton related the story of Mrs. Anderton's lost sister, and the singular bond which had existed between them. The conversation appears to have continued for some time, and in the course of it a jesting remark was made by one of the party in allusion to the story of eating by deputy, to which I am inclined to look as the key-note of this horrible affair.

"I said," deposes Mr. Morton, *"I said it was lucky for the young woman that the fellow didn't eat anything unwholesome."*

From the moment these words were spoken the Baron appears to have dropped out of the conversation altogether. More than this, he was clearly in a condition of great mental pre-occupation and disturbance. Mr. Morton goes on to describe the singularity of his manner, the letting his cigar expire between his teeth, and the tremulousness of his hands, so excessive, that in attempting to re-light it he only succeeded in destroying that of his friend. There can, I think, be no doubt whatever that from that moment he believed thoroughly in the identity of Rosalie with the lost sister of Mrs. Anderton. What other ideas the conversation had suggested to him we must endeavour to ascertain from the evidence that follows.

On the morning of the day succeeding that on the evening of which he had become convinced of Rosalie's identity, we find Baron R** at Doctors' Commons* inquiring into the particulars of a will by which the sum of £25,000 had been bequeathed, under certain conditions, to the children of Lady Boleton. Under the provisions of this will, the girl Rosalie was, after her sister and Mr. Anderton, the heir to this legacy. We need, I think, have no difficulty in connecting the

---

* A society of London lawyers specializing in civil law, including the laws of inheritance.

acquisition of this intelligence with the steps by which it was immediately followed. Mr. Anderton at once received an intimation of the Baron's approaching departure for the continent, and at the end of the third week from that time leave was taken, and he apparently started upon his journey. In point of fact, however, his plans were of a very different character. During the three weeks which intervened between his visit to Doctors' Commons and his farewell to Mr. Anderton, there had been advertised in the parish church of Kensington the banns of marriage between himself and his "medium," Rosalie,—not, indeed, in the names by which they were ordinarily known, and which would very probably have excited attention, but in the family name—if so it be—of the Baron and in that by which Rosalie was originally known when with the travelling circus. By what means he prevailed upon his victim to consent to such a step is not important to the matter in hand. The general tenour of the subsequent evidence shows clearly that it must have been under some form of compulsion, and, indeed, the unfortunate girl seems to have been made by some means altogether subservient to his will.

The marriage thus secretly effected, the Baron and his wife leave town, not for the continent, as stated to Mr. Anderton, but for Bognor, an out-of-the-way little watering-place on the Sussex coast, deserted save for the week of the Goodwood races, where, at that time of the year, he was not likely to meet with any one to whom he was known. Before endeavouring to investigate the motive of all this mystery, it is necessary to bear in mind one important fact:—

Between the wife of Baron R** and Mr. Wilson's legacy of £25,000, the lives of Mr. and Mrs. Anderton now alone intervened.

The first few days of the Baron's stay in Bognor seem to have been devoted to the search for a servant, he having insisted on the unusual arrangement of himself providing one in the house where he lodged.* It is worthy of note that the one finally selected was in a position, with respect to character, that placed her entirely in her master's power. It is unfortunate that this same defect of character necessarily lessens the value of evidence from such a source. We must, however, take it for what it is worth, remembering at the same time, that there is a total absence of any apparent motive, save that of telling the truth, for the statement she has made.

It appears, then, from her account, that after trying by every means to tempt her into some repetition of her former error, the Baron at last seized upon the pretext of her taking from the breakfast table a single taste of jam upon her finger,

---

* It was usual at the time for servants to be included with a house that was rented for a short term.

to threaten her with immediate and utter ruin. One only loop-hole was left by which she could escape. The alternative was, indeed, most ingeniously and delicately veiled under the pretext of seeking a plausible reason for her dismissal; but, in point of fact, it amounted to this, that as a condition of her alleged offence not being recorded against her, she would own to the commission of another with which she had nothing whatever to do.

The offence to which she was falsely to plead guilty was this. On the night succeeding the commission of the fault of which, such as it was, she was really guilty, Madame R** was taken suddenly ill. The symptoms were those of antimonial poisoning. The presence of antimony in the stomach was clearly shown. In the presence of the medical man who had been called in, the girl was taxed by the Baron with having administered, by way of a trick, a dose of tartar emetic; and she, in obedience to a strong hint from her master, confessed to the delinquency, and was thereupon dismissed with a good character in other respects. Freed from the dread of exposure, she now flatly denies the whole affair, both of the trick and of the quarrel which was supposed to have led to it, and I am bound to say, that looking both to external and internal evidence, her statement seems worthy of credit.

Nevertheless the poison was unquestionably administered. By whom?

Cui bono? Certainly, it will be said, not for that of the Baron; for until at least the death of Mr. and Mrs. Anderton his interest was clearly in the life of his wife. It is not, therefore, by any means to be supposed that he would before that event attempt to poison her. Of this mystery, then, it appears that we must seek the solution elsewhere.

Returning then for a time to Mr. and Mrs. Anderton, we find that the latter has also suffered from an attack of illness. Comparing her journal, and the evidence of her doctor, with that given in the case of Madame R**, it appears that the symptoms were identical in every respect, with this single but important exception, that in this case there is no apparent cause for the attack, nor can any trace of poison be found. A little further inquiry, and we arrive at a yet more mysterious coincidence.

It is a matter of universal experience, that almost the most fatal enemy of crime is over-precaution. In this particular case the precautions of the Baron R** appear to have been dictated by a skill and forethought almost superhuman, and so admirably have they been taken, that, save in the concealment of the marriage,

---

*   Latin: "for whose good?" A legal term, used when considering suspects for a crime.

it is almost impossible to recognise in them any sinister motive whatever. His course with respect to the servant girl, though dictated, as we believe, by the most criminal designs, is perfectly consistent with motives of the very highest philanthropy. Even in the concealment of the marriage, once granting—as I think may very fairly be granted—that such a marriage might be concealed without any necessary imputation of evil, the means adopted were equally simple, effective, and unblameable. They consisted merely in the use of the real, instead of the stage names of the contracting parties, and in the very proper avoidance of all ground for scandal by hiring another lodging, in order that before marriage the address of both parties might not be the same. In the illness of Madame R**, too, at Bognor, nothing can, to all appearance, be more straightforward than the Baron's conduct. He at once proclaims his suspicion of poison, sends for an eminent physician, verifies his doubts, administers the proper remedies, and dismisses the servant by whose fault the attack has been occasioned. Viewed with an eye of suspicion, there is indeed something questionable in the selection of the medical attendant. Why should the Baron refuse to send for either of the local practitioners, both gentlemen of skill and reputation, and insist on calling in a stranger to the place, who in a very few days would leave it, and very probably return no more? Distrust of country doctors, and decided preference for London skill, furnishes us, as usual, with a prompt and plausible reply. It does not, however, exclude the possibility that the expediency of removing as far as possible all evidence of what had passed may have in some degree affected the choice. Be that as it may, this precaution, whether originally for good or for evil, has enabled us to fix with certainty a very important point.

*Mrs. Anderton was taken ill, not only with the same symptoms, but at the same time, with Madame R**.*

Before proceeding to consider the events which followed, there are one or two points in the history of this first illness of the sisters on which it is needful to remark. The action of these metallic poisons, among which we may undoubtedly rank antimony, is as yet but very little understood. We know, however, from the statements of Professor Taylor,* certainly by far the first English authority upon the subject, that peculiarities of constitution, or, as they are termed, "idiosyncracies," frequently assist or impede to a very extraordinary extent the action of such drugs. The constitution of Madame R** appears to have been thus idiosyncratically disposed to favour the action of antimony. There can be no doubt that the

---

* Original footnote: "Taylor on Poisons." 2nd edition, p. 98, et inf.

action of the poison upon her system was very greatly in excess of that which under ordinary circumstances would have been expected from a similar dose. The poison, therefore, by whomsoever administered, was not intended to prove fatal, though from the peculiar idiosyncracy of Madame R** it was very nearly doing so.

The narrowness of Madame R**'s escape seems to have struck the Baron, and to have exercised a strong influence over his future proceedings. Whether or not he knew or believed her to be exposed to any peculiar influences which might tend to render her life less secure than that of her delicate and invalid sister, it is impossible positively to say. There was no question, however, that her death before that of Mrs. Anderton would destroy all prospect of his succession to the £25,000, and with this view he proceeded to take as speedily as possible the necessary steps to secure himself against such an event. The obvious course, and indeed that suggested at once by Dr. Jones, was that of assurance, and this course he accordingly adopted, after having previously, by a tour of several months, restored his wife to a state of health in which her life would probably be accepted by the offices concerned. The insurances, therefore, with which we are concerned, were effected in consequence of a previous administration of poison to Madame R**, producing an illness far more serious than could have been anticipated, and accompanied by precisely similar symptoms on the part of her delicate sister, Mrs. Anderton, whose death, *if preceding that of Madame R***, would more than double the Baron's prospect of succession.

Between him, therefore, and the sum of either £25,000 or £50,000 there now intervened three lives, those of Mr. and Mrs. Anderton, and of his own wife, Madame R**, and on the order in which they fell depended the amount of his gain by their demise. The death of Mr. Anderton before that of Mrs. Anderton, would open the possibility of a second marriage, from which might arise issue, whose claim would precede his; that of his own wife preceding that of either Mr. or Mrs. Anderton, would destroy altogether his own claim to the larger sum. It was only in the event of Mrs. Anderton's death being followed first by that of her husband, and afterwards by that of her sister, that the Baron's entire claim would be secured.

Within one year from the time at which matters assumed this position, these three lives fell in, and in precisely the order in which the Baron would most largely and securely profit by their demise.

We now proceed to examine the circumstances under which they fell.

Immediately on his return to England, and before apparently completing his arrangements with respect to the policies of insurance, the Baron, we find, calls upon Mr. Anderton, and by dint of minute inquiries draws from him the entire history of the attack from which Mrs. Anderton had suffered several months before. Supposing, therefore, that the information was of any practical interest, the Baron was now fully aware of the perfect similarity, both of time and symptom, between the cases of his wife and her sister. It is essential that this should be borne in mind.

He now proceeds to establish himself in lodgings in Russell Place, in a house in which, for five days and every night in the week, he is entirely alone. The only other tenant is a medical man, whose visits are confined to a few hours on two days in the week, and who lives at too great a distance to be called in on any sudden emergency. Here he establishes himself upon the first and second floors with a laboratory in a small detached room upon the basement floor, where his chemical experiments can be carried on without inconvenience to the rest of the house. It is essential that the position of this laboratory should be very clearly borne in mind, as it plays a most important part in the story which is now to follow.

In these lodgings, then, Madame R,** is again taken ill with a return, though in a greatly mitigated form, of the same symptoms from which she had previously suffered at Bognor. The attack, however, though less violent in its immediate effects, was succeeded at regular intervals of about a fortnight by others of a precisely similar character. And here we arrive at what is at once the most significant, the most extraordinary, and the most questionable of the evidence we have been able to collect.

It appears, then, that upon a night in August, a young man of the name of Aldridge, who, as a matter of special favour, had been taken into the house since the arrival of the Baron, saw Madame R** leave her bedroom, and, apparently in her sleep, walk down the stairs in the dark to the lower part of the house. The room in which the Baron slept was next to hers, and on the wall of that room, projected by the night-lamp burning on the table, the young man saw what seemed to be the shadow of a man watching Madame R** as she went by. He looked again and the shadow was gone—so rapidly that at first he could scarcely believe his eyes, and was only, after consideration, satisfied that it really had been there. He went down to the room, but the Baron was asleep. He told him what had happened to Madame R**, and he at once followed her. Young Aldridge watched him until he had descended the kitchen-stairs and returned, followed closely by the sleep-walker. He then went back to his room, to which the Baron shortly afterwards came to thank him for his warning, and to tell him that, in some freak of slumber, Madame R** *had visited the kitchen.*

THE NOTTING HILL MYSTERY | 117

So far the story is simple enough. There is nothing extraordinary in a sick woman of exciteable nerves taking a sudden fit of somnambulism, and walking down even into the kitchen of a house that was not her own. The Baron's conduct—in all respects but that of the watching shadow—was precisely that which, from a sensible and affectionate husband, might most naturally have been expected. Nor is it very difficult, even setting aside all idea of malice, to set down the shadow portion of the story to a mere freak of imagination on the part of the young man who, though "not drunk," was nevertheless on his own admission, "perhaps a little excited," and who had been "drinking a good deal of beer and shandy-gaff."* But the evidence does not end here.

By one of those extraordinary coincidences by which the simple course of ordinary events so often baffles the best laid schemes of crime, there were others in the house, besides the young man Aldridge, who witnessed the movements of the Baron and Madame R**. It so happened that, on the afternoon of that particular day, the woman of the house had hampered the little latch-lock by which young Aldridge usually admitted himself, and, as this occurred late in the day, it is more than probable that the Baron was unaware of it, as also of the fact that in consequence the servant-girl Susan Turner, sat up beyond the usual hour of going to bed for the purpose of letting the young man in. This girl, it seems, had a lover—a stoker on one of the northern lines—and him she appears to have invited to keep her company on her watch. Aldridge returned and went up to bed, but the lover—who was to be on duty with his engine at two o'clock, and who was doubtlessly interrupted in a most interesting conversation by the arrival of the lodger—still remained in the kitchen, and was only just leaving it when Madame R** came down stairs. Taking her at first to be the mistress of the house, and fearful lest the street-lamp gleaming through the glass parti- tion should betray her "young man's" presence, Susan Turner draws him to the lumber-room, the window of which, it appears, looks into a sort of well between the house and the two rooms built out at the back, after a fashion not unusual in London houses. Into this well, also, immediately opposite to the window of the lumber-room, looks that of the backroom or laboratory, furnished with what the witness describes as a "tin looking-glass," but which is really one of those metal reflectors, in common use, for increasing the light of rooms in such a position. The distance between the two windows is little more than eight feet. The night was clear, with a bright, full harvest moon, and its rays, thrown by the reflector into

---

* Known as shandy today.

the laboratory, made every part of its interior distinctly visible from the lumber-room. The door of the latter room was open, and the staircase illuminated by the Baron's approaching light. The hiders in the lumber-room could see distinctly the whole proceedings of both Baron and Madame R**, from the time Aldridge lost sight of them to the moment they again emerged into his view.

And this was what they saw:

*"Madame R** never went into the kitchen at all;" "she went straight into the laboratory," and "the Baron watched her as she came out."*

A glance at the place will show the bearing of this evidence and the impossibility of the Baron (who, if he had not been in the kitchen, must at least have thoroughly known the position of his own laboratory) having made any mistake on this point.

What, then, was his motive in thus imposing upon Aldridge, to whose interference he professed himself so much indebted, with this false statement of the place to which Madame R** had been?

There does not seem the slightest reason for discrediting the evidence of these two witnesses. Their story is perfectly simple and coherent. There is neither malice against the Baron nor collusion with Aldridge, in whose case such malice is supposed to exist. The only weak point in their position is the fact, that they were both doing wrong in being in that place at that time; but the admission of this, in truth, rather strengthens than injures the testimony which involves it. We must seek the clue, then, not in their motives, but in those of the Baron. The errand of Madame R**, in her strange expedition, may perhaps afford it. What did she do in the laboratory?

"She drank something from a bottle." "It smelt and tasted like sherry." "It was marked VIN. ANT. POT. TART." That label designates antimonial wine, which is a mixture of sherry and tartar emetic.

Let us see if from this point we can feel our way, as it were, backwards, to the motive for concealment. The life of Madame R** was, as we know, heavily insured. It had already been seriously endangered by the effects of precisely the same drug as that she was now seen to take. If the Baron knew or suspected the motive of her visit, here is at once a motive sufficient, if not perhaps very creditable, for the concealment of a fact, the knowledge of which might very probably lead to difficulty with respect to payment of the policy in case of death.

But here another difficulty meets us. The incident in question occurred at about the middle of the long illness of Madame R**. That illness consisted of a series of attacks, occurring as nearly as possible at intervals of a fortnight, and exhibiting the exact symptoms of the poison here shown to have been taken. One of these attacks followed within a very few hours of the occurrence into which we are examining. Was it the only one of the kind?

The evidence of the night-nurse bears with terrible weight upon this point. Her orders are strict, on no account to close her eyes. Her hours of watch are short, and the repose of the entire day leaves her without the slightest cause for unusual drowsiness. The testimonials of twenty years bear unvarying witness to her care and trustworthiness. Yet every alternate Saturday for eight or ten, or it may even have been nearly twelve weeks, at one regular hour she falls asleep. It is in vain that she watches and fights against it—in vain even that, suspecting "some trick" she on one occasion abstains entirely from food, and drinks nothing but that peculiarly wakeful decoction, strong green tea. On every other night she keeps awake with ease, but surely as the fatal Saturday comes round she again succumbs, and surely as sleep steals over her is it followed by a fresh attack of the symptoms we so plainly recognise. She cannot in any way account for such an extraordinary fatality. She is positive that such a thing never happened to her before. We also are at an equal loss. We can but pause upon the reflection that twice before the periodic drowsiness began, a similarly irresistible sleep had been induced by the so-called mesmeric powers of the Baron himself. And then we pass naturally to her who had been for years habituated to such control, and we cannot but call to mind the statement of Mr. Hands—"I have often *willed* her (S. Parsons) to go into a dark room and pick up a pin, or some article equally minute."

And then we again remember the watching shadow on the wall.

And yet, after all, at what have we arrived? Grant that the Baron knew the nature of his wife's errand in the laboratory; that the singular power—call it what we will—by which he had before in jest compelled the nurse to sleep, was really employed in enabling the somnambulist to elude her watch. Grant even that the pretensions of the mesmerist are true, and that it was in obedience to his direct will that Madame R** acted as she did, we are no nearer a solution than before.

It was not the Baron's interest that his wife should die.

We must then seek further afield for any explanation of this terrible enigma. Let us see how it fared with Mrs. Anderton while these events were passing at her sister's house.

And here we seem to have another instance of the manner in which the wisest precautions so often turn against those by whom they are taken. Admitting that the illness of Madame R** was really caused by criminal means, nothing could be wiser than the precaution which selected for their first essay a night on which they could be tried without fear of observation. Yet this very circumstance enables us to fix a date of the last importance, which without it must have remained uncertain. Madame R**, then, was taken ill on Saturday, the 5th April. On that very night—at, as nearly as can be ascertained, the very same hour, Mrs. Anderton was unaccountably seized with an illness in all respects resembling hers. Like hers, too, the attacks returned at fortnightly intervals: For a few days, on the Baron's advice, a particular medicine is given, and at first with apparently good effect. At the same date the diary of Dr. Marsden shows a similar amelioration of symptoms in the case of Madame R**. In both cases the amendment is but short, and the disease again pursues its course. The result in both is utter exhaustion. In the case of Madame R** reducing the sufferer to death's door; in the *weaker constitution* of her sister terminating in death. Examination is made. The appearances of the body, no less than the symptoms exhibited in life, are all those of antimonial poisoning. No antimony is, however, found; and from this and other circumstances, results a verdict of "Natural Death." On the 12th October, then, Mrs. Anderton's story ends.

*From that time dates the recovery of Madame R**.*

The first life is now removed from between Baron R** and the full sum of £50,000. Let us examine briefly the circumstances attending the lapse of the second. Here again events, each in itself quite simple and natural, combine to form a story fraught with terrible suspicion. I have alluded to the inquest which followed on the death of Mrs. Anderton. That inquiry originated in circumstances which cast upon her husband the entire suspicion of her murder. To whose agency, whether direct or indirect, voluntary or involuntary, is an after question, may every one of these circumstances be traced? Mr. Anderton insists on being the only one from whom the patient shall receive either medicine or food. It is the Baron who applauds and encourages a line of conduct diametrically opposed to his own, and tending more than any other circumstance to fix suspicion on his friend. A remedy is suggested, the recommending of which points strongly to the idea of poison, and it is from the Baron that the suggestion comes. Two papers are found, the one bearing in part the other in full, the name of the poison suspected to have been used. The first of these is brought to light by the Baron himself,—the second is found in a place where he has just been, and by a person whom he has himself despatched to search there for something else. He draws continual attention to that point of exclusive attendance from which suspicion chiefly springs. His replies to Dr. Dodsworth respecting the recommendation of the antimonial antidote are so given as to confirm the worst interpretation to which it had given rise, and even when, on the discovery of the second paper, he advises the nurse that it should be destroyed, he does so in a manner that ensures not only its preservation but its immediate employment in the manner most dangerous to his friend.

The evidence fails. What is the Baron's connection with the catastrophe that follows? He knows well the accused man's nervous anxiety for his own good name. He procures, on the ground of his friendly anxiety, the earliest intelligence of his friend's probable acquittal. He enters that friend's room to acquaint him with the good news. Returning he takes measures to secure the prisoner throughout the night from interruption or interference. In the morning Mr. Anderton is a corpse, and on his pillow is found the phial in which the poison had been contained, and a written statement that the desperate step* had been taken in despair of an acquittal. By what marvellous accident was the hopeful news of the chemical investigation thus misinterpreted? By what negligence or connivance was the fatal drug placed within his reach? One thing only we know—

It was the Baron who conveyed the news. It was from his pocket medicine case, left by him within the sick man's reach, that the poison came.

Thus fell the second of the two lives which stood between the Baron and the full sum of £50,000. Of this sum the £25,000 which accrues from the relationship between Mrs. Anderton and Madame R** is already his as soon as claimed†, but there is no immediate necessity for the claim to be preferred. He may perhaps have thought it better to wait before making such a claim until the first sensation occasioned by the double deaths through which he inherited had passed away. He may have been merely putting in train some plausible story to account for his only now proclaiming a fact of which he had certainly been aware for at least a year. Whatever his reason, however, he certainly for some weeks after Mr. Anderton's death made no movement to establish his claim upon the property, and during this time Madame R** was slowly but surely recovering her strength.

But while wisdom thus dictated a policy of delay, the irresistible course of events hurried on the crisis. A letter comes, filled with threats of the vengeance of jealous love if its cause be not that night removed.‡ It is but a fragment of that

---

* i.e. suicide.

† According to English law at that time, any money earned or inherited by a married woman belonged to her husband.

‡ A fragment of a letter, found in the Baron's room after the death of his wife, was described in an earlier instalment. Written in French, it was addressed to "Philip" from "a jealous woman" and demanded a meeting, making threatening references to the death of a child.

letter that is preserved, but its meaning is clear enough, and it is that under threat of revelation of some capital crime, the connection between himself and Madame R** should be finally brought to an end.

"*N'en sais-tu bien le moyen?*"*

That night the condition is fulfilled. Once more the sleeping lady takes her midnight journey to her husband's laboratory. Once more her unconscious hand pours out the deadly draught. But this time it is no slow poison that she takes. It is a powerful and burning acid that even as it awakes her from her trance, shrivels her with a horrible and instant death. One shrill and quickly stifled shriek alarms the inmates of the house, and when they hurry to the spot they find only a disfigured corpse, lying with bare feet and disordered night dress in the darkness of the stormy November night, and with the fatal glass still clasped in its hand.

My task is done. In possession of the evidence thus placed before you, your judgment of its result will be as good as mine. Link by link you have now been put in possession of the entire chain. Is that chain one of purely accidental coincidences, or does it point with terrible certainty to a series of crimes, in their nature and execution almost too horrible to contemplate? That is the first question to be asked, and it is one to which I confess myself unable to reply. The second is more strange, and perhaps even more difficult still. Supposing the latter to be the case, are crimes thus committed susceptible of proof, or even if proved, are they of a kind for which the criminal can be brought to punishment?

---

* French: "Do you not know well the means?"

THE MYSTERY OF ORCIVAL

(EXTRACT)

by Émile Gaboriau

1867

Monsieur Lecoq ("Mr. Rooster") of the Sûreté was the creation of French writer Émile Gaboriau, and drew on the same source of inspiration as Edgar Allan Poe's great detective, C. Auguste Dupin: the former criminal, founder of the Sûreté, and head of the first known private detective agency, Eugène François Vidocq. Lecoq stars in five novels and one short story by Gaboriau and at least four novels by other authors; his exploits have been adapted for film and television in France.

English translations of all five novels were published, and it is clear that Doyle was familiar with them: in *A Study in Scarlet,* Holmes describes Lecoq as "a miserable bungler." Whatever Holmes thought, though, Lecoq was a careful and scientific detective, and Doyle admitted that he admired Gaboriau's plots.

Published in 1867, *Le Crime d'Orcival* was the second of Lecoq's adventures to see print. Set primarily in a series of small towns on the Seine that are now suburbs of Paris, the story revolves around a love triangle consisting of the wealthy Clement Sauvresy, his beautiful but modestly-born wife Bertha, and his old college friend, Count Hector de Tremorel. Stricken with a sudden illness, Sauvresy begs the other two to marry after his death, which they do.

The couple lived happily, bound together by the memory of Sauvresy, until the body of the Countess is found floating in the Seine by a poacher named Bertaud and, a short time later, the Count's body is also found. Suspicion falls upon Guespin, a gardener on their estate of Valfeuillu, who maintains his innocence in the face of some damning but circumstantial evidence.

After a careful investigation, Monsieur Lecoq, accompanied by Monsieur Plantat, the local justice of the peace, presents his findings to Monsieur Domini, the presiding judge, and sets in motion the climactic hunt for the true murderer.

M. Plantat, in speaking of M. Domini's impatience, did not exaggerate the truth. That personage was furious; he could not comprehend the reason of the prolonged absence of his three fellow-workers of the previous evening. He had installed himself early in the morning in his cabinet, at the court-house, enveloped in his judicial robe; and he counted the minutes as they passed. His reflections during the night, far from shaking, had only confirmed his opinion. As he receded from the period of the crime, he found it very simple and natural—indeed, the easiest thing in the world to account for. He was annoyed that the rest did not share his convictions, and he awaited their report in a state of irritation which his clerk only too well perceived. He had eaten his breakfast in his cabinet, so as to be sure and be beforehand with M. Lecoq. It was a useless precaution; for the hours passed on and no one arrived.

To kill time, he sent for Guespin and Bertaud and questioned them anew, but learned nothing more than he had extracted from them the night before. One of the prisoners swore by all things sacred that he knew nothing except what he had already told; the other preserved an obstinate and ferocious silence, confining himself to the remark: "I know that I am lost; do with me what you please."

M. Domini was just going to send a mounted gendarme to Orcival to find out the cause of the delay, when those whom he awaited were announced. He quickly gave the order to admit them, and so keen was his curiosity, despite what he called his dignity, that he got up and went forward to meet them.

"How late you are!" said he.

"And yet we haven't lost a minute," replied M. Plantat. "We haven't even been in bed."

"There is news, then? Has the count's body been found?"

"There is much news, Monsieur," said M. Lecoq. "But the count's body has not been found, and I dare even say that it will not be found—for the very simple fact that he has not been killed. The reason is that he was not one of the victims, as at first supposed, but the assassin."

At this distinct declaration on M. Lecoq's part, the judge started in his seat. "Why, this is folly!" cried he.

M. Lecoq never smiled in a magistrate's presence. "I do not think so," said he, coolly; "I am persuaded that if Monsieur Domini will grant me his attention for half an hour I will have the honor of persuading him to share my opinion."

M. Domini's slight shrug of the shoulders did not escape the detective, but he calmly continued:

"More; I am sure that Monsieur Domini will not permit me to leave his cabinet without a warrant to arrest Count Hector de Tremorel, whom at present he thinks to be dead."

"Possibly," said M. Domini. "Proceed."

M. Lecoq then rapidly detailed the facts gathered by himself and M. Plantat from the beginning of the inquest. He narrated them not as if he had guessed or been told of them, but in their order of time and in such a manner that each new incident which he mentioned followed naturally from the preceding one. He had completely resumed his character of a retired haberdasher, with a little piping voice, and such obsequious expressions as, "I have the honor," and "If Monsieur the Judge will deign to permit me;" he resorted to the candy-box with the portrait, and, as the night before at Valfeuillu,* chewed a lozenge when he came to the more striking points. M. Domini's surprise increased every minute as he proceeded; while at times, exclamations of astonishment passed his lips: "Is it possible?" "That is hard to believe!"

M. Lecoq finished his recital; he tranquilly munched a lozenge, and added:

"What does Monsieur the Judge of Instruction think now?"

M. Domini was fain to confess that he was almost satisfied. A man, however, never permits an opinion deliberately and carefully formed to be refuted by one whom he looks on as an inferior, without a secret chagrin. But in this case the evidence was too abundant, and too positive to be resisted.

"I am convinced," said he, "that a crime was committed on Monsieur Sauvresy with the dearly paid assistance of this Robelot. To-morrow I shall give instructions to Doctor Gendron to proceed at once to an exhumation and autopsy of the late master of Valfeuillu."

"And you may be sure that I shall find the poison," chimed in the doctor.

---

* The home of the Count de Tremorel.

"Very well," resumed M. Domini. "But does it necessarily follow that because Monsieur Tremorel poisoned his friend to marry his widow, he yesterday killed his wife and then fled? I don't think so."

"Pardon me," objected Lecoq, gently. "It seems to me that Mademoiselle Courtois's supposed suicide proves at least something."

"That needs clearing up. This coincidence can only be a matter of pure chance."

"But I am sure that Monsieur Tremorel shaved himself—of that we have proof; then, we did not find the boots which, according to the valet, he put on the morning of the murder."

"Softly, softly," interrupted the judge. "I don't pretend that you are absolutely wrong; it must be as you say; only I give you my objections. Let us admit that Tremorel killed his wife, that he fled and is alive. Does that clear Guespin, and show that he took no part in the murder?"

This was evidently the flaw in Lecoq's case; but being convinced of Hector's guilt, he had given little heed to the poor gardener, thinking that his innocence would appear of itself when the real criminal was arrested. He was about to reply, when footsteps and voices were heard in the corridor.

"Stop," said M. Domini. "Doubtless we shall now hear something important about Guespin."

"Are you expecting some new witness?" asked M. Plantat.

"No; I expect one of the Corbeil police to whom I have given an important mission."

"Regarding Guespin?"

"Yes. Very early this morning a young working-woman of the town, whom Guespin has been courting, brought me an excellent photograph of him. I gave this portrait to the agent with instructions to go to the Vulcan's Forges* and ascertain if Guespin had been seen there, and whether he bought anything there night before last."

M. Lecoq was inclined to be jealous; the judge's proceeding ruffled him, and he could not conceal an expressive grimace.

"I am truly grieved," said he, dryly, "that Monsieur the Judge has so little confidence in me that he thinks it necessary to give me assistance."

This sensitiveness aroused M. Domini, who replied:

"Eh! my dear man, you can't be everywhere at once. I think you very shrewd, but you were not here, and I was in a hurry."

---

* A hardware store.

"A false step is often irreparable."

"Make yourself easy; I've sent an intelligent man." At this moment the door opened, and the policeman referred to by the judge appeared on the threshold. He was a muscular man about forty years old, with a military pose, a heavy mustache, and thick brows, meeting over the nose. He had a sly rather than a shrewd expression, so that his appearance alone seemed to awake all sorts of suspicions and put one instinctively on his guard.

"Good news!" said he in a big voice: "I didn't make the journey to Paris for the King of Prussia; we are right on the track of this rogue of a Guespin."

M. Domini encouraged him with an approving gesture.

"See here, Goulard," said he, "let us go on in order if we can. You went then, according to my instructions, to the Vulcan's Forges?"

"At once, Monsieur."

"Precisely. Had they seen the prisoner there?"

"Yes; on the evening of Wednesday, July 8th."

"At what hour?"

"About ten o'clock, a few minutes before they shut up; so that he was remarked, and the more distinctly observed."

The judge moved his lips as if to make an objection, but was stopped by a gesture from M. Lecoq.

"And who recognized the photograph?"

"Three of the clerks. Guespin's manner first attracted their attention. It was strange, so they said, and they thought he was drunk, or at least tipsy. Then their recollection was fixed by his talking very fast, saying that he was going to patronize them a great deal, and that if they would make a reduction in their prices he would procure for them the custom of an establishment whose confidence he possessed, the *Gentil Jardinier*,* which bought a great many gardening tools."

M. Domini interrupted the examination to consult some papers which lay before him on his desk. It was, he found, the *Gentil Jardinier* which had procured Guespin his place in Tremorel's household. The judge remarked this aloud, and added:

"The question of identity seems to be settled. Guespin was undoubtedly at the Vulcan's Forges on Wednesday night."

"So much the better for him," M. Lecoq could not help muttering.

---

* French: "Kindly Gardener."

The judge heard him, but though the remark seemed singular to him he did not notice it, and went on questioning the agent.

"Well, did they tell you what Guespin went there to obtain?"

"The clerks recollected it perfectly. He first bought a hammer, a cold chisel, and a file."

"I knew it," exclaimed the judge. "And then?"

"Then—"

Here the man, ambitious to make a sensation among his hearers, rolled his eyes tragically, and in a dramatic tone, added:

"Then he bought a dirk knife!"

The judge felt that he was triumphing over M. Lecoq.

"Well," said he to the detective in his most ironical tone, "what do you think of your friend now? What do you say to this honest and worthy young man, who, on the very night of the crime, leaves a wedding where he would have had a good time, to go and buy a hammer, a chisel, and a dirk—everything, in short, used in the murder and the mutilation of the body?"

Dr. Gendron seemed a little disconcerted at this, but a sly smile overspread M. Plantat's face. As for M. Lecoq, he had the air of one who is shocked by objections which he knows he ought to annihilate by a word, and yet who is fain to be resigned to waste time in useless talk, which he might put to great profit.

"I think, Monsieur," said he, very humbly, "that the murderers at Valfeuillu did not use either a hammer or a chisel, or a file, and that they brought no instrument at all from outside—since they used a hammer."

"And didn't they have a dirk besides?" asked the judge in a bantering tone, confident that he was on the right path.

"That is another question, I confess; but it is a difficult one to answer."

He began to lose patience. He turned toward the Corbeil policeman, and abruptly asked him:

"Is this all you know?"

The big man with the thick eyebrows superciliously eyed this little Parisian who dared to question him thus. He hesitated so long that M. Lecoq, more rudely than before, repeated his question.

"Yes, that's all," said Goulard at last, "and I think it's sufficient; the judge thinks so too; and he is the only person who gives me orders, and whose approbation I wish for."

M. Lecoq shrugged his shoulders, and proceeded:

"Let's see; did you ask what was the shape of the dirk bought by Guespin? Was it long or short, wide or narrow?"

"Faith, no. What was the use?"

"Simply, my brave fellow, to compare this weapon with the victim's wounds, and to see whether its handle corresponds to that which left a distinct and visible imprint between the victim's shoulders."

"I forgot it; but it is easily remedied."

"An oversight may, of course, be pardoned; but you can at least tell us in what sort of money Guespin paid for his purchases?"

The poor man seemed so embarrassed, humiliated, and vexed, that the judge hastened to his assistance.

"The money is of little consequence, it seems to me," said he.

"I beg you to excuse me; I don't agree with you," returned M. Lecoq. "This matter may be a very grave one. What is the most serious evidence against Guespin? The money found in his pocket. Let us suppose for a moment that night before last, at ten o'clock, he changed a one-thousand-franc note* in Paris. Could the obtaining of that note have been the motive of the crime at Valfeuillu? No, for up to that hour the crime had not been committed. Where could it have come from? That is no concern of mine, at present. But if my theory is correct, justice will be forced to agree that the several hundred francs found in Guespin's possession can and must be the change for the note."

"That is only a theory," urged M. Domini in an irritated tone.

"That is true; but one which may turn out a certainty. It remains for me to ask this man how Guespin carried away the articles which he bought? Did he simply slip them into his pocket, or did he have them done up in a bundle, and if so, how?"

The detective spoke in a sharp, hard, freezing tone, with a bitter raillery in it, frightening his Corbeil colleague out of his assurance.

"I don't know," stammered the latter. "They didn't tell me—I thought—"

M. Lecoq raised his hands as if to call the heavens to witness: in his heart, he was charmed with this fine occasion to revenge himself for M. Domini's disdain. He could not, dared not say anything to the judge; but he had the right to banter the agent and visit his wrath upon him.

"Ah so, my lad," said he, "what did you go to Paris for? To show Guespin's picture and detail the crime to the people at Vulcan's Forges? They ought to be

---

* According to online sources, 1,000 francs in 1876 would have the same value as about U.S. $13,000 today.

very grateful to you; but Madame Petit, Monsieur Plantat's housekeeper, would have done as much."

At this stroke the man began to get angry; he frowned, and in his bluffest tone, began:

"Look here now, you—"

"Ta, ta, ta," interrupted M. Lecoq. "Let me alone, and know who is talking to you. I am Monsieur Lecoq."

The effect of the famous detective's name on his antagonist was magical. He naturally laid down his arms and surrendered, straightway becoming respectful and obsequious. It almost flattered him to be roughly handled by such a celebrity. He muttered, in an abashed and admiring tone:

"What, is it possible? You, Monsieur Lecoq!"

"Yes, it is I, young man; but console yourself; I bear no grudge against you. You don't know your trade, but you have done me a service and you have brought us a convincing proof of Guespin's innocence."

M. Domini looked on at this scene with secret chagrin. His recruit went over to the enemy, yielding without a struggle to a confessed superiority. M. Lecoq's presumption, in speaking of a prisoner's innocence whose guilt seemed to the judge indisputable, exasperated him.

"And what is this tremendous proof, if you please?" asked he.

"It is simple and striking," answered M. Lecoq, putting on his most frivolous air as his conclusions narrowed the field of probabilities.

"You doubtless recollect that when we were at Valfeuillu we found the hands of the clock in the bedroom stopped at twenty minutes past three. Distrusting foul play, I put the striking apparatus in motion—do you recall it? What happened? The clock struck eleven. That convinced us that the crime was committed before that hour. But don't you see that if Guespin was at the Vulcan's Forges at ten he could not have got back to Valfeuillu before midnight? Therefore it was not—he who did the deed."

The detective, as he came to this conclusion, pulled out the inevitable box and helped himself to a lozenge, at the same time bestowing upon the judge a smile which said:

"Get out of that, if you can."

The judge's whole theory tumbled to pieces if M. Lecoq's deductions were right; but he could not admit that he had been so much deceived; he could not renounce an opinion formed by deliberate reflection.

"I don't pretend that Guespin is the only criminal," said he. "He could only have been an accomplice; and that he was."

"An accomplice? No, Judge, he was a victim. Ah, Tremorel is a great rascal! Don't you see now why he put forward the hands? At first I didn't perceive the object of advancing the time five hours; now it is clear. In order to implicate Guespin the crime must appear to have been committed after midnight, and—"

He suddenly checked himself and stopped with open mouth and fixed eyes as a new idea crossed his mind. The judge, who was bending over his papers trying to find something to sustain his position, did not perceive this.

"But then," said the latter, "how do you explain Guespin's refusal to speak and to give an account of where he spent the night?"

M. Lecoq had now recovered from his emotion, and Dr. Gendron and M. Plantat, who were watching him with the deepest attention, saw a triumphant light in his eyes. Doubtless he had just found a solution of the problem which had been put to him.

"I understand," replied he, "and can explain Guespin's obstinate silence. I should be perfectly amazed if he decided to speak just now."

M. Domini misconstrued the meaning of this; he thought he saw in it a covert intention to banter him.

"He has had a night to reflect upon it," he answered. "Is not twelve hours enough to mature a system of defense?"

The detective shook his head doubtfully.

"It is certain that he does not need it," said he. "Our prisoner doesn't trouble himself about a system of defense, that I'll swear to."

"He keeps quiet, because he hasn't been able to get up a plausible story."

"No, no; believe me, he isn't trying to get up one. In my opinion, Guespin is a victim; that is, I suspect Tremorel of having set an infamous trap for him, into which he has fallen, and in which he sees himself so completely caught that he thinks it useless to struggle. The poor wretch is convinced that the more he resists the more surely he will tighten the web that is woven around him."

"I think so, too," said M. Plantat.

"The true criminal, Count Hector," resumed the detective, "lost his presence of mind at the last moment, and thus lost all the advantages which his previous caution had gained. Don't let us forget that he is an able man, perfidious enough to mature the most infamous stratagems, and unscrupulous enough to execute them. He knows that justice must have its victims, one for every crime; he does not forget that the police, as long as it has not the criminal, is always on the search with eye and ear open; and he has thrown us Guespin as a huntsman, closely pressed, throws his glove to the bear that is close upon him. Perhaps he thought that the innocent man would not be in danger of his life; at all events he hoped to gain time by this ruse; while the bear is smelling and turning over the glove, the huntsman gains ground, escapes and reaches his place of refuge; that was what Tremorel proposed to do."

The Corbeil policeman was now undoubtedly Lecoq's most enthusiastic listener. Goulard literally drank in his chief's words. He had never heard any of his colleagues express themselves with such fervor and authority; he had had no idea of such eloquence, and he stood erect, as if some of the admiration which he saw in all the faces were reflected back on him. He grew in his own esteem as he thought that he was a soldier in an army commanded by such generals. He had no longer any opinion excepting that of his superior. It was not so easy to persuade, subjugate, and convince the judge.

"But," objected the latter, "you saw Guespin's countenance?"

"Ah, what matters the countenance—what does that prove? Don't we know if you and I were arrested to-morrow on a terrible charge, what our bearing would be?"

M. Domini gave a significant start; this hypothesis scarcely pleased him.

"And yet you and I are familiar with the machinery of justice. When I arrested Lanscot, the poor servant in the Rue Marignan, his first words were: 'Come on, my account is good.' The morning that Papa Tabaret and I took the Viscount de Commarin as he was getting out of bed, on the accusation of having murdered the widow Lerouge, he cried: 'I am lost.' Yet neither of them was guilty; but both of them, the viscount and the valet, equal before the terror of a possible mistake of justice, and running over in their thoughts the charges which would be brought against them, had a moment of overwhelming discouragement."

"But such discouragement does not last two days," said M. Domini.

M. Lecoq did not answer this; he went on, growing more animated as he proceeded.

"You and I have seen enough prisoners to know how deceitful appearances are, and how little they are to be trusted. It would be foolish to base a theory upon a prisoner's bearing. He who talked about 'the cry of innocence' was an idiot, just as the man was who prated about the 'pale stupor' of guilt. Neither crime nor virtue have, unhappily, any especial countenance. The Simon girl, who was accused of having killed her father, absolutely refused to answer any questions for twenty-two days; on the twenty-third, the murderer was caught. As to the Sylvain affair—"

M. Domini rapped lightly on his desk to check the detective. As a man, the judge held too obstinately to his opinions; as a magistrate he was equally obstinate, but was at the same time ready to make any sacrifice of his self-esteem if the voice of duty prompted it. M. Lecoq's arguments had not shaken his convictions, but they imposed on him the duty of informing himself at once, and to either conquer the detective or avow himself conquered.

"You seem to be pleading," said he to M. Lecoq. "There is no need of that here. We are not counsel and judge; the same honorable intentions animate us both. Each, in his sphere, is searching after the truth. You think you see it shining where I only discern clouds; and you may be mistaken as well as I."

Then by an act of heroism, he condescended to add:

"What do you think I ought to do?"

The judge was at least rewarded for the effort he made by approving glances from M. Plantat and the doctor. But M. Lecoq did not hasten to respond; he had many weighty reasons to advance; that, he saw, was not what was necessary. He ought to present the facts, there and at once, and produce one of those proofs which can be touched with the finger. How should he do it? His active mind searched eagerly for such a proof.

"Well?" insisted M. Domini.

"Ah," cried the detective. "Why can't I ask Guespin two or three questions?"

The judge frowned; the suggestion seemed to him rather presumptuous. It is formally laid down that the questioning of the accused should be done in secret, and by the judge alone, aided by his clerk. On the other hand it is decided, that after he has once been interrogated he may be confronted with witnesses. There are, besides, exceptions in favor of the members of the police force. M. Domini reflected whether there were any precedents to apply to the case.

"I don't know," he answered at last, "to what point the law permits me to consent to what you ask. However, as I am convinced the interests of truth outweigh all rules, I shall take it on myself to let you question Guespin."

He rang; a bailiff appeared.

"Has Guespin been carried back to prison?"

"Not yet, Monsieur."

"So much the better; have him brought in here."

M. Lecoq was beside himself with joy; he had not hoped to achieve such a victory over one so determined as M. Domini.

"He will speak now," said he, so full of confidence that his eyes shone, and he forgot the portrait of the dear defunct, "for I have three means of unloosening his tongue, one of which is sure to succeed. But before he comes I should like to know one thing. Do you know whether Tremorel saw Jenny after Sauvresy's death?"

"Jenny?" asked M. Plantat, a little surprised.

"Yes."

"Certainly he did."

"Several times?"

"Pretty often. After the scene at the *Belle Image*⁎ the poor girl plunged into terrible dissipation. Whether she was smitten with remorse, or understood that it was her conduct which had killed Sauvresy, or suspected the crime, I don't know. She began, however, to drink furiously, falling lower and lower every week—"

"And the count really consented to see her again?"

"He was forced to do so; she tormented him, and he was afraid of her. When she had spent all her money she sent to him for more, and he gave it. Once he refused; and that very evening she went to him the worse for wine, and he had the greatest difficulty in the world to send her away again. In short, she knew what his relations with Madame Sauvresy had been, and she threatened him; it was a regular black-mailing operation. He told me all about the trouble she gave him, and added that he would not be able to get rid of her without shutting her up, which he could not bring himself to do."

"How long ago was their last interview?"

"Why," answered the doctor, "not three weeks ago, when I had a consultation at Melun, I saw the count and this demoiselle at a hotel window; when he saw me he suddenly drew back."

"Then," said the detective, "there is no longer any doubt—"

He stopped. Guespin came in between two gendarmes.

The unhappy gardener had aged twenty years in twenty-four hours. His eyes were haggard, his dry lips were bordered with foam.

"Let us see," said the judge. "Have you changed your mind about speaking?"

The prisoner did not answer.

"Have you decided to tell us about yourself?"

Guespin's rage made him tremble from head to foot, and his eyes became fiery.

"Speak!" said he hoarsely. "Why should I?"

He added with the gesture of a desperate man who abandons himself, renounces all struggling and all hope:

"What have I done to you, my God, that you torture me this way? What do you want me to say? That I did this crime—is that what you want? Well,

---

⁎ A hotel in Corbeil, where de Tremorel had been seen to quarrel with her.

then—yes—it was I. Now you are satisfied. Now cut my head off, and do it quick—for I don't want to suffer any longer."

A mournful silence welcomed Guespin's declaration. What, he confessed it!

M. Domini had at least the good taste not to exult; he kept still, and yet this avowal surprised him beyond all expression.

M. Lecoq alone, although surprised, was not absolutely put out of countenance. He approached Guespin and tapping him on the shoulder, said in a paternal tone:

"Come, comrade, what you are telling us is absurd. Do you think the judge has any secret grudge against you? No, eh? Do you suppose I am interested to have you guillotined? Not at all. A crime has been committed, and we are trying to find the assassin. If you are innocent, help us to find the man who isn't: What were you doing from Wednesday evening till Thursday morning?"

But Guespin persisted in his ferocious and stupid obstinacy.

"I've said what I have to say," said he.

M. Lecoq changed his tone to one of severity, stepping back to watch the effect he was about to produce upon Guespin.

"You haven't any right to hold your tongue. And even if you do, you fool, the police know everything. Your master sent you on an errand, didn't he, on Wednesday night; what did he give you? A one-thousand-franc note?"

The prisoner looked at M. Lecoq in speechless amazement.

"No," he stammered. "It was a five-hundred-franc note."

The detective, like all great artists in a critical scene, was really moved. His surprising genius for investigation had just inspired him with a bold stroke, which, if it succeeded, would assure him the victory.

"Now," said he, "tell me the woman's name."

"I don't know."

"You are only a fool then. She is short, isn't she, quite pretty, brown and pale, with very large eyes?"

"You know her, then?" said Guespin, in a voice trembling with emotion.

"Yes, comrade, and if you want to know her name, to put in your prayers, she is called—Jenny."

Men who are really able in some specialty, whatever it may be, never uselessly abuse their superiority; their satisfaction at seeing it recognized is sufficient reward. M. Lecoq softly enjoyed his triumph, while his hearers wondered at his perspicacity. A rapid chain of reasoning had shown him not only Tremorel's thoughts, but also the means he had employed to accomplish his purpose.

Guespin's astonishment soon changed to anger. He asked himself how this man could have been informed of things which he had every reason to believe were secret. Lecoq continued:

"Since I have told you the woman's name, tell me now, how and why the count gave you a five-hundred-franc note."

"It was just as I was going out. The count had no change, and did not want to send me to Orcival for it. I was to bring back the rest."

"And why didn't you rejoin your companions at the wedding in the Batignolles?"*

No answer.

"What was the errand which you were to do for the count?"

Guespin hesitated. His eyes wandered from one to another of those present, and he seemed to discover an ironical expression on all the faces. It occurred to him that they were making sport of him, and had set a snare into which he had fallen. A great despair took possession of him.

"Ah," cried he, addressing M. Lecoq, "you have deceived me. You have been lying so as to find out the truth. I have been such a fool as to answer you, and you are going to turn it all against me."

"What? Are you going to talk nonsense again?"

"No, but I see just how it is, and you won't catch me again! Now I'd rather die than say a word."

The detective tried to reassure him; but he added:

"Besides, I'm as sly as you; I've told you nothing but lies."

This sudden whim surprised no one. Some prisoners entrench themselves behind a system of defense, and nothing can divert them from it; others vary with each new question, denying what they have just affirmed, and constantly inventing some new absurdity which anon they reject again. M. Lecoq tried in vain to draw Guespin from his silence; M. Domini made the same attempt, and also failed; to all questions he only answered, "I don't know."

At last the detective waxed impatient.

"See here," said he to Guespin, "I took you for a young man of sense, and you are only an ass. Do you imagine that we don't know anything? Listen: On the night of Madame Denis's wedding, you were getting ready to go off with your comrades, and had just borrowed twenty francs from the valet, when the count called you. He made you promise absolute secrecy (a promise which, to do you

---

* A district on the edge of Paris.

justice, you kept); he told you to leave the other servants at the station and go to Vulcan's Forges, where you were to buy for him a hammer, a file, a chisel, and a dirk; these you were to carry to a certain woman. Then he gave you this famous five-hundred-franc note, telling you to bring him back the change when you returned next day. Isn't that so?"

An affirmative response glistened in the prisoner's eyes; still, he answered, "I don't recollect it."

"Now," pursued M. Lecoq, "I'm going to tell you what happened afterwards. You drank something and got tipsy, and in short spent a part of the change of the note. That explains your fright when you were seized yesterday morning, before anybody said a word to you. You thought you were being arrested for spending that money. Then, when you learned that the count had been murdered during the night, recollecting that on the evening before you had bought all kinds of instruments of theft and murder, and that you didn't know either the address or the name of the woman to whom you gave up the package, convinced that if you explained the source of the money found in your pocket, you would not be believed—then, instead of thinking of the means to prove your innocence, you became afraid, and thought you would save yourself by holding your tongue."

The prisoner's countenance visibly changed; his nerves relaxed; his tight lips fell apart; his mind opened itself to hope. But he still resisted.

"Do with me as you like," said he.

"Eh! What should we do with such a fool as you?" cried M. Lecoq angrily. "I begin to think you are a rascal too. A decent fellow would see that we wanted to get him out of a scrape, and he'd tell us the truth. You are prolonging your imprisonment by your own will. You'd better learn that the greatest shrewdness consists in telling the truth. A last time, will you answer?"

Guespin shook his head; no.

"Go back to prison, then; since it pleases you," concluded the detective. He looked at the judge for his approval, and added:

"Gendarmes, remove the prisoner."

The judge's last doubt was dissipated like the mist before the sun. He was, to tell the truth, a little uneasy at having treated the detective so rudely; and he tried to repair it as much as he could.

"You are an able man, Monsieur Lecoq," said he. "Without speaking of your clear-sightedness, which is so prompt as to seem almost like second sight, your examination just now was a master-piece of its kind. Receive my congratulations, to say nothing of the reward which I propose to recommend in your favor to your chiefs."

The detective at these compliments cast down his eyes with the abashed air of a virgin. He looked tenderly at the dear defunct's portrait, and doubtless said to it:

"At last, darling, we have defeated him—this austere judge who so heartily detests the force of which we are the brightest ornament, makes his apologies; he recognizes and applauds our services."

He answered aloud:

"I can only accept half of your eulogies, Monsieur; permit me to offer the other half to my friend Monsieur Plantat."

M. Plantat tried to protest.

"Oh," said he, "only for some bits of information! You would have ferreted out the truth without me all the same."

The judge arose and graciously, but not without effort, extended his hand to M. Lecoq, who respectfully pressed it.

"You have spared me," said the judge, "a great remorse. Guespin's innocence would surely sooner or later have been recognized; but the idea of having imprisoned an innocent man and harassed him with my interrogatories, would have disturbed my sleep and tormented my conscience for a long time."

"God knows this poor Guespin is not an interesting youth," returned the detective. "I should be disposed to press him hard were I not certain that he's half a fool."

M. Domini gave a start.

"I shall discharge him this very day," said he, "this very hour."

"It will be an act of charity," said M. Lecoq; "but confound his obstinacy; it was so easy for him to simplify my task. I might be able, by the aid of chance, to collect the principal facts—the errand, and a woman being mixed up in the affair; but as I'm no magician, I couldn't guess all the details. How is Jenny mixed up in this affair? Is she an accomplice, or has she only been made to play an ignorant part in it? Where did she meet Guespin and whither did she lead him? It is clear that she made the poor fellow tipsy so as to prevent his going to the Batignolles. Tremorel must have told her some false story—but what?"

"I don't think Tremorel troubled his head about so small a matter," said M. Plantat. "He gave Guespin and Jenny some task, without explaining it at all."

M. Lecoq reflected a moment.

"Perhaps you are right. But Jenny must have had special orders to prevent Guespin from putting in an alibi."

"But," said M. Domini, "Jenny will explain it all to us."

"That is what I rely on; and I hope that within forty-eight hours I shall have found her and brought her safely to Corbeil."

He rose at these words, took his cane and hat, and turning to the judge, said:

"Before retiring—"

"Yes, I know," interrupted M. Domini, "you want a warrant to arrest Hector de Tremorel."

"I do, as you are now of my opinion that he is still alive."

"I am sure of it."

M. Domini opened his portfolio and wrote off a warrant as follows:

"By the law: "We, judge of instruction of the first tribunal, etc., considering articles 91 and 94 of the code of criminal instruction, command and ordain to all the agents of the police to arrest, in conformity with the law, one Hector de Tremorel, etc."

When he had finished, he said:

"Here it is, and may you succeed in speedily finding this great criminal."

"Oh, he'll find him," cried the Corbeil policeman.

"I hope so, at least. As to how I shall go to work, I don't know yet. I will arrange my plan of battle to-night."

The detective then took leave of M. Domini and retired, followed by M. Plantat. The doctor remained with the judge to make arrangements for Sauvresy's exhumation.

M. Lecoq was just leaving the court-house when he felt himself pulled by the arm. He turned and found that it was Goulard who came to beg his favor and to ask him to take him along, persuaded that after having served under so great a captain he must inevitably become a famous man himself. M. Lecoq had some difficulty in getting rid of him; but he at length found himself alone in the street with the old justice of the peace.

"It is late," said the latter. "Would it be agreeable to you to partake of another modest dinner with me, and accept my cordial hospitality?"

"I am chagrined to be obliged to refuse you," replied M. Lecoq. "But I ought to be in Paris this evening."

"But I—in fact, I—was very anxious to talk to you—about—"

"About Mademoiselle Laurence?"

"Yes; I have a plan, and if you would help me—"

M. Lecoq affectionately pressed his friend's hand.

"I have only known you a few hours," said he, "and yet I am as devoted to you as I would be to an old friend. All that is humanly possible for me to do to serve you, I shall certainly do."

"But where shall I see you? They expect me to-day at Orcival."

"Very well; to-morrow morning at nine, at my rooms. No—Rue Montmartre."

"A thousand thanks; I shall be there."

When they had reached the *Belle Image* they separated.

MR. POLICEMAN AND THE COOK

by Wilkie Collins

1880

Wilkie Collins is another writer credited with the creation of the detective genre. His 1859 novel *The Woman in White* has been hailed as the first great English mystery novel, although it might be argued that it really belongs in the earlier category of "sensation fiction," from which the detective story emerged. Walter Hartright, the novel's protagonist, is a drawing teacher, an everyman character who, while he turns out to be a capable investigator, is unexceptional compared to Dupin and Holmes.

In 1868, Collins published *The Moonstone,* another novel which has been hailed as the first English detective novel. Called "A Romance" on its flyleaf, *The Moonstone* features a fabulous jewel, a party in an English country house, and an elaborate plot involving robbery, revenge, and other features that came to characterize detective fiction: a brilliant detective outwitting the bungling local constabulary, a liberal sprinkling of red herrings, a large number of suspects, and a twist that pins the crime on the least likely of them. On the basis of *The Moonstone,* T. S. Eliot credited Collins with creating the English detective novel, "a genre invented by Collins and not by Poe." Dorothy L. Sayers, a leading light of the so-called "Golden Age of Detective Fiction," called it "probably the very finest detective story ever written."

Both *The Moonstone* and *The Woman in White* are widely available, but Collins's shorter fiction is less well-known. This tale was first published as a serial in *The Spirit of the Times,* under the title "Who Killed Zebedee?" It was later collected in his three-volume collection *Little Novels.* It takes the form of a deathbed confession, as an unnamed police officer remembers a case from the beginning of his career, which has haunted him for his whole life.

A FIRST WORD FOR MYSELF.

Before the doctor left me one evening, I asked him how much longer I was likely to live. He answered: "It's not easy to say; you may die before I can get back to you in the morning, or you may live to the end of the month."

I was alive enough on the next morning to think of the needs of my soul, and (being a member of the Roman Catholic Church) to send for the priest.

The history of my sins, related in confession, included blameworthy neglect of a duty which I owed to the laws of my country. In the priest's opinion—and I agreed with him—I was bound to make public acknowledgment of my fault, as an act of penance becoming to a Catholic Englishman. We concluded, thereupon, to try a division of labor. I related the circumstances, while his reverence took the pen and put the matter into shape.

Here follows what came of it:

I.

When I was a young man of five-and-twenty, I became a member of the London police force. After nearly two years' ordinary experience of the responsible and ill-paid duties of that vocation, I found myself employed on my first serious and terrible case of official inquiry—relating to nothing less than the crime of Murder.

The circumstances were these:

I was then attached to a station in the northern district of London—which I beg permission not to mention more particularly. On a certain Monday in the week, I took my turn of night duty. Up to four in the morning, nothing occurred at the station-house out of the ordinary way. It was then springtime, and, between the gas and the fire, the room became rather hot. I went to the door to get a breath of fresh air—much to the surprise of our Inspector on duty, who was constitutionally a chilly man. There was a fine rain falling; and a nasty damp in the air sent me back to the fireside. I don't suppose I had sat down for more than a minute when the swinging-door was violently pushed open. A frantic woman ran in with a scream, and said: "Is this the station-house?"

Our Inspector (otherwise an excellent officer) had, by some perversity of nature, a hot temper in his chilly constitution. "Why, bless the woman, can't you see it is?" he says. "What's the matter now?"

"Murder's the matter!" she burst out. "For God's sake, come back with me. It's at Mrs. Crosscapel's lodging-house, number 14 Lehigh Street. A young woman has murdered her husband in the night! With a knife, sir. She says she thinks she did it in her sleep."

I confess I was startled by this; and the third man on duty (a sergeant) seemed to feel it too. She was a nice-looking young woman, even in her terrified condition, just out of bed, with her clothes huddled on anyhow. I was partial in those days to a tall figure—and she was, as they say, my style. I put a chair for her; and the sergeant poked the fire. As for the Inspector, nothing ever upset *him*. He questioned her as coolly as if it had been a case of petty larceny.

"Have you seen the murdered man?" he asked.

"No, sir."

"Or the wife?"

"No, sir. I didn't dare go into the room; I only heard about it!"

"Oh? And who are You? One of the lodgers?"

"No, sir. I'm the cook."

"Isn't there a master in the house?"

"Yes, sir. He's frightened out of his wits. And the housemaid's gone for the doctor. It all falls on the poor servants, of course. Oh, why did I ever set foot in that horrible house?"

The poor soul burst out crying, and shivered from head to foot. The Inspector made a note of her statement, and then asked her to read it, and sign it with her name. The object of this proceeding was to get her to come near enough to give him the opportunity of smelling her breath. "When people make extraordinary statements," he afterward said to me, "it sometimes saves trouble to satisfy yourself that they are not drunk. I've known them to be mad—but not often. You will generally find *that* in their eyes."

She roused herself and signed her name—"Priscilla Thurlby." The Inspector's own test proved her to be sober; and her eyes—a nice light blue color, mild and pleasant, no doubt, when they were not staring with fear, and red with crying—satisfied him (as I supposed) that she was not mad. He turned the case over to me, in the first instance. I saw that he didn't believe in it, even yet.

"Go back with her to the house," he says. "This may be a stupid hoax, or a quarrel exaggerated. See to it yourself, and hear what the doctor says. If it is serious, send word back here directly, and let nobody enter the place or leave it till we come. Stop! You know the form if any statement is volunteered?"

"Yes, sir. I am to caution the persons that whatever they say will be taken down, and may be used against them."

"Quite right. You'll be an Inspector yourself one of these days. Now, miss!" With that he dismissed her, under my care.

Lehigh Street was not very far off—about twenty minutes' walk from the station. I confess I thought the Inspector had been rather hard on Priscilla. She was herself naturally angry with him. "What does he mean," she says, "by talking of a hoax? I wish he was as frightened as I am. This is the first time I have been out at service, sir—and I did think I had found a respectable place."

I said very little to her—feeling, if the truth must be told, rather anxious about the duty committed to me. On reaching the house the door was opened from within, before I could knock. A gentleman stepped out, who proved to be the doctor. He stopped the moment he saw me.

"You must be careful, policeman," he says. "I found the man lying on his back, in bed, dead—with the knife that had killed him left sticking in the wound."

Hearing this, I felt the necessity of sending at once to the station. Where could I find a trustworthy messenger? I took the liberty of asking the doctor if he would repeat to the police what he had already said to me. The station was not much out of his way home. He kindly granted my request.

The landlady (Mrs. Crosscapel) joined us while we were talking. She was still a young woman; not easily frightened, as far as I could see, even by a murder in the house. Her husband was in the passage behind her. He looked old enough to be her father; and he so trembled with terror that some people might have taken him for the guilty person. I removed the key from the street door, after locking it; and I said to the landlady: "Nobody must leave the house, or enter the house, till the Inspector comes. I must examine the premises to see if any one has broken in."

"There is the key of the area gate," she said, in answer to me. "It's always kept locked. Come downstairs and see for yourself." Priscilla went with us. Her mistress set her to work to light the kitchen fire. "Some of us," says Mrs. Crosscapel, "may be the better for a cup of tea." I remarked that she took things easy, under the circumstances. She answered that the landlady of a London lodging-house could not afford to lose her wits, no matter what might happen.

I found the gate locked, and the shutters of the kitchen window fastened. The back kitchen and back door were secured in the same way. No person was concealed anywhere. Returning upstairs, I examined the front parlor window. There, again, the barred shutters answered for the security of that room. A cracked voice spoke through the door of the back parlor. "The policeman can come in," it said, "if he will promise not to look at me." I turned to the landlady for information. "It's my parlor lodger, Miss Mybus," she said, "a most respectable lady." Going into the room, I saw something rolled up perpendicularly in the bed curtains. Miss Mybus had made herself modestly invisible in that way. Having now satisfied my mind about the security of the lower part of the house, and having the keys safe in my pocket, I was ready to go upstairs.

On our way to the upper regions I asked if there had been any visitors on the previous day. There had been only two visitors, friends of the lodgers—and Mrs. Crosscapel herself had let them both out. My next inquiry related to the lodgers themselves. On the ground floor there was Miss Mybus. On the first floor (occupying both rooms) Mr. Barfield, an old bachelor, employed in a merchant's office. On the second floor, in the front room, Mr. John Zebedee, the murdered man, and his wife. In the back room, Mr. Deluc; described as a cigar agent, and supposed to be a Creole gentleman from Martinique. In the front garret, Mr. and Mrs. Crosscapel. In the back garret, the cook and the housemaid. These were the inhabitants, regularly accounted for. I asked about the servants. "Both excellent characters," says the landlady, "or they would not be in my service."

We reached the second floor, and found the housemaid on the watch outside the door of the front room. Not as nice a woman, personally, as the cook, and sadly frightened of course. Her mistress had posted her, to give the alarm in the case of an outbreak on the part of Mrs. Zebedee, kept locked up in the room. My arrival relieved the housemaid of further responsibility. She ran downstairs to her fellow-servant in the kitchen.

I asked Mrs. Crosscapel how and when the alarm of the murder had been given.

"Soon after three this morning," says she, "I was woke by the screams of Mrs. Zebedee. I found her out here on the landing, and Mr. Deluc, in great alarm, trying to quiet her. Sleeping in the next room he had only to open his door, when her screams woke him. 'My dear John's murdered! I am the miserable wretch—I did it in my sleep!' She repeated these frantic words over and over again, until she dropped in a swoon. Mr. Deluc and I carried her back into the bedroom. We both thought the poor creature had been driven distracted by some dreadful dream. But when we got to the bedside—don't ask me what we saw; the doctor has told you about it already. I was once a nurse in a hospital, and accustomed, as such, to horrid sights. It turned me cold and giddy, notwithstanding. As for Mr. Deluc, I thought *he* would have had a fainting fit next."

Hearing this, I inquired if Mrs. Zebedee had said or done any strange things since she had been Mrs. Crosscapel's lodger.

"You think she's mad?" says the landlady. "And anybody would be of your mind, when a woman accuses herself of murdering her husband in her sleep. All I can say is that, up to this morning, a more quiet, sensible, well-behaved little person than Mrs. Zebedee I never met with. Only just married, mind, and as fond of her unfortunate husband as a woman could be. I should have called them a pattern couple, in their own line of life."

There was no more to be said on the landing. We unlocked the door and went into the room.

II.

He lay in bed on his back as the doctor had described him. On the left side of his nightgown, just over his heart, the blood on the linen told its terrible tale. As well as one could judge, looking unwillingly at a dead face, he must have been a handsome young man in his lifetime. It was a sight to sadden anybody—but I think the most painful sensation was when my eyes fell next on his miserable wife.

She was down on the floor, crouched up in a corner—a dark little woman, smartly dressed in gay colors. Her black hair and her big brown eyes made the horrid paleness of her face look even more deadly white than perhaps it really was. She stared straight at us without appearing to see us. We spoke to her, and she never answered a word. She might have been dead—like her husband—except that she perpetually picked at her fingers, and shuddered every now and then as if she was cold. I went to her and tried to lift her up. She shrank back with a cry that well-nigh frightened me—not because it was loud, but because it was more like the cry of some animal than of a human being. However quietly she might have behaved in the landlady's previous experience of her, she was beside herself now. I might have been moved by a natural pity for her, or I might have been completely upset in my mind—I only know this, I could not persuade myself that she was guilty. I even said to Mrs. Crosscapel, "I don't believe she did it."

While I spoke there was a knock at the door. I went downstairs at once, and admitted (to my great relief) the Inspector, accompanied by one of our men.

He waited downstairs to hear my report, and he approved of what I had done. "It looks as if the murder had been committed by somebody in the house." Saying this, he left the man below, and went up with me to the second floor.

Before he had been a minute in the room, he discovered an object which had escaped my observation.

It was the knife that had done the deed.

The doctor had found it left in the body—had withdrawn it to probe the wound—and had laid it on the bedside table. It was one of those useful knives which contain a saw, a corkscrew, and other like implements. The big blade fastened back, when open, with a spring. Except where the blood was on it, it was as bright as when it had been purchased. A small metal plate was fastened to the horn handle, containing an inscription, only partly engraved, which ran thus: "To John Zebedee, from—" There it stopped, strangely enough.

Who or what had interrupted the engraver's work? It was impossible even to guess. Nevertheless, the Inspector was encouraged.

"This ought to help us," he said—and then he gave an attentive ear (looking all the while at the poor creature in the corner) to what Mrs. Crosscapel had to tell him.

The landlady having done, he said he must now see the lodger who slept in the next bed-chamber.

Mr. Deluc made his appearance, standing at the door of the room, and turning away his head with horror from the sight inside.

He was wrapped in a splendid blue dressing-gown, with a golden girdle and trimmings. His scanty brownish hair curled (whether artificially or not, I am unable to say) in little ringlets. His complexion was yellow; his greenish-brown eyes were of the sort called "goggle"—they looked as if they might drop out of his face, if you held a spoon under them. His mustache and goat's beard were beautifully oiled; and, to complete his equipment, he had a long black cigar in his mouth.

"It isn't insensibility to this terrible tragedy," he explained. "My nerves have been shattered, Mr. Policeman, and I can only repair the mischief in this way. Be pleased to excuse and feel for me."

The Inspector questioned this witness sharply and closely. He was not a man to be misled by appearances; but I could see that he was far from liking, or even trusting, Mr. Deluc. Nothing came of the examination, except what Mrs. Crosscapel had in substance already mentioned to me. Mr. Deluc returned to his room.

"How long has he been lodging with you?" the Inspector asked, as soon as his back was turned.

"Nearly a year," the landlady answered.

"Did he give you a reference?"

"As good a reference as I could wish for." Thereupon, she mentioned the names of a well-known firm of cigar merchants in the city. The Inspector noted the information in his pocketbook.

I would rather not relate in detail what happened next: it is too distressing to be dwelt on. Let me only say that the poor demented woman was taken away in a cab to the station-house. The Inspector possessed himself of the knife, and of a book found on the floor, called "The World of Sleep." The portmanteau containing the luggage was locked—and then the door of the room was secured, the keys in both cases being left in my charge. My instructions were to remain in the house, and allow nobody to leave it, until I heard again shortly from the Inspector.

III.

The coroner's inquest was adjourned; and the examination before the magistrate ended in a remand—Mrs. Zebedee being in no condition to understand the proceedings in either case. The surgeon reported her to be completely prostrated by a terrible nervous shock. When he was asked if he considered her to have been a sane woman before the murder took place, he refused to answer positively at that time.

A week passed. The murdered man was buried; his old father attending the funeral. I occasionally saw Mrs. Crosscapel, and the two servants, for the purpose of getting such further information as was thought desirable. Both the cook and the housemaid had given their month's notice to quit; declining, in the interest of their characters, to remain in a house which had been the scene of a murder. Mr. Deluc's nerves led also to his removal; his rest was now disturbed by frightful dreams. He paid the necessary forfeit-money, and left without notice. The first-floor lodger, Mr. Barfield, kept his rooms, but obtained leave of absence from his employers, and took refuge with some friends in the country. Miss Mybus alone remained in the parlors. "When I am comfortable," the old lady said, "nothing moves me, at my age. A murder up two pairs of stairs is nearly the same thing as a murder in the next house. Distance, you see, makes all the difference."

It mattered little to the police what the lodgers did. We had men in plain clothes watching the house night and day. Everybody who went away was privately followed; and the police in the district to which they retired were warned to keep an eye on them, after that. As long as we failed to put Mrs. Zebedee's extraordinary statement to any sort of test—to say nothing of having proved unsuccessful, thus far, in tracing the knife to its purchaser—we were bound to let no person living under Mr. Crosscapel's roof, on the night of the murder, slip through our fingers.

IV.

In a fortnight more, Mrs. Zebedee had sufficiently recovered to make the necessary statement—after the preliminary caution addressed to persons in such cases. The surgeon had no hesitation, now, in reporting her to be a sane woman.

Her station in life had been domestic service. She had lived for four years in her last place as lady's-maid, with a family residing in Dorsetshire. The one objection to her had been the occasional infirmity of sleep-walking, which made it necessary that one of the other female servants should sleep in the same room, with the door locked and the key under her pillow. In all other respects the lady's-maid was described by her mistress as "a perfect treasure."

In the last six months of her service, a young man named John Zebedee entered the house (with a written character) as a footman. He soon fell in love with the nice little lady's-maid, and she heartily returned the feeling. They might have waited for years before they were in a pecuniary position to marry, but for the death of Zebedee's uncle, who left him a little fortune of two thousand pounds. They were now, for persons in their station, rich enough to please themselves; and they were married from the house in which they had served together, the little daughters of the family showing their affection for Mrs. Zebedee by acting as her bridesmaids.

The young husband was a careful man. He decided to employ his small capital to the best advantage, by sheep-farming in Australia. His wife made no objection; she was ready to go wherever John went.

Accordingly they spent their short honeymoon in London, so as to see for themselves the vessel in which their passage was to be taken. They went to Mrs. Crosscapel's lodging-house because Zebedee's uncle had always stayed there when in London. Ten days were to pass before the day of embarkation arrived. This gave the young couple a welcome holiday, and a prospect of amusing themselves to their heart's content among the sights and shows of the great city.

On their first evening in London they went to the theater. They were both accustomed to the fresh air of the country, and they felt half stifled by the heat and the gas. However, they were so pleased with an amusement which was new to them that they went to another theater on the next evening. On this second occasion, John Zebedee found the heat unendurable. They left the theater, and got back to their lodgings toward ten o'clock.

Let the rest be told in the words used by Mrs. Zebedee herself. She said:

"We sat talking for a little while in our room, and John's headache got worse and worse. I persuaded him to go to bed, and I put out the candle (the fire giving sufficient light to undress by), so that he might the sooner fall asleep. But he was too restless to sleep. He asked me to read him something. Books always made him drowsy at the best of times.

"I had not myself begun to undress. So I lit the candle again, and I opened the only book I had. John had noticed it at the railway bookstall by the name of 'The World of Sleep.' He used to joke with me about my being a sleepwalker; and he said, 'Here's something that's sure to interest you'—and he made me a present of the book.

"Before I had read to him for more than half an hour he was fast asleep. Not feeling that way inclined, I went on reading to myself.

"The book did indeed interest me. There was one terrible story which took a hold on my mind—the story of a man who stabbed his own wife in a sleep-walking dream. I thought of putting down my book after that, and then changed my mind again and went on. The next chapters were not so interesting; they were full of learned accounts of why we fall asleep, and what our brains do in that state, and such like. It ended in my falling asleep, too, in my armchair by the fireside.

"I don't know what o'clock it was when I went to sleep. I don't know how long I slept, or whether I dreamed or not. The candle and the fire had both burned out, and it was pitch dark when I woke. I can't even say why I woke—unless it was the coldness of the room.

"There was a spare candle on the chimney-piece. I found the matchbox, and got a light. Then for the first time, I turned round toward the bed; and I saw—"

She had seen the dead body of her husband, murdered while she was unconsciously at his side—and she fainted, poor creature, at the bare remembrance of it.

The proceedings were adjourned. She received every possible care and attention; the chaplain looking after her welfare as well as the surgeon.

I have said nothing of the evidence of the landlady and servants. It was taken as a mere formality. What little they knew proved nothing against Mrs. Zebedee. The police made no discoveries that supported her first frantic accusation of herself. Her master and mistress, where she had been last in service, spoke of her in the highest terms. We were at a complete deadlock.

It had been thought best not to surprise Mr. Deluc, as yet, by citing him as a witness. The action of the law was, however, hurried in this case by a private communication received from the chaplain.

After twice seeing, and speaking with, Mrs. Zebedee, the reverend gentleman was persuaded that she had no more to do than himself with the murder of her husband. He did not consider that he was justified in repeating a confidential communication—he would only recommend that Mr. Deluc should be summoned to appear at the next examination. This advice was followed.

The police had no evidence against Mrs. Zebedee when the inquiry was resumed. To assist the ends of justice she was now put into the witness-box. The discovery of her murdered husband, when she woke in the small hours of the morning, was passed over as rapidly as possible. Only three questions of importance were put to her.

First, the knife was produced. Had she ever seen it in her husband's possession? Never. Did she know anything about it? Nothing whatever.

Secondly: Did she, or did her husband, lock the bedroom door when they returned from the theater? No. Did she afterward lock the door herself? No.

Thirdly: Had she any sort of reason to give for supposing that she had murdered her husband in a sleep-walking dream? No reason, except that she was beside herself at the time, and the book put the thought into her head.

After this the other witnesses were sent out of court The motive for the chaplain's communication now appeared. Mrs. Zebedee was asked if anything unpleasant had occurred between Mr. Deluc and herself.

Yes. He had caught her alone on the stairs at the lodging-house; had presumed to make love to her; and had carried the insult still farther by attempting to kiss her. She had slapped his face, and had declared that her husband should know of it, if his misconduct was repeated. He was in a furious rage at having his face slapped; and he said to her: "Madam, you may live to regret this."

After consultation, and at the request of our Inspector, it was decided to keep Mr. Deluc in ignorance of Mrs. Zebedee's statement for the present. When the witnesses were recalled, he gave the same evidence which he had already given to the Inspector—and he was then asked if he knew anything of the knife. He looked at it without any guilty signs in his face, and swore that he had never seen it until that moment. The resumed inquiry ended, and still nothing had been discovered.

But we kept an eye on Mr. Deluc. Our next effort was to try if we could associate him with the purchase of the knife.

Here again (there really did seem to be a sort of fatality in this case) we reached no useful result. It was easy enough to find out the wholesale cutlers, who had manufactured the knife at Sheffield, by the mark on the blade. But they made tens of thousands of such knives, and disposed of them to retail dealers all over Great Britain—to say nothing of foreign parts. As to finding out the person who had engraved the imperfect inscription (without knowing where, or by whom, the knife had been purchased) we might as well have looked for the proverbial needle in the bundle of hay. Our last resource was to have the knife photographed, with the inscribed side uppermost, and to send copies to every police-station in the kingdom.

At the same time we reckoned up Mr. Deluc—I mean that we made investigations into his past life—on the chance that he and the murdered man might have known each other, and might have had a quarrel, or a rivalry about a woman, on some former occasion. No such discovery rewarded us.

We found Deluc to have led a dissipated life, and to have mixed with very bad company. But he had kept out of reach of the law. A man may be a profligate vagabond; may insult a lady; may say threatening things to her, in the first stinging sensation of having his face slapped—but it doesn't follow from these blots on his character that he has murdered her husband in the dead of the night.

Once more, then, when we were called upon to report ourselves, we had no evidence to produce. The photographs failed to discover the owner of the knife, and to explain its interrupted inscription. Poor Mrs. Zebedee was allowed to go back to her friends, on entering into her own recognizance to appear again if called upon. Articles in the newspapers began to inquire how many more murderers would succeed in baffling the police. The authorities at the Treasury offered a reward of a hundred pounds for the necessary information. And the weeks passed and nobody claimed the reward.

Our Inspector was not a man to be easily beaten. More inquiries and examinations followed. It is needless to say anything about them. We were defeated—and there, so far as the police and the public were concerned, was an end of it.

The assassination of the poor young husband soon passed out of notice, like other undiscovered murders. One obscure person only was foolish enough, in his leisure hours, to persist in trying to solve the problem of Who Killed Zebedee? He felt that he might rise to the highest position in the police force if he succeeded where his elders and betters had failed—and he held to his own little ambition, though everybody laughed at him. In plain English, I was the man.

V.

Without meaning it, I have told my story ungratefully.

There were two persons who saw nothing ridiculous in my resolution to continue the investigation, single-handed. One of them was Miss Mybus; and the other was the cook, Priscilla Thurlby.

Mentioning the lady first, Miss Mybus was indignant at the resigned manner in which the police accepted their defeat. She was a little bright-eyed wiry woman; and she spoke her mind freely.

"This comes home to me," she said. "Just look back for a year or two. I can call to mind two cases of persons found murdered in London—and the assassins have never been traced. I am a person, too; and I ask myself if my turn is not coming next. You're a nice-looking fellow and I like your pluck and perseverance. Come here as often as you think right; and say you are my visitor, if they make any difficulty about letting you in. One thing more! I have nothing particular to do, and I am no fool. Here, in the parlors, I see everybody who comes into the house or goes out of the house. Leave me your address—I may get some information for you yet."

With the best intentions, Miss Mybus found no opportunity of helping me. Of the two, Priscilla Thurlby seemed more likely to be of use.

In the first place, she was sharp and active, and (not having succeeded in getting another situation as yet) was mistress of her own movements.

In the second place, she was a woman I could trust. Before she left home to try domestic service in London, the parson of her native parish gave her a written testimonial, of which I append a copy. Thus it ran:

> "I gladly recommend Priscilla Thurlby for any respectable employment which she may be competent to undertake. Her father and mother are infirm old people, who have lately suffered a diminution of their income; and they have a younger daughter to maintain. Rather than be a burden on her parents, Priscilla goes to London to find domestic employment, and to devote her earnings to the assistance of her father and mother. This circumstance speaks for itself. I have

known the family many years; and I only regret that I have no vacant place in my own household which I can offer to this good girl,

(Signed) "HENRY DEERINGTON, Rector of Roth."

After reading those words, I could safely ask Priscilla to help me in reopening the mysterious murder case to some good purpose.

My notion was that the proceedings of the persons in Mrs. Crosscapel's house had not been closely enough inquired into yet. By way of continuing the investigation, I asked Priscilla if she could tell me anything which associated the housemaid with Mr. Deluc. She was unwilling to answer. "I may be casting suspicion on an innocent person," she said. "Besides, I was for so short a time the housemaid's fellow servant—"

"You slept in the same room with her," I remarked; "and you had opportunities of observing her conduct toward the lodgers. If they had asked you, at the examination, what I now ask, you would have answered as an honest woman."

To this argument she yielded. I heard from her certain particulars, which threw a new light on Mr. Deluc, and on the case generally. On that information I acted. It was slow work, owing to the claims on me of my regular duties; but with Priscilla's help, I steadily advanced toward the end I had in view.

Besides this, I owed another obligation to Mrs. Crosscapel's nice-looking cook. The confession must be made sooner or later—and I may as well make it now. I first knew what love was, thanks to Priscilla. I had delicious kisses, thanks to Priscilla. And, when I asked if she would marry me, she didn't say No. She looked, I must own, a little sadly, and she said: "How can two such poor people as we are ever hope to marry?" To this I answered: "It won't be long before I lay my hand on the clew which my Inspector has failed to find. I shall be in a position to marry you, my dear, when that time comes."

At our next meeting we spoke of her parents. I was now her promised husband. Judging by what I had heard of the proceedings of other people in my position, it seemed to be only right that I should be made known to her father and mother. She entirely agreed with me; and she wrote home that day to tell them to expect us at the end of the week.

I took my turn of night-duty, and so gained my liberty for the greater part of the next day. I dressed myself in plain clothes, and we took our tickets on the railway for Yateland, being the nearest station to the village in which Priscilla's parents lived.

VI.

The train stopped, as usual, at the big town of Waterbank. Supporting herself by her needle, while she was still unprovided with a situation, Priscilla had been at work late in the night—she was tired and thirsty. I left the carriage to get her some soda-water. The stupid girl in the refreshment room failed to pull the cork out of the bottle, and refused to let me help her. She took a corkscrew, and used it crookedly. I lost all patience, and snatched the bottle out of her hand. Just as I drew the cork, the bell rang on the platform. I only waited to pour the soda-water into a glass—but the train was moving as I left the refreshment room. The porters stopped me when I tried to jump on to the step of the carriage. I was left behind.

As soon as I had recovered my temper, I looked at the time-table. We had reached Waterbank at five minutes past one. By good luck, the next train was due at forty-four minutes past one, and arrived at Yateland (the next station) ten minutes afterward. I could only hope that Priscilla would look at the time-table too, and wait for me. If I had attempted to walk the distance between the two places, I should have lost time instead of saving it. The interval before me was not very long; I occupied it in looking over the town.

Speaking with all due respect to the inhabitants, Waterbank (to other people) is a dull place. I went up one street and down another—and stopped to look at a shop which struck me; not from anything in itself, but because it was the only shop in the street with the shutters closed.

A bill was posted on the shutters, announcing that the place was to let. The outgoing tradesman's name and business, announced in the customary painted letters, ran thus: *James Wycomb, Cutler, etc.*

For the first time, it occurred to me that we had forgotten an obstacle in our way, when we distributed our photographs of the knife. We had none of us remembered that a certain proportion of cutlers might be placed, by circumstances, out of our reach—either by retiring from business or by becoming bankrupt. I always carried a copy of the photograph about me; and I thought to myself, "Here is the ghost of a chance of tracing the knife to Mr. Deluc!"

The shop door was opened, after I had twice rung the bell, by an old man, very dirty and very deaf. He said "You had better go upstairs, and speak to Mr. Scorrier—top of the house."

I put my lips to the old fellow's ear-trumpet, and asked who Mr. Scorrier was.

"Brother-in-law to Mr. Wycomb. Mr. Wycomb's dead. If you want to buy the business apply to Mr. Scorrier."

Receiving that reply, I went upstairs, and found Mr. Scorrier engaged in engraving a brass door-plate. He was a middle-aged man, with a cadaverous face and dim eyes. After the necessary apologies, I produced my photograph.

"May I ask, sir, if you know anything of the inscription on that knife?" I said.

He took his magnifying glass to look at it.

"This is curious," he remarked quietly. "I remember the queer name—Zebedee. Yes, sir; I did the engraving, as far as it goes. I wonder what prevented me from finishing it?"

The name of Zebedee, and the unfinished inscription on the knife, had appeared in every English newspaper. He took the matter so coolly that I was doubtful how to interpret his answer. Was it possible that he had not seen the account of the murder? Or was he an accomplice with prodigious powers of self-control?

"Excuse me," I said, "do you read the newspapers?"

"Never! My eyesight is failing me. I abstain from reading, in the interests of my occupation."

"Have you not heard the name of Zebedee mentioned—particularly by people who do read the newspapers?"

"Very likely; but I didn't attend to it. When the day's work is done, I take my walk. Then I have my supper, my drop of grog, and my pipe. Then I go to bed. A dull existence you think, I daresay! I had a miserable life, sir, when I was young. A bare subsistence, and a little rest, before the last perfect rest in the grave—that is all I want. The world has gone by me long ago. So much the better."

The poor man spoke honestly. I was ashamed of having doubted him. I returned to the subject of the knife.

"Do you know where it was purchased, and by whom?" I asked.

"My memory is not so good as it was," he said; "but I have got something by me that helps it."

He took from a cupboard a dirty old scrapbook. Strips of paper, with writing on them, were pasted on the pages, as well as I could see. He turned to an index, or table of contents, and opened a page. Something like a flash of life showed itself on his dismal face.

"Ha! now I remember," he said. "The knife was bought of my late brother-in-law, in the shop downstairs. It all comes back to me, sir. A person in a state of frenzy burst into this very room, and snatched the knife away from me, when I was only half way through the inscription!"

I felt that I was now close on discovery. "May I see what it is that has assisted your memory?" I asked.

"Oh yes. You must know, sir, I live by engraving inscriptions and addresses, and I paste in this book the manuscript instructions which I receive, with marks of my own on the margin. For one thing, they serve as a reference to new customers. And for another thing, they do certainly help my memory."

He turned the book toward me, and pointed to a slip of paper which occupied the lower half of a page.

I read the complete inscription, intended for the knife that killed Zebedee, and written as follows:

"To John Zebedee. From Priscilla Thurlby."

VII.

I declare that it is impossible for me to describe what I felt when Priscilla's name confronted me like a written confession of guilt. How long it was before I recovered myself in some degree, I cannot say. The only thing I can clearly call to mind is, that I frightened the poor engraver.

My first desire was to get possession of the manuscript inscription. I told him I was a policeman, and summoned him to assist me in the discovery of a crime. I even offered him money. He drew back from my hand. "You shall have it for nothing," he said, "if you will only go away and never come here again." He tried to cut it out of the page—but his trembling hands were helpless. I cut it out myself, and attempted to thank him. He wouldn't hear me. "Go away!" he said, "I don't like the look of you."

It may be here objected that I ought not to have felt so sure as I did of the woman's guilt, until I had got more evidence against her. The knife might have been stolen from her, supposing she was the person who had snatched it out of the engraver's hands, and might have been afterward used by the thief to commit the murder. All very true. But I never had a moment's doubt in my own mind, from the time when I read the damnable line in the engraver's book.

I went back to the railway without any plan in my head. The train by which I had proposed to follow her had left Waterbank. The next train that arrived was for London. I took my place in it—still without any plan in my head.

At Charing Cross a friend met me. He said, "You're looking miserably ill. Come and have a drink."

I went with him. The liquor was what I really wanted; it strung me up, and cleared my head. He went his way, and I went mine. In a little while more, I determined what I would do.

In the first place, I decided to resign my situation in the police, from a motive which will presently appear. In the second place, I took a bed at a public-house. She would no doubt return to London, and she would go to my lodgings to find out why I had broken my appointment. To bring to justice the one woman whom I had dearly loved was too cruel a duty for a poor creature like me. I preferred leaving the police force. On the other hand, if she and I met before time had helped me to control myself, I had a horrid fear that I might turn murderer next, and kill her then and there. The wretch had not only all but misled me into marrying her, but also into charging the innocent housemaid with being concerned in the murder.

The same night I hit on a way of clearing up such doubts as still harassed my mind. I wrote to the rector of Roth, informing him that I was engaged to marry her, and asking if he would tell me (in consideration of my position) what her former relations might have been with the person named John Zebedee.

By return of post I got this reply:

"SIR—Under the circumstances, I think I am bound to tell you confidentially what the friends and well-wishers of Priscilla have kept secret, for her sake.

"Zebedee was in service in this neighborhood. I am sorry to say it, of a man who has come to such a miserable end—but his behavior to Priscilla proves him to have been a vicious and heartless wretch. They were engaged—and, I add with indignation, he tried to seduce her under a promise of marriage. Her virtue resisted him, and he pretended to be ashamed of himself. The banns were published in my church. On the next day Zebedee disappeared, and cruelly deserted her. He was a capable servant; and I believe he got another place. I leave you to imagine what the poor girl suffered under the outrage inflicted on her. Going to London, with my recommendation, she answered the first advertisement that she saw, and was unfortunate enough to begin her career in domestic service in the very lodging-house to which (as I gather from the newspaper report of the murder) the man Zebedee took the person whom he married, after deserting Priscilla. Be assured that you are about to unite yourself to an excellent girl, and accept my best wishes for your happiness."

It was plain from this that neither the rector nor the parents and friends knew anything of the purchase of the knife. The one miserable man who knew the truth was the man who had asked her to be his wife.

I owed it to myself—at least so it seemed to me—not to let it be supposed that I, too, had meanly deserted her. Dreadful as the prospect was, I felt that I must see her once more, and for the last time.

She was at work when I went into her room. As I opened the door she started to her feet. Her cheeks reddened, and her eyes flashed with anger. I stepped forward—and she saw my face. My face silenced her.

I spoke in the fewest words I could find.

"I have been to the cutler's shop at Waterbank," I said. "There is the unfinished inscription on the knife, complete in your handwriting. I could hang you by a word. God forgive me—I can't say the word."

Her bright complexion turned to a dreadful clay-color. Her eyes were fixed and staring, like the eyes of a person in a fit. She stood before me, still and silent. Without saying more, I dropped the inscription into the fire. Without saying more, I left her.

I never saw her again.

VIII.

But I heard from her a few days later. The letter has long since been burned. I wish I could have forgotten it as well. It sticks to my memory. If I die with my senses about me, Priscilla's letter will be my last recollection on earth.

In substance it repeated what the rector had already told me. Further, it informed me that she had bought the knife as a keepsake for Zebedee, in place of a similar knife which he had lost. On the Saturday, she made the purchase, and left it to be engraved. On the Sunday, the banns were put up. On the Monday, she was deserted; and she snatched the knife from the table while the engraver was at work.

She only knew that Zebedee had added a new sting to the insult inflicted on her when he arrived at the lodgings with his wife. Her duties as cook kept her in the kitchen—and Zebedee never discovered that she was in the house. I still remember the last lines of her confession:

"The devil entered into me when I tried their door, on my way up to bed, and found it unlocked, and listened a while, and peeped in. I saw them by the dying light of the candle—one asleep on the bed, the other asleep by the fireside. I had the knife in my hand, and the thought came to me to do it, so that they might hang *her* for the murder. I couldn't take the knife out again, when I had done it. Mind this! I did really like you—I didn't say Yes, because you could hardly hang your own wife, if you found out who killed Zebedee."

Since the past time I have never heard again of Priscilla Thurlby; I don't know whether she is living or dead. Many people may think I deserve to be hanged myself for not having given her up to the gallows. They may, perhaps, be disappointed when they see this confession, and hear that I have died decently in my bed. I don't blame them. I am a penitent sinner. I wish all merciful Christians good-by forever.

THE LENTON CROFT ROBBERIES

by Arthur Morrison

1894

Arthur Morrison was born in Poplar in London's East End, the son of an engine fitter at the London docks who died when he was barely eight years old. He worked as an office boy, haunting used bookstores in his free time, and published his first work, a humorous poem, at seventeen. As he matured, he published novels and stories with titles like *Tales of Mean Streets* (1895) and *A Child of the Jago* (1897), which depicted East End life with unflinching realism.

Unlike Holmes, Morrison's detective Martin Hewitt is unassuming, middle-class, and of unremarkable appearance. He relies more on logic than on science, and in place of Holmes's almost godlike fund of skills and knowledge, Hewitt has a sharp eye, a logical mind, and an abundance of common sense. He is less prone to lecture on points of science, promising instead to "explain all my tricks when the job's done," and his solutions, the reader feels, are never guilty of scientific or intellectual *deus ex machina* tricks; when all is revealed, anyone can see that it all makes perfect sense.

"The Lenton Croft Robberies" was the first of the Hewitt stories, appearing in the *Strand* magazine in March 1894—three months after Holmes and Moriarty's struggle by the Reichenbach Falls. No fresh Holmes stories appeared in the *Strand* until the first installment of *The Hound of the Baskervilles* was published in August 1901, and during that hiatus Morrison published seventeen Hewitt stories in the *Strand* and elsewhere, collecting them in three volumes: *Martin Hewitt, Investigator* (1894), *The Chronicles of Martin Hewitt* (1895), and *The Adventures of Martin Hewitt* (1896). Eight more were published in *The Harmsworthy Magazine* in 1902–3; six of which were collected in *The Red Triangle* (1904).

The first Hewitt story provides a perfect introduction to the character, involving him in a country house mystery with a solution that is at once unexpected and logical.

T hose who retain any memory of the great law cases of fifteen or twenty years back will remember, at least, the title of that extraordinary will case, "Bartley *v.* Bartley and others," which occupied the Probate Court for some weeks on end, and caused an amount of public interest rarely accorded to any but the cases considered in the other division of the same court. The case itself was noted for the large quantity of remarkable and unusual evidence presented by the plaintiff's side—evidence that took the other party completely by surprise, and overthrew their case like a house of cards. The affair will, perhaps, be more readily recalled as the occasion of the sudden rise to eminence in their profession of Messrs. Crellan, Hunt & Crellan, solicitors for the plaintiff—a result due entirely to the wonderful ability shown in this case of building up, apparently out of nothing, a smashing weight of irresistible evidence. That the firm has since maintained—indeed enhanced—the position it then won for itself need scarcely be said here; its name is familiar to everybody. But there are not many of the outside public who know that the credit of the whole performance was primarily due to a young clerk in the employ of Messrs. Crellan, who had been given charge of the seemingly desperate task of collecting evidence in the case.

This Mr. Martin Hewitt had, however, full credit and reward for his exploit from his firm and from their client, and more than one other firm of lawyers engaged in contentious work made good offers to entice Hewitt to change his employers. Instead of this, however, he determined to work independently for the future, having conceived the idea of making a regular business of doing, on behalf of such clients as might retain him, similar work to that he had just done with such conspicuous success for Messrs. Crellan, Hunt & Crellan. This was the beginning of the private detective business of Martin Hewitt, and his action at that time has been completely justified by the brilliant professional successes he has since achieved.

His business has always been conducted in the most private manner, and he has always declined the help of professional assistants, preferring to carry out himself such of the many investigations offered him as he could manage. He has always maintained that he has never lost by this policy, since the chance of his refusing a case begets competition for his services, and his fees rise by a natural process. At the same time, no man could know better how to employ casual assistance at the right time.

Some curiosity has been expressed as to Mr. Martin Hewitt's system, and, as he himself always consistently maintains that he has no system beyond a judicious use of ordinary faculties, I intend setting forth in detail a few of the more interesting of his cases in order that the public may judge for itself if I am right in estimating Mr. Hewitt's "ordinary faculties" as faculties very extraordinary indeed. He is not a man who has made many friendships (this, probably, for professional reasons), notwithstanding his genial and companionable manners. I myself first made his acquaintance as a result of an accident resulting in a fire at the old house in which Hewitt's office was situated, and in an upper floor of which I occupied bachelor chambers. I was able to help in saving a quantity of extremely important papers relating to his business, and, while repairs were being made, allowed him to lock them in an old wall-safe in one of my rooms which the fire had scarcely damaged.

The acquaintance thus begun has lasted many years, and has become a rather close friendship. I have even accompanied Hewitt on some of his expeditions, and, in a humble way, helped him. Such of the cases, however, as I personally saw nothing of I have put into narrative form from the particulars given me.

"I consider you, Brett," he said, addressing me, "the most remarkable journalist alive. Not because you're particularly clever, you know, because, between ourselves, I hope you'll admit you're not; but because you have known something of me and my doings for some years, and have never yet been guilty of giving away any of my little business secrets you may have become acquainted with. I'm afraid you're not so enterprising a journalist as some, Brett. But now, since you ask, you shall write something—if you think it worth while."

This he said, as he said most things, with a cheery, chaffing good-nature that would have been, perhaps, surprising to a stranger who thought of him only as a grim and mysterious discoverer of secrets and crimes. Indeed, the man had always as little of the aspect of the conventional detective as may be imagined. Nobody could appear more cordial or less observant in manner, although there was to be seen a certain sharpness of the eye—which might, after all, only be the twinkle of good humor.

I *did* think it worth while to write something of Martin Hewitt's investigations, and a description of one of his adventures follows.

At the head of the first flight of a dingy staircase leading up from an ever-open portal in a street by the Strand stood a door, the dusty ground-glass upper panel of which carried in its center the single word "Hewitt," while at its right-hand lower corner, in smaller letters, "Clerk's Office" appeared. On a morning when the clerks in the ground-floor offices had barely hung up their hats, a short, well-dressed young man, wearing spectacles, hastening to open the dusty door, ran into the arms of another man who suddenly issued from it.

"I beg pardon," the first said. "Is this Hewitt's Detective Agency Office?"

"Yes, I believe you will find it so," the other replied. He was a stoutish, clean-shaven man, of middle height, and of a cheerful, round countenance. "You'd better speak to the clerk."

In the little outer office the visitor was met by a sharp lad with inky fingers, who presented him with a pen and a printed slip. The printed slip having been filled with the visitor's name and present business, and conveyed through an inner door, the lad reappeared with an invitation to the private office. There, behind a writing-table, sat the stoutish man himself, who had only just advised an appeal to the clerk.

"Good-morning, Mr. Lloyd—Mr. Vernon Lloyd," he said, affably, looking again at the slip. "You'll excuse my care to start even with my visitors—I must, you know. You come from Sir James Norris, I see."

"Yes; I am his secretary. I have only to ask you to go straight to Lenton Croft at once, if you can, on very important business. Sir James would have wired, but had not your precise address. Can you go by the next train? Eleven-thirty is the first available from Paddington."

"Quite possibly. Do you know any thing of the business?"

"It is a case of a robbery in the house, or, rather, I fancy, of several robberies. Jewelry has been stolen from rooms occupied by visitors to the Croft. The first case occurred some months ago—nearly a year ago, in fact. Last night there was another. But I think you had better get the details on the spot. Sir James has told me to telegraph if you are coming, so that he may meet you himself at the station; and I must hurry, as his drive to the station will be rather a long one. Then I take it you will go, Mr. Hewitt? Twyford is the station."

"Yes, I shall come, and by the 11.30. Are you going by that train yourself?"

"No, I have several things to attend to now I am in town. Good-morning; I shall wire at once."

Mr. Martin Hewitt locked the drawer of his table and sent his clerk for a cab.

At Twyford Station Sir James Norris was waiting with a dog-cart. Sir James was a tall, florid man of fifty or thereabout, known away from home as something of a county historian, and nearer his own parts as a great supporter of the hunt, and a gentleman much troubled with poachers. As soon as he and Hewitt had found one another the baronet hurried the detective into his dog-cart. "We've something over seven miles to drive," he said, "and I can tell you all about this wretched business as we go. That is why I came for you myself, and alone."

Hewitt nodded.

"I have sent for you, as Lloyd probably told you, because of a robbery at my place last evening. It appears, as far as I can guess, to be one of three by the same hand, or by the same gang. Late yesterday afternoon—"

"Pardon me, Sir James," Hewitt interrupted, "but I think I must ask you to begin at the first robbery and tell me the whole tale in proper order. It makes things clearer, and sets them in their proper shape."

"Very well! Eleven months ago, or thereabout, I had rather a large party of visitors, and among them Colonel Heath and Mrs. Heath—the lady being a relative of my own late wife. Colonel Heath has not been long retired, you know—used to be political resident in an Indian native state. Mrs. Heath had rather a good stock of jewelry of one sort and another, about the most valuable piece being a bracelet set with a particularly fine pearl—quite an exceptional pearl, in fact—that had been one of a heap of presents from the maharajah of his state when Heath left India.

"It was a very noticeable bracelet, the gold setting being a mere feather-weight piece of native filigree work—almost too fragile to trust on the wrist—and the pearl being, as I have said, of a size and quality not often seen. Well, Heath and his wife arrived late one evening, and after lunch the following day, most of the men being off by themselves—shooting, I think—my daughter, my sister (who is very often down here), and Mrs. Heath took it into their heads to go walking—fern-hunting, and so on. My sister was rather long dressing, and, while they waited, my daughter went into Mrs. Heath's room, where Mrs. Heath turned over all her treasures to show her, as women do, you know. When my sister was at last ready, they came straight away, leaving the things littering about the room rather than stay longer to pack them up. The bracelet, with other things, was on the dressing-table then."

"One moment. As to the door?"

"They locked it. As they came away my daughter suggested turning the key, as we had one or two new servants about."

"And the window?"

"That they left open, as I was going to tell you. Well, they went on their walk and came back, with Lloyd (whom they had met somewhere) carrying their ferns for them. It was dusk and almost dinner-time. Mrs. Heath went straight to her room, and—the bracelet was gone."

"Was the room disturbed?"

"Not a bit. Everything was precisely where it had been left, except the bracelet. The door hadn't been tampered with, but of course the window was open, as I have told you."

"You called the police, of course?"

"Yes, and had a man from Scotland Yard down in the morning. He seemed a pretty smart fellow, and the first thing he noticed on the dressing-table, within an inch or two of where the bracelet had been, was a match, which had been lit and thrown down. Now nobody about the house had had occasion to use a match in that room that day, and, if they had, certainly wouldn't have thrown it on the cover of the dressing-table. So that, presuming the thief to have used that match, the robbery must have been committed when the room was getting dark—immediately before Mrs. Heath returned, in fact. The thief had evidently struck the match, passed it hurriedly over the various trinkets lying about, and taken the most valuable."

"Nothing else was even moved?"

"Nothing at all. Then the thief must have escaped by the window, although it was not quite clear how. The walking party approached the house with a full view of the window, but saw nothing, although the robbery must have been actually taking place a moment or two before they turned up.

"There was no water-pipe within any practicable distance of the window, but a ladder usually kept in the stable-yard was found lying along the edge of the lawn. The gardener explained, however, that he had put the ladder there after using it himself early in the afternoon."

"Of course it might easily have been used again after that and put back."

"Just what the Scotland Yard man said. He was pretty sharp, too, on the gardener, but very soon decided that he knew nothing of it. No stranger had been seen in the neighborhood, nor had passed the lodge gates. Besides, as the detective said, it scarcely seemed the work of a stranger. A stranger could scarcely have known enough to go straight to the room where a lady—only arrived the day before—had left a valuable jewel, and away again without being seen. So all the people about the house were suspected in turn. The servants offered, in a body, to have their boxes searched, and this was done; everything was turned over, from the butler's to the new kitchen-maid's. I don't know that I should have had this carried quite so far if I had been the loser myself, but it was my guest, and

I was in such a horrible position. Well, there's little more to be said about that, unfortunately. Nothing came of it all, and the thing's as great a mystery now as ever. I believe the Scotland Yard man got as far as suspecting *me* before he gave it up altogether, but give it up he did in the end. I think that's all I know about the first robbery. Is it clear?"

"Oh, yes; I shall probably want to ask a few questions when I have seen the place, but they can wait. What next?"

"Well," Sir James pursued, "the next was a very trumpery* affair, that I should have forgotten all about, probably, if it hadn't been for one circumstance. Even now I hardly think it could have been the work of the same hand. Four months or thereabout after Mrs. Heath's disaster—in February of this year, in fact—Mrs. Armitage, a young widow, who had been a school-fellow of my daughter's, stayed with us for a week or so. The girls don't trouble about the London season, you know, and I have no town house, so they were glad to have their old friend here for a little in the dull time. Mrs. Armitage is a very active young lady, and was scarcely in the house half an hour before she arranged a drive in a pony-cart with Eva—my daughter—to look up old people in the village that she used to know before she was married. So they set off in the afternoon, and made such a round of it that they were late for dinner. Mrs. Armitage had a small plain gold brooch—not at all valuable, you know; two or three pounds, I suppose—which she used to pin up a cloak or anything of that sort. Before she went out she stuck this in the pin-cushion on her dressing-table, and left a ring—rather a good one, I believe—lying close by."

"This," asked Hewitt, "was not in the room that Mrs. Heath had occupied, I take it?"

"No; this was in another part of the building. Well, the brooch went—taken, evidently, by some one in a deuce of a hurry, for, when Mrs. Armitage got back to her room, there was the pin-cushion with a little tear in it, where the brooch had been simply snatched off. But the curious thing was that the ring—worth a dozen of the brooch—was left where it had been put. Mrs. Armitage didn't remember whether or not she had locked the door herself, although she found it locked when she returned; but my niece, who was indoors all the time, went and tried it once—because she remembered that a gas-fitter was at work on the landing near by—and found it safely locked. The gas-fitter, whom we didn't know at the time, but who since seems to be quite an honest fellow, was ready to swear that

---

* Of little account.

nobody but my niece had been to the door while he was in sight of it—which was almost all the time. As to the window, the sash-line had broken that very morning, and Mrs. Armitage had propped open the bottom half about eight or ten inches with a brush; and, when she returned, that brush, sash, and all were exactly as she had left them. Now I scarcely need tell *you* what an awkward job it must have been for anybody to get noiselessly in at that unsupported window; and how unlikely he would have been to replace it, with the brush, exactly as he found it."

"Just so. I suppose the brooch, was really gone? I mean, there was no chance of Mrs. Armitage having mislaid it?"

"Oh, none at all! There was a most careful search."

"Then, as to getting in at the window, would it have been easy?"

"Well, yes," Sir James replied; "yes, perhaps it would. It was a first-floor window, and it looks over the roof and skylight of the billiard-room. I built the billiard-room myself—built it out from a smoking-room just at this corner. It would be easy enough to get at the window from the billiard-room roof. But, then," he added, "that couldn't have been the way. Somebody or other was in the billiard-room the whole time, and nobody could have got over the roof (which is nearly all skylight) without being seen and heard. I was there myself for an hour or two, taking a little practice."

"Well, was anything done?"

"Strict inquiry was made among the servants, of course, but nothing came of it. It was such a small matter that Mrs. Armitage wouldn't hear of my calling in the police or anything of that sort, although I felt pretty certain that there must be a dishonest servant about somewhere. A servant might take a plain brooch, you know, who would feel afraid of a valuable ring, the loss of which would be made a greater matter of."

"Well, yes, perhaps so, in the case of an inexperienced thief, who also would be likely to snatch up whatever she took in a hurry. But I'm doubtful. What made you connect these two robberies together?"

"Nothing whatever—for some months. They seemed quite of a different sort. But scarcely more than a month ago I met Mrs. Armitage at Brighton, and we talked, among other things, of the previous robbery—that of Mrs. Heath's bracelet. I described the circumstances pretty minutely, and, when I mentioned the match found on the table, she said: 'How strange! Why, *my* thief left a match on the dressing-table when he took my poor little brooch!'"

Hewitt nodded. "Yes," he said. "A spent match, of course?"

"Yes, of course, a spent match. She noticed it lying close by the pin-cushion, but threw it away without mentioning the circumstance. Still, it seemed rather curious to me that a match should be lit and dropped, in each case, on the dressing-cover an inch from where the article was taken. I mentioned it to Lloyd when I got back, and he agreed that it seemed significant."

"Scarcely," said Hewitt, shaking his head. "Scarcely, so far, to be called significant, although worth following up. Everybody uses matches in the dark, you know."

"Well, at any rate, the coincidence appealed to me so far that it struck me it might be worth while to describe the brooch to the police in order that they could trace it if it had been pawned. They had tried that, of course, over the bracelet without any result, but I fancied the shot might be worth making, and might possibly lead us on the track of the more serious robbery."

"Quite so. It was the right thing to do. Well?"

"Well, they found it. A woman had pawned it in London—at a shop in Chelsea. But that was some time before, and the pawnbroker had clean forgotten all about the woman's appearance. The name and address she gave were false. So that was the end of that business."

"Had any of the servants left you between the time the brooch was lost and the date of the pawn ticket?"

"No."

"Were all your servants at home on the day the brooch was pawned?"

"Oh, yes! I made that inquiry myself."

"Very good! What next?"

"Yesterday—and this is what made me send for you. My late wife's sister came here last Tuesday, and we gave her the room from which Mrs. Heath lost her bracelet. She had with her a very old-fashioned brooch, containing a miniature of her father, and set in front with three very fine brilliants and a few smaller stones. Here we are, though, at the Croft. I'll tell you the rest indoors."

Hewitt laid his hand on the baronet's arm. "Don't pull up, Sir James," he said. "Drive a little farther. I should like to have a general idea of the whole case before we go in."

"Very good!" Sir James Norris straightened the horse's head again and went on. "Late yesterday afternoon, as my sister-in-law was changing her dress, she left her room for a moment to speak to my daughter in her room, almost adjoining. She was gone no more than three minutes, or five at most, but on her return the brooch, which had been left on the table, had gone. Now the window was shut fast, and had not been tampered with. Of course the door was open, but so was my daughter's, and anybody walking near must have been heard. But the strangest circumstance, and one that almost makes me wonder whether I have been awake to-day or not, was that there lay *a used match* on the very spot, as nearly as possible, where the brooch had been—and it was broad daylight!"

Hewitt rubbed his nose and looked thoughtfully before him. "Um—curious, certainly," he said, "Anything else?"

"Nothing more than you shall see for yourself. I have had the room locked and watched till you could examine it. My sister-in-law had heard of your name, and suggested that you should be called in; so, of course, I did exactly as she wanted. That she should have lost that brooch, of all things, in my house is most unfortunate; you see, there was some small difference about the thing between my late wife and her sister when their mother died and left it. It's almost worse than the Heaths' bracelet business, and altogether I'm not pleased with things, I can assure you. See what a position it is for me! Here are three ladies, in the space of one year, robbed one after another in this mysterious fashion in my house, and I can't find the thief! It's horrible! People will be afraid to come near the place. And I can do nothing!"

"Ah, well, we'll see. Perhaps we had better turn back now. By-the-by, were you thinking of having any alterations or additions made to your house?"

"No. What makes you ask?"

"I think you might at least consider the question of painting and decorating, Sir James—or, say, putting up another coach-house, or something. Because I should like to be (to the servants) the architect—or the builder, if you please—come to look around. You haven't told any of them about this business?"

"Not a word. Nobody knows but my relatives and Lloyd. I took every precaution myself, at once. As to your little disguise, be the architect by all means, and do as you please. If you can only find this thief and put an end to this horrible state of affairs, you'll do me the greatest service I've ever asked for—and as to your fee, I'll gladly make it whatever is usual, and three hundred in addition."

Martin Hewitt bowed. "You're very generous, Sir James, and you may be sure I'll do what I can. As a professional man, of course, a good fee always stimulates my interest, although this case of yours certainly seems interesting enough by itself."

"Most extraordinary! Don't you think so? Here are three persons, all ladies, all in my house, two even in the same room, each successively robbed of a piece of jewelry, each from a dressing-table, and a used match left behind in every case. All in the most difficult—one would say impossible—circumstances for a thief, and yet there is no clue!"

THE LENTON CROFT ROBBERIES | 171

"Well, we won't say that just yet, Sir James; we must see. And we must guard against any undue predisposition to consider the robberies in a lump. Here we are at the lodge gate again. Is that your gardener—the man who left the ladder by the lawn on the first occasion you spoke of?"

Mr. Hewitt nodded in the direction of a man who was clipping a box border.

"Yes; will you ask him anything?"

"No, no; at any rate, not now. Remember the building alterations. I think, if there is no objection, I will look first at the room that the lady—Mrs.—" Hewitt looked up, inquiringly.

"My sister-in-law? Mrs. Cazenove. Oh, yes! you shall come to her room at once."

"Thank you. And I think Mrs. Cazenove had better be there."

They alighted, and a boy from the lodge led the horse and dog-cart away.

Mrs. Cazenove was a thin and faded, but quick and energetic, lady of middle age. She bent her head very slightly on learning Martin Hewitt's name, and said: "I must thank you, Mr. Hewitt, for your very prompt attention. I need scarcely say that any help you can afford in tracing the thief who has my property—whoever it may be—will make me most grateful. My room is quite ready for you to examine."

The room was on the second floor—the top floor at that part of the building. Some slight confusion of small articles of dress was observable in parts of the room.

"This, I take it," inquired Hewitt, "is exactly as it was at the time the brooch was missed?"

"Precisely," Mrs. Cazenove answered. "I have used another room, and put myself to some other inconveniences, to avoid any disturbance."

Hewitt stood before the dressing-table. "Then this is the used match," he observed, "exactly where it was found?"

"Yes."

"Where was the brooch?"

"I should say almost on the very same spot. Certainly no more than a very few inches away."

Hewitt examined the match closely. "It is burned very little," he remarked. "It would appear to have gone out at once. Could you hear it struck?"

"I heard nothing whatever; absolutely nothing."

"If you will step into Miss Norris' room now for a moment," Hewitt suggested, "we will try an experiment. Tell me if you hear matches struck, and how many. Where is the match-stand?"

The match-stand proved to be empty, but matches were found in Miss Norris' room, and the test was made. Each striking could be heard distinctly, even with one of the doors pushed to.

"Both your own door and Miss Norris' were open, I understand; the window shut and fastened inside as it is now, and nothing but the brooch was disturbed?"

"Yes, that was so."

"Thank you, Mrs. Cazenove. I don't think I need trouble you any further just at present. I think, Sir James," Hewitt added, turning to the baronet, who was standing by the door—"I think we will see the other room and take a walk outside the house, if you please. I suppose, by the by, that there is no getting at the matches left behind on the first and second occasions?"

"No," Sir James answered. "Certainly not here. The Scotland Yard man may have kept his."

The room that Mrs. Armitage had occupied presented no peculiar feature. A few feet below the window the roof of the billiard-room was visible, consisting largely of skylight. Hewitt glanced casually about the walls, ascertained that the furniture and hangings had not been materially changed since the second robbery, and expressed his desire to see the windows from the outside. Before leaving the room, however, he wished to know the names of any persons who were known to have been about the house on the occasions of all three robberies.

"Just carry your mind back, Sir James," he said. "Begin with yourself, for instance. Where were you at these times?"

"When Mrs. Heath lost her bracelet, I was in Tagley Wood all the afternoon. When Mrs. Armitage was robbed, I believe I was somewhere about the place most of the time she was out. Yesterday I was down at the farm." Sir James' face broadened. "I don't know whether you call those suspicious movements," he added, and laughed.

"Not at all; I only asked you so that, remembering your own movements, you might the better recall those of the rest of the household. Was anybody, to your knowledge—*anybody*, mind—in the house on all three occasions?"

"Well, you know, it's quite impossible to answer for all the servants. You'll only get that by direct questioning—I can't possibly remember things of that sort. As to the family and visitors—why, you don't suspect any of them, do you?"

"I don't suspect a soul, Sir James," Hewitt answered, beaming genially, "not a soul. You see, I can't suspect people till I know something about where they were. It's quite possible there will be independent evidence enough as it is, but you must help me if you can. The visitors, now. Was there any visitor here each time—or even on the first and last occasions only?"

"No, not one. And my own sister, perhaps you will be pleased to know, was only there at the time of the first robbery."

"Just so! And your daughter, as I have gathered, was clearly absent from the spot each time—indeed, was in company with the party robbed. Your niece, now?"

"Why hang it all, Mr. Hewitt, I can't talk of my niece as a suspected criminal! The poor girl's under my protection, and I really can't allow—"

Hewitt raised his hand, and shook his head deprecatingly.

"My dear sir, haven't I said that I don't suspect a soul? *Do* let me know how the people were distributed, as nearly as possible. Let me see. It was your, niece, I think, who found that Mrs. Armitage's door was locked—this door, in fact—on the day she lost her brooch?"

"Yes, it was."

"Just so—at the time when Mrs. Armitage herself had forgotten whether she locked it or not. And yesterday—was she out then?"

"No, I think not. Indeed, she goes out very little—her health is usually bad. She was indoors, too, at the time of the Heath robbery, since you ask. But come, now, I don't like this. It's ridiculous to suppose that *she* knows anything of it."

"I don't suppose it, as I have said. I am only asking for information. That is all your resident family, I take it, and you know nothing of anybody else's movements—except, perhaps, Mr. Lloyd's?"

"Lloyd? Well, you know yourself that he was out with the ladies when the first robbery took place. As to the others, I don't remember. Yesterday he was probably in his room, writing. I think that acquits *him*, eh?" Sir James looked quizzically into the broad face of the affable detective, who smiled and replied:

"Oh, of course nobody can be in two places at once, else what would become of the *alibi* as an institution? But, as I have said, I am only setting my facts in order. Now, you see, we get down to the servants—unless some stranger is the party wanted. Shall we go outside now?"

Lenton Croft was a large, desultory sort of house, nowhere more than three floors high, and mostly only two. It had been added to bit by bit, till it zigzagged about its site, as Sir James Norris expressed it, "like a game of dominoes." Hewitt scrutinized its external features carefully as they strolled around, and stopped some little while before the windows of the two bed-rooms he had just seen from the inside. Presently they approached the stables and coach-house, where a groom was washing the wheels of the dog-cart.

"Do you mind my smoking?" Hewitt asked Sir James. "Perhaps you will take a cigar yourself—they are not so bad, I think. I will ask your man for a light."

Sir James felt for his own match-box, but Hewitt had gone, and was lighting his cigar with a match from a box handed him by the groom. A smart little terrier was trotting about by the coach-house, and Hewitt stooped to rub its head. Then he made some observation about the dog, which enlisted the groom's interest, and was soon absorbed in a chat with the man. Sir James, waiting a little way off, tapped the stones rather impatiently with his foot, and presently moved away.

For full a quarter of an hour Hewitt chatted with the groom, and, when at last he came away and overtook Sir James, that gentleman was about re-entering the house.

"I beg your pardon, Sir James," Hewitt said, "for leaving you in that unceremonious fashion to talk to your groom, but a dog, Sir James—a good dog—will draw me anywhere."

"Oh!" replied Sir James, shortly.

"There is one other thing," Hewitt went on, disregarding the other's curtness, "that I should like to know: There are two windows directly below that of the room occupied yesterday by Mrs. Cazenove—one on each floor. What rooms do they light?"

"That on the ground floor is the morning-room; the other is Mr. Lloyd's—my secretary. A sort of study or sitting-room."

"Now you will see at once, Sir James," Hewitt pursued, with an affable determination to win the baronet back to good-humor—"you will see at once that, if a ladder had been used in Mrs. Heath's case, anybody looking from either of these rooms would have seen it."

"Of course! The Scotland Yard man questioned everybody as to that, but nobody seemed to have been in either of the rooms when the thing occurred; at any rate, nobody saw anything."

"Still, I think I should like to look out of those windows myself; it will, at least, give me an idea of what *was* in view and what was not, if anybody had been there."

Sir James Norris led the way to the morning-room. As they reached the door a young lady, carrying a book and walking very languidly, came out. Hewitt stepped aside to let her pass, and afterward said interrogatively: "Miss Norris, your daughter, Sir James?"

"No, my niece. Do you want to ask her anything? Dora, my dear," Sir James added, following her in the corridor, "this is Mr. Hewitt, who is investigating these wretched robberies for me. I think he would like to hear if you remember anything happening at any of the three times."

The lady bowed slightly, and said in a plaintive drawl: "I, uncle? Really, I don't remember anything; nothing at all."

"You found Mrs. Armitage's door locked, I believe," asked Hewitt, "when you tried it, on the afternoon when she lost her brooch?"

"Oh, yes; I believe it was locked. Yes, it was."

"Had the key been left in?"

"The key? Oh, no! I think not; no."

"Do you remember anything out of the common happening—anything whatever, no matter how trivial—on the day Mrs. Heath lost her bracelet?"

"No, really, I don't. I can't remember at all."

"Nor yesterday?"

"No, nothing. I don't remember anything."

"Thank you," said Hewitt, hastily; "thank you. Now the morning-room, Sir James."

In the morning-room Hewitt stayed but a few seconds, doing little more than casually glance out of the windows. In the room above he took a little longer time. It was a comfortable room, but with rather effeminate indications about its contents. Little pieces of draped silk-work hung about the furniture, and Japanese silk fans decorated the mantel-piece. Near the window was a cage containing a gray parrot, and the writing-table was decorated with two vases of flowers.

"Lloyd makes himself pretty comfortable, eh?" Sir James observed. "But it isn't likely anybody would be here while he was out, at the time that bracelet went."

"No," replied Hewitt, meditatively. "No, I suppose not."

He stared thoughtfully out of the window, and then, still deep in thought, rattled at the wires of the cage with a quill toothpick and played a moment with the parrot. Then, looking up at the window again, he said: "That is Mr. Lloyd, isn't it, coming back in a fly?"

"Yes, I think so. Is there anything else you would care to see here?"

"No, thank you," Hewitt replied; "I don't think there is."

They went down to the smoking-room, and Sir James went away to speak to his secretary. When he returned, Hewitt said quietly: "I think, Sir James—I *think* that I shall be able to give you your thief presently."

"What! Have you a clue? Who do you think? I began to believe you were hopelessly stumped."

"Well, yes. I have rather a good clue, although I can't tell you much about it just yet. But it is so good a clue that I should like to know now whether you are determined to prosecute when you have the criminal?"

"Why, bless me, of course," Sir James replied, with surprise. "It doesn't rest with me, you know—the property belongs to my friends. And even if they were disposed to let the thing slide, I shouldn't allow it—I couldn't, after they had been robbed in my house."

"Of course, of course! Then, if I can, I should like to send a message to Twyford by somebody perfectly trustworthy—not a servant. Could anybody go?"

"Well, there's Lloyd, although he's only just back from his journey. But, if it's important, he'll go."

"It is important. The fact is we must have a policeman or two here this evening, and I'd like Mr. Lloyd to fetch them without telling anybody else."

Sir James rang, and, in response to his message, Mr. Lloyd appeared. While Sir James gave his secretary his instructions, Hewitt strolled to the door of the smoking-room, and intercepted the latter as he came out.

"I'm sorry to give you this trouble, Mr. Lloyd," he said, "but I must stay here myself for a little, and somebody who can be trusted must go. Will you just bring back a police-constable with you? or rather two—two would be better. That is all that is wanted. You won't let the servants know, will you? Of course there will be a female searcher at the Twyford police-station? Ah—of course. Well, you needn't bring her, you know. That sort of thing is done at the station." And, chatting thus confidentially, Martin Hewitt saw him off.

When Hewitt returned to the smoking-room, Sir James said, suddenly: "Why, bless my soul, Mr. Hewitt, we haven't fed you! I'm awfully sorry. We came in rather late for lunch, you know, and this business has bothered me so I clean forgot everything else. There's no dinner till seven, so you'd better let me give you something now. I'm really sorry. Come along."

"Thank you, Sir James," Hewitt replied; "I won't take much. A few biscuits, perhaps, or something of that sort. And, by the by, if you don't mind, I rather think I should like to take it alone. The fact is I want to go over this case thoroughly by myself. Can you put me in a room?"

"Any room you like. Where will you go? The dining-room's rather large, but there's my study, that's pretty snug, or—"

"Perhaps I can go into Mr. Lloyd's room for half an hour or so; I don't think he'll mind, and it's pretty comfortable."

"Certainly, if you'd like. I'll tell them to send you whatever they've got."

"Thank you very much. Perhaps they'll also send me a lump of sugar and a walnut; it's—it's a little fad of mine."

"A—what? A lump of sugar and a walnut?" Sir James stopped for a moment, with his hand on the bell-rope. "Oh, certainly, if you'd like it; certainly," he added, and stared after this detective with curious tastes as he left the room.

When the vehicle, bringing back the secretary and the policeman, drew up on the drive, Martin Hewitt left the room on the first floor and proceeded down-stairs. On the landing he met Sir James Norris and Mrs. Cazenove, who stared with astonishment on perceiving that the detective carried in his hand the parrot-cage.

"I think our business is about brought to a head now," Hewitt remarked, on the stairs. "Here are the police officers from Twyford." The men were standing in the hall with Mr. Lloyd, who, on catching sight of the cage in Hewitt's hand, paled suddenly.

"This is the person who will be charged, I think," Hewitt pursued, addressing the officers, and indicating Lloyd with his finger.

"What, Lloyd?" gasped Sir James, aghast. "No—not Lloyd—nonsense!"

"He doesn't seem to think it nonsense himself, does he?" Hewitt placidly observed. Lloyd had sunk on a chair, and, gray of face, was staring blindly at the man he had run against at the office door that morning. His lips moved in spasms, but there was no sound. The wilted flower fell from his button-hole to the floor, but he did not move.

"This is his accomplice," Hewitt went on, placing the parrot and cage on the hall table, "though I doubt whether there will be any use in charging *him*. Eh, Polly?"

The parrot put his head aside and chuckled. "Hullo, Polly!" it quietly gurgled. "Come along!"

Sir James Norris was hopelessly bewildered. "Lloyd—Lloyd," he said, under his breath. "Lloyd—and that!"

"This was his little messenger, his useful Mercury," Hewitt explained, tapping the cage complacently; "in fact, the actual lifter. Hold him up!"

The last remark referred to the wretched Lloyd, who had fallen forward with something between a sob and a loud sigh. The policemen took him by the arms and propped him in his chair.

"System?" said Hewitt, with a shrug of the shoulders, an hour or two after in Sir James' study. "I can't say I have a system. I call it nothing but common-sense and a sharp pair of eyes. Nobody using these could help taking the right road in this case. I began at the match, just as the Scotland Yard man did, but I had the advantage of taking a line through three cases. To begin with, it was plain that that match, being left there in daylight, in Mrs. Cazenove's room, could not have been used to light the table-top, in the full glare of the window; therefore it had been used for some other purpose—*what* purpose I could not, at the moment, guess. Habitual thieves, you know, often have curious superstitions, and some will never take anything without leaving something behind—a pebble or a piece of coal, or something like that—in the premises they have been robbing. It seemed at first extremely likely that this was a case of that kind. The match had clearly been *brought in*—because, when I asked for matches, there were none in the stand, not even an empty box, and the room had not been disturbed. Also the match probably had not been struck there, nothing having been heard, although, of course, a mistake in this matter was just possible. This match, then, it was fair to assume, had been lit somewhere else and blown out immediately—I remarked at the time that it was very little burned. Plainly it could not have been treated thus for nothing, and the only possible object would have been to prevent it igniting accidentally. Following on this, it became obvious that the match was used, for whatever purpose, not *as* a match, but merely as a convenient splinter of wood.

"So far so good. But on examining the match very closely I observed, as you can see for yourself, certain rather sharp indentations in the wood. They are very small, you see, and scarcely visible, except upon narrow inspection; but there they are, and their positions are regular. See, there are two on each side, each opposite the corresponding mark of the other pair. The match, in fact, would seem to have been gripped in some fairly sharp instrument, holding it at two points above and two below—an instrument, as it may at once strike you, not unlike the beak of a bird.

"Now here was an idea. What living creature but a bird could possibly have entered Mrs. Heath's window without a ladder—supposing no ladder to have been used—or could have got into Mrs. Armitage's window without lifting the sash higher than the eight or ten inches it was already open? Plainly, nothing. Further, it is significant that only *one* article was stolen at a time, although others were about. A human being could have carried any reasonable number, but a bird could only take one at a time. But why should a bird carry a match in its beak? Certainly it must have been trained to do that for a purpose, and a little consideration made that purpose pretty clear. A noisy, chattering bird would probably betray itself at once. Therefore it must be trained to keep quiet both while going for and coming away with its plunder. What readier or more probably effectual way than, while teaching it to carry without dropping, to teach it also to keep quiet while carrying? The one thing would practically cover the other.

"I thought at once, of course, of a jackdaw or a magpie—these birds' thievish reputations made the guess natural. But the marks on the match were much too wide apart to have been made by the beak of either. I conjectured, therefore, that it must be a raven. So that, when we arrived near the coach-house, I seized the opportunity of a little chat with your groom on the subject of dogs and pets in general, and ascertained that there was no tame raven in the place. I also, incidentally, by getting a light from the coach-house box of matches, ascertained that the match found was of the sort generally used about the establishment—the large, thick, red-topped English match. But I further found that Mr. Lloyd had a parrot which was a most intelligent pet, and had been trained into comparative quietness—for a parrot. Also, I learned that more than once the groom had met Mr. Lloyd carrying his parrot under his coat, it having, as its owner explained, learned the trick of opening its cage-door and escaping.

"I said nothing, of course, to you of all this, because I had as yet nothing but a train of argument and no results. I got to Lloyd's room as soon as possible. My chief object in going there was achieved when I played with the parrot, and induced it to bite a quill toothpick.

"When you left me in the smoking-room, I compared the quill and the match very carefully, and found that the marks corresponded exactly. After this I felt very little doubt indeed. The fact of Lloyd having met the ladies walking before dark on the day of the first robbery proved nothing, because, since it was clear that the match had *not* been used to procure a light, the robbery might as easily have taken place in daylight as not—must have so taken place, in fact, if my conjectures were right. That they were right I felt no doubt. There could be no other explanation.

"When Mrs. Heath left her window open and her door shut, anybody climbing upon the open sash of Lloyd's high window could have put the bird upon the sill above. The match placed in the bird's beak for the purpose I have indicated, and struck first, in case by accident it should ignite by rubbing against something and startle the bird—this match would, of course, be dropped just where the object to be removed was taken up; as you know, in every case the match was found almost upon the spot where the missing article had been left—scarcely a likely triple coincidence had the match been used by a human thief. This would have been done as soon after the ladies had left as possible, and there would then have been plenty of time for Lloyd to hurry out and meet them before dark—especially plenty of time to meet them *coming back*, as they must have been, since they were carrying their ferns. The match was an article well chosen for its purpose, as being a not altogether unlikely thing to find on a dressing-table, and, if noticed, likely to lead to the wrong conclusions adopted by the official detective.

"In Mrs. Armitage's case the taking of an inferior brooch and the leaving of a more valuable ring pointed clearly either to the operator being a fool or unable to distinguish values, and certainly, from other indications, the thief seemed no fool. The door was locked, and the gas-fitter, so to speak, on guard, and the window was only eight or ten inches open and propped with a brush. A human thief entering the window would have disturbed this arrangement, and would scarcely risk discovery by attempting to replace it, especially a thief in so great a hurry as to snatch the brooch up without unfastening the pin. The bird could pass through the opening as it was, and *would have* to tear the pin-cushion to pull the brooch off, probably holding the cushion down with its claw the while.

"Now in yesterday's case we had an alteration of conditions. The window was shut and fastened, but the door was open—but only left for a few minutes, during which time no sound was heard either of coming or going. Was it not possible, then, that the thief was *already* in the room, in hiding, while Mrs. Cazenove was there, and seized its first opportunity on her temporary absence? The room is full of draperies, hangings, and what not, allowing of plenty of concealment for a bird, and a bird could leave the place noiselessly and quickly. That the whole scheme was strange mattered not at all. Robberies presenting such unaccountable features must have been effected by strange means of one sort or another. There was no improbability. Consider how many hundreds of examples of infinitely higher degrees of bird-training are exhibited in the London streets every week for coppers.

"So that, on the whole, I felt pretty sure of my ground. But before taking any definite steps I resolved to see if Polly could not be persuaded to exhibit his accomplishments to an indulgent stranger. For that purpose I contrived to send Lloyd away again and have a quiet hour alone with his bird. A piece of sugar, as everybody knows, is a good parrot bribe; but a walnut, split in half, is a better—especially if the bird be used to it; so I got you to furnish me with both. Polly was shy at first, but I generally get along very well with pets, and a little perseverance soon led to a complete private performance for my benefit. Polly would take the match, mute as wax, jump on the table, pick up the brightest thing he could see, in a great hurry, leave the match behind, and scuttle away round the room; but at first wouldn't give up the plunder to *me*. It was enough. I also took the liberty, as you know, of a general look round, and discovered that little collection of Brummagem* rings and trinkets that you have just seen—used in Polly's education, no doubt. When we sent Lloyd away, it struck me that he might as well be usefully employed as not, so I got him to fetch the police, deluding him a little, I fear, by talking about the servants and a female searcher. There will be no trouble about evidence; he'll confess. Of that I'm sure. I know the sort of man. But I doubt if you'll get Mrs. Cazenove's brooch back. You see, he has been to London to-day, and by this time the swag is probably broken up."

Sir James listened to Hewitt's explanation with many expressions of assent and some of surprise. When it was over, he smoked a few whiffs and then said: "But Mrs. Armitage's brooch was pawned, and by a woman."

"Exactly. I expect our friend Lloyd was rather disgusted at his small luck—probably gave the brooch to some female connection in London, and she realized on it. Such persons don't always trouble to give a correct address."

The two smoked in silence for a few minutes, and then Hewitt continued: "I don't expect our friend has had an easy job altogether with that bird. His successes at most have only been three, and I suspect he had many failures and not a few anxious moments that we know nothing of. I should judge as much merely from what the groom told me of frequently meeting Lloyd with his parrot. But the plan was not a bad one—not at all. Even if the bird had been caught in the act, it would only have been 'That mischievous parrot!' you see. And his master would only have been looking for him."

---

* A nickname for the city of Birmingham, and people or things from there. The city's fame for manufacturing cheap metal buttons and trinkets led to the term's adoption for cheap, showy, or counterfeit items.

GENTLEMEN AND PLAYERS
AND THE RETURN MATCH

by E. W. Hornung

1899

Ernest William Hornung was Conan Doyle's brother-in-law. Like Doyle, he was a prolific author, and like Doyle, he is mainly remembered for one character—the cricketer
and gentleman thief A. J. Raffles—whose adventures have been adapted for stage
and screen down the years and continued in print by other writers. Raffles has been
portrayed by John Barrymore (1917), David Niven (1939), and Nigel Havers (2001),
among others; British author Graham Greene wrote a play in 1974 that speculated
about the nature of the relationship between Raffles and his nervous sidekick, Bunny
Manders; and he has appeared in a number of pastiches, sometimes as an opponent
of Holmes.

   As a gentleman thief who commits crimes for sport, Raffles is the direct ancestor of
later antiheroes such as Leslie Charteris's Simon "The Saint" Templar, *The Pink Panther*'s
Sir Charles "The Phantom" Lytton—also played by David Niven in the first movie, twenty-
four years after his turn as Raffles on the silver screen—Thomas Crown, and, most
recently, Neal Caffrey in the 2009–2014 TV series *White Collar*.

   Raffles has been extensively pastiched, crossing swords with Holmes on numerous
non-canonical occasions. As early as 1906, American humorist John Kendrick Bangs
wrote *R. Holmes & Co.*, whose hero, Raffles Holmes, is the offspring of the great detective with the cracksman's daughter.

"Gentlemen and Players"—presented here with its sequel "The Return Match"—goes to the heart of Raffles's character. Cricketers of the time were divided into two classes: the "Gentlemen" who played for sport, and the "Players," usually of a lower social status, who played for pay. Raffles regards crime in exactly the same light, and when he gets word that a gang of "pros" plans a jewel robbery, he decides to thwart their scheme and take the jewels for himself. "The Return Match" sees the leader of the gang, recently escaped from one of England's most secure prisons, returning to collect what he believes he is owed.

GENTLEMEN AND PLAYERS

O ld Raffles may or may not have been an exceptional criminal, but as a cricketer I dare swear he was unique. Himself a dangerous bat, a brilliant field, and perhaps the very finest slow bowler of his decade, he took incredibly little interest in the game at large. He never went up to Lord's* without his cricket-bag, or showed the slightest interest in the result of a match in which he was not himself engaged. Nor was this mere hateful egotism on his part. He professed to have lost all enthusiasm for the game, and to keep it up only from the very lowest motives.

"Cricket," said Raffles, "like everything else, is good enough sport until you discover a better. As a source of excitement it isn't in it with other things you wot† of, Bunny, and the involuntary comparison becomes a bore. What's the satisfaction of taking a man's wicket‡ when you want his spoons? Still, if you can bowl a bit your low cunning won't get rusty, and always looking for the weak spot's just the kind of mental exercise one wants. Yes, perhaps there's some affinity between the two things after all. But I'd chuck up cricket to-morrow, Bunny, if it wasn't for the glorious protection it affords a person of my proclivities."

"How so?" said I. "It brings you before the public, I should have thought, far more than is either safe or wise."

"My dear Bunny, that's exactly where you make a mistake. To follow Crime with reasonable impunity you simply *must* have a parallel, ostensible career—the

---

* Lord's cricket ground, the home of the famous Marylebone Cricket Club and the "Mecca of Cricket."

† Know.

‡ Taking a batsman out of the game.

more public the better. The principle is obvious. Mr. Peace,* of pious memory, disarmed suspicion by acquiring a local reputation for playing the fiddle and taming animals, and it's my profound conviction that Jack the Ripper was a really eminent public man, whose speeches were very likely reported alongside his atrocities. Fill the bill in some prominent part, and you'll never be suspected of doubling it with another of equal prominence. That's why I want you to cultivate journalism, my boy, and sign all you can. And it's the one and only reason why I don't burn my bats for firewood."

Nevertheless, when he did play there was no keener performer on the field, nor one more anxious to do well for his side. I remember how he went to the nets, before the first match of the season, with his pocket full of sovereigns, which he put on the stumps instead of bails. It was a sight to see the professionals bowling like demons for the hard cash, for whenever a stump was hit a pound was tossed to the bowler and another balanced in its stead, while one man took £3 with a ball that spreadeagled the wicket. Raffles's practice cost him either eight or nine sovereigns; but he had absolutely first-class bowling all the time; and he made fifty-seven runs next day.

It became my pleasure to accompany him to all his matches, to watch every ball he bowled, or played, or fielded, and to sit chatting with him in the pavilion when he was doing none of these three things. You might have seen us there, side by side, during the greater part of the Gentlemen's first innings against the Players[†] (who had lost the toss) on the second Monday in July. We were to be seen, but not heard, for Raffles had failed to score, and was uncommonly cross for a player who cared so little for the game. Merely taciturn with me, he was positively rude to more than one member who wanted to know how it had happened, or who ventured to commiserate him on his luck; there he sat, with a straw hat tilted over his nose and a cigarette stuck between lips that curled disagreeably at every advance. I was therefore much surprised when a young fellow of the exquisite type came and squeezed himself in between us, and met with a perfectly civil reception despite the liberty. I did not know the boy by sight, nor did Raffles introduce us; but their conversation proclaimed at once a slightness of acquaintanceship and a license on the lad's part which combined to puzzle me. Mystification reached

---

* Charles Peace, a notorious burglar and murderer, was hanged in 1879 after a criminal career of more than thirty years. He dressed well and played the violin well enough to perform at local concerts, diverting suspicion in a time when criminals were thought to be ill-kempt and aggressive members of the lower classes.

† An annual cricket match. The Gentlemen were upper-class and middle-class cricketers who played as a hobby; the Players were mostly working-class and were paid by their clubs or by match organizers.

its height when Raffles was informed that the other's father was anxious to meet him, and he instantly consented to gratify that whim.

"He's in the Ladies' Enclosure. Will you come round now?"

"With pleasure," says Raffles. "Keep a place for me, Bunny."

And they were gone.

"Young Crowley," said some voice further back. "Last year's Harrow* Eleven."

"I remember him. Worst man in the team."

"Keen cricketer, however. Stopped till he was twenty to get his colours.† Governor made him. Keen breed. Oh, pretty, sir! Very pretty!"

The game was boring me. I only came to see old Raffles perform. Soon I was looking wistfully for his return, and at length I saw him beckoning me from the palings to the right.

"Want to introduce you to old Amersteth," he whispered, when I joined him. "They've a cricket week next month, when this boy Crowley comes of age, and we've both got to go down and play."

"Both!" I echoed. "But I'm no cricketer!"

"Shut up," says Raffles. "Leave that to me. I've been lying for all I'm worth," he added sepulchrally as we reached the bottom of the steps. "I trust to you not to give the show away."

There was a gleam in his eye that I knew well enough elsewhere, but was unprepared for in those healthy, sane surroundings; and it was with very definite misgivings and surmises that I followed the Zingari‡ blazer through the vast flower-bed of hats and bonnets that bloomed beneath the ladies' awning.

Lord Amersteth was a fine-looking man with a short mustache and a double chin. He received me with much dry courtesy, through which, however, it was not difficult to read a less flattering tale. I was accepted as the inevitable appendage of the invaluable Raffles, with whom I felt deeply incensed as I made my bow.

"I have been bold enough," said Lord Amersteth, "to ask one of the Gentlemen of England to come down and play some rustic cricket for us next month. He is kind enough to say that he would have liked nothing better, but for this little

---

*   Harrow is a famous English public school, second only to Eton in prestige.

†   The British equivalent of a varsity letter; the school color is worn in or on scarves, ties, blazers, gowns, cuff-links, and other items of apparel. Best known are the "blues" awarded by Oxford and Cambridge Universities.

‡   I Zingari ("the Gypsies") is an amateur cricket club, named for its lack of a home ground. It was particularly formidable between 1849 and 1904.

fishing expedition of yours, Mr.—, Mr.—," and Lord Amersteth succeeded in remembering my name.

It was, of course, the first I had ever heard of that fishing expedition, but I made haste to say that it could easily, and should certainly, be put off. Raffles gleamed approval through his eyelashes. Lord Amersteth bowed and shrugged.

"You're very good, I'm sure," said he. "But I understand you're a cricketer yourself?"

"He was one at school," said Raffles, with infamous readiness.

"Not a real cricketer," I was stammering meanwhile.

"In the eleven?"* said Lord Amersteth.

"I'm afraid not," said I.

"But only just out of it," declared Raffles, to my horror.

"Well, well, we can't all play for the Gentlemen," said Lord Amersteth slyly. "My son Crowley only just scraped into the eleven at Harrow, and *he's* going to play. I may even come in myself at a pinch; so you won't be the only duffer, if you are one, and I shall be very glad if you will come down and help us too. You shall flog a stream† before breakfast and after dinner, if you like."

"I should be very proud," I was beginning, as the mere prelude to resolute excuses; but the eye of Raffles opened wide upon me; and I hesitated weakly, to be duly lost.

"Then that's settled," said Lord Amersteth, with the slightest suspicion of grimness. "It's to be a little week, you know, when my son comes of age. We play the Free Foresters, the Dorsetshire Gentlemen, and probably some local lot as well. But Mr. Raffles will tell you all about it, and Crowley shall write. Another wicket! By Jove, they're all out! Then I rely on you both." And, with a little nod, Lord Amersteth rose and sidled to the gangway.

Raffles rose also, but I caught the sleeve of his blazer.

"What are you thinking of?" I whispered savagely. "I was nowhere near the eleven. I'm no sort of cricketer. I shall have to get out of this!"

"Not you," he whispered back. "You needn't play, but come you must. If you wait for me after half-past six I'll tell you why."

But I could guess the reason; and I am ashamed to say that it revolted me much less than did the notion of making a public fool of myself on a cricket-field. My gorge rose at this as it no longer rose at crime, and it was in no tranquil

---

* On the team. A cricket team consists of eleven players.

† Meaning unknown. Possibly a reference to the fly fishing mentioned later.

humor that I strolled about the ground while Raffles disappeared in the pavilion. Nor was my annoyance lessened by a little meeting I witnessed between young Crowley and his father, who shrugged as he stopped and stooped to convey some information which made the young man look a little blank. It may have been pure self-consciousness on my part, but I could have sworn that the trouble was their inability to secure the great Raffles without his insignificant friend.

Then the bell rang, and I climbed to the top of the pavilion to watch Raffles bowl. No subtleties are lost up there; and if ever a bowler was full of them, it was A. J. Raffles on this day, as, indeed, all the cricket world remembers. One had not to be a cricketer oneself to appreciate his perfect command of pitch and break, his beautifully easy action, which never varied with the varying pace, his great ball on the leg-stump—his dropping head-ball—in a word, the infinite ingenuity of that versatile attack. It was no mere exhibition of athletic prowess, it was an intellectual treat, and one with a special significance in my eyes. I saw the "affinity between the two things," saw it in that afternoon's tireless warfare against the flower of professional cricket. It was not that Raffles took many wickets for few runs; he was too fine a bowler to mind being hit; and time was short, and the wicket good. What I admired, and what I remember, was the combination of resource and cunning, of patience and precision, of head-work and handiwork, which made every over an artistic whole. It was all so characteristic of that other Raffles whom I alone knew!

"I felt like bowling this afternoon," he told me later in the hansom. "With a pitch to help me, I'd have done something big; as it is, three for forty-one,* out of the four that fell, isn't so bad for a slow bowler on a plumb wicket against those fellows. But I felt venomous! Nothing riles me more than being asked about for my cricket as though I were a pro myself."

"Then why on earth go?"

"To punish them, and—because we shall be jolly hard up, Bunny, before the season's over!"

"Ah!" said I. "I thought it was that."

"Of course, it was! It seems they're going to have the very devil of a week of it—balls—dinner parties—swagger house party—general junketings—and obviously a houseful of diamonds as well. Diamonds galore! As a general rule nothing would induce me to abuse my position as a guest. I've never done it, Bunny. But in this case we're engaged like the waiters and the band, and by heaven we'll take our toll! Let's have a quiet dinner somewhere and talk it over."

---

* Three players out, for forty-one runs conceded.

"It seems rather a vulgar sort of theft," I could not help saying; and to this, my single protest, Raffles instantly assented.

"It is a vulgar sort," said he; "but I can't help that. We're getting vulgarly hard up again, and there's an end on't. Besides, these people deserve it, and can afford it. And don't you run away with the idea that all will be plain sailing; nothing will be easier than getting some stuff, and nothing harder than avoiding all suspicion, as, of course, we must. We may come away with no more than a good working plan of the premises. Who knows? In any case there's weeks of thinking in it for you and me."

But with those weeks I will not weary you further than by remarking that the "thinking," was done entirely by Raffles, who did not always trouble to communicate his thoughts to me. His reticence, however, was no longer an irritant. I began to accept it as a necessary convention of these little enterprises. And, after our last adventure of the kind, more especially after its denouement, my trust in Raffles was much too solid to be shaken by a want of trust in me, which I still believe to have been more the instinct of the criminal than the judgment of the man.

It was on Monday, the tenth of August, that we were due at Milchester Abbey, Dorset; and the beginning of the month found us cruising about that very county, with fly-rods actually in our hands. The idea was that we should acquire at once a local reputation as decent fishermen, and some knowledge of the countryside, with a view to further and more deliberate operations in the event of an unprofitable week. There was another idea which Raffles kept to himself until he had got me down there. Then one day he produced a cricket-ball in a meadow we were crossing, and threw me catches for an hour together. More hours he spent in bowling to me on the nearest green; and, if I was never a cricketer, at least I came nearer to being one, by the end of that week, than ever before or since.

Incident began early on the Monday. We had sallied forth from a desolate little junction within quite a few miles of Milchester, had been caught in a shower, had run for shelter to a wayside inn. A florid, overdressed man was drinking in the parlor, and I could have sworn it was at the sight of him that Raffles recoiled on the threshold, and afterwards insisted on returning to the station through the rain. He assured me, however, that the odor of stale ale had almost knocked him down. And I had to make what I could of his speculative, downcast eyes and knitted brows.

Milchester Abbey is a gray, quadrangular pile, deep-set in rich woody country, and twinkling with triple rows of quaint windows, every one of which seemed alight as we drove up just in time to dress for dinner. The carriage had whirled us under I know not how many triumphal arches in process of construction, and past the tents and flag-poles of a juicy-looking cricket-field, on which Raffles undertook to bowl up to his reputation. But the chief signs of festival were within, where we found an enormous house-party assembled, including more persons of pomp, majesty, and dominion than I had ever encountered in one room before. I confess I felt overpowered. Our errand and my own presences combined to rob me of an address upon which I have sometimes plumed myself; and I have a grim recollection of my nervous relief when dinner was at last announced. I little knew what an ordeal it was to prove.

I had taken in a much less formidable young lady than might have fallen to my lot. Indeed I began by blessing my good fortune in this respect. Miss Melhuish was merely the rector's daughter, and she had only been asked to make an even number. She informed me of both facts before the soup reached us, and her subsequent conversation was characterized by the same engaging candor. It exposed what was little short of a mania for imparting information. I had simply to listen, to nod, and to be thankful.

When I confessed to knowing very few of those present, even by sight, my entertaining companion proceeded to tell me who everybody was, beginning on my left and working conscientiously round to her right. This lasted quite a long time, and really interested me; but a great deal that followed did not, and, obviously to recapture my unworthy attention, Miss Melhuish suddenly asked me, in a sensational whisper, whether I could keep a secret.

I said I thought I might, whereupon another question followed, in still lower and more thrilling accents:

"Are you afraid of burglars?"

Burglars! I was roused at last. The word stabbed me. I repeated it in horrified query.

"So I've found something to interest you at last!" said Miss Melhuish, in naive triumph. "Yes—burglars! But don't speak so loud. It's supposed to be kept a great secret. I really oughtn't to tell you at all!"

"But what is there to tell?" I whispered with satisfactory impatience.

"You promise not to speak of it?"

"Of course!"

"Well, then, there are burglars in the neighborhood."

"Have they committed any robberies?"

"Not yet."

"Then how do you know?"

"They've been seen. In the district. Two well-known London thieves!"

Two! I looked at Raffles. I had done so often during the evening, envying him his high spirits, his iron nerve, his buoyant wit, his perfect ease and self-possession. But now I pitied him; through all my own terror and consternation, I pitied him as he sat eating and drinking, and laughing and talking, without a cloud of fear or of embarrassment on his handsome, taking,* daredevil face. I caught up my champagne and emptied the glass.

"Who has seen them?" I then asked calmly.

"A detective. They were traced down from town a few days ago. They are believed to have designs on the Abbey!"

"But why aren't they run in?"

"Exactly what I asked papa on the way here this evening; he says there is no warrant out against the men at present, and all that can be done is to watch their movements."

"Oh! so they are being watched?"

"Yes, by a detective who is down here on purpose. And I heard Lord Amersteth tell papa that they had been seen this afternoon at Warbeck Junction!"

The very place where Raffles and I had been caught in the rain! Our stampede from the inn was now explained; on the other hand, I was no longer to be taken by surprise by anything that my companion might have to tell me; and I succeeded in looking her in the face with a smile.

"This is really quite exciting, Miss Melhuish," said I. "May I ask how you come to know so much about it?"

"It's papa," was the confidential reply. "Lord Amersteth consulted him, and he consulted me. But for goodness' sake don't let it get about! I can't think WHAT tempted me to tell you!"

"You may trust me, Miss Melhuish. But—aren't you frightened?"

Miss Melhuish giggled.

"Not a bit! They won't come to the rectory. There's nothing for them there. But look round the table: look at the diamonds: look at old Lady Melrose's necklace alone!"

The Dowager Marchioness of Melrose was one of the few persons whom it had been unnecessary to point out to me. She sat on Lord Amersteth's right, flourishing her ear-trumpet, and drinking champagne with her usual notorious freedom, as dissipated and kindly a dame as the world has ever seen. It was a necklace of diamonds and sapphires that rose and fell about her ample neck.

---

* Not a term commonly used today, although one may still read of someone being "taken" with the face of another person.

"They say it's worth five thousand pounds at least,"* continued my companion. "Lady Margaret told me so this morning (that's Lady Margaret next your Mr. Raffles, you know); and the old dear WILL wear them every night. Think what a haul they would be! No; we don't feel in immediate danger at the rectory."

When the ladies rose, Miss Melhuish bound me to fresh vows of secrecy; and left me, I should think, with some remorse for her indiscretion, but more satisfaction at the importance which it had undoubtedly given her in my eyes. The opinion may smack of vanity, though, in reality, the very springs of conversation reside in that same human, universal itch to thrill the auditor. The peculiarity of Miss Melhuish was that she must be thrilling at all costs. And thrilling she had surely been.

I spare you my feelings of the next two hours. I tried hard to get a word with Raffles, but again and again I failed. In the dining-room he and Crowley lit their cigarettes with the same match, and had their heads together all the time. In the drawing-room I had the mortification of hearing him talk interminable nonsense into the ear-trumpet of Lady Melrose, whom he knew in town. Lastly, in the billiard-room, they had a great and lengthy pool, while I sat aloof and chafed more than ever in the company of a very serious Scotchman, who had arrived since dinner, and who would talk of nothing but the recent improvements in instantaneous photography. He had not come to play in the matches (he told me), but to obtain for Lord Amersteth such a series of cricket photographs as had never been taken before; whether as an amateur or a professional photographer I was unable to determine. I remember, however, seeking distraction in little bursts of resolute attention to the conversation of this bore. And so at last the long ordeal ended; glasses were emptied, men said good-night, and I followed Raffles to his room.

"It's all up!" I gasped, as he turned up the gas and I shut the door. "We're being watched. We've been followed down from town. There's a detective here on the spot!"

"How do YOU know?" asked Raffles, turning upon me quite sharply, but without the least dismay. And I told him how I knew.

"Of course," I added, "it was the fellow we saw in the inn this afternoon."

"The detective?" said Raffles. "Do you mean to say you don't know a detective when you see one, Bunny?"

"If that wasn't the fellow, which is?"

Raffles shook his head.

---

* The equivalent of £620,000 (about US $830,000) in 2018.

"To think that you've been talking to him for the last hour in the billiard-room and couldn't spot what he was!"

"The Scotch photographer—"

I paused aghast.

"Scotch he is," said Raffles, "and photographer he may be. He is also Inspector Mackenzie of Scotland Yard—the very man I sent the message to that night last April. And you couldn't spot who he was in a whole hour! O Bunny, Bunny, you were never built for crime!"

"But," said I, "if that was Mackenzie, who was the fellow you bolted from at Warbeck?"

"The man he's watching."

"But he's watching us!"

Raffles looked at me with a pitying eye, and shook his head again before handing me his open cigarette-case.

"I don't know whether smoking's forbidden in one's bedroom, but you'd better take one of these and stand tight, Bunny, because I'm going to say something offensive."

I helped myself with a laugh.

"Say what you like, my dear fellow, if it really isn't you and I that Mackenzie's after."

"Well, then, it isn't, and it couldn't be, and nobody but a born Bunny would suppose for a moment that it was! Do you seriously think he would sit there and knowingly watch his man playing pool under his nose? Well, he might; he's a cool hand, Mackenzie; but I'm not cool enough to win a pool under such conditions. At least I don't think I am; it would be interesting to see. The situation wasn't free from strain as it was, though I knew he wasn't thinking of us. Crowley told me all about it after dinner, you see, and then I'd seen one of the men for myself this afternoon. You thought it was a detective who made me turn tail at that inn. I really don't know why I didn't tell you at the time, but it was just the opposite. That loud, red-faced brute is one of the cleverest thieves in London, and I once had a drink with him and our mutual fence. I was an Eastender from tongue to toe at the moment, but you will understand that I don't run unnecessary risks of recognition by a brute like that."

"He's not alone, I hear."

"By no means; there's at least one other man with him; and it's suggested that there may be an accomplice here in the house."

"Did Lord Crowley tell you so?"

"Crowley and the champagne between them. In confidence, of course, just as your girl told you; but even in confidence he never let on about Mackenzie. He told me there was a detective in the background, but that was all. Putting him up as a guest is evidently their big secret, to be kept from the other guests because it might offend them, but more particularly from the servants whom he's here to watch. That's my reading of the situation, Bunny, and you will agree with me that it's infinitely more interesting than we could have imagined it would prove."

"But infinitely more difficult for us," said I, with a sigh of pusillanimous relief. "Our hands are tied for this week, at all events."

"Not necessarily, my dear Bunny, though I admit that the chances are against us. Yet I'm not so sure of that either. There are all sorts of possibilities in these three-cornered combinations. Set A to watch B, and he won't have an eye left for C. That's the obvious theory, but then Mackenzie's a very big A. I should be sorry to have any boodle* about me with that man in the house. Yet it would be great to nip in between A and B and score off them both at once! It would be worth a risk, Bunny, to do that; it would be worth risking something merely to take on old hands like B and his men at their own old game! Eh, Bunny? That would be something like a match. Gentlemen and Players at single wicket, by Jove!"

His eyes were brighter than I had known them for many a day. They shone with the perverted enthusiasm which was roused in him only by the contemplation of some new audacity. He kicked off his shoes and began pacing his room with noiseless rapidity; not since the night of the Old Bohemian dinner to Reuben Rosenthall had Raffles exhibited such excitement in my presence; and I was not sorry at the moment to be reminded of the fiasco to which that banquet had been the prelude.

"My dear A. J.," said I in his very own tone, "you're far too fond of the uphill game; you will eventually fall a victim to the sporting spirit and nothing else. Take a lesson from our last escape, and fly lower as you value our skins. Study the house as much as you like, but do—not—go and shove your head into Mackenzie's mouth!"

My wealth of metaphor brought him to a stand-still, with his cigarette between his fingers and a grin beneath his shining eyes.

"You're quite right, Bunny. I won't. I really won't. Yet—you saw old Lady Melrose's necklace? I've been wanting it for years! But I'm not going to play the

---

* Valuables.

fool; honor bright, I'm not; yet—by Jove!—to get to windward of the professors*
and Mackenzie too! It would be a great game, Bunny, it would be a great game!"

"Well, you mustn't play it this week."

"No, no, I won't. But I wonder how the professors think of going to work?
That's what one wants to know. I wonder if they've really got an accomplice in
the house? How I wish I knew their game! But it's all right, Bunny; don't you be
jealous; it shall be as you wish."

And with that assurance I went off to my own room, and so to bed with an
incredibly light heart. I had still enough of the honest man in me to welcome the
postponement of our actual felonies, to dread their performance, to deplore their
necessity: which is merely another way of stating the too patent fact that I was an
incomparably weaker man than Raffles, while every whit as wicked.

I had, however, one rather strong point. I possessed the gift of dismissing
unpleasant considerations, not intimately connected with the passing moment,
entirely from my mind. Through the exercise of this faculty I had lately been
living my frivolous life in town with as much ignoble enjoyment as I had derived
from it the year before; and similarly, here at Milchester, in the long-dreaded
cricket-week, I had after all a quite excellent time.

It is true that there were other factors in this pleasing disappointment. In the
first place, *mirabile dictu*,[†] there were one or two even greater duffers than I on
the Abbey cricket-field. Indeed, quite early in the week, when it was of most value
to me, I gained considerable *kudos* for a lucky catch; a ball, of which I had merely
heard the hum, stuck fast in my hand, which Lord Amersteth himself grasped in
public congratulation. This happy accident was not to be undone even by me, and,
as nothing succeeds like success, and the constant encouragement of the one great
cricketer on the field was in itself an immense stimulus, I actually made a run or
two in my very next innings. Miss Melhuish said pretty things to me that night at
the great ball in honor of Viscount Crowley's majority; she also told me that was the
night on which the robbers would assuredly make their raid, and was full of arch
tremors when we sat out in the garden, though the entire premises were illuminated
all night long. Meanwhile the quiet Scotchman took countless photographs by day,
which he developed by night in a dark room admirably situated in the servants'
part of the house; and it is my firm belief that only two of his fellow-guests knew
Mr. Clephane of Dundee for Inspector Mackenzie of Scotland Yard.

---

* Professional or master criminals.

† Latin: "wonderful to say."

The week was to end with a trumpery match on the Saturday, which two or three of us intended abandoning early in order to return to town that night. The match, however, was never played. In the small hours of the Saturday morning a tragedy took place at Milchester Abbey.

Let me tell of the thing as I saw and heard it. My room opened upon the central gallery, and was not even on the same floor as that on which Raffles—and I think all the other men—were quartered. I had been put, in fact, into the dressing-room of one of the grand suites, and my too near neighbors were old Lady Melrose and my host and hostess. Now, by the Friday evening the actual festivities were at an end, and, for the first time that week, I must have been sound asleep since midnight, when all at once I found myself sitting up breathless. A heavy thud had come against my door, and now I heard hard breathing and the dull stamp of muffled feet.

"I've got ye," muttered a voice. "It's no use struggling."

It was the Scotch detective, and a new fear turned me cold. There was no reply, but the hard breathing grew harder still, and the muffled feet beat the floor to a quicker measure. In sudden panic I sprang out of bed and flung open my door. A light burnt low on the landing, and by it I could see Mackenzie swaying and staggering in a silent tussle with some powerful adversary.

"Hold this man!" he cried, as I appeared. "Hold the rascal!"

But I stood like a fool until the pair of them backed into me, when, with a deep breath I flung myself on the fellow, whose face I had seen at last. He was one of the footmen who waited at table; and no sooner had I pinned him than the detective loosed his hold.

"Hang on to him," he cried. "There's more of 'em below."

And he went leaping down the stairs, as other doors opened and Lord Amersteth and his son appeared simultaneously in their pyjamas. At that my man ceased struggling; but I was still holding him when Crowley turned up the gas.

"What the devil's all this?" asked Lord Amersteth, blinking. "Who was that ran downstairs?"

"Mac—Clephane!" said I hastily.

"Aha!" said he, turning to the footman. "So you're the scoundrel, are you? Well done! Well done! Where was he caught?"

I had no idea.

"Here's Lady Melrose's door open," said Crowley. "Lady Melrose! Lady Melrose!"

"You forget she's deaf," said Lord Amersteth. "Ah! that'll be her maid."

An inner door had opened; next instant there was a little shriek, and a white figure gesticulated on the threshold.

"Ou donc est l'ecrin de Madame la Marquise? La fenetre est ouverte. Il a disparu!"*

"Window open and jewel-case gone, by Jove!" exclaimed Lord Amersteth.

"Mais comment est Madame la Marquise? Est elle bien?"

"Oui, milor. Elle dort."†

"Sleeps through it all," said my lord. "She's the only one, then!"

"What made Mackenzie—Clephane—bolt?" young Crowley asked me.

"Said there were more of them below."

"Why the devil couldn't you tell us so before?" he cried, and went leaping downstairs in his turn.

He was followed by nearly all the cricketers, who now burst upon the scene in a body, only to desert it for the chase. Raffles was one of them, and I would gladly have been another, had not the footman chosen this moment to hurl me from him, and to make a dash in the direction from which they had come. Lord Amersteth had him in an instant; but the fellow fought desperately, and it took the two of us to drag him downstairs, amid a terrified chorus from half-open doors. Eventually we handed him over to two other footmen who appeared with their nightshirts tucked into their trousers, and my host was good enough to compliment me as he led the way outside.

"I thought I heard a shot," he added. "Didn't you?"

"I thought I heard three."

And out we dashed into the darkness.

I remember how the gravel pricked my feet, how the wet grass numbed them as we made for the sound of voices on an outlying lawn. So dark was the night that we were in the cricketers' midst before we saw the shimmer of their pyjamas; and then Lord Amersteth almost trod on Mackenzie as he lay prostrate in the dew.

"Who's this?" he cried. "What on earth's happened?"

"It's Clephane," said a man who knelt over him. "He's got a bullet in him somewhere."

"Is he alive?"

"Barely."

"Good God! Where's Crowley?"

---

* French: "Where is the Marchioness's [i.e. Lady Melrose's] case? The window is open. It's gone!"

† "How is the Marchioness? Is she well?" "Yes, my lord. She is asleep."

"Here I am," called a breathless voice. "It's no good, you fellows. There's nothing to show which way they've gone. Here's Raffles; he's chucked it, too." And they ran up panting.

"Well, we've got one of them, at all events," muttered Lord Amersteth. "The next thing is to get this poor fellow indoors. Take his shoulders, somebody. Now his middle. Join hands under him. All together, now; that's the way. Poor fellow! Poor fellow! His name isn't Clephane at all. He's a Scotland Yard detective, down here for these very villains!"

Raffles was the first to express surprise; but he had also been the first to raise the wounded man. Nor had any of them a stronger or more tender hand in the slow procession to the house.

In a little we had the senseless man stretched on a sofa in the library. And there, with ice on his wound and brandy in his throat, his eyes opened and his lips moved.

Lord Amersteth bent down to catch the words.

"Yes, yes," said he; "we've got one of them safe and sound. The brute you collared upstairs." Lord Amersteth bent lower. "By Jove! Lowered the jewel-case out of the window, did he? And they've got clean away with it! Well, well! I only hope we'll be able to pull this good fellow through. He's off again."

An hour passed: the sun was rising.

It found a dozen young fellows on the settees in the billiard-room, drinking whiskey and soda-water in their overcoats and pyjamas, and still talking excitedly in one breath. A time-table was being passed from hand to hand: the doctor was still in the library. At last the door opened, and Lord Amersteth put in his head.

"It isn't hopeless," said he, "but it's bad enough. There'll be no cricket to-day."

Another hour, and most of us were on our way to catch the early train; between us we filled a compartment almost to suffocation. And still we talked all together of the night's event; and still I was a little hero in my way, for having kept my hold of the one ruffian who had been taken; and my gratification was subtle and intense. Raffles watched me under lowered lids. Not a word had we had together; not a word did we have until we had left the others at Paddington, and were skimming through the streets in a hansom with noiseless tires and a tinkling bell.

"Well, Bunny," said Raffles, "so the professors have it, eh?"

"Yes," said I. "And I'm jolly glad!"

"That poor Mackenzie has a ball in his chest?"

"That you and I have been on the decent side for once."

He shrugged his shoulders.

"You're hopeless, Bunny, quite hopeless! I take it you wouldn't have refused your share if the boodle had fallen to us? Yet you positively enjoy coming off second best—for the second time running! I confess, however, that the professors' methods were full of interest to me. I, for one, have probably gained as much in experience as I have lost in other things. That lowering the jewel-case out of the window was a very simple and effective expedient; two of them had been waiting below for it for hours."

"How do you know?" I asked.

"I saw them from my own window, which was just above the dear old lady's. I was fretting for that necklace in particular, when I went up to turn in for our last night—and I happened to look out of my window. In point of fact, I wanted to see whether the one below was open, and whether there was the slightest chance of working the oracle with my sheet for a rope. Of course I took the precaution of turning my light off first, and it was a lucky thing I did. I saw the pros right down below, and they never saw me. I saw a little tiny luminous disk just for an instant, and then again for an instant a few minutes later. Of course I knew what it was, for I have my own watch-dial daubed with luminous paint; it makes a lantern of sorts when you can get no better. But these fellows were not using theirs as a lantern. They were under the old lady's window. They were watching the time. The whole thing was arranged with their accomplice inside. Set a thief to catch a thief: in a minute I had guessed what the whole thing proved to be."

"And you did nothing!" I exclaimed.

"On the contrary, I went downstairs and straight into Lady Melrose's room—"

"You did?"

"Without a moment's hesitation. To save her jewels. And I was prepared to yell as much into her ear-trumpet for all the house to hear. But the dear lady is too deaf and too fond of her dinner to wake easily."

"Well?"

"She didn't stir."

"And yet you allowed the professors, as you call them, to take her jewels, case and all!"

"All but this," said Raffles, thrusting his fist into my lap. "I would have shown it you before, but really, old fellow, your face all day has been worth a fortune to the firm!"

And he opened his fist, to shut it next instant on the bunch of diamonds and of sapphires that I had last seen encircling the neck of Lady Melrose.

THE RETURN MATCH

I had turned into Piccadilly, one thick evening in the following November, when my guilty heart stood still at the sudden grip of a hand upon my arm. I thought—I was always thinking—that my inevitable hour was come at last. It was only Raffles, however, who stood smiling at me through the fog.

"Well met!" said he. "I've been looking for you at the club."

"I was just on my way there," I returned, with an attempt to hide my tremors. It was an ineffectual attempt, as I saw from his broader smile, and by the indulgent shake of his head.

"Come up to my place instead," said he. "I've something amusing to tell you."

I made excuses, for his tone foretold the kind of amusement, and it was a kind against which I had successfully set my face for months. I have stated before, however, and I can but reiterate, that to me, at all events, there was never anybody in the world so irresistible as Raffles when his mind was made up. That we had both been independent of crime since our little service to Sir Bernard Debenham—that there had been no occasion for that masterful mind to be made up in any such direction for many a day—was the undeniable basis of a longer spell of honesty than I had hitherto enjoyed during the term of our mutual intimacy. Be sure I would deny it if I could; the very thing I am to tell you would discredit such a boast. I made my excuses, as I have said.

But his arm slid through mine, with his little laugh of light-hearted mastery. And even while I argued we were on his staircase in the Albany.

His fire had fallen low. He poked and replenished it after lighting the gas. As for me, I stood by sullenly in my overcoat until he dragged it off my back.

"What a chap you are!" said Raffles, playfully. "One would really think I had proposed to crack another crib this blessed night! Well, it isn't that, Bunny; so get into that chair, and take one of these Sullivans and sit tight."

He held the match to my cigarette; he brought me a whiskey and soda. Then he went out into the lobby, and, just as I was beginning to feel happy, I heard a bolt shot home. It cost me an effort to remain in that chair; next moment he was straddling another and gloating over my discomfiture across his folded arms.

"You remember Milchester, Bunny, old boy?"

His tone was as bland as mine was grim when I answered that I did.

"We had a little match there that wasn't down on the card. Gentlemen and Players, if you recollect?"

"I don't forget it."

"Seeing that you never got an innings, so to speak, I thought you might. Well, the Gentlemen scored pretty freely, but the Players were all caught."

"Poor devils!"

"Don't be too sure. You remember the fellow we saw in the inn? The florid, over-dressed chap who I told you was one of the cleverest thieves in town?"

"I remember him. Crawshay his name turned out to be."

"Well, it was certainly the name he was convicted under, so Crawshay let it be. You needn't waste any pity on HIM, old chap; he escaped from Dartmoor* yesterday afternoon."

"Well done!"

Raffles smiled, but his eyebrows had gone up, and his shoulders followed suit.

"You are perfectly right; it was very well done indeed. I wonder you didn't see it in the paper. In a dense fog on the moor yesterday good old Crawshay made a bolt for it, and got away without a scratch under heavy fire. All honor to him, I agree; a fellow with that much grit deserves his liberty. But Crawshay has a good deal more. They hunted him all night long; couldn't find him for nuts; and that was all you missed in the morning papers."

He unfolded a *Pall Mall*,† which he had brought in with him.

"But listen to this; here's an account of the escape, with just the addition which puts the thing on a higher level. 'The fugitive has been traced to Totnes, where he appears to have committed a peculiarly daring outrage in the early hours of this morning. He is reported to have entered the lodgings of the Rev. A. H. Ellingworth, curate of the parish, who missed his clothes on rising at the usual hour; later in the morning those of the convict were discovered neatly folded at the bottom of a drawer. Meanwhile Crawshay had made good his second escape, though it is believed that so distinctive a guise will lead to his recapture during the day.' What do you think of that, Bunny?"

"He is certainly a sportsman," said I, reaching for the paper.

"He's more," said Raffles, "he's an artist, and I envy him. The curate, of all men! Beautiful—beautiful! But that's not all. I saw just now on the board at the club that there's been an outrage on the line near Dawlish. Parson found insensible in the six-foot way.‡ Our friend again! The telegram doesn't say so, but it's obvious; he's

---

*   A high-security prison in a remote area of south-western England, with a reputation for being escape-proof.

†   A London magazine of the time.

‡   The space between two adjacent tracks.

simply knocked some other fellow out, changed clothes again, and come on gayly to town. Isn't it great? I do believe it's the best thing of the kind that's ever been done!"

"But why should he come to town?"

In an instant the enthusiasm faded from Raffles's face; clearly I had reminded him of some prime anxiety, forgotten in his impersonal joy over the exploit of a fellow-criminal. He looked over his shoulder towards the lobby before replying.

"I believe," said he, "that the beggar's on MY tracks!"

And as he spoke he was himself again—quietly amused—cynically unperturbed—characteristically enjoying the situation and my surprise.

"But look here, what do you mean?" said I. "What does Crawshay know about you?"

"Not much; but he suspects."

"Why should he?"

"Because, in his way he's very nearly as good a man as I am; because, my dear Bunny, with eyes in his head and brains behind them, he couldn't help suspecting. He saw me once in town with old Baird. He must have seen me that day in the pub on the way to Milchester, as well as afterwards on the cricket-field. As a matter of fact, I know he did, for he wrote and told me so before his trial."

"He wrote to you! And you never told me!"

The old shrug answered the old grievance.

"What was the good, my dear fellow? It would only have worried you."

"Well, what did he say?"

"That he was sorry he had been run in before getting back to town, as he had proposed doing himself the honor of paying me a call; however, he trusted it was only a pleasure deferred, and he begged me not to go and get lagged* myself before he came out. Of course he knew the Melrose necklace was gone, though he hadn't got it; and he said that the man who could take that and leave the rest was a man after his own heart. And so on, with certain little proposals for the far future, which I fear may be the very near future indeed! I'm only surprised he hasn't turned up yet."

He looked again towards the lobby, which he had left in darkness, with the inner door shut as carefully as the outer one. I asked him what he meant to do.

"Let him knock—if he gets so far. The porter is to say I'm out of town; it will be true, too, in another hour or so."

"You're going off to-night?"

"By the 7.15 from Liverpool Street. I don't say much about my people, Bunny, but I have the best of sisters married to a country parson in the eastern counties.

---

* Imprisoned.

202 | E. W. HORNUNG

They always make me welcome, and let me read the lessons for the sake of getting me to church. I'm sorry you won't be there to hear me on Sunday, Bunny. I've figured out some of my best schemes in that parish, and I know of no better port in a storm. But I must pack. I thought I'd just let you know where I was going, and why, in case you cared to follow my example."

He flung the stump of his cigarette into the fire, stretched himself as he rose, and remained so long in the inelegant attitude that my eyes mounted from his body to his face; a second later they had followed his eyes across the room, and I also was on my legs. On the threshold of the folding doors that divided bedroom and sitting-room, a well-built man stood in ill-fitting broadcloth, and bowed to us until his bullet head presented an unbroken disk of short red hair.

Brief as was my survey of this astounding apparition, the interval was long enough for Raffles to recover his composure; his hands were in his pockets, and a smile upon his face, when my eyes flew back to him.

"Let me introduce you, Bunny," said he, "to our distinguished colleague, Mr. Reginald Crawshay."

The bullet head bobbed up, and there was a wrinkled brow above the coarse, shaven face, crimson also, I remember, from the grip of a collar several sizes too small. But I noted nothing consciously at the time. I had jumped to my own conclusion, and I turned on Raffles with an oath.

"It's a trick!" I cried. "It's another of your cursed tricks! You got him here, and then you got me. You want me to join you, I suppose? I'll see you damned!"

So cold was the stare which met this outburst that I became ashamed of my words while they were yet upon my lips.

"Really, Bunny!" said Raffles, and turned his shoulder with a shrug.

"Lord love yer," cried Crawshay, "'E knew nothin'. 'E didn't expect me; 'E's all right. And you're the cool canary, YOU are," he went on to Raffles. "I knoo you were, but, do me proud, you're one after my own kidney!" And he thrust out a shaggy hand.

"After that," said Raffles, taking it, "what am I to say? But you must have heard my opinion of you. I am proud to make your acquaintance. How the deuce did you get in?"

"Never you mind," said Crawshay, loosening his collar; "let's talk about how I'm to get out. Lord love yer, but that's better!"

There was a livid ring round his bull-neck, that he fingered tenderly. "Didn't know how much longer I might have to play the gent," he explained; "didn't know who you'd bring in."

"Drink whiskey and soda?" inquired Raffles, when the convict was in the chair from which I had leapt.

"No, I drink it neat," replied Crawshay, "but I talk business first. You don't get over me like that, Lor' love yer!"

"Well, then, what can I do for you?"

"You know without me tellin' you."

"Give it a name."

"Clean heels,* then; that's what I want to show, and I leaves the way to you. We're brothers in arms, though I ain't armed this time. It ain't necessary. You've too much sense. But brothers we are, and you'll see a brother through. Let's put it at that. You'll see me through in yer own way. I leaves it all to you."

His tone was rich with conciliation and concession; he bent over and tore a pair of button boots from his bare feet, which he stretched towards the fire, painfully uncurling his toes.

"I hope you take a larger size than them," said he. "I'd have had a see if you'd given me time. I wasn't in long afore you."

"And you won't tell me how you got in?"

"Wot's the use? I can't teach YOU nothin'. Besides, I want out. I want out of London, an' England, an' bloomin' Europe too. That's all I want of you, mister. I don't arst how YOU go on the job. You know where I come from, 'cos I 'eard you say; you know where I want to 'ead for, 'cos I've just told yer; the details I leaves entirely to you."

"Well," said Raffles, "we must see what can be done."

"We must," said Mr. Crawshay, and leaned back comfortably, and began twirling his stubby thumbs.

Raffles turned to me with a twinkle in his eye; but his forehead was scored with thought, and resolve mingled with resignation in the lines of his mouth. And he spoke exactly as though he and I were alone in the room.

"You seize the situation, Bunny? If our friend here is 'copped,' to speak his language, he means to 'blow the gaff' on you and me. He is considerate enough not to say so in so many words, but it's plain enough, and natural enough for that matter. I would do the same in his place. We had the bulge† before; he has it now; it's perfectly fair. We must take on this job; we aren't in a position to refuse it; even if we were, I should take it on! Our friend is a great sportsman; he has

---

* A clean escape. In the slang of the time, to "show a clean pair of heels" was to flee.

† Advantage.

got clear away from Dartmoor; it would be a thousand pities to let him go back. Nor shall he; not if I can think of a way of getting him abroad."

"Any way you like," murmured Crawshay, with his eyes shut. "I leaves the 'ole thing to you."

"But you'll have to wake up and tell us things."

"All right, mister; but I'm fair on the rocks for a sleep!"

And he stood up, blinking.

"Think you were traced to town?"

"Must have been."

"And here?"

"Not in this fog—not with any luck."

Raffles went into the bedroom, lit the gas there, and returned next minute.

"So you got in by the window?"

"That's about it."

"It was devilish smart of you to know which one; it beats me how you brought it off in daylight, fog or no fog! But let that pass. You don't think you were seen?"

"I don't think it, sir."

"Well, let's hope you are right. I shall reconnoitre and soon find out. And you'd better come too, Bunny, and have something to eat and talk it over."

As Raffles looked at me, I looked at Crawshay, anticipating trouble; and trouble brewed in his blank, fierce face, in the glitter of his startled eyes, in the sudden closing of his fists.

"And what's to become o' me?" he cried out with an oath.

"You wait here."

"No, you don't," he roared, and at a bound had his back to the door. "You don't get round me like that, you cuckoos!"

Raffles turned to me with a twitch of the shoulders. "That's the worst of these professors," said he; "they never will use their heads. They see the pegs, and they mean to hit 'em; but that's all they do see and mean, and they think we're the same. No wonder we licked them last time!"

"Don't talk through yer neck," snarled the convict. "Talk out straight, curse you!"

"Right," said Raffles. "I'll talk as straight as you like. You say you put yourself in my hands—you leave it all to me—yet you don't trust me an inch! I know what's to happen if I fail. I accept the risk. I take this thing on. Yet you think I'm going straight out to give you away and make you give me away in my turn. You're a fool, Mr. Crawshay, though you have broken Dartmoor; you've got to listen to a better man, and obey him. I see you through in my own way, or not at all. I come and go as I like, and with whom I like, without your interference; you stay here and lie just as low as you know how, be as wise as your word, and leave the whole thing to me. If you won't—if you're fool enough not to trust me—there's the door. Go out and say what you like, and be damned to you!"

Crawshay slapped his thigh.

"That's talking!" said he. "Lord love yer, I know where I am when you talk like that. I'll trust yer. I know a man when he gets his tongue between his teeth; you're all right. I don't say so much about this other gent, though I saw him along with you on the job that time in the provinces; but if he's a pal of yours, Mr. Raffles, he'll be all right too. I only hope you gents ain't too stony—"*

And he touched his pockets with a rueful face.

"I only went for their togs," said he. "You never struck two such stony-broke cusses in yer life!"

"That's all right," said Raffles. "We'll see you through properly. Leave it to us, and you sit tight."

"Rightum!" said Crawshay. "And I'll have a sleep time you're gone. But no sperrits—no, thank'ee—not yet! Once let me loose on the lush, and, Lord love yer, I'm a gone coon!"†

Raffles got his overcoat, a long, light driving-coat, I remember, and even as he put it on our fugitive was dozing in the chair; we left him murmuring incoherently, with the gas out, and his bare feet toasting.

"Not such a bad chap, that professor," said Raffles on the stairs; "a real genius in his way, too, though his methods are a little elementary for my taste. But technique isn't everything; to get out of Dartmoor and into the Albany in the same twenty-four hours is a whole that justifies its parts. Good Lord!"

We had passed a man in the foggy courtyard, and Raffles had nipped my arm.

"Who was it?"

"The last man we want to see! I hope to heaven he didn't hear me!"

"But who is he, Raffles?"

"Our old friend Mackenzie, from the Yard!"

I stood still with horror.

"Do you think he's on Crawshay's track?"

"I don't know. I'll find out."

---

* Broke.

† Past saving.

And before I could remonstrate he had wheeled me round; when I found my voice he merely laughed, and whispered that the bold course was the safe one every time.

"But it's madness—"

"Not it. Shut up! Is that *you*, Mr. Mackenzie?"

The detective turned about and scrutinized us keenly; and through the gaslit mist I noticed that his hair was grizzled at the temples, and his face still cadaverous, from the wound that had nearly been his death.

"Ye have the advantage o' me, sirs," said he.

"I hope you're fit again," said my companion. "My name is Raffles, and we met at Milchester last year."

"Is that a fact?" cried the Scotchman, with quite a start. "Yes, now I remember your face, and yours too, sir. Ay, yon was a bad business, but it ended vera well, an' that's the main thing."

His native caution had returned to him. Raffles pinched my arm.

"Yes, it ended splendidly, but for you," said he. "But what about this escape of the leader of the gang, that fellow Crawshay? What do you think of that, eh?"

"I havena the parteeculars," replied the Scot.

"Good!" cried Raffles. "I was only afraid you might be on his tracks once more!"

Mackenzie shook his head with a dry smile, and wished us good evening as an invisible window was thrown up, and a whistle blown softly through the fog.

"We must see this out," whispered Raffles. "Nothing more natural than a little curiosity on our part. After him, quick!"

And we followed the detective into another entrance on the same side as that from which we had emerged, the left-hand side on one's way to Piccadilly; quite openly we followed him, and at the foot of the stairs met one of the porters of the place. Raffles asked him what was wrong.

"Nothing, sir," said the fellow glibly.

"Rot!" said Raffles. "That was Mackenzie, the detective. I've just been speaking to him. What's he here for? Come on, my good fellow; we won't give you away, if you've instructions not to tell."

The man looked quaintly wistful, the temptation of an audience hot upon him; a door shut upstairs, and he fell.

"It's like this," he whispered. "This afternoon a gen'leman comes arfter rooms, and I sent him to the orfice; one of the clurks, 'e goes round with 'im an' shows 'im the empties, an' the gen'leman's partic'ly struck on the set the coppers is up in now. So he sends the clurk to fetch the manager, as there was one or two things he wished to speak about; an' when they come back, blowed if the gent isn't gone!

Beg yer pardon, sir, but he's clean disappeared off the face o' the premises!" And the porter looked at us with shining eyes.

"Well?" said Raffles.

"Well, sir, they looked about, an' looked about, an' at larst they give him up for a bad job; thought he'd changed his mind an' didn't want to tip the clurk; so they shut up the place an' come away. An' that's all till about 'alf an hour ago, when I takes the manager his extry-speshul *Star;* in about ten minutes he comes running out with a note, an' sends me with it to Scotland Yard in a hansom. An' that's all I know, sir—straight. The coppers is up there now, and the tec,[†] and the manager, and they think their gent is about the place somewhere still. Least, I reckon that's their idea; but who he is, or what they want him for, I dunno."

"Jolly interesting!" said Raffles. "I'm going up to inquire. Come on, Bunny; there should be some fun."

"Beg yer pardon, Mr. Raffles, but you won't say nothing about me?"

"Not I; you're a good fellow. I won't forget it if this leads to sport. Sport!" he whispered as we reached the landing. "It looks like precious poor sport for you and me, Bunny!"

"What are you going to do?"

"I don't know. There's no time to think. This, to start with."

And he thundered on the shut door; a policeman opened it. Raffles strode past him with the air of a chief commissioner, and I followed before the man had recovered from his astonishment. The bare boards rang under us; in the bedroom we found a knot of officers stooping over the window-ledge with a constable's lantern. Mackenzie was the first to stand upright, and he greeted us with a glare.

"May I ask what you gentlemen want?" said he.

"We want to lend a hand," said Raffles briskly. "We lent one once before, and it was my friend here who took over from you the fellow who split on all the rest, and held him tightly. Surely that entitles him, at all events, to see any fun that's going? As for myself, well, it's true I only helped to carry you to the house; but for old acquaintance I do hope, my dear Mr. Mackenzie, that you will permit us to share such sport as there may be. I myself can only stop a few minutes, in any case."

"Then ye'll not see much," growled the detective, "for he's not up here. Constable, go you and stand at the foot o' the stairs, and let no other body come up on any conseederation; these gentlemen may be able to help us after all."

<hr />

* An evening newspaper.

† Detective.

"That's kind of you, Mackenzie!" cried Raffles warmly. "But what is it all? I questioned a porter I met coming down, but could get nothing out of him, except that somebody had been to see these rooms and not since been seen himself."

"He's a man we want," said Mackenzie. "He's concealed himself somewhere about these premises, or I'm vera much mistaken. D'ye reside in the Albany, Mr. Raffles?"

"I do."

"Will your rooms be near these?"

"On the next staircase but one."

"Ye'll just have left them?"

"Just."

"Been in all the afternoon, likely?"

"Not all."

"Then I may have to search your rooms, sir. I am prepared to search every room in the Albany! Our man seems to have gone for the leads;* but unless he's left more marks outside than in, or we find him up there, I shall have the entire building to ransack."

"I will leave you my key," said Raffles at once. "I am dining out, but I'll leave it with the officer down below."

I caught my breath in mute amazement. What was the meaning of this insane promise? It was wilful, gratuitous, suicidal; it made me catch at his sleeve in open horror and disgust; but, with a word of thanks, Mackenzie had returned to his window-sill, and we sauntered unwatched through the folding-doors into the adjoining room. Here the window looked down into the courtyard; it was still open; and as we gazed out in apparent idleness, Raffles reassured me.

"It's all right, Bunny; you do what I tell you and leave the rest to me. It's a tight corner, but I don't despair. What you've got to do is to stick to these chaps, especially if they search my rooms; they mustn't poke about more than necessary, and they won't if you're there."

"But where will you be? You're never going to leave me to be landed alone?"

"If I do, it will be to turn up trumps at the right moment. Besides, there are such things as windows, and Crawshay's the man to take his risks. You must trust me, Bunny; you've known me long enough."

"Are you going now?"

---

* The roof.

"There's no time to lose. Stick to them, old chap; don't let them suspect YOU, whatever else you do." His hand lay an instant on my shoulder; then he left me at the window, and recrossed the room.

"I've got to go now," I heard him say; "but my friend will stay and see this through, and I'll leave the gas on in my rooms, and my key with the constable downstairs. Good luck, Mackenzie; only wish I could stay."

"Good-by, sir," came in a preoccupied voice, "and many thanks."

Mackenzie was still busy at his window, and I remained at mine, a prey to mingled fear and wrath, for all my knowledge of Raffles and of his infinite resource. By this time I felt that I knew more or less what he would do in any given emergency; at least I could conjecture a characteristic course of equal cunning and audacity. He would return to his rooms, put Crawshay on his guard, and—stow him away? No—there were such things as windows. Then why was Raffles going to desert us all? I thought of many things—lastly of a cab. These bedroom windows looked into a narrow side-street; they were not very high; from them a man might drop on to the roof of a cab—even as it passed—and be driven away even under the noses of the police! I pictured Raffles driving that cab, unrecognizable in the foggy night; the vision came to me as he passed under the window, tucking up the collar of his great driving-coat on the way to his rooms; it was still with me when he passed again on his way back, and stopped to hand the constable his key.

"We're on his track," said a voice behind me. "He's got up on the leads, sure enough, though how he managed it from yon window is a myst'ry to me. We're going to lock up here and try what like it is from the attics. So you'd better come with us if you've a mind."

The top floor at the Albany, as elsewhere, is devoted to the servants—a *congerie* of little kitchens and cubicles, used by many as lumber-rooms—by Raffles among the many. The annex in this case was, of course, empty as the rooms below; and that was lucky, for we filled it, what with the manager, who now joined us, and another tenant whom he brought with him to Mackenzie's undisguised annoyance.

"Better let in all Piccadilly at a crown a head," said he. "Here, my man, out you go on the roof to make one less, and have your truncheon handy."

We crowded to the little window, which Mackenzie took care to fill; and a minute yielded no sound but the crunch and slither of constabulary boots upon sooty slates. Then came a shout.

"What now?" cried Mackenzie.

"A rope," we heard, "hanging from the spout by a hook!"

"Sirs," purred Mackenzie, "yon's how he got up from below! He would do it with one o' they telescope sticks, an' I never thocht o't! How long a rope, my lad?"

"Quite short. I've got it."

"Did it hang over a window? Ask him that!" cried the manager. "He can see by leaning over the parapet."

The question was repeated by Mackenzie; a pause, then "Yes, it did."

"Ask him how many windows along!" shouted the manager in high excitement.

"Six, he says," said Mackenzie next minute; and he drew in his head and shoulders. "I should just like to see those rooms, six windows along."

"Mr. Raffles," announced the manager after a mental calculation.

"Is that a fact?" cried Mackenzie. "Then we shall have no difficulty at all. He's left me his key down below."

The words had a dry, speculative intonation, which even then I found time to dislike; it was as though the coincidence had already struck the Scotchman as something more.

"Where is Mr. Raffles?" asked the manager, as we all filed downstairs.

"He's gone out to his dinner," said Mackenzie.

"Are you sure?"

"I saw him go," said I. My heart was beating horribly. I would not trust myself to speak again. But I wormed my way to a front place in the little procession, and was, in fact, the second man to cross the threshold that had been the Rubicon of my life. As I did so I uttered a cry of pain, for Mackenzie had trod back heavily on my toes; in another second I saw the reason, and saw it with another and a louder cry.

A man was lying at full length before the fire on his back, with a little wound in the white forehead, and the blood draining into his eyes. And the man was Raffles himself!

"Suicide," said Mackenzie calmly. "No—here's the poker—looks more like murder." He went on his knees and shook his head quite cheerfully. "An' it's not even murder," said he, with a shade of disgust in his matter-of-fact voice; "yon's no more than a flesh-wound, and I have my doubts whether it felled him; but, sirs, he just stinks o' chloryform!"

He got up and fixed his keen gray eyes upon me; my own were full of tears, but they faced him unashamed.

"I understood ye to say ye saw him go out?" said he sternly.

"I saw that long driving-coat; of course, I thought he was inside it."

"And I could ha' sworn it was the same gent when he give me the key!"

It was the disconsolate voice of the constable in the background; on him turned Mackenzie, white to the lips.

"You'd think anything, some of you damned policemen," said he. "What's your number, you rotter? P 34? You'll be hearing more of this, Mr. P 34! If that gentleman was dead—instead of coming to himself while I'm talking—do you know what you'd be? Guilty of his manslaughter, you stuck pig in buttons! Do you know who you've let slip, butter-fingers? Crawshay—no less—him that broke Dartmoor yesterday. By the God that made ye, P 34, if I lose him I'll hound ye from the forrce!"*

Working face—shaking fist—a calm man on fire. It was a new side of Mackenzie, and one to mark and to digest. Next moment he had flounced from our midst.

ↄ

"Difficult thing to break your own head," said Raffles later; "infinitely easier to cut your own throat. Chloroform's another matter; when you've used it on others, you know the dose to a nicety. So you thought I was really gone? Poor old Bunny! But I hope Mackenzie saw your face?"

"He did," said I. I would not tell him all Mackenzie must have seen, however.

"That's all right. I wouldn't have had him miss it for worlds; and you mustn't think me a brute, old boy, for I fear that man, and, know, we sink or swim together."

"And now we sink or swim with Crawshay, too," said I dolefully.

"Not we!" said Raffles with conviction. "Old Crawshay's a true sportsman, and he'll do by us as we've done by him; besides, this makes us quits; and I don't think, Bunny, that we'll take on the professors again!"

---

* The spelling is Hornung's attempt to convey the hard "r" sound of Mackenzie's Scottish accent.

THE SECRET OF
THE FOX HUNTER

by William le Queux

1903

The Anglo-French writer William le Queux was a prolific writer of thrillers, mysteries, and spy fiction, including two invasion scare stories, *The Great War in England in 1897* (1894) and *The Invasion of 1910* (1906) which remain his best-known works. Both are marked by an almost hysterical xenophobia, and at the outbreak of World War I le Queux pestered the police constantly, seemingly convinced that German agents were out to get him for "rumbling their schemes" in his books. His appeals were not taken seriously, and he survived the war unscathed.

Le Queux was also a diplomat, a wireless pioneer, and a flying enthusiast at a time when both radio and aviation were in their infancies.

Duckworth Drew of the Foreign Office was created in 1903, and it has been claimed that his adventures influenced a young Ian Fleming, who would go on to create James Bond, the most famous fictional spy in history. Like the early Bond, Drew made occasional use of gadgets—drugged cigars, poisoned pins, and other devices are found in his adventures—and he reports to the Marquis of Macclesfield, to whom he sometimes refers by the initials "M.M." It has also been observed that the author's last name is pronounced "Q."

Fourteen of Drew's adventures were collected in the resoundingly-titled *Secrets of the Foreign Office: Describing the Doings of Duckworth Drew, of the Secret Service*

(1903), but le Queux seems to have lost interest in him after that. Perhaps he suffered from too many ideas: at that time it was not unusual for him to publish six or seven novels in a year.

Though le Queux has been credited with inventing spy fiction, Drew's adventures also owe something to the detective genre, whose conventions were well established by now. "The Secret of the Fox Hunter" revolves around the hunt for a stolen treaty with vast geopolitical ramifications, but it starts—like so many detective stories, from Holmes to Agatha Christie—with a seemingly inexplicable murder at an English country house.

It happened three winters ago. Having just returned from Stuttgart, where I had spent some weeks at the Marquardt in the guise I so often assumed, that of Monsieur Gustav Dreux, commercial traveller, of Paris, and where I had been engaged in watching the movements of two persons staying in the hotel, a man and a woman, I was glad to be back again in Bloomsbury to enjoy the ease of my armchair and pipe.

I was much gratified that I had concluded a very difficult piece of espionage, and having obtained the information I sought, had been able to place certain facts before my Chief, the Marquess of Macclesfield, which had very materially strengthened his hands in some very delicate diplomatic negotiations with Germany. Perhaps the most exacting position in the whole of British diplomacy is the post of Ambassador at Berlin, for the Germans are at once our foes, as well as our friends, and are at this moment only too ready to pick a quarrel with us from motives of jealousy which may have serious results.

The war cloud was still hovering over Europe; hence a swarm of spies, male and female, were plotting, scheming, and working in secret in our very midst. The reader would be amazed if he could but glance at a certain red-bound book, kept under lock and key at the Foreign Office, in which are registered the names, personal descriptions and other facts concerning all the known foreign spies living in London and in other towns in England.

But active as are the agents of our enemies, so also are we active in the opposition camp. Our Empire has such tremendous responsibilities that we cannot now depend upon mere birth, wealth and honest dealing, but must call in shrewdness, tact, subterfuge and the employment of secret agents in order to combat the plots of those ever seeking to accomplish England's overthrow.

Careful student of international affairs that I was, I knew that trouble was brewing in China. Certain confidential despatches from our Minister in Pekin* had been shown to me by the Marquess, who, on occasion, flattered me by placing implicit trust in me, and from them I gathered that Russia was at work in secret to undermine our influence in the Far East.

I knew that the grave, kindly old statesman was greatly perturbed by the grim shadows that were slowly rising, but when we consulted on the day after my return from Stuttgart, his lordship was of opinion that at present I had not sufficient ground upon which to institute inquiries.

"For the present, Drew," he said, "we must watch and wait. There is war in the air—first at Pekin, and then in Europe. But we must prevent it at all costs. Huntley leaves for Pekin tonight with despatches in which I have fully explained the line which Sir Henry is to follow. Hold yourself in readiness, for you may have to return to Germany or Russia tomorrow. We cannot afford to remain long in the dark. We must crush any alliance between Petersburg and Berlin."

"A telegram to my rooms will bring me to your lordship at any moment," was my answer.

"Ready to go anywhere—eh, Drew?" he smiled; and then, after a further chat, I left Downing Street and returned to Bloomsbury.

Knowing that for at least a week or two I should be free, I left my address with Boyd, and went down to Cotterstock, in Northamptonshire, to stay with my old friend of college days, George Hamilton, who rented a hunting-box† and rode with the Fitzwilliam Pack.

I had had a long-standing engagement with him to go down and get a few runs with the hounds, but my constant absence abroad had always prevented it until then. Of course none of my friends knew my real position at the Foreign Office. I was believed to be an attaché.

Personally, I am extremely fond of riding to hounds, therefore, when that night I sat at dinner with George, his wife, and the latter's cousin, Beatrice Graham, I was full of expectation of some good runs. An English country house, with its old oak, old silver and air of solidity, is always delightful to me after the flimsy gimcracks of Continental life. The evening proved a very pleasant one. Never having met Beatrice Graham before, I was much attracted by her striking beauty. She was tall and dark, about twenty-two, with a remarkable figure which was shown to advantage by

---

* Beijing.

† Hunting lodge.

her dinner-gown of turquoise blue. So well did she talk, so splendidly did she sing Dupont's "Jeune Fille", and so enthusiastic was she regarding hunting, that, before I had been an hour with her, I found myself thoroughly entranced.

The meet, three days afterwards, was at Wansford, that old-time hunting centre by the Nene, about six miles distant, and as I rode at her side along the road through historic Fotheringhay and Nassington, I noticed what a splendid horsewoman she was. Her dark hair was coiled tightly behind, and her bowler hat suited her face admirably while her habit fitted as though it had been moulded to her figure. In her mare's tail was a tiny piece of scarlet silk to warn others that she was a kicker.

At Wansford, opposite the old Haycock, once a hunting inn in the old coaching days, but now Lord Chesham's hunting-box, the gathering was a large one. From the great rambling old house servants carried glasses of sloe gin to all who cared to partake of his lordship's hospitality, while every moment the meet grew larger and the crowd of horses and vehicles more congested.

George had crossed to chat with the Master, Mr. George Fitzwilliam, who had just driven up and was still in his overcoat, therefore I found myself alone with my handsome companion, who appeared to be most popular everywhere. Dozens of men and women rode up to her and exchanged greetings, the men more especially, until at last Barnard, the huntsman, drew his hounds together, the word was given, and they went leisurely up the hill to draw the first cover.

The morning was one of those damp cold ones of mid-February; the frost had given and everyone expected a good run, for the scent would be excellent. Riding side by side with my fair companion, we chatted and laughed as we went along, until, on reaching the cover, we drew up with the others and halted while hounds went in.

The first cover was, however, drawn blank, but from the second a fox went away straight for Elton, and soon the hounds were in full cry after him and we followed at a gallop. After a couple of miles more than half the field was left behind, still we kept on, until of a sudden, and without effort, my companion took a high hedge and was cutting across the pastures ere I knew that she had left the road. That she was a straight rider I at once saw, and I must confess that I preferred the gate to the hedge and ditch which she had taken so easily.

Half an hour later the kill took place near Haddon Hall, and of the half dozen in at the death Beatrice Graham was one.

When I rode up, five minutes afterwards, she smiled at me. Her face was a trifle flushed by hard riding, yet her hair was in no way awry, and she declared that she had thoroughly enjoyed that tearing gallop.

Just, however, as we sat watching Barnard cut off the brush,* a tall, rather good-looking man rode up, having apparently been left just as I had. As he approached I noticed that he gave my pretty friend a strange look, almost as of warning, while she on her part, refrained from acknowledging him. It was as though he had made her some secret sign which she had understood.

But there was a further fact that puzzled me greatly. I had recognized in that well-turned-out hunting man someone whom I had had distinct occasion to recollect. At first I failed to recall the man's identity, but when I did, a few moments later, I sat regarding his retreating figure like one in a dream. The horseman who rode with such military bearing was none other than the renowned spy, one of the cleverest secret agents in the world, Otto Krempelstein, Chief of the German Secret Service.

That my charming little friend knew him was apparent. The slightest quiver in his eyelids and the almost imperceptible curl of his lip had not passed me unnoticed. There was some secret between them, of what nature I, of course, knew not. But all through that day my eyes were ever open to re-discover the man whose ingenuity and cunning had so often been in competition with my own. Twice I saw him again, once riding with a big, dark-haired man in pink,† on a splendid bay and followed by a groom with a second horse, and on the second occasion, at the edge of Stockhill Wood while we were waiting together he galloped past us, but without the slightest look of recognition.

"I wonder who that man is?" I remarked casually, as soon as he was out of hearing.

"I don't know," was her prompt reply. "He's often out with the hounds—a foreigner, I believe. Probably he's one of those who come to England for the hunting season. Since the late Empress of Austria came here to hunt, the Fitzwilliam has always been a favourite pack with the foreigners."

I saw that she did not intend to admit that she had any knowledge of him. Like all women, she was a clever diplomatist. But he had made a sign to her—a sign of secrecy.

Did Krempelstein recognize me, I wondered? I could not think so, because we had never met face to face. He had once been pointed out to me in the Wilhelmstrasse in Berlin by one of our secret agents who knew him, and his features had ever since been graven on my memory.

---

* The fox's tail, traditionally kept as a trophy.

† Although red in color, traditional fox-hunting jackets are known as "pinks."

That night, when I sat alone with my friend George, I learned from him that Mr. Graham, his wife's uncle, had lived a long time on the Continent as manager to a large commercial firm, and that Beatrice had been born in France and had lived there a good many years. I made inquiries regarding the foreigners who were hunting that season with the Fitzwilliam, but he, with an Englishman's prejudice, declared that he knew none of them, and didn't want to know them.

The days passed and we went to several meets together—at Apethorpe, at Castor Hanglands, at Laxton Park and other places, but I saw no more of Krempelstein. His distinguished-looking friend, however, I met on several occasions, and discovered that his name was Baron Stern, a wealthy Viennese, who had taken a hunting-box near Stoke Doyle, and had as friend a young man named Percival, who was frequently out with the hounds.

But the discovery there of Krempelstein had thoroughly aroused my curiosity. He had been there for some distinct purpose, without a doubt. Therefore I made inquiry of Kersch, one of our secret agents in Berlin, a man employed in the Ministry of Foreign Affairs, and from him received word that Krempelstein was back in Berlin, and further warning me that something unusual was on foot in England. This aroused me at once to activity. I knew that Krempelstein and his agents were ever endeavouring to obtain the secrets of our guns, our ships, and our diplomacy with other nations, and I therefore determined that on this occasion he should not succeed. However much I admired Beatrice Graham, I now knew that she had lied to me, and that she was in all probability his associate. So I watched her carefully, and when she went out for a stroll or a ride, as she often did, I followed her.

How far I was justified in this action does not concern me. I had quite unexpectedly alighted upon certain suspicious facts, and was determined to elucidate them. The only stranger she met was Percival. Late one afternoon, just as dusk was deepening into night, she pulled up her mare beneath the bare black trees while crossing Burghley Park, and after a few minutes was joined by the young foreigner, who, having greeted her, chatted for a long time in a low, earnest tone, as though giving her directions. She seemed to remonstrate with him, but at the place I was concealed I was unable to distinguish what was said. I saw him, however, hand her something, and then, raising his hat, he turned his horse and galloped away down the avenue in the opposite direction.

I did not meet her again until I sat beside her at the dinner-table that night, and then I noticed how pale and anxious she was, entirely changed from her usual sweet, light-hearted self.

She told me that she had ridden into Stamford for exercise, but told me nothing of the clandestine meeting. How I longed to know what the young foreigner had given her. Whatever it was, she kept it a close secret to herself.

More than once I felt impelled to go to her room in her absence and search her cupboards, drawers and travelling trunks. My attitude towards her was that of a man fallen entirely in love, for I had discovered that she was easily flattered by a little attention.

I was searching for some excuse to know Baron Stern, but often for a week he never went to the meets. It was as though he purposely avoided me. He was still at Weldon Lodge, near Stoke Doyle, for George told me that he had met him in Oundle only two days before.

Three whole weeks went by, and I remained just as puzzled as ever. Beatrice Graham was, after all, a most delightful companion, and although she was to me a mystery, yet we had become excellent friends.

One afternoon, just as I entered the drawing-room where she stood alone, she hurriedly tore up a note, and threw the pieces on the great log fire. I noticed one tiny piece about an inch square remained unconsumed, and managed, half an hour later, to get possession of it.

The writing upon it was, I found, in German, four words in all, which, without context, conveyed to me no meaning.

On the following night Mrs. Hamilton and Beatrice remained with us in the smoking-room till nearly eleven o'clock, and at midnight I bade my host good night, and ascended the stairs to retire. I had been in my room about half an hour when I heard stealthy footsteps. In an instant the truth flashed upon me. It was Beatrice on her way downstairs.

Quickly I slipped on some things and noiselessly followed my pretty fellow-guest through the drawing-room out across the lawn and into the lane beyond. White mists had risen from the river, and the low roaring of the weir prevented her hearing my footsteps behind her. Fearing lest I should lose her I kept close behind, following her across several grass fields until she came to Southwick Wood, a dark, deserted spot, away from road or habitation.

Her intention was evidently to meet someone, so when, presently, she halted beneath a clump of high black firs, I also took shelter a short distance away.

She sat on the fallen trunk of a tree and waited in patience. Time went on, and so cold was it that I became chilled to the bones. I longed for a pipe, but feared that the smell of tobacco or the light might attract her. Therefore I was compelled to crouch and await the clandestine meeting.

She remained very quiet. Not a dead leaf was stirred; not a sound came from her direction. I wondered why she waited in such complete silence.

Nearly two hours passed, when, at last, cramped and half frozen, I raised myself in order to peer into the darkness in her direction.

At first I could see no one, but, on straining my eyes, I saw, to my dismay, that she had fallen forward from the tree trunk, and was lying motionless in a heap upon the ground.

I called to her, but received no reply. Then rising, I walked to the spot, and in dismay threw myself on my knees and tried to raise her. My hand touched her white cheek. It was as cold as stone.

Next instant I undid her fur cape and bodice, and placed my hand upon her heart. There was no movement.

Beatrice Graham was dead.

The shock of the discovery held me spellbound. But when, a few moments later, I aroused myself to action, a difficult problem presented itself. Should I creep back to my room and say nothing, or should I raise the alarm, and admit that I had been watching her? My first care was to search the unfortunate girl's pocket, but I found nothing save a handkerchief and purse.

Then I walked back, and, regardless of the consequences, gave the alarm.

It is unnecessary here to describe the sensation caused by the discovery, or of how we carried the body back to the house. Suffice it to say that we called the doctor, who could find no mark of violence, or anything to account for death.

And yet she had expired suddenly, without a cry.

One feature, however, puzzled the doctor—namely, that her left hand and arm were much swollen, and had turned almost black, while the spine was curved—a fact which aroused a suspicion of some poison akin to strychnia.*

From the very first, I held a theory that she had been secretly poisoned, but with what motive I could not imagine.

A post-mortem examination was made by three doctors on the following day, but, beyond confirming the theory I held, they discovered nothing.

On the day following, a few hours before the inquest, I was recalled to the Foreign Office by telegraph, and that same afternoon sat with the Marquess of Macclesfield in his private room receiving his instructions.

An urgent despatch from Lord Rockingham, our Ambassador at Petersburg, made it plain that an alliance had been proposed by Russia to Germany, the effect

---

* A solution of strychnine.

of which would be to break British power in the Far East. His Excellency knew that the terms of the secret agreement had been settled, and all that remained was its signature. Indeed, it would have already been signed save for opposition in some quarters unknown, and while that opposition existed I might gain time to ascertain the exact terms of the proposed alliance—no light task in Russia, be it said, for police spies exist there in thousands, and my disguise had always to be very carefully thought out whenever I passed the frontier at Wirballen.*

The Marquess urged upon me to put all our secret machinery in motion in order to discover the terms of the proposed agreement, and more particularly as regards the extension of Russian influence in Manchuria.

"I know well the enormous difficulties of the inquiry," his lordship said; "but recollect, Drew, that in this matter you may be the means of saving the situation in the Far East. If we gain knowledge of the truth, we may be able to act promptly and effectively. If not—well—" and the grey-headed statesman shrugged his shoulders expressively without concluding the sentence.

Full of regret that I was unable to remain at Cotterstock and sift the mystery surrounding Beatrice Graham's death, I left London that night for Berlin, where, on the following evening, I called upon our secret agent, Kersch, who lived in a small but comfortable house at Teltow, one of the suburbs of the German capital. He occupied a responsible position in the German Foreign Office, but, having expensive tastes and a penchant for cards, was not averse to receiving British gold in exchange for the confidential information with which he furnished us from time to time. I sat with him, discussing the situation for a long time. It was true, he said, that a draft agreement had been prepared and placed before the Tzar and the Kaiser, but it had not yet been signed. He knew nothing of the clauses, however, as they had been prepared in secret by the Minister's own hand, neither could he suggest any means of obtaining knowledge of them.

My impulse was to go on next day to Petersburg. Yet somehow I felt that I might be more successful in Germany than in Russia, so resolved to continue my inquiries.

"By the way," the German said, "you wrote me about Krempelstein. He has been absent a great deal lately, but I had no idea he had been to England. Can he be interested in the same matter on which you are now engaged?"

"Is he now in Berlin?" I inquired eagerly.

"I met him at Boxhagen three days ago. He seems extremely active just now."

---

* German name of the Lithuanian border town Virbalis.

"Three days ago!" I echoed. "You are quite certain of the day?" I asked him this because, if his statement were true, it was proved beyond doubt that the German spy had no hand in the unfortunate girl's death.

"I am quite certain," was his reply. "I saw him entering the station on Monday morning."

At eleven o'clock that same night, I called at the British Embassy and sat for a long time with the Ambassador in his private room. His Excellency told me all he knew regarding the international complication which the Marquess, sitting in Downing Street, had foreseen weeks ago, but could make no suggestion as to my course of action. The war clouds had gathered undoubtedly, and the signing of the agreement between our enemies would cause it at once to burst over Europe. The crisis was one of the most serious in English history.

One fact puzzled us both, just as it puzzled our Chief at home—namely, if the agreement had been seen and approved by both Emperors,* why was it not signed? Whatever hitch had occurred, it was more potent than the will of the two most powerful monarchs in Europe.

On my return to the hotel I scribbled a hasty note and sent it by messenger to the house of the Imperial Chancellor's son in Charlottenburg. It was addressed to Miss Maud Baines, the English governess of the Count's children, who, I may as well admit, was in our employ. She was a young, ingenuous† and fascinating little woman. She had, at my direction, acted as governess in many of the great families in France, Russia and Germany, and was now in the employ of the Chancellor's son, in order to have opportunity of keeping a watchful eye on the great statesman himself.

She kept the appointment next morning at an obscure cafe near the Behrenstrasse. She was a neatly dressed, rather petite person, with a face that entirely concealed her keen intelligence and marvellous cunning.

As she sat at the little table with me, I told her in low tones of the object of my visit to Berlin, and sought her aid.

"A serious complication has arisen. I was about to report to you through the Embassy," was her answer. "Last night the Chancellor dined with us, and I overheard him discussing the affair with his son as they sat alone smoking after the ladies had left. I listened at the door and heard the Chancellor distinctly say that the draft treaty had been stolen."

---

*   i.e. The German Kaiser and the Russian Czar.

†   This seems like a misprint for "ingenious," but has not been changed.

"Stolen!" I gasped. "By whom?"

"Ah! that's evidently the mystery—a mystery for us to fathom. But the fact that somebody else is in possession of the intentions of Germany and Russia against England, believed to be a secret, is no doubt the reason why the agreement has not been signed."

"Because it is no longer secret!" I suggested. "Are you quite certain you've made no mistake?"

"Quite," was her prompt answer. "You can surely trust me after the intricate little affairs which I have assisted you in unravelling? When may I return to Gloucester to see my friends?"

"Soon, Miss Baines—as soon as this affair is cleared up. But tell me, does the Chancellor betray any fear of awkward complications when the secret of the proposed plot against England is exposed?"

"Yes. The Prince told his son in confidence that his only fear was of England's retaliation. He explained that, as far as was known, the secret document, after being put before the Tzar and approved, mysteriously disappeared.

Every inquiry was being made by the confidential agents of Russia and Germany, and further, he added, that even his trusted Krempelstein was utterly nonplussed."

Mention of Krempelstein brought back to me the recollection of the tragedy in rural England.

"You've done us a great service, Miss Baines," I said. "This information is of highest importance. I shall telegraph in cipher at once to Lord Macclesfield. Do you, by any chance, happen to know a young lady named Graham?" I inquired, recollecting that the deceased woman had lived in Germany for several years.

She responded in the negative, whereupon I drew from my pocket a snap-shot photograph, which I had taken of one of the meets of hounds at Wansford, and handing it to her inquired if she recognized any of the persons in it.

Having carefully examined it, she pointed to Baron Stern, whom I had taken in the act of lighting a cigarette, and exclaimed—

"Why! that's Colonel Davidoff, who was secretary to Prince Obolenski when I was in his service. Do you know him?"

"No," I answered. "But he has been hunting in England as Baron Stern, of Vienna. This man is his friend," I added, indicating Percival.

"And that's undoubtedly a man whom you know well by repute—Moore, Chief of the Russian Secret Service in England. He came to Prince Obolenski's once, when he was in Petersburg, and the Princess told me who he was."

Unfortunately, I had not been able to include Beatrice in the group, therefore I had only her description to place before the clever young woman, who had, on so many occasions, gained knowledge of secrets where I and my agents had failed. Her part was always a difficult one to play, but she was well paid, was a marvellous linguist, and for patience and cunning was unequalled.

I described her as minutely as I could, but still she had no knowledge of her. She remained thoughtful a long time, and then observed:

"You have said that she apparently knew Moore? He has, I know, recently been back in Petersburg, therefore they may have met there. She may be known. Why not seek for traces of her in Russia?"

It seemed something of a wild-goose chase, yet with the whole affair shrouded in mystery and tragedy as it was, I was glad to adopt any suggestion that might lead to a solution of the enigma. The reticence of Mrs. Hamilton regarding her cousin, and the apparent secret association of the dead girl with those two notorious spies, had formed a problem which puzzled me almost to the point of madness.

The English governess told me where in Petersburg I should be likely to find either the two Russian agents, Davidoff or Moore, who had been posing in England for some unknown purpose as hunting men of means; therefore I left by the night mail for the Russian capital. I put up at a small, and not over-clean hotel, in preference to the Europe,* and, compelled to carefully conceal my identity, I at once set about making inquiries in various quarters, whether the two men had returned to Russia. They had, and had both had long interviews, two days before, with General Zouboff, Chief of the Secret Service, and with the Russian Foreign Minister.

At the Embassy, and in various English quarters, I sought trace of the woman whose death was such a profound mystery, but all in vain. At last I suddenly thought of another source of information as yet untried—namely, the register of the English Charity in Petersburg, and on searching it, I found, to my complete satisfaction, that about six weeks before Beatrice Graham applied to the administration, and was granted money to take her back to England. She was the daughter, it was registered, of a Mr. Charles Graham, the English manager of a cotton mill in Moscow, who had been killed by an accident, and had left her penniless. For some months she had tried to earn her own living, in a costumier's shop in the Nevski, and, not knowing Russian sufficiently well, had been discharged. Before her father's death she had been engaged to marry a young

---

* One of the top hotels in St. Petersburg, opened in 1875 and still in business at the time of publication.

Englishman, whose name was not given, but who was said to be tutor to the children of General Vraski, Governor-General of Warsaw.

The information was interesting, but carried me no further, therefore I set myself to watch the two men who had travelled from England to consult the Tzar's chief adviser. Aided by two Russians, who were in British pay, I shadowed them day and night for six days, until, one evening, I followed Davidoff down to the railway station, where he took a ticket for the frontier. Without baggage I followed him, for his movements were of a man who was escaping from the country. He passed out across the frontier, and went on to Vienna, and thence direct to Paris, where he put up at the Hotel Terminus, Gare St Lazare.

Until our arrival at the hotel he had never detected that I was following him, but on the second day in Paris we came face to face in the large central hall, used as a reading room. He glanced at me quickly, but whether he recognized me as the companion of Beatrice Graham in the hunting field I have no idea. All I know is that his movements were extremely suspicious, and that I invoked the aid of all three of our secret agents in Paris to keep watch on him, just as had been done in Petersburg.

On the fourth night of our arrival in the French capital I returned to the hotel about midnight, having dined at the Café Americain with Greville, the naval attaché at the Embassy. In washing my hands prior to turning in, I received a nasty scratch on my left wrist from a pin which a careless laundress had left in the towel. There was a little blood, but I tied my handkerchief around it, and, tired out, lay down and was soon asleep.

Half an hour afterwards, however, I was aroused by an excruciating pain over my whole left side, a strange twitching of the muscles of my face and hands, and a contraction of the throat which prevented me from breathing or crying out.

I tried to rise and press the electric bell for assistance, but could not. My whole body seemed entirely paralysed. Then the ghastly truth flashed upon me, causing me to break out into a cold sweat.

That pin had been placed there purposely. I had been poisoned and in the same manner as Beatrice Graham!

I recollect that my heart seemed to stop, and my nails clenched themselves in the palms in agony. Then next moment I knew no more.

When I recovered consciousness, Ted Greville, together with a tall, black-bearded man named Delisle, who was in the confidential department of the Quai d'Orsay* and who often furnished us with information—at a very high figure,

---

* Home of the French Ministry of Foreign Affairs.

be it said—were standing by my bedside, while a French doctor was leaning over the foot rail watching me.

"Thank heaven you're better, old chap!" Greville exclaimed. "They thought you were dead. You've had a narrow squeak. How did it happen?"

"That pin!" I cried, pointing to the towel.

"What pin?" he asked.

"Mind! don't touch the towel," I cried. "There's a pin in it—a pin that's poisoned! That Russian evidently came here in my absence and very cunningly laid a deathtrap for me."

"You mean Davidoff," chimed in the Frenchman. "When, *m'sieur*, the doctor has left the room I can tell you something in confidence."

The doctor discreetly withdrew, and then our spy said:

"Davidoff has turned traitor to his own country. I have discovered that the reason of his visit here is because he has in his possession the original draft of a proposed secret agreement between Russia and Germany against England, and is negotiating for its sale to us for one hundred thousand francs. He had a secret interview with our Chief last night at his private house in the Avenue des Champs Elysées."

"Then it is he who stole it, after it had the Tzar's approval!" I cried, starting up in bed, aroused at once to action by the information. "Has he disposed of it to France?"

"Not yet. It is still in his possession."

"And he is here?"

"No. He has hidden himself in lodgings in the Rue Lafayette, No. 247, until the Foreign Minister decides whether he shall buy the document."

"And the name by which he is known there?"

"He is passing as a Greek named Geunadios."

"Keep a strict watch on him. He must not escape," I said. "He has endeavoured to murder me."

"A watch is being kept," was the Frenchman's answer, as, exhausted, I sank again upon the pillow.

Just before midnight I entered the traitor's room in the Rue Lafayette, and when he saw me he fell back with blanched face and trembling hands.

"No doubt my presence here surprises you," I said, "but I may as well at once state my reason for coming here. I want a certain document which concerns Germany and your own country—the document which you have stolen to sell to France."

"What do you mean, *m'sieur?*" he asked, with an attempted hauteur.

"My meaning is simple. I require that document, otherwise I shall give you into the hands of the police for attempted murder. The Paris police will detain you until the police of Petersburg apply for your extradition as a traitor. You know what that means—Schlüsselburg."

Mention of that terrible island fortress, dreaded by every Russian, caused him to quiver. He looked me straight in the face, and saw determination written there, yet he was unyielding, and refused for a long time to give the precious document into my hands. I referred to his stay at Stoke Doyle, and spoke of his friendship with the spy Moore, so that he should know that I was aware of the truth, until at last he suggested a bargain with me, namely, that in exchange for the draft agreement against England I should preserve silence and permit him to return to Russia.

To this course I acceded, and then the fellow took from a secret cavity of his travelling bag a long official envelope, which contained the innocent-looking paper, which would, if signed, have destroyed England's prestige in the Far East. He handed it to me, the document for which he hoped to obtain one hundred thousand francs, and in return I gave him his liberty to go back to Russia unmolested.

Our parting was the reverse of cordial, for undoubtedly he had placed in my towel the pin which had been steeped in some subtle and deadly poison, and then escaped from the hotel, in the knowledge that I must sooner or later become scratched and fall a victim.

I had had a very narrow escape, it was true, but I did not think so much of my good fortune in regaining my life as the rapid delivery of the all-important document into Lord Macclesfield's hands, which I effected at noon next day.

My life had been at stake, for I afterwards found that a second man had been his accomplice, but happily I had succeeded in obtaining possession of the actual document, the result being that England acted so promptly and vigorously that the situation was saved, and the way was, as you know, opened for the Anglo-Japanese Treaty,* which, to the discomfiture of Germany, was effected a few months later.

Nearly two years have gone by since then, and it was only the other day, by mere accident, that I made a further discovery which explained the death of the unfortunate Beatrice Graham.

A young infantry lieutenant, named Bellingham, having passed in Russian, had some four years before entered our Secret Service, and been employed in Russia on

---

* The Anglo-Japanese Alliance of 1902, which, together with other treaties already in place, ensured that Russia was left without allies in the Far East and ultimately brought Japan into World War I on the British side.

certain missions. A few days ago, on his return to London, after performing a perilous piece of espionage on the Russo-German frontier, he called upon me in Bloomsbury, and in course of conversation, mentioned that about two years ago, in order to get access to certain documents relating to the Russian mobilisation scheme for her western frontier, he acted as tutor to the sons of the Governor-General of Warsaw.

In an instant a strange conjecture flashed across my mind.

"Am I correct in assuming that you knew a young English lady in Russia named Graham—Beatrice Graham?"

He looked me straight in the face, open-mouthed in astonishment, yet I saw that a cloud of sadness overshadowed him instantly.

"Yes," he said. "I knew her. Our meeting resulted in a terrible tragedy. Owing to the position I hold I have been compelled to keep the details to myself—although it is the tragedy of my life."

"How? Tell me," I urged sympathetically.

"Ah!" he sighed, "it is a strange story. We met in Petersburg; where she was employed in a shop in the Nevski. I loved her, and we became engaged. Withholding nothing from her I told her who I was and the reason I was in the service of the Governor-General. At once, instead of despising me as a spy, she became enthusiastic as an Englishwoman, and declared her readiness to assist me. She was looking forward to our marriage, and saw that if I could effect a big coup my position would at once be improved, and we could then be united."

He broke off, and remained silent for a few moments, looking blankly down into the grey London street. Then he said,

"I explained to her the suspicion that Germany and Russia were conspiring in the Far East, and told her that a draft treaty was probably in existence, and that it was a document of supreme importance to British interests. Judge my utter surprise when, a week later, she came to me with the actual document which she said she had managed to secure from the private cabinet of Prince Korolkoff, director of the private Chancellerie of the Emperor, to whose house she had gone on a commission to the Princess. Truly she had acted with a boldness and cleverness that were amazing. Knowing the supreme importance of the document, I urged her to leave Russia at once, and conceal herself with friends in England, taking care always that the draft treaty never left her possession. This plan she adopted, first, however, placing herself under the protection of the English charity, thus allaying any suspicions that the police might entertain.

"Poor Beatrice went to stay with her cousin, a lady named Hamilton, in Northamptonshire, but the instant the document was missed the Secret Services of Germany and Russia were at once agog, and the whole machinery was set in motion, with the result that two Russian agents—an Englishman named Moore, and a Russian named Davidoff—as well as Krempelstein, chief of the German Service, had suspicions, and followed her to England with the purpose of obtaining re-possession of the precious document. For some weeks they plotted in vain, although both the German and the Englishman succeeded in getting on friendly terms with her.

"She telegraphed to me, asking how she should dispose of the document, fearing to keep it long in her possession, but not being aware of the desperate character of the game, I replied that there was nothing to be feared. I was wrong," he cried, bitterly. "I did not recognize the vital importance of the information; I did not know that Empires were at stake. The man Davidoff, who posed as a wealthy Austrian Baron, had by some means discovered that she always carried the precious draft concealed in the bodice of her dress, therefore he had recourse to a dastardly ruse. From what I have since discovered he one day succeeded in concealing in the fur of her cape a pin impregnated with a certain deadly arrow poison unknown to toxicologists. Then he caused to be dispatched from London a telegram purporting to come from me, urging her to meet me in secret at a certain spot on that same night. In eager expectation the poor girl went forth to meet me, believing I had returned unexpectedly from Russia, but in putting on her cape, she tore her finger with the poisoned pin. While waiting for me the fatal paralysis seized her, and she expired, after which Davidoff crept up, secured the missing document and escaped. His anxiety to get hold of it was to sell it at a high price to a foreign country, nevertheless he was compelled first to return to Russia and report. No one knew that he actually held the draft, for to Krempelstein, as well as to Moore, my poor love's death was believed to be due to natural causes, while Davidoff, on his part, took care to so arrange matters, that his presence at the spot where poor Beatrice expired could never be proved. The spies therefore left England reluctantly after the tragedy, believing that the document, if ever possessed by my unfortunate love, had passed out of her possession into unknown hands."

"And what of the assassin Davidoff now?" I inquired.

"I have avenged her death," answered Bellingham with set teeth. "I gave information to General Zouboff of the traitor's attempted sale of the draft treaty to France, with the result that the court martial has condemned him to incarceration for life in the cells below the lake at Schlüsselburg."

THE SUPERFLUOUS FINGER

by Jacques Futrelle

1906

Jacques Futrelle started as a newspaperman. He wrote for the sports section of the *Atlanta Journal* before moving on to the *New York Herald,* the *Boston Post,* and the *Boston American.* It was there that he published his first story featuring Professor Augustus S. F. X. van Dusen, "the Thinking Machine." Titled "The Problem of Cell 13," it involved an experiment in which van Dusen undertook to escape from a prison cell within one week to prove his proposition that nothing is impossible when the human mind is properly applied.

The Thinking Machine went on to appear in fifty-one short stories and one novel—compared to fifty-six stories and four novels in the Sherlock Holmes canon. Although van Dusen is American, the influence of Holmes on his character is plain. He solves problems by remorseless logic, and unfurls his thinking at the end of a tale. He works with the police on occasion, but is not one of them; and he has a resourceful side-kick, the reporter Hutchinson Hatch, who combines the roles of Watson and the Baker Street Irregulars—although, perhaps strangely for a reporter, he does not narrate the tales of the Thinking Machine.

Unlike Holmes, though, van Dusen is little represented in other media. "The Problem of Cell 13" and "The Superfluous Finger" were adapted for television and radio by the BBC in 1973 and 2011 respectively, both for short-lived series presenting the rivals of Sherlock Holmes. He made a brief appearance in the graphic novel series *The League of Extraordinary Gentlemen,* which features an enormous cast of characters from literature.

Germany was more accepting of the Thinking Machine: between 1978 and 1999 the radio station RIAS broadcast seventy-nine Augustus van Dusen plays, a few based on stories by Futrelle, but most new creations by German author Michael Koser. All featured Hutchinson Hatch in the Watson role of narrator.

"The Superfluous Finger" first appeared in the *Sunday Magazine,* 25 November, 1906. Futrelle died on the *Titanic* in 1912, after forcibly placing his wife in a lifeboat.

S he drew off her left glove, a delicate, crinkled suede affair, and offered her bare hand to the surgeon. An artist would have called it beautiful, perfect, even; the surgeon, professionally enough, set it down as an excellent structural specimen. From the polished pink nails of the tapering fingers to the firm, well moulded wrist, it was distinctly the hand of a woman of ease—one that had never known labour, a pampered hand Dr. Prescott told himself.

"The fore-finger," she explained calmly. "I should like to have it amputated at the first joint, please."

"Amputated?" gasped Dr. Prescott. He stared into the pretty face of his caller. It was flushed softly, and the red lips were parted in a slight smile. It seemed quite an ordinary affair to her. The surgeon bent over the hand with quick interest. "Amputated!" he repeated.

"I came to you," she went on with a nod, "because I have been informed that you are one of the most skilful men of your profession, and the cost of the operation is quite immaterial."

Dr. Prescott pressed the pink nail of the fore-finger then permitted the blood to rush back into it. Several times he did this, then he turned the hand over and scrutinized it closely inside from the delicately lined palm to the tips of the fingers. When he looked up at last there was an expression of frank bewilderment on his face.

"What's the matter with it?" he asked.

"Nothing," the woman replied pleasantly. "I merely want it off from the first joint."

The surgeon leaned back in his chair with a frown of perplexity on his brow, and his visitor was subjected to a sharp, professional stare. She bore it unflinchingly and even smiled a little at his obvious perturbation.

"Why do you want it off?" he demanded.

The woman shrugged her shoulders a little impatiently.

"I can't tell you that," she replied. "It really is not necessary that you should know. You are a surgeon, I want an operation performed. That is all."

There was a long pause; the mutual stare didn't waver.

"You must understand, Miss—Miss—er—" began Dr. Prescott at last. "By the way, you have not introduced yourself?" She was silent. "May I ask your name?"

"My name is of no consequence," she replied calmly. "I might, of course, give you a name, but it would not be mine, therefore any name would be superfluous."

Again the surgeon stared.

"When do you want the operation performed?" he inquired.

"Now," she replied. "I am ready."

"You must understand," he said severely, "that surgery is a profession for the relief of human suffering, not for mutilation—wilful mutilation I might say."

"I understand that perfectly," she said. "But where a person submits of her own desire to—to mutilation as you call it, I can see no valid objection on your part."

"It would be criminal to remove a finger where there is no necessity for it," continued the surgeon bluntly. "No good end could be served."

A trace of disappointment showed in the young woman's face, and again she shrugged her shoulders.

"The question after all," she said finally, "is not one of ethics but is simply whether or not you will perform the operation. Would you do it for, say, a thousand dollars?"

"Not for five thousand dollars," blurted the surgeon,

"Well, for ten thousand then?" she asked, quiet casually.

All sorts of questions were pounding in Dr. Prescott's mind. Why did a young and beautiful woman desire—why was she anxious even—to sacrifice a perfectly healthy finger? What possible purpose would it serve to mar a hand which was as nearly perfect as any he had ever seen? Was it some insane caprice? Staring deeply into her steady, quiet eyes he could only be convinced of her sanity. Then what?

"No, madam," he said at last, vehemently, "I would not perform the operation for any sum you might mention, unless I was first convinced that the removal of that finger was absolutely necessary. That, I think, is all."

He arose as if to end the consultation. The woman remained seated and continued thoughtful for a minute.

"As I understand it," she said, "you would perform the operation if I could convince you that it was absolutely necessary?"

"Certainly," he replied promptly, almost eagerly. His curiosity was aroused. "Then it would come well within the range of my professional duties."

"Won't you take my word that it is necessary, and that it is impossible for me to explain why?"

"No. I must know why."

The woman arose and stood facing him. The disappointment had gone from her face now.

"Very well," she remarked steadily. "You will perform the operation if it is necessary, therefore if I should shoot the finger off, perhaps—?"

"Shoot it off?" exclaimed Dr. Prescott in amazement. "Shoot it off?"

"That is what I said," she replied calmly. "If I should shoot the finger off you would consent to dress the wound? You would make any necessary amputation?"

She held up the finger under discussion and looked at it curiously. Dr. Prescott himself stared at it with a sudden new interest.

"Shoot it off?" he repeated. "Why, you must be mad to contemplate such a thing," he exploded, and his face flushed in sheer anger. "I—I will have nothing whatever to do with the affair, madam. Good day."

"I should have to be very careful, of course," she mused, "but I think perhaps one shot would be sufficient, then I should come to you and demand that you dress it?"

There was a question in the tone. Dr. Prescott stared at her for a full minute then walked over and opened the door.

"In my profession, madam," he said coldly, "there is too much possibility of doing good and relieving actual suffering for me to consider this matter or discuss it further with you. There are three persons now waiting in the ante-room who need my services. I shall be compelled to ask you to excuse me."

"But you will dress the wound?" the woman insisted, undaunted by his forbidding tone and manner.

"I shall have nothing whatever to do with it," declared the surgeon, positively, finally. "If you need the services of any medical man permit me to suggest that it is an alienist* and not a surgeon."

The woman didn't appear to take offence.

"Someone would have to dress it," she continued insistently. "I should much prefer that it be a man of undisputed skill—you, I mean—therefore I shall call again. Good day."

There was a rustle of silken skirts and she was gone. Dr. Prescott stood for an instant gazing after her with frank wonder and annoyance in his eyes, his

---

* Psychiatrist (archaic).

attitude, then he went back and sat down at the desk. The crinkled suede glove still lay where she had left it. He examined it gingerly then with a final shake of his head dismissed the affair and turned to other things.

ᘐ

Early next afternoon Dr. Prescott was sitting in his office writing when the door from the ante-room where patients awaited his leisure was thrown open and the young man in attendance rushed in.

"A lady has fainted, sir," he said hurriedly. "She seems to be hurt."

Dr. Prescott arose quickly and strode out. There, lying helplessly back in her chair with white face and closed eyes, was his visitor of the day before. He stepped toward her quickly then hesitated as he recalled their conversation. Finally, however, professional instinct, the desire to relieve suffering, and perhaps curiosity too, caused him to go to her. The left hand was wrapped in an improvised bandage through which there was a trickle of blood. He glared at it with incredulous eyes.

"Hanged if she didn't do it," he blurted angrily.

The fainting spell, Dr. Prescott saw, was due only to loss of blood and physical pain, and he busied himself trying to restore her to consciousness. Meanwhile he gave some hurried instructions to the young man who was in attendance in the ante-room.

"Call up Professor Van Dusen on the 'phone," he directed his assistant, "and ask him if he can assist me in a minor operation. Tell him it's rather a curious case and I am sure it will interest him."

It was in this manner that the problem of the superfluous finger first came to the attention of The Thinking Machine. He arrived just as the mysterious woman was opening her eyes to consciousness from the fainting spell. She stared at him glassily, unrecognizingly; then her glance wandered to Dr. Prescott. She smiled.

"I knew you'd have to do it," she murmured weakly.

After the ether had been administered for the operation, a simple and an easy one, Dr. Prescott stated the circumstances of the case to The Thinking Machine. The scientist stood with his long, slender fingers resting lightly on the young woman's pulse, listening in silence.

"What do you make of it?" demanded the surgeon.

The Thinking Machine didn't say. At the moment he was leaning over the unconscious woman squinting at her forehead. With his disengaged hand he stroked the delicately pencilled eye-brows several times the wrong way, and again at close range squinted at them. Dr. Prescott saw and seeing, understood.

"No, it isn't that," he said and he shuddered a little. "I thought of it myself. Her bodily condition is excellent, splendid."

It was some time later when the young woman was sleeping lightly, placidly under the influence of a soothing potion, that The Thinking Machine spoke of the peculiar events which had preceded the operation. Then he was sitting in Dr. Prescott's private office. He had picked up a woman's glove from the desk.

"This is the glove she left when she first called, isn't it?" he inquired.

"Yes."

"Did you happen to see her remove it?"

"Yes."

The Thinking Machine curiously examined the dainty, perfumed trifle, then, arising suddenly, went into the adjoining room where the woman lay asleep. He stood for an instant gazing down admiringly at the exquisite, slender figure; then, bending over, he looked closely at her left hand. When at last he straightened up it seemed that some unspoken question in his mind had been answered. He rejoined Dr. Prescott.

"It's difficult to say what motive is back of her desire to have the finger amputated," he said musingly. "I could perhaps venture a conjecture but if the matter is of no importance to you beyond mere curiosity, I should not like to do so. Within a few months from now, I daresay, important developments will result and I should like to find out something more about her. That I can do when she returns to wherever she is stopping in the city. I'll 'phone to Mr. Hatch and have him ascertain for me where she goes, her name and other things which may throw a light on the matter."

"He will follow her?"

"Yes, precisely. Now we only seem to know two facts in connection with her. First, she is English."

"Yes," Dr. Prescott agreed. "Her accent, her appearance, everything about her suggests that."

"And the second fact is of no consequence at the moment," resumed The Thinking Machine. "Let me use your 'phone, please."

৶

Hutchinson Hatch, reporter, was talking.

"When the young woman left Dr. Prescott's she took the cab which had been ordered for her and told the driver to go ahead until she stopped him. I got a

THE SUPERFLUOUS FINGER | 235

good look at her, by the way. I managed to pass just as she entered the cab and walking on down got into another cab which was waiting for me. Her cab drove for three or four blocks, aimlessly, and finally stopped. The driver stooped down as if to listen to someone inside, and my cab passed. Then the other cab turned across a side street and after going eight or ten blocks pulled up in front of an apartment house. The young woman got out and went inside. Her cab went away. Inside I found out that she was Mrs. Frederick Chevedon Morey. She came there last Tuesday—this is Friday—with her husband, and they engaged—"

"Yes, I knew she had a husband," interrupted The Thinking Machine.

"—engaged apartments for three months. When I had learned this much I remembered your instructions as to steamers from Europe landing on the day they took apartments or possibly a day or so before. I was just going out when Mrs. Morey stepped out of the elevator and preceded me to the door. She had changed her clothing and wore a different hat.

"It didn't seem to be necessary then to find out where she was going, for I knew I could find her when I wanted to, so I went down and made inquiries at the steamship offices. I found, after a great deal of work, that no one of the three steamers which arrived the day they took apartments brought a Mr. and Mrs. Morey, but one steamer on the day before brought a Mr. and Mrs. David Girardeau from Liverpool. Mrs. Girardeau answered Mrs. Morey's description to the minutest detail, even to the gown she wore when she left the steamer—that is the same she wore when she left Dr. Prescott's after the operation."

That was all. The Thinking Machine sat with his enormous yellow head pillowed against a high-backed chair and his long slender fingers pressed tip to tip. He asked no questions and made no comment for a long time, then:

"About how many minutes was it from the time she entered the house until she came out again?"

"Not more than ten or fifteen," was the reply. "I was still talking casually to the people down stairs trying to find out something about them."

"What do they pay for their apartment?" asked the scientist, irrelevantly.

"Three hundred dollars a month."

The Thinking Machine's squint eyes were fixed immovably on a small discoloured spot on the ceiling of his laboratory.

"Whatever else may develop in this matter, Mr. Hatch," he said after a time, "we must admit that we have met a woman with extraordinary courage—nerve, I daresay you'd call it. When Mrs. Morey left Dr. Prescott's operating room she was so ill and weak from the shock that she could hardly stand, and now you tell me she changed her dress and went out immediately after she returned home."

"Well, of course—" Hatch said, apologetically.

"In that event," resumed the scientist, "we must assume also that the matter is one of the utmost importance to her, and yet the nature of the case had led me to believe that it might be months, perhaps, before there would be any particular development in it."

"What? How?" asked the reporter.

"The final development doesn't seem, from what I know, to belong on this side of the ocean at all," explained The Thinking Machine. "I imagine it is a case for Scotland Yard. The problem of course is: What made it necessary for her to get rid of that finger? If we admit her sanity we can count the possible answers to this question on one hand, and at least three of these answers take the case back to England." He paused. "By the way, was Mrs. Morey's hand bound up in the same way when you saw her the second time?"

"Her left hand was in a muff," explained the reporter. "I couldn't see but it seems to me that she wouldn't have had time to change the manner of its dressing."

"It's extraordinary," commented the scientist. He arose and paced back and forth across the room. "Extraordinary," he repeated. "One can't help but admire the fortitude of women under certain circumstances, Mr. Hatch. I think perhaps this particular case had better be called to the attention of Scotland Yard, but first I think it would be best for you to call on the Moreys tomorrow—you can find some pretext—and see what you can learn about them. You are an ingenious young man—I'll leave it all to you."

⌇

Hatch did call at the Morey apartments on the morrow, but under circumstances which were not at all what he expected. He went there with Detective Mallory, and Detective Mallory went there in a cab at full speed because the manager of the apartment house had 'phoned that Mrs. Frederick Chevedon Morey had been found murdered in her apartments. The detective ran up two flights of stairs and blundered heavy-footed into the rooms, and there he paused in the presence of death.

The body of the woman lay on the floor, and some one had mercifully covered it with a cloth from the bed. Detective Mallory drew the covering down from over the face and Hatch stared with a feeling of awe at the beautiful countenance which had, on the day before, been so radiant with life. Now it was distorted into an expression of awful agony and the limbs were drawn up convulsively. The mark of the murderer was at the white, exquisitely rounded throat—great black bruises where powerful, merciless fingers had sunk deeply into the soft flesh.

A physician in the house had preceded the police. After one glance at the woman and a swift, comprehensive look about the room Detective Mallory turned to him inquiringly.

"She has been dead for several hours," the doctor volunteered, "possibly since early last night. It appears that some virulent, burning poison was administered and then she was choked. I gather this from an examination of her mouth."

These things were readily to be seen; also it was plainly evident for many reasons that the finger marks at the throat were those of a man, but each step beyond these obvious facts only served to further bewilder the investigators. First was the statement of the night elevator boy.

"Mr. and Mrs. Morey left here last night about eleven o'clock," he said. "I know because I telephoned for a cab, and later brought them down from the third floor. They went into the manager's office leaving two suit cases in the hall. When they came out I took the suit cases to a cab that was waiting. They got in it and drove away."

"When did they return?" inquired the detective.

"They didn't return, sir," responded the boy. "I was on duty until six o'clock this morning. It just happened that no one came in after they went out until I was off duty at six."

The detective turned to the physician again.

"Then she couldn't have been dead since early last night," he said.

"She has been dead for several hours—at least twelve, possibly longer," said the physician firmly. "There's no possible argument about that."

The detective stared at him scornfully for an instant, then looked at the manager of the house.

"What was said when Mr. and Mrs. Morey entered your office last night?" he asked. "Were you there?"

"I was there, yes," was the reply. "Mr. Morey explained that they had been called away for a few days unexpectedly, and left the keys of the apartment with me. That was all that was said; I saw the elevator boy take the suit cases out for them as they went to the cab."

"How did it come, then, if you knew they were away that some one entered here this morning, and so found the body?"

"I discovered the body myself," replied the manager. "There was some electric wiring to be done in here, and I thought their absence would be a good time for it. I came up to see about it and saw—that."

He glanced at the covered body with a little shiver and a grimace. Detective Mallory was deeply thoughtful for several minutes.

"The woman is here and she's dead," he said finally. "If she is here she came back here, dead or alive, last night between the time she went out with her husband and the time her body was found this morning. Now that's an absolute fact. But how did she come here?"

Of the three employees of the apartment house only the elevator boy on duty had not spoken. Now he spoke because the detective glared at him fiercely.

"I didn't see either Mr. or Mrs. Morey come in this morning," he explained hastily. "Nobody had come in at all except the postman and some delivery wagon drivers up to the time the body was found."

Again Detective Mallory turned on the manager.

"Does any window of this apartment open on a fire escape?" he demanded.

"Yes—this way."

They passed through the short hallway to the back. Both the windows were locked on the inside, so instantly it appeared that even if the woman had been brought into the room that way the windows would not have been fastened unless her murderer went out of the house the front way. When Detective Mallory reached this stage of the investigation he sat down and stared from one to the other of the silent little party as if he considered the entire matter some affair which they had perpetrated to annoy him.

Hutchinson Hatch started to say something, then thought better of it, and turning, went to the telephone below. Within a few minutes The Thinking Machine stepped out of a cab in front and paused in the lower hall long enough to listen to the facts developed. There was a perfect network of wrinkles in the dome-like brow when the reporter concluded.

"It's merely a transfer of the final development in the affair from England to this country," he said enigmatically. "Please 'phone for Dr. Prescott to come here immediately."

He went on to the Morey apartments. With only a curt nod for Detective Mallory, the only one of the small party who knew him, he proceeded to the body of the dead woman and squinted down without a trace of emotion into the white, pallid face. After a moment he dropped on his knees beside the inert body and examined the mouth and the finger marks about the white throat.

"Carbolic acid and strangulation," he remarked tersely to Detective Mallory who was leaning over watching him with something of hopeful eagerness in his stolid face. The Thinking Machine glanced past him to the manager of the house. "Mr. Morey is a powerful, athletic man in appearance?" he asked.

"Oh no," was the reply. "He's short and slight, only a little larger than you are."

The scientist squinted aggressively at the manager as if the description were not quite what he expected. Then the slightly puzzled expression passed.

"Oh, I see," he remarked. "Played the piano." This was not a question; it was a statement.

"Yes, a great deal," was the reply, "so much so in fact that twice we had complaints from other persons in the house despite the fact that they had been here only a few days."

"Of course," mused the scientist abstractedly. "Of course. Perhaps Mrs. Morey did not play at all?"

"I believe she told me she did not."

The Thinking Machine drew down the thin cloth which had been thrown over the body and glanced at the left hand.

"Dear me! Dear me!" he exclaimed suddenly, and he arose. "Dear me!" he repeated. "That's the—" He turned to the manager and the two elevator boys. "This is Mrs. Morey beyond any question?"

The answer was a chorus of affirmation accompanied by some startling facial expressions.

"Did Mr. and Mrs. Morey employ any servants?"

"No," was the reply. "They had their meals in the café below most of the time. There is no housekeeping in these apartments at all."

"How many persons live in the building?"

"A hundred, I should say."

"There is a great deal of passing to and fro, then?"

"Certainly. It was rather unusual that so few persons passed in and out last night and this morning, and certainly Mrs. Morey and her husband were not among them, if that's what you're trying to find out."

The Thinking Machine glanced at the physician who was standing by silently.

"How long do you make it that she's been dead?" he asked.

"At least twelve hours," replied the physician. "Possibly longer."

"Yes, nearer fourteen, I imagine."

Abruptly he left the group and walked through the apartment and back again slowly. As he re-entered the room where the body lay, the door from the hall opened and Dr. Prescott entered, followed by Hutchinson Hatch. The Thinking Machine led the surgeon straight to the body and drew the cloth down from the face. Dr. Prescott started back with an exclamation of astonishment, recognition.

"There's no doubt about it at all in your mind?" inquired the scientist.

"Not the slightest," replied Dr. Prescott positively. "It's the same woman."

"Yet, look here!"

With a quick movement The Thinking Machine drew down the cloth still more. Dr. Prescott, together with those who had no idea of what to expect, peered down at the body. After one glance the surgeon dropped on his knees and examined closely the dead left hand. The fore-finger was off at the first joint. Dr. Prescott stared, stared incredulously. After a moment his eyes left the maimed hand and settled again on her face.

"I have never seen—never dreamed—of such a startling—" he began.

"That settles it all, of course," interrupted The Thinking Machine. "It solves and proves the problem at once. Now, Mr. Mallory, if we can go to your office or some place where we will be undisturbed I will—"

"But who killed her?" demanded the detective abruptly.

"I have the photograph of her murderer in my pocket," returned The Thinking Machine. "Also a photograph of an accomplice."

ᕃ

Detective Mallory, Dr. Prescott, The Thinking Machine, Hutchinson Hatch, and the apartment house physician were seated in the front room of the Morey apartments with all doors closed against prying, inquisitive eyes. At the scientist's request, Dr. Prescott repeated the circumstances leading up to the removal of a woman's left fore-finger, and there The Thinking Machine took up the story.

"Suppose, Mr. Mallory," and the scientist turned to the detective, "a woman should walk into your office and say she must have a finger cut off, what would you think?"

"I'd think she was crazy," was the prompt reply.

"Naturally, in your position," The Thinking Machine went on, "you are acquainted with many strange happenings. Wouldn't this one instantly suggest something to you. Something that was to happen months off."

Detective Mallory considered it wisely, but was silent.

"Well here," declared The Thinking Machine. "A woman whom we now know to be Mrs. Morey wanted her finger cut off. It instantly suggested three, four, five, a dozen possibilities. Of course only one, or possibly two in combination, could be true. Therefore, which one? A little logic now to prove that two and two always make four—not some times but all the time.

"Naturally the first supposition was insanity. We pass that as absurd on its face. Then disease—a taint of leprosy perhaps which had been visible on the left fore-finger. I tested for that, and that was eliminated. Three strong reasons for desiring the finger off, either of which is strongly probable, remained. The fact that the woman was English unmistakably was obvious. From the mark of a wedding ring on her glove and a corresponding mark on her finger—she wore no such ring—we could safely surmise that she was married. These were the two first facts I learned. Substantiative evidence that she was married and not a widow came partly from her extreme youth and the lack of mourning in her attire.

"Then Mr. Hatch followed her, learned her name, where she lived, and later the fact that she had arrived with her husband on a steamer a day or so before they took apartments here. This was proof that she was English, and proof that she had a husband. They came over on the steamer as Mr. and Mrs. David Girardeau—here they were Mr. and Mrs. Frederick Chevedon Morey. Why this difference in name? The circumstance in itself pointed to irregularity—crime committed or contemplated. Other things made me think it was merely contemplated and that it could be prevented; for then the absence of every fact gave me no intimation that there would be murder. Then came the murder presumably of—Mrs. Morey?"

"Isn't it Mrs. Morey?" demanded the detective.

"Mr. Hatch recognized the woman as the one he had followed, I recognized her as the one on whom there had been an operation, Dr. Prescott also recognized her," continued the Thinking Machine. "To convince myself, after I had found the manner of death, that it was the woman, I looked at her left hand. I found that the fore-finger was gone—it had been removed by a skilled surgeon at the first joint. And this fact instantly showed me that the dead woman was not Mrs. Morey at all, but somebody else; and incidentally cleared up the entire affair."

"How?" demanded the detective. "I thought you just said that you had helped cut off her fore-finger."

"Dr. Prescott and I cut off that finger yesterday," replied The Thinking Machine calmly. "The finger of the dead woman had been cut off months, perhaps years, ago."

There was blank amazement on Detective Mallory's face, and Hatch was staring straight into the squint eyes of the scientist. Vaguely, as through a mist, he was beginning to account for many things which had been hitherto inexplicable.

"The perfectly healed wound on the hand eliminated every possibility but one," The Thinking Machine resumed. "Previously I had been informed that Mrs. Morey did not—or said she did not—play the piano. I had seen the bare possibility of an immense insurance on her hands, and some trick to defraud an insurance company by marring one. Of course against this was the fact that she had offered to pay a large sum for the operation; that their expenses here must have been enormous, so I was beginning to doubt the tenability of this supposition. The fact that the dead woman's finger was off removed that possibility completely, as it also removed the possibility of a crime of some sort in which there might have been left behind a tell-tale print of that fore-finger. If there had been a serious crime with the trace of the finger as evidence, its removal would have been necessary to her.

"Then the one thing remained—that is that Mrs. Morey, or whatever her name is—was in a conspiracy with her husband to get possession of certain properties, perhaps a title—remember she is English—by sacrificing that finger so that identification might be in accordance with the description of an heir whom she was to impersonate. We may well believe that she was provided with the necessary documentary evidence, and we know conclusively—we don't conjecture but we know—that the dead woman in there is the woman whose rights were to have been stolen by the so-called Mrs. Morey."

"But that is Mrs. Morey, isn't it?" demanded the detective again.

"No," was the sharp retort. "The perfect resemblance to Mrs. Morey, and the finger removed long ago, makes that clear. There is, I imagine, a relationship between them—perhaps they are cousins. I can hardly believe they are twins because the necessity, then of one impersonating the other to obtain either money or a title, would not have existed so palpably although it is possible that Mrs. Morey, if disinherited or disowned, would have resorted to such a course. This dead woman is Miss—Miss—" and he glanced at the back of a photograph, "Miss Evelyn Rossmore, and she has evidently been living in this city for some time. This is her picture, and it was made at least a year ago by Harkinson here. Perhaps he can give you her address as well."

There was silence for several minutes. Each member of the little group was turning over the stated facts mentally, and Detective Mallory was staring at the photograph, studying the handwriting on the back.

"But how did she come here—like this?" Hatch inquired.

"You remember, Mr. Hatch, when you followed Mrs. Morey here you told me she dressed again and went out?" asked the scientist in turn. "It was not Mrs. Morey you saw then—she was ill and I knew it from the operation—it was Miss Rossmore. The manager says a hundred persons live in this house—that there is a great deal of passing in and out. Can't you see that when there is such a startling resemblance Miss Rossmore could pass in and out at will and always be mistaken for Mrs. Morey? That no one would ever notice the difference?"

"But who killed her?" asked Detective Mallory, curiously. "How? Why?"

"Morey killed her," said The Thinking Machine flatly and he produced two other photographs from his pocket. "There's his picture and his wife's picture for identification purposes. How did he kill her? We can fairly presume that first he tricked her into drinking the acid, then perhaps she was screaming with the pain of it, and he choked her to death. I imagined first he was a large, powerful man because his grip on her throat was so powerful that he ruptured the jugular inside; but instead of that he plays the piano a great deal, which would give him the handpower to choke her. And why? We can suppose only that it was because she had in some way learned of their purpose. That would have established the motive. The crowning delicacy of the affair was Morey's act in leaving his keys with the manager here. He did not anticipate that the apartments would be entered for several days—after they were safely away—while there was a chance that if neither of them had been seen here and their disappearance was unexplained, the rooms would have been opened to ascertain why. That is all, I think."

"Except to catch Morey and his wife," said the detective grimly.

"Easily done with those photographs," said The Thinking Machine. "I imagine, if this murder is kept out of the newspapers for a couple of hours you can find them about to sail for Europe. Suppose you try the line they came over on?"

‿

It was just three hours later that the accused man and wife were taken prisoner. They had just engaged passage on the steamer which sailed at half-past four o'clock. Their trial was a famous one and resulted in conviction after an astonishing story of an attempt to seize an estate and title belonging rightfully to Miss Evelyn Rossmore who had mysteriously disappeared years before.

THE MYSTERY OF
THE YELLOW ROOM
(EXTRACT)

by Gaston Leroux

1907

The author of *The Phantom of the Opera* was born in Paris in 1868. He studied law in Paris before inheriting a fortune and almost spending himself into bankruptcy. Starting as a court reporter and theater critic, he spent seventeen years as a journalist, covering the Russian Revolution and the former Paris Opera, in whose basement a cell had held members of the Paris Commune, a revolutionary socialist government that ruled the city for ten weeks in 1871 before being violently put down by the French Army. This must surely have played some part in inspiring his most famous work.

In 1907, Leroux abruptly left journalism. He began writing fiction, and formed a film company with fellow writer Arthur Bernède to adapt their novels for the new medium. *Le mystère de la chambre jaune* (*The Mystery of the Yellow Room*) was his first novel, and introduces his detective Joseph Rouletabille—whose name, translatable as "roll your marble," was contemporary slang for a globetrotter who has been everywhere and seen everything.

Rouletabille's opponent in this tale is the international criminal Ballmayer, a villain cut from the same cloth as Doyle's Professor Moriarty and Maurice Leblanc's Arsène Lupin, one of whose adventures will be found later in this book. He reappears in another of the

Rouletabille novels, *The Perfume of the Lady in Black,* as does the Lady in Black herself, the American heiress Mathilde Stangerson.

Leroux wrote seven Rouletabille novels in all, and two authorized sequels were published in 1947. The detective's adventures have been filmed several times in France—most recently in 2005—and *The Mystery of the Yellow Room* was filmed in 1919 by the Boston-based Mayflower Photoplay Company and in 1947 by the Argentinian studio Film Andes. In his native France, Rouletabille has also appeared on television and in comics.

In this extract from *The Mystery of the Yellow Room,* Rouletabille dramatically hijacks the court proceedings to present new evidence and unmask the true murderer—with whom he has made a highly questionable deal.

CHAPTER XXVII
IN WHICH JOSEPH ROULETABILLE APPEARS IN ALL HIS GLORY

T he excitement was extreme. Cries from fainting women were to be heard amid the extraordinary bustle and stir. The "majesty of the law" was utterly forgotten. The President tried in vain to make himself heard. Rouletabille made his way forward with difficulty, but by dint of much elbowing reached his manager and greeted him cordially. The letter was passed to him and pocketing it he turned to the witness-box. He was dressed exactly as on the day he left me even to the ulster over his arm. Turning to the President, he said:

"I beg your pardon, Monsieur President, but I have only just arrived from America. The steamer was late. My name is Joseph Rouletabille!"

The silence which followed his stepping into the witness-box was broken by laughter when his words were heard. Everybody seemed relieved and glad to find him there, as if in the expectation of hearing the truth at last.

But the President was extremely incensed:

"So, you are Joseph Rouletabille," he replied; "well, young man, I'll teach you what comes of making a farce of justice. By virtue of my discretionary power, I hold you at the court's disposition."

"I ask nothing better, Monsieur President. I have come here for that purpose. I humbly beg the court's pardon for the disturbance of which I have been the innocent cause. I beg you to believe that nobody has a greater respect for the court than I have. I came in as I could." He smiled.

"Take him away!" ordered the President.

Maitre Henri Robert intervened. He began by apologising for the young man, who, he said, was moved only by the best intentions. He made the President understand that the evidence of a witness who had slept at the Glandier during the whole of that eventful week could not be omitted, and the present witness, moreover, had come to name the real murderer.

"Are you going to tell us who the murderer was?" asked the President, somewhat convinced though still sceptical.

"I have come for that purpose, Monsieur President!" replied Rouletabille.

An attempt at applause was silenced by the usher.

"Joseph Rouletabille," said Maitre Henri Robert, "has not been regularly subpoenaed as a witness, but I hope, Monsieur President, you will examine him in virtue of your discretionary powers."

"Very well!" said the President, "we will question him. But we must proceed in order."

The Advocate-General rose:

"It would, perhaps, be better," he said, "if the young man were to tell us now whom he suspects."

The President nodded ironically:

"If the Advocate-General attaches importance to the deposition of Monsieur Joseph Rouletabille, I see no reason why this witness should not give us the name of the murderer."

A pin drop could have been heard. Rouletabille stood silent looking sympathetically at Darzac, who, for the first time since the opening of the trial, showed himself agitated.

"Well," cried the President, "we wait for the name of the murderer." Rouletabille, feeling in his waistcoat pocket, drew his watch and, looking at it, said:

"Monsieur President, I cannot name the murderer before half-past six o'clock!"

Loud murmurs of disappointment filled the room. Some of the lawyers were heard to say: "He's making fun of us!"

The President in a stern voice, said:

"This joke has gone far enough. You may retire, Monsieur, into the witnesses' room. I hold you at our disposition."

Rouletabille protested.

"I assure you, Monsieur President," he cried in his sharp, clear voice, "that when I do name the murderer you will understand why I could not speak before half-past six. I assert this on my honour. I can, however, give you now some explanation of the murder of the keeper. Monsieur Frederic Larsan, who has seen me at work at the Glandier, can tell you with what care I studied this case. I found myself compelled to differ with him in arresting Monsieur Robert Darzac, who is innocent. Monsieur Larsan knows of my good faith and knows that some importance may be attached to my discoveries, which have often corroborated his own."

Frederic Larsan said:

"Monsieur President, it will be interesting to hear Monsieur Joseph Rouletabille, especially as he differs from me."

A murmur of approbation greeted the detective's speech. He was a good sportsman and accepted the challenge. The struggle between the two promised to be exciting.

As the President remained silent, Frederic Larsan continued:

"We agree that the murderer of the keeper was the assailant of Mademoiselle Stangerson; but as we are not agreed as to how the murderer escaped, I am curious to hear Monsieur Rouletabille's explanation."

"I have no doubt you are," said my friend.

General laughter followed this remark. The President angrily declared that if it was repeated, he would have the court cleared.

"Now, young man," said the President, "you have heard Monsieur Frederic Larsan; how did the murderer get away from the court?"

Rouletabille looked at Madame Mathieu, who smiled back at him sadly.

"Since Madame Mathieu," he said, "has freely admitted her intimacy with the keeper—"

"Why, it's the boy!" exclaimed Daddy Mathieu.

"Remove that man!" ordered the President.

Mathieu was removed from the court. Rouletabille went on:

"Since she has made this confession, I am free to tell you that she often met the keeper at night on the first floor of the donjon, in the room which was once an oratory. These meetings became more frequent when her husband was laid up by his rheumatism. She gave him morphine to ease his pain and to give herself more time for the meetings. Madame Mathieu came to the chateau that night, enveloped in a large black shawl which served also as a disguise. This was the phantom that disturbed Daddy Jacques. She knew how to imitate the mewing of Mother Angenoux' cat and she would make the cries to advise the keeper of her presence. The recent repairs of the donjon* did not interfere with their meetings

---

* An old French word for a castle keep.

in the keeper's old room, in the donjon, since the new room assigned to him at the end of the right wing was separated from the steward's room by a partition only.

"Previous to the tragedy in the courtyard Madame Mathieu and the keeper left the donjon together. I learnt these facts from my examination of the footmarks in the court the next morning. Bernier, the concierge, whom I had stationed behind the donjon—as he will explain himself—could not see what passed in the court. He did not reach the court until he heard the revolver shots, and then he fired. When the woman parted from the man she went towards the open gate of the court, while he returned to his room.

"He had almost reached the door when the revolvers rang out. He had just reached the corner when a shadow bounded by. Meanwhile, Madame Mathieu, surprised by the revolver shots and by the entrance of people into the court, crouched in the darkness. The court is a large one and, being near the gate, she might easily have passed out unseen. But she remained and saw the body being carried away. In great agony of mind she neared the vestibule and saw the dead body of her lover on the stairs lit up by Daddy Jacques' lantern. She then fled; and Daddy Jacques joined her.

"That same night, before the murder, Daddy Jacques had been awakened by the cat's cry, and, looking through his window, had seen the black phantom. Hastily dressing himself he went out and recognised her. He is an old friend of Madame Mathieu, and when she saw him she had to tell him of her relations with the keeper and begged his assistance. Daddy Jacques took pity on her and accompanied her through the oak grove out of the park, past the border of the lake to the road to Epinay. From there it was but a very short distance to her home.

"Daddy Jacques returned to the chateau, and, seeing how important it was for Madame Mathieu's presence at the chateau to remain unknown, he did all he could to hide it. I appeal to Monsieur Larsan, who saw me, next morning, examine the two sets of footprints."

Here Rouletabille turning towards Madame Mathieu, with a bow, said:

"The footprints of Madame bear a strange resemblance to the neat footprints of the murderer."

Madame Mathieu trembled and looked at him with wide eyes as if in wonder at what he would say next.

"Madame has a shapely foot, long and rather large for a woman. The imprint, with its pointed toe, is very like that of the murderer's."

A movement in the court was repressed by Rouletabille. He held their attention at once.

"I hasten to add," he went on, "that I attach no importance to this. Outward signs like these are often liable to lead us into error, if we do not reason rightly. Monsieur Robert Darzac's footprints are also like the murderer's, and yet he is not the murderer!"

The President turning to Madame Mathieu asked:

"Is that in accordance with what you know occurred?"

"Yes, Monsieur President," she replied, "it is as if Monsieur Rouletabille had been behind us."

"Did you see the murderer running towards the end of the right wing?"

"Yes, as clearly as I saw them afterwards carrying the keeper's body."

"What became of the murderer?—You were in the courtyard and could easily have seen."

"I saw nothing of him, Monsieur President. It became quite dark just then."

"Then Monsieur Rouletabille," said the President, "must explain how the murderer made his escape."

Rouletabille continued:

"It was impossible for the murderer to escape by the way he had entered the court without our seeing him; or if we couldn't see him we must certainly have felt him, since the court is a very narrow one enclosed in high iron railings."

"Then if the man was hemmed in that narrow square, how is it you did not find him?—I have been asking you that for the last half hour."

"Monsieur President," replied Rouletabille, "I cannot answer that question before half-past six!"

By this time the people in the court-room were beginning to believe in this new witness. They were amused by his melodramatic action in thus fixing the hour; but they seemed to have confidence in the outcome. As for the President, it looked as if he also had made up his mind to take the young man in the same way. He had certainly been impressed by Rouletabille's explanation of Madame Mathieu's part.

"Well, Monsieur Rouletabille," he said, "as you say; but don't let us see any more of you before half-past six."

Rouletabille bowed to the President, and made his way to the door of the witnesses' room.

I quietly made my way through the crowd and left the court almost at the same time as Rouletabille. He greeted me heartily, and looked happy.

"I'll not ask you, my dear fellow," I said, smiling, "what you've been doing in America; because I've no doubt you'll say you can't tell me until after half-past six."

"No, my dear Sainclair, I'll tell you right now why I went to America. I went in search of the name of the other half of the murderer!"

"The name of the other half?"

"Exactly. When we last left the Glandier I knew there were two halves to the murderer and the name of only one of them. I went to America for the name of the other half."

I was too puzzled to answer. Just then we entered the witnesses' room, and Rouletabille was immediately surrounded. He showed himself very friendly to all except Arthur Rance to whom he exhibited a marked coldness of manner. Frederic Larsan came in also. Rouletabille went up and shook him heartily by the hand. His manner toward the detective showed that he had got the better of the policeman. Larsan smiled and asked him what he had been doing in America, Rouletabille began by telling him some anecdotes of his voyage. They then turned aside together apparently with the object of speaking confidentially. I, therefore, discreetly left them and, being curious to hear the evidence, returned to my seat in the court-room where the public plainly showed its lack of interest in what was going on in their impatience for Rouletabille's return at the appointed time.

On the stroke of half-past six Joseph Rouletabille was again brought in. It is impossible for me to picture the tense excitement which appeared on every face, as he made his way to the bar. Darzac rose to his feet, frightfully pale.

The President, addressing Rouletabille, said gravely:

"I will not ask you to take the oath, because you have not been regularly summoned; but I trust there is no need to urge upon you the gravity of the statement you are about to make."

Rouletabille looked the President quite calmly and steadily in the face, and replied:

"Yes, Monsieur."

"At your last appearance here," said the President, "we had arrived at the point where you were to tell us how the murderer escaped, and also his name. Now, Monsieur Rouletabille, we await your explanation."

"Very well, Monsieur," began my friend amidst a profound silence. "I had explained how it was impossible for the murderer to get away without being seen. And yet he was there with us in the courtyard."

"And you did not see him? At least that is what the prosecution declares."

"No! We all of us saw him, Monsieur le President!" cried Rouletabille.

"Then why was he not arrested?"

"Because no one, besides myself, knew that he was the murderer. It would have spoiled my plans to have had him arrested, and I had then no proof other than my own reasoning. I was convinced we had the murderer before us and that we were actually looking at him. I have now brought what I consider the indisputable proof."

"Speak out, Monsieur! Tell us the murderer's name."

"You will find it on the list of names present in the court on the night of the tragedy," replied Rouletabille.

The people present in the court-room began showing impatience. Some of them even called for the name, and were silenced by the usher.

"The list includes Daddy Jacques, Bernier the concierge, and Mr. Arthur Rance," said the President. "Do you accuse any of these?"

"No, Monsieur!"

"Then I do not understand what you are driving at. There was no other person at the end of the court."

"Yes, Monsieur, there was, not at the end, but above the court, who was leaning out of the window."

"Do you mean Frederic Larsan!" exclaimed the President.

"Yes! Frederic Larsan!" replied Rouletabille in a ringing tone. "Frederic Larsan is the murderer!"

The court-room became immediately filled with loud and indignant protests. So astonished was he that the President did not attempt to quiet it. The quick silence which followed was broken by the distinctly whispered words from the lips of Robert Darzac:

"It's impossible! He's mad!"

"You dare to accuse Frederic Larsan, Monsieur?" asked the President. "If you are not mad, what are your proofs?"

"Proofs, Monsieur?—Do you want proofs? Well, here is one," cried Rouletabille shrilly. "Let Frederic Larsan be called!"

"Usher, call Frederic Larsan."

The usher hurried to the side door, opened it, and disappeared. The door remained open, while all eyes turned expectantly towards it. The clerk re-appeared and, stepping forward, said:

"Monsieur President, Frederic Larsan is not here. He left at about four o'clock and has not been seen since."

"That is my proof!" cried Rouletabille, triumphantly.

"Explain yourself?" demanded the President.

"My proof is Larsan's flight," said the young reporter. "He will not come back. You will see no more of Frederic Larsan."

"Unless you are playing with the court, Monsieur, why did you not accuse him when he was present? He would then have answered you."

"He could give no other answer than the one he has now given by his flight."

"We cannot believe that Larsan has fled. There was no reason for his doing so. Did he know you'd make this charge?"

"He did. I told him I would."

"Do you mean to say that knowing Larsan was the murderer you gave him the opportunity to escape?"

"Yes, Monsieur President, I did," replied Rouletabille, proudly. "I am not a policeman, I am a journalist; and my business is not to arrest people. My business is in the service of truth, and is not that of an executioner. If you are just, Monsieur, you will see that I am right. You can now understand why I refrained until this hour to divulge the name. I gave Larsan time to catch the 4:17 train for Paris, where he would know where to hide himself, and leave no traces. You will not find Frederic Larsan," declared Rouletabille, fixing his eyes on Monsieur Robert Darzac. "He is too cunning. He is a man who has always escaped you and whom you have long searched for in vain. If he did not succeed in outwitting me, he can yet easily outwit any police. This man who, four years ago, introduced himself to the *Sûreté*, and became celebrated as Frederic Larsan, is notorious under another name—a name well known to crime. Frederic Larsan, Monsieur President, is Ballmeyer!"

"Ballmeyer!" cried the President.

"Ballmeyer!" exclaimed Robert Darzac, springing to his feet. "Ballmeyer!—It was true, then!"

"Ah! Monsieur Darzac; you don't think I am mad, now!" cried Rouletabille.

Ballmeyer! Ballmeyer! No other word could be heard in the courtroom. The President adjourned the hearing.

Those of my readers who may not have heard of Ballmeyer will wonder at the excitement the name caused. And yet the doings of this remarkable criminal form the subject-matter of the most dramatic narratives of the newspapers and criminal records of the past twenty years. It had been reported that he was dead, and thus had eluded the police as he had eluded them throughout the whole of his career.

Ballmeyer was the best specimen of the high-class "gentleman swindler." He was adept at sleight of hand tricks, and no bolder or more ruthless crook ever lived. He was received in the best society, and was a member of some of the most exclusive clubs. On many of his depredatory expeditions he had not hesitated to use the knife and the mutton-bone.* No difficulty stopped him and no "operation" was too dangerous. He had been caught, but escaped on the very morning of his trial, by throwing pepper into the eyes of the guards who were conducting him to Court. It was known later that, in spite of the keen hunt after him by the most expert of detectives, he had sat that same evening at a first performance in the *Theatre Français*, without the slightest disguise.

He left France, later, to "work" America. The police there succeeded in capturing him once, but the extraordinary man escaped the next day. It would need a volume to recount the adventures of this master-criminal. And yet this was the man Rouletabille had allowed to get away! Knowing all about him and who he was, he afforded the criminal an opportunity for another laugh at the society he had defied! I could not help admiring the bold stroke of the young journalist, because I felt certain his motive had been to protect both Mademoiselle Stangerson and rid Darzac of an enemy at the same time.

The crowd had barely recovered from the effect of the astonishing revelation when the hearing was resumed. The question in everybody's mind was: Admitting that Larsan was the murderer, how did he get out of The Yellow Room?

Rouletabille was immediately called to the bar and his examination continued.

"You have told us," said the President, "that it was impossible to escape from the end of the court. Since Larsan was leaning out of his window, he had left the court. How did he do that?"

"He escaped by a most unusual way. He climbed the wall, sprang onto the terrace, and, while we were engaged with the keeper's body, reached the gallery by the window. He then had little else to do than to open the window, get in and call out to us, as if he had just come from his own room. To a man of Ballmeyer's strength all that was mere child's play. And here, Monsieur, is the proof of what I say."

Rouletabille drew from his pocket a small packet, from which he produced a strong iron peg.

"This, Monsieur," he said, "is a spike which perfectly fits a hole still to be seen in the cornice supporting the terrace. Larsan, who thought and prepared for everything in case of any emergency, had fixed this spike into the cornice. All he had to do to make his escape good was to plant one foot on a stone which is placed at the corner of the chateau, another on this support, one hand on the

---

* The suspected murder weapon, and from references elsewhere in the story, a fairly common type of club used by Parisian criminals at the time.

cornice of the keeper's door and the other on the terrace, and Larsan was clear of
the ground. The rest was easy. His acting after dinner as if he had been drugged
was make believe. He was not drugged; but he did drug me. Of course he had
to make it appear as if he also had been drugged so that no suspicion should fall
on him for my condition. Had I not been thus overpowered, Larsan would never
have entered Mademoiselle Stangerson's chamber that night, and the attack on
her would not have taken place."

A groan came from Darzac, who appeared to be unable to control his suffering.

"You can understand," added Rouletabille, "that Larsan would feel himself
hampered from the fact that my room was so close to his, and from a suspicion
that I would be on the watch that night. Naturally, he could not for a moment
believe that I suspected him! But I might see him leaving his room when he was
about to go to Mademoiselle Stangerson. He waited till I was asleep, and my friend
Sainclair was busy trying to rouse me. Ten minutes after that Mademoiselle was
calling out, "Murder!""

"How did you come to suspect Larsan?" asked the President.

"My pure reason pointed to him. That was why I watched him. But I did not
foresee the drugging. He is very cunning. Yes, my pure reason pointed to him;
but I required tangible proof so that my eyes could see him as my pure reason
saw him."

"What do you mean by your pure reason?"

"That power of one's mind which admits of no disturbing elements to a conclusion. The day following the incident of 'the inexplicable gallery,'* I felt myself
losing control of it. I had allowed myself to be diverted by fallacious evidence;
but I recovered and again took hold of the right end. I satisfied myself that the
murderer could not have left the gallery, either naturally or supernaturally. I narrowed the field of consideration to that small circle, so to speak. The murderer
could not be outside that circle. Now who was in it? There was, first, the murderer. Then there were Daddy Jacques, Monsieur Stangerson, Frederic Larsan,
and myself. Five persons in all, counting in the murderer. And yet, in the gallery,
there were but four. Now since it had been demonstrated to me that the fifth
could not have escaped, it was evident that one of the four present in the gallery
must be a double—he must be himself and the murderer also. Why had I not
seen this before? Simply because the phenomenon of the double personality had
not occurred before in this inquiry.

---

* An earlier incident in which the murderer, surrounded by Rouletabille and others, had apparently
vanished.

"Now who of the four persons in the gallery was both that person and the assassin? I went over in my mind what I had seen. I had seen at one and the same time, Monsieur Stangerson and the murderer, Daddy Jacques and the murderer, myself and the murderer; so that the murderer, then, could not be either Monsieur Stangerson, Daddy Jacques, or myself. Had I seen Frederic Larsan and the murderer at the same time?—No!—Two seconds had passed, during which I lost sight of the murderer; for, as I have noted in my papers, he arrived two seconds before Monsieur Stangerson, Daddy Jacques, and myself at the meeting-point of the two galleries. That would have given Larsan time to go through the 'off-turning' gallery, snatch off his false beard, return, and hurry with us as if, like us, in pursuit of the murderer. I was sure now I had got hold of the right end in my reasoning. With Frederic Larsan was now always associated, in my mind, the personality of the unknown of whom I was in pursuit—the murderer, in other words.

"That revelation staggered me. I tried to regain my balance by going over the evidences previously traced, but which had diverted my mind and led me away from Frederic Larsan. What were these evidences?

"1st. I had seen the unknown in Mademoiselle Stangerson's chamber. On going to Frederic Larsan's room, I had found Larsan sound asleep.

"2nd. The ladder.

"3rd. I had placed Frederic Larsan at the end of the 'off-turning' gallery and had told him that I would rush into Mademoiselle Stangerson's room to try to capture the murderer. Then I returned to Mademoiselle Stangerson's chamber where I had seen the unknown.

"The first evidence did not disturb me much. It is likely that, when I descended from my ladder, after having seen the unknown in Mademoiselle Stangerson's chamber, Larsan had already finished what he was doing there. Then, while I was re-entering the chateau, Larsan went back to his own room and, undressing himself, went to sleep.

"Nor did the second evidence trouble me. If Larsan were the murderer, he could have no use for a ladder; but the ladder might have been placed there to give an appearance to the murderer's entrance from without the chateau; especially as Larsan had accused Darzac and Darzac was not in the chateau that night. Further, the ladder might have been placed there to facilitate Larsan's flight in case of absolute necessity.

"But the third evidence puzzled me altogether. Having placed Larsan at the end of the 'off-turning gallery,' I could not explain how he had taken advantage of the moment when I had gone to the left wing of the chateau to find Monsieur

Stangerson and Daddy Jacques, to return to Mademoiselle Stangerson's room. It was a very dangerous thing to do. He risked being captured,—and he knew it. And he was very nearly captured. He had not had time to regain his post, as he had certainly hoped to do. He had then a very strong reason for returning to his room. As for myself, when I sent Daddy Jacques to the end of the 'right gallery,' I naturally thought that Larsan was still at his post. Daddy Jacques, in going to his post, had not looked, when he passed, to see whether Larsan was at his post or not.

"What, then, was the urgent reason which had compelled Larsan to go to the room a second time? I guessed it to be some evidence of his presence there. He had left something very important in that room. What was it? And had he recovered it? I begged Madame Bernier who was accustomed to clean the room to look, and she found a pair of eye-glasses—this pair, Monsieur President!"

And Rouletabille drew the eye-glasses, of which we know, from his pocket.

"When I saw these eye-glasses," he continued, "I was utterly nonplussed. I had never seen Larsan wear eye-glasses. What did they mean? Suddenly I exclaimed to myself: 'I wonder if he is long-sighted?' I had never seen Larsan write. He might, then, be long-sighted. They would certainly know at the *Sûreté*, and also know if the glasses were his. Such evidence would be damning. That explained Larsan's return. I know now that Larsan, or Ballmeyer, is long-sighted and that these glasses belonged to him.

"I now made one mistake. I was not satisfied with the evidence I had obtained. I wished to see the man's face. Had I refrained from this, the second terrible attack would not have occurred."

"But," asked the President, "why should Larsan go to Mademoiselle Stangerson's room, at all? Why should he twice attempt to murder her?"

"Because he loves her, Monsieur President."

"That is certainly a reason, but—"

"It is the only reason. He was madly in love, and because of that, and—other things, he was capable of committing any crime."

"Did Mademoiselle Stangerson know this?"

"Yes, Monsieur; but she was ignorant of the fact that the man who was pursuing her was Frederic Larsan, otherwise, of course, he would not have been allowed to be at the chateau. I noticed, when he was in her room after the incident in the gallery, that he kept himself in the shadow, and that he kept his head bent down. He was looking for the lost eye-glasses. Mademoiselle Stangerson knew Larsan under another name."

"Monsieur Darzac," asked the President, "did Mademoiselle Stangerson in any way confide in you on this matter? How is it that she has never spoken about it to anyone? If you are innocent, she would have wished to spare you the pain of being accused."

"Mademoiselle Stangerson told me nothing," replied Monsieur Darzac.

"Does what this young man says appear probable to you?" the President asked.

"Mademoiselle Stangerson has told me nothing," he replied stolidly.

"How do you explain that, on the night of the murder of the keeper," the President asked, turning to Rouletabille, "the murderer brought back the papers stolen from Monsieur Stangerson?—How do you explain how the murderer gained entrance into Mademoiselle Stangerson's locked room?"

"The last question is easily answered. A man like Larsan, or Ballmeyer, could have had made duplicate keys. As to the documents, I think Larsan had not intended to steal them, at first. Closely watching Mademoiselle with the purpose of preventing her marriage with Monsieur Robert Darzac, he one day followed her and Monsieur into the Grands Magasins de la Louvre.˙ There he got possession of the reticule† which she lost, or left behind. In that reticule was a key with a brass head. He did not know there was any value attached to the key till the advertisement in the newspapers revealed it. He then wrote to Mademoiselle, as the advertisement requested. No doubt he asked for a meeting, making known to her that he was also the person who had for some time pursued her with his love. He received no answer. He went to the Post Office and ascertained that his letter was no longer there. He had already taken complete stock of Monsieur Darzac, and, having decided to go to any lengths to gain Mademoiselle Stangerson, he had planned that, whatever might happen, Monsieur Darzac, his hated rival, should be the man to be suspected.

"I do not think that Larsan had as yet thought of murdering Mademoiselle Stangerson; but whatever he might do, he made sure that Monsieur Darzac should suffer for it. He was very nearly of the same height as Monsieur Darzac and had almost the same sized feet. It would not be difficult, to take an impression of Monsieur Darzac's footprints, and have similar boots made for himself. Such tricks were mere child's play for Larsan, or Ballmeyer.

"Receiving no reply to his letter, he determined, since Mademoiselle Stangerson would not come to him, that he would go to her. His plan had long been formed.

---

* A Paris department store.

† A type of small handbag.

He had made himself master of the plans of the chateau and the pavilion. So that, one afternoon, while Monsieur and Mademoiselle Stangerson were out for a walk, and while Daddy Jacques was away, he entered the latter by the vestibule window. He was alone, and, being in no hurry, he began examining the furniture. One of the pieces, resembling a safe, had a very small keyhole. That interested him! He had with him the little key with the brass head, and, associating one with the other, he tried the key in the lock. The door opened. He saw nothing but papers. They must be very valuable to have been put away in a safe, and the key to which to be of so much importance. Perhaps a thought of blackmail occurred to him as a useful possibility in helping him in his designs on Mademoiselle Stangerson. He quickly made a parcel of the papers and took it to the lavatory in the vestibule. Between the time of his first examination of the pavilion and the night of the murder of the keeper, Larsan had had time to find out what those papers contained. He could do nothing with them, and they were rather compromising. That night he took them back to the chateau. Perhaps he hoped that, by returning the papers he might obtain some gratitude from Mademoiselle Stangerson. But whatever may have been his reasons, he took the papers back and so rid himself of an encumbrance."

Rouletabille coughed. It was evident to me that he was embarrassed. He had arrived at a point where he had to keep back his knowledge of Larsan's true motive. The explanation he had given had evidently been unsatisfactory. Rouletabille was quick enough to note the bad impression he had made, for, turning to the President, he said: "And now we come to the explanation of the Mystery of the Yellow Room!"

A movement of chairs in the court with a rustling of dresses and an energetic whispering of "Hush!" showed the curiosity that had been aroused.

"It seems to me," said the President, "that the Mystery of the Yellow Room, Monsieur Rouletabille, is wholly explained by your hypothesis. Frederic Larsan is the explanation. We have merely to substitute him for Monsieur Robert Darzac. Evidently the door of the Yellow Room was open at the time Monsieur Stangerson was alone, and that he allowed the man who was coming out of his daughter's chamber to pass without arresting him—perhaps at her entreaty to avoid all scandal."

"No, Monsieur President," protested the young man. "You forget that, stunned by the attack made on her, Mademoiselle Stangerson was not in a condition to have made such an appeal. Nor could she have locked and bolted herself in her room. You must also remember that Monsieur Stangerson has sworn that the door was not open."

"That, however, is the only way in which it can be explained. The Yellow Room was as closely shut as an iron safe. To use your own expression, it was impossible for the murderer to make his escape either naturally or supernaturally. When the room was broken into he was not there! He must, therefore, have escaped."

"That does not follow."

"What do you mean?"

"There was no need for him to escape—if he was not there!"

"Not there!"

"Evidently, not. He could not have been there, if he were not found there."

"But, what about the evidences of his presence?" asked the President.

"That, Monsieur President, is where we have taken hold of the wrong end. From the time Mademoiselle Stangerson shut herself in the room to the time her door was burst open, it was impossible for the murderer to escape. He was not found because he was not there during that time."

"But the evidences?"

"They have led us astray. In reasoning on this mystery we must not take them to mean what they apparently mean. Why do we conclude the murderer was there?—Because he left his tracks in the room? Good! But may he not have been there before the room was locked? Nay, he must have been there before! Let us look into the matter of these traces and see if they do not point to my conclusion.

"After the publication of the article in the *Matin* and my conversation with the examining magistrate on the journey from Paris to Epinay-sur-Orge, I was certain that the Yellow Room had been hermetically sealed, so to speak, and that consequently the murderer had escaped before Mademoiselle Stangerson had gone into her chamber at midnight.

"At the time I was much puzzled. Mademoiselle Stangerson could not have been her own murderer, since the evidences pointed to some other person. The assassin, then, had come before. If that were so, how was it that Mademoiselle had been attacked after? or rather, that she appeared to have been attacked after? It was necessary for me to reconstruct the occurrence and make of it two phases—each separated from the other, in time, by the space of several hours. One phase in which Mademoiselle Stangerson had really been attacked—the other phase in which those who heard her cries thought she was being attacked. I had not then examined the Yellow Room. What were the marks on Mademoiselle Stangerson? There were marks of strangulation and the wound from a hard blow on the temple. The marks of strangulation did not interest me much; they might have been made before, and Mademoiselle Stangerson could have concealed them by a collarette, or any similar article of apparel. I had to suppose this the moment I was compelled to reconstruct the occurrence by two phases. Mademoiselle Stangerson had, no doubt, her own reasons for so doing, since she had told her father nothing of it, and had made it understood to the examining magistrate that the attack had taken place in the night, during the second phase. She was forced to say that, otherwise her father would have questioned her as to her reason for having said nothing about it.

"But I could not explain the blow on the temple. I understood it even less when I learned that the mutton-bone had been found in her room. She could not hide the fact that she had been struck on the head, and yet that wound appeared evidently to have been inflicted during the first phase, since it required the presence of the murderer! I thought Mademoiselle Stangerson had hidden the wound by arranging her hair in bands on her forehead.

"As to the mark of the hand on the wall, that had evidently been made during the first phase—when the murderer was really there. All the traces of his presence had naturally been left during the first phase; the mutton-bone, the black footprints, the Basque cap, the handkerchief, the blood on the wall, on the door, and on the floor. If those traces were still all there, they showed that Mademoiselle Stangerson—who desired that nothing should be known—had not yet had time to clear them away. This led me to the conclusion that the two phases had taken place one shortly after the other. She had not had the opportunity, after leaving her room and going back to the laboratory to her father, to get back again to her room and put it in order. Her father was all the time with her, working. So that after the first phase she did not re-enter her chamber till midnight. Daddy Jacques was there at ten o'clock, as he was every night; but he went in merely to close the blinds and light the night-light. Owing to her disturbed state of mind she had forgotten that Daddy Jacques would go into her room and had begged him not to trouble himself. All this was set forth in the article in the *Matin*. Daddy Jacques did go, however, and, in the dim light of the room, saw nothing.

"Mademoiselle Stangerson must have lived some anxious moments while Daddy Jacques was absent; but I think she was not aware that so many evidences had been left. After she had been attacked she had only time to hide the traces of the man's fingers on her neck and to hurry to the laboratory. Had she known of the bone, the cap, and the handkerchief, she would have made away with them after she had gone back to her chamber at midnight. She did not see them, and undressed by the uncertain glimmer of the night light. She went to bed, worn-out by anxiety and fear—a fear that had made her remain in the laboratory as late as possible.

"My reasoning had thus brought me to the second phase of the tragedy, when Mademoiselle Stangerson was alone in the room. I had now to explain the revolver shots fired during the second phase. Cries of 'Help!—Murder!' had been heard. How to explain these? As to the cries, I was in no difficulty; since she was alone in her room these could result from nightmare only. My explanation of the struggle and noise that were heard is simply that in her nightmare she was haunted by the terrible experience she had passed through in the afternoon. In her dream she sees the murderer about to spring upon her and she cries, 'Help! Murder!' Her hand wildly seeks the revolver she had placed within her reach on the night-table by the side of her bed, but her hand, striking the table, overturns it, and the revolver, falling to the floor, discharges itself, the bullet lodging in the ceiling. I knew from the first that the bullet in the ceiling must have resulted from an accident. Its very position suggested an accident to my mind, and so fell in with my theory of a nightmare. I no longer doubted that the attack had taken place before Mademoiselle had retired for the night. After wakening from her frightful dream and crying aloud for help, she had fainted.

"My theory, based on the evidence of the shots that were heard at midnight, demanded two shots—one which wounded the murderer at the time of his attack, and one fired at the time of the nightmare. The evidence given by the Berniers before the examining magistrate was to the effect that only one shot had been heard. Monsieur Stangerson testified to hearing a dull sound first followed by a sharp ringing sound. The dull sound I explained by the falling of the marble-topped table; the ringing sound was the shot from the revolver. I was now convinced I was right. The shot that had wounded the hand of the murderer and had caused it to bleed so that he left the bloody imprint on the wall was fired by Mademoiselle in self-defence, before the second phase, when she had been really attacked. The shot in the ceiling which the Berniers heard was the accidental shot during the nightmare.

"I had now to explain the wound on the temple. It was not severe enough to have been made by means of the mutton-bone, and Mademoiselle had not attempted to hide it. It must have been made during the second phase. It was to find this out that I went to the Yellow Room, and I obtained my answer there."

Rouletabille drew a piece of white folded paper from his pocket, and drew out of it an almost invisible object which he held between his thumb and forefinger.

"This, Monsieur President," he said, "is a hair—a blond hair stained with blood;—it is a hair from the head of Mademoiselle Stangerson. I found it sticking to one of the corners of the overturned table. The corner of the table was itself stained with blood—a tiny stain—hardly visible; but it told me that, on rising from her bed, Mademoiselle Stangerson had fallen heavily and had struck her head on the corner of its marble top.

"I still had to learn, in addition to the name of the assassin, which I did later, the time of the original attack. I learned this from the examination of Mademoiselle Stangerson and her father, though the answers given by the former were well calculated to deceive the examining magistrate—Mademoiselle Stangerson had stated very minutely how she had spent the whole of her time that day. We established the fact that the murderer had introduced himself into the pavilion between five and six o'clock. At a quarter past six the professor and his daughter had resumed their work. At five the professor had been with his daughter, and since the attack took place in the professor's absence from his daughter, I had to find out just when he left her. The professor had stated that at the time when he and his daughter were about to re-enter the laboratory he was met by the keeper and held in conversation about the cutting of some wood and the poachers. Mademoiselle Stangerson was not with him then since the professor said: 'I left the keeper and rejoined my daughter who was at work in the laboratory.'

"It was during that short interval of time that the tragedy took place. That is certain. In my mind's eye I saw Mademoiselle Stangerson re-enter the pavilion, go to her room to take off her hat, and find herself faced by the murderer. He had been in the pavilion for some time waiting for her. He had arranged to pass the whole night there. He had taken off Daddy Jacques's boots; he had removed the papers from the cabinet; and had then slipped under the bed. Finding the time long, he had risen, gone again into the laboratory, then into the vestibule, looked into the garden, and had seen, coming towards the pavilion, Mademoiselle Stangerson—alone. He would never have dared to attack her at that hour, if he had not found her alone. His mind was made up. He would be more at ease alone with Mademoiselle Stangerson in the pavilion, than he would have been in the middle of the night, with Daddy Jacques sleeping in the attic. So he shut the vestibule window. That explains why neither Monsieur Stangerson, nor the keeper, who were at some distance from the pavilion, had heard the revolver shot.

"Then he went back to 'The Yellow Room.' Mademoiselle Stangerson came in. What passed must have taken place very quickly. Mademoiselle tried to call for help; but the man had seized her by the throat. Her hand had sought and grasped the revolver which she had been keeping in the drawer of her night-table, since she had come to fear the threats of her pursuer. The murderer was about to strike her on the head with the mutton-bone—a terrible weapon in the hands of a Larsan or Ballmeyer; but she fired in time, and the shot wounded the hand that held the weapon. The bone fell to the floor covered with the blood of the murderer, who staggered, clutched at the wall for support—imprinting on it the red marks—and, fearing another bullet, fled.

"She saw him pass through the laboratory, and listened. He was long at the window. At length he jumped from it. She flew to it and shut it. The danger past, all her thoughts were of her father. Had he either seen or heard? At any cost to herself she must keep this from him. Thus when Monsieur Stangerson returned, he found the door of the Yellow Room closed, and his daughter in the laboratory, bending over her desk, at work!"

Turning towards Monsieur Darzac, Rouletabille cried: "You know the truth! Tell us, then, if that is not how things happened."

"I don't know anything about it," replied Monsieur Darzac.

"I admire you for your silence," said Rouletabille, "but if Mademoiselle Stangerson knew of your danger, she would release you from your oath. She would beg of you to tell all she has confided to you. She would be here to defend you!"

Monsieur Darzac made no movement, nor uttered a word. He looked at Rouletabille sadly.

"However," said the young reporter, "since Mademoiselle is not here, I must do it myself. But, believe me, Monsieur Darzac, the only means to save Mademoiselle Stangerson and restore her to her reason, is to secure your acquittal."

"What is this secret motive that compels Mademoiselle Stangerson to hide her knowledge from her father?" asked the President.

"That, Monsieur, I do not know," said Rouletabille. "It is no business of mine."

The President, turning to Monsieur Darzac, endeavoured to induce him to tell what he knew.

"Do you still refuse, Monsieur, to tell us how you employed your time during the attempts on the life of Mademoiselle Stangerson?"

"I cannot tell you anything, Monsieur."

The President turned to Rouletabille as if appealing for an explanation.

"We must assume, Monsieur President, that Monsieur Robert Darzac's absences are closely connected with Mademoiselle Stangerson's secret, and that Monsieur Darzac feels himself in honour bound to remain silent. It may be that Larsan, who, since his three attempts, has had everything in training to cast suspicion on Monsieur Darzac, had fixed on just those occasions for a meeting with Monsieur Darzac at a spot most compromising. Larsan is cunning enough to have done that."

The President seemed partly convinced, but still curious, he asked:

"But what is this secret of Mademoiselle Stangerson?"

"That I cannot tell you," said Rouletabille. "I think, however, you know enough now to acquit Monsieur Robert Darzac! Unless Larsan should return, and I don't think he will," he added, with a laugh.

"One question more," said the President. "Admitting your explanation, we know that Larsan wished to turn suspicion on Monsieur Robert Darzac, but why should he throw suspicion on Daddy Jacques also?"

"There came in the professional detective, Monsieur, who proves himself an unraveller of mysteries, by annihilating the very proofs he had accumulated. He's a very cunning man, and a similar trick had often enabled him to turn suspicion from himself. He proved the innocence of one before accusing the other. You can easily believe, Monsieur, that so complicated a scheme as this must have been long and carefully thought out in advance by Larsan. I can tell you that he had long been engaged on its elaboration. If you care to learn how he had gathered information, you will find that he had, on one occasion, disguised himself as the commissionaire between the Laboratory of the *Sûreté* and Monsieur Stangerson, of whom 'experiments' were demanded. In this way he had been able before the crime, on two occasions to take stock of the pavilion. He had 'made up' so that Daddy Jacques had not recognised him. And yet Larsan had found the opportunity to rob the old man of a pair of old boots and a cast-off Basque cap, which the servant had tied up in a handkerchief, with the intention of carrying them to a friend, a charcoal-burner on the road to Epinay. When the crime was discovered, Daddy Jacques had immediately recognised these objects as his. They were extremely compromising, which explains his distress at the time when we spoke to him about them. Larsan confessed it all to me. He is an artist at the game. He did a similar thing in the affair of the 'Credit Universel,' and in that of the 'Gold Ingots of the Mint.' Both these cases should be revised. Since Ballmeyer or Larsan has been in the *Sûreté* a number of innocent persons have been sent to prison."

THE JEWISH LAMP

(EXTRACT)

by Maurice Leblanc

1908

Born in Normandy, Maurice Leblanc studied in several countries before dropping out of law school to become a writer. His novels, influenced by great French writers like Gustav Flaubert and Guy de Maupassant, were critical successes but sold poorly; his crime fiction proved to be much more commercial.

Leblanc's anti-hero Arsène Lupin is often cited as the prototype of the gentleman thief character, although E. W. Hornung had created A. J. Raffles several years before the publication of the first Lupin story. Lupin was not even the first gentleman thief character to appear in French: the novelist and playwright Octave Mirabeau created Arthur Lebeau in his 1901 novel *Les 21 jours d'un neurasthénique* (*Twenty-one Days of a Neurasthenic*), and the following year his play *Scrupules* featured a similar character.

Leblanc wasted no time in throwing down the gauntlet to Doyle and Holmes. In June 1906, the French Magazine *Je sais tout* ("I know all") published a Lupin story titled "Sherlock Holmes Arrives Too Late," prompting legal objections from Doyle. Leblanc responded by changing a few key names when the story was collected in book form: Herlock Sholmes and his faithful sidekick Wilson appeared in two further stories, "The Blonde Lady" and "The Jewish Lamp," which were collected in book form as *Arsène Lupin contre Herlock Sholmes*. "Herlock Sholmes" seems to have been too much for the publishers of the first English translations, who came up with *Arsène Lupin versus*

Holmlock Shears instead. One wonders why they bothered, and so, apparently, did they: subsequent U.S. printings changed the book's title to *The Blonde Lady.*

"The Jewish Lamp" consists of two chapters, the first of which is presented here. In the second part, "The Shipwreck," Sholmes confronts Lupin on a boat on the Seine; Lupin appears to drown, but reappears later, after Sholmes has solved the mystery, and the two exchange some rather unconvincing words of mutual admiration.

H erlock Sholmes and Wilson were sitting in front of the fireplace, in comfortable armchairs, with the feet extended toward the grateful warmth of a glowing coke fire.

Sholmes' pipe, a short brier with a silver band, had gone out. He knocked out the ashes, filled it, lighted it, pulled the skirts of his dressing-gown over his knees, and drew from his pipe great puffs of smoke, which ascended toward the ceiling in scores of shadow rings.

Wilson gazed at him, as a dog lying curled up on a rug before the fire might look at his master, with great round eyes which have no hope other than to obey the least gesture of his owner. Was the master going to break the silence? Would he reveal to Wilson the subject of his reverie and admit his satellite into the charmed realm of his thoughts? When Sholmes had maintained his silent attitude for some time. Wilson ventured to speak:

"Everything seems quiet now. Not the shadow of a case to occupy our leisure moments."

Sholmes did not reply, but the rings of smoke emitted by Sholmes were better formed, and Wilson observed that his companion drew considerable pleasure from that trifling fact—an indication that the great man was not absorbed in any serious meditation. Wilson, discouraged, arose and went to the window.

The lonely street extended between the gloomy façades of grimy houses, unusually gloomy this morning by reason of a heavy downfall of rain. A cab passed; then another. Wilson made an entry of their numbers in his memorandum-book. One never knows!

"Ah!" he exclaimed, "the postman."

The man entered, shown in by the servant.

"Two registered letters, sir . . . if you will sign, please?"

Sholmes signed the receipts, accompanied the man to the door, and was opening one of the letters as he returned.

"It seems to please you," remarked Wilson, after a moment's silence.

"This letter contains a very interesting proposition. You are anxious for a case—here's one. Read—"

Wilson read:

> "Monsieur,
>
> "I desire the benefit of your services and experience. I have been the victim of a serious theft, and the investigation has as yet been unsuccessful. I am sending to you by this mail a number of newspapers which will inform you of the affair, and if you will undertake the case, I will place my house at your disposal and ask you to fill in the enclosed check, signed by me, for whatever sum you require for your expenses.
>
> "Kindly reply by telegraph, and much oblige,
>
> "Your humble servant,
>
> "Baron Victor d'Imblevalle,
>
> "18 Rue Murillo, Paris."

"Ah!" exclaimed Sholmes, "that sounds good . . . a little trip to Paris . . . and why not, Wilson? Since my famous duel with Arsène Lupin, I have not had an excuse to go there. I should be pleased to visit the capital of the world under less strenuous conditions."

He tore the check into four pieces and, while Wilson, whose arm had not yet regained its former strength,* uttered bitter words against Paris and the Parisians, Sholmes opened the second envelope. Immediately, he made a gesture of annoyance, and a wrinkle appeared on his forehead during the reading of the letter; then, crushing the paper into a ball, he threw it, angrily, on the floor.

"Well! What's the matter?" asked Wilson, anxiously.

He picked up the ball of paper, unfolded it, and read, with increasing amazement:

> "My Dear Monsieur:
>
> "You know full well the admiration I have for you and the interest I take in your renown. Well, believe me, when I warn you to have

---

* Wilson's arm was broken by Lupin's men in the previous story, "The Blonde Lady."

nothing whatever to do with the case on which you have just now been called to Paris. Your intervention will cause much harm; your efforts will produce a most lamentable result; and you will be obliged to make a public confession of your defeat.

"Having a sincere desire to spare you such humiliation, I implore you, in the name of the friendship that unites us, to remain peacefully reposing at your own fireside.

"My best wishes to Monsieur Wilson, and, for yourself, the sincere regards of your devoted ARSÈNE LUPIN."

"Arsène Lupin!" repeated Wilson, astounded.

Sholmes struck the table with his fist, and exclaimed:

"Ah! he is pestering me already, the fool! He laughs at me as if I were a schoolboy! The public confession of my defeat! Didn't I force him to disgorge the blue diamond?"

"I tell you—he's afraid," suggested Wilson.

"Nonsense! Arsène Lupin is not afraid, and this taunting letter proves it."

"But how did he know that the Baron d'Imblevalle had written to you?"

"What do I know about it? You do ask some stupid questions, my boy."

"I thought . . . I supposed—"

"What? That I am a clairvoyant? Or a sorcerer?"

"No, but I have seen you do some marvellous things."

"No person can perform *marvellous* things. I no more than you. I reflect, I deduct, I conclude—that is all; but I do not divine. Only fools divine."

Wilson assumed the attitude of a whipped cur, and resolved not to make a fool of himself by trying to divine why Sholmes paced the room with quick, nervous strides. But when Sholmes rang for the servant and ordered his valise, Wilson thought that he was in possession of a material fact which gave him the right to reflect, deduct and conclude that his associate was about to take a journey. The same mental operation permitted him to assert, with almost mathematical exactness:

"Sholmes, you are going to Paris."

"Possibly."

"And Lupin's affront impels you to go, rather than the desire to assist the Baron d'Imblevalle."

"Possibly."

"Sholmes, I shall go with you."

"Ah; ah! my old friend," exclaimed Sholmes, interrupting his walking, "you are not afraid that your right arm will meet the same fate as your left?"

"What can happen to me? You will be there."

"That's the way to talk, Wilson. We will show that clever Frenchman that he made a mistake when he threw his glove in our faces. Be quick, Wilson, we must catch the first train."

"Without waiting for the papers the baron has sent you?"

"What good are they?"

"I will send a telegram."

"No; if you do that, Arsène Lupin will know of my arrival. I wish to avoid that. This time, Wilson, we must fight under cover."

That afternoon, the two friends embarked at Dover. The passage was a delightful one. In the train from Calais to Paris, Sholmes had three hours' sound sleep, while Wilson guarded the door of the compartment.

Sholmes awoke in good spirits. He was delighted at the idea of another duel with Arsène Lupin, and he rubbed his hands with the satisfied air of a man who looks forward to a pleasant vacation.

"At last!" exclaimed Wilson, "we are getting to work again."

And he rubbed his hands with the same satisfied air.

At the station, Sholmes took the wraps and, followed by Wilson, who carried the valises, he gave up his tickets and started off briskly.

"Fine weather, Wilson. . . . Blue sky and sunshine! Paris is giving us a royal reception."

"Yes, but what a crowd!"

"So much the better, Wilson, we will pass unnoticed. No one will recognize us in such a crowd."

"Is this Monsieur Sholmes?"

He stopped, somewhat puzzled. Who the deuce could thus address him by his name? A woman stood beside him; a young girl whose simple dress outlined her slender form and whose pretty face had a sad and anxious expression. She repeated her enquiry:

"You are Monsieur Sholmes?"

As he still remained silent, as much from confusion as from a habit of prudence, the girl asked a third time:

"Have I the honor of addressing Monsieur Sholmes?"

"What do you want?" he replied, testily, considering the incident a suspicious one.

"You must listen to me, Monsieur Sholmes, as it is a serious matter. I know that you are going to the Rue Murillo."

"What do you say?"

"I know . . . I know . . . Rue Murillo . . . number 18. Well, you must not go . . . no, you must not. I assure you that you will regret it. Do not think that I have any interest in the matter. I do it because it is right . . . because my conscience tells me to do it."

Sholmes tried to get away, but she persisted:

"Oh! I beg of you, don't neglect my advice. . . . Ah! if I only knew how to convince you! Look at me! Look into my eyes! They are sincere . . . they speak the truth."

She gazed at Sholmes, fearlessly but innocently, with those beautiful eyes, serious and clear, in which her very soul seemed to be reflected.

Wilson nodded his head, as he said:

"Mademoiselle looks honest."

"Yes," she implored, "and you must have confidence—"

"I have confidence in you, mademoiselle," replied Wilson.

"Oh, how happy you make me! And so has your friend? I feel it . . . I am sure of it! What happiness! Everything will be all right now! . . . What a good idea of mine! . . . Ah! yes, there is a train for Calais in twenty minutes. You will take it. . . . Quick, follow me . . . you must come this way . . . there is just time."

She tried to drag them along. Sholmes seized her arm, and in as gentle a voice as he could assume, said to her:

"Excuse me, mademoiselle, if I cannot yield to your wishes, but I never abandon a task that I have once undertaken."

"I beseech you . . . I implore you. . . . Ah if you could only understand!"

Sholmes passed outside and walked away at a quick pace. Wilson said to the girl:

"Have no fear . . . he will be in at the finish. He never failed yet."

And he ran to overtake Sholmes.

HERLOCK SHOLMES—ARSÈNE LUPIN.

These words, in great black letters, met their gaze as soon as they left the railway station. A number of sandwich-men were parading through the street, one behind the other, carrying heavy canes with iron ferrules with which they struck the pavement in harmony, and, on their backs, they carried large posters, on which one could read the following notice:

THE MATCH BETWEEN HERLOCK SHOLMES AND ARSÈNE LUPIN. ARRIVAL OF THE ENGLISH CHAMPION. THE GREAT DETECTIVE ATTACKS THE MYSTERY OF THE Rue MURILLO. READ THE DETAILS IN THE "ECHO DE FRANCE".

Wilson shook his head, and said:

"Look at that, Sholmes, and we thought we were traveling incognito! I shouldn't be surprised to find the Republican Guard waiting for us at the Rue Murillo to give us an official reception with toasts and champagne."

"Wilson, when you get funny, you get beastly funny," growled Sholmes.

Then he approached one of the sandwich-men with the obvious intention of seizing him in his powerful grip and crushing him, together with his infernal sign-board. There was quite a crowd gathered about the men, reading the notices, and joking and laughing.

Repressing a furious access of rage, Sholmes said to the man:

"When did they hire you?"

"This morning."

"How long have you been parading?"

"About an hour."

"But the boards were ready before that?"

"Oh, yes, they were ready when we went to the agency this morning."

So then it appears that Arsène Lupin had foreseen that he, Sholmes, would accept the challenge. More than that, the letter written by Lupin showed that he was eager for the fray and that he was prepared to measure swords once more with his formidable rival. Why! What motive could Arsène Lupin have in renewing the struggle!

Sholmes hesitated for a moment. Lupin must be very confident of his success to show so much insolence in advance; and was not he, Sholmes, falling into a trap by rushing into the battle at the first call for help?

However, he called a carriage.

"Come, Wilson! . . . Driver, 18 Rue Murillo!" he exclaimed, with an outburst of his accustomed energy. With distended veins and clenched fists, as if he were about to engage in a boxing bout, he jumped into the carriage.

ᘡ

The Rue Murillo is bordered with magnificent private residences, the rear of which overlook the Parc Monceau. One of the most pretentious of these houses is number 18, owned and occupied by the Baron d'Imblevalle and furnished in a luxurious manner consistent with the owner's taste and wealth. There was a courtyard in front of the house, and, in the rear, a garden well filled with trees whose branches mingle with those of the park.

After ringing the bell, the two Englishmen were admitted, crossed the courtyard, and were received at the door by a footman who showed them into a small parlor facing the garden in the rear of the house. They sat down and, glancing about, made a rapid inspection of the many valuable objects with which the room was filled.

"Everything very choice," murmured Wilson, "and in the best of taste. It is a safe deduction to make that those who had the leisure to collect these articles must now be at least fifty years of age."

The door opened, and the Baron d'Imblevalle entered, followed by his wife. Contrary to the deduction made by Wilson, they were both quite young, of elegant appearance, and vivacious in speech and action. They were profuse in their expressions of gratitude.

"So kind of you to come! Sorry to have caused you so much trouble! The theft now seems of little consequence, since it has procured us this pleasure."

"How charming these French people are!" thought Wilson, evolving one of his commonplace deductions.

"But time is money," exclaimed the baron, "especially your time, Monsieur Sholmes. So I will come to the point. Now, what do you think of the affair? Do you think you can succeed in it?"

"Before I can answer that I must know what it is about."

"I thought you knew."

"No; so I must ask you for full particulars, even to the smallest detail. First, what is the nature of the case?"

"A theft."

"When did it take place?"

"Last Saturday," replied the baron, "or, at least, some time during Saturday night or Sunday morning."

"That was six days ago. Now, you can tell me all about it."

"In the first place, monsieur, I must tell you that my wife and I, conforming to the manner of life that our position demands, go out very little. The education of our children, a few receptions, and the care and decoration of our house—such constitutes our life; and nearly all our evenings are spent in this little room, which is my wife's boudoir, and in which we have gathered a few artistic objects. Last Saturday night, about eleven o'clock, I turned off the electric lights, and my wife and I retired, as usual, to our room."

"Where is your room?"

"It adjoins this. That is the door. Next morning, that is to say, Sunday morning, I arose quite early. As Suzanne, my wife, was still asleep, I passed into the boudoir as quietly as possible so as not to wake her. What was my astonishment when I found that window open—as we had left it closed the evening before!"

"A servant—"

"No one enters here in the morning until we ring. Besides, I always take the precaution to bolt the second door which communicates with the ante-chamber. Therefore, the window must have been opened from the outside. Besides, I have some evidence of that: the second pane of glass from the right—close to the fastening—had been cut."

"And what does that window overlook?"

"As you can see for yourself, it opens on a little balcony, surrounded by a stone railing. Here, we are on the first floor, and you can see the garden behind the house and the iron fence which separates it from the Parc Monceau. It is quite certain that the thief came through the park, climbed the fence by the aid of a ladder, and thus reached the terrace below the window."

"That is quite certain, you say!"

"Well, in the soft earth on either side of the fence, they found the two holes made by the bottom of the ladder, and two similar holes can be seen below the window. And the stone railing of the balcony shows two scratches which were doubtless made by the contact of the ladder."

"Is the Parc Monceau closed at night?"

"No; but if it were, there is a house in course of erection at number 14, and a person could enter that way."

Herlock Sholmes reflected for a few minutes, and then said:

"Let us come down to the theft. It must have been committed in this room?"

"Yes; there was here, between that twelfth-century Virgin and that tabernacle of chased silver, a small Jewish lamp. It has disappeared."

"And is that all?"

"That is all."

"Ah! . . . And what is a Jewish lamp!"

"One of those copper lamps used by the ancient Jews, consisting of a standard which supported a bowl containing the oil, and from this bowl projected several burners intended for the wicks."

"Upon the whole, an object of small value."

"No great value, of course. But this one contained a secret hiding-place in which we were accustomed to place a magnificent jewel, a chimera in gold, set with rubies and emeralds, which was of great value."

"Why did you hide it there?"

"Oh! I can't give any reason, monsieur, unless it was an odd fancy to utilize a hiding-place of that kind."

"Did anyone know it?"

"No."

"No one—except the thief," said Sholmes. "Otherwise he would not have taken the trouble to steal the lamp."

"Of course. But how could he know it, as it was only by accident that the secret mechanism of the lamp was revealed to us."

"A similar accident has revealed it to some one else . . . a servant . . . or an acquaintance. But let us proceed: I suppose the police have been notified?"

"Yes. The examining magistrate has completed his investigation. The reporter-detectives attached to the leading newspapers have also made their investigations. But, as I wrote to you, it seems to me the mystery will never be solved."

Sholmes arose, went to the window, examined the casement, the balcony, the terrace, studied the scratches on the stone railing with his magnifying-glass, and then requested M. d'Imblevalle to show him the garden.

Outside, Sholmes sat down in a rattan chair and gazed at the roof of the house in a dreamy way. Then he walked over to the two little wooden boxes with which they had covered the holes made in the ground by the bottom of the ladder with a view of preserving them intact. He raised the boxes, kneeled on the ground, scrutinized the holes and made some measurements. After making a similar examination of the holes near the fence, he and the baron returned to the boudoir where Madame d'Imblevalle was waiting for them. After a short silence Sholmes said:

"At the very outset of your story, baron, I was surprised at the very simple methods employed by the thief. To raise a ladder, cut a window-pane, select a valuable article, and walk out again—no, that is not the way such things are done. All that is too plain, too simple."

"Well, what do you think!"

"That the Jewish lamp was stolen under the direction of Arsène Lupin."

"Arsène Lupin!" exclaimed the baron.

"Yes, but he did not do it himself, as no one came from the outside. Perhaps a servant descended from the upper floor by means of a waterspout that I noticed when I was in the garden."

"What makes you think so!"

"Arsène Lupin would not leave this room empty-handed."

"Empty-handed! But he had the lamp."

"But that would not have prevented his taking that snuff-box, set with diamonds, or that opal necklace. When he leaves anything, it is because he can't carry it away."

"But the marks of the ladder outside!"

"A false scent. Placed there simply to avert suspicion."

"And the scratches on the balustrade?"

"A farce! They were made with a piece of sandpaper. See, here are scraps of the paper that I picked up in the garden."

"And what about the marks made by the bottom of the ladder?"

"Counterfeit! Examine the two rectangular holes below the window, and the two holes near the fence. They are of a similar form, but I find that the two holes near the house are closer to each other than the two holes near the fence. What does that fact suggest? To me, it suggested that the four holes were made by a piece of wood prepared for the purpose."

"The better proof would be the piece of wood itself."

"Here it is," said Sholmes, "I found it in the garden, under the box of a laurel tree."

The baron bowed to Sholmes in recognition of his skill. Only forty minutes had elapsed since the Englishman had entered the house, and he had already exploded all the theories theretofore formed, and which had been based on what appeared to be obvious and undeniable facts. But what now appeared to be the real facts of the case rested upon a more solid foundation, to-wit, the astute reasoning of a Herlock Sholmes.

"The accusation which you make against one of our household is a very serious matter," said the baroness. "Our servants have been with us a long time and none of them would betray our trust."

"If none of them has betrayed you, how can you explain the fact that I received this letter on the same day and by the same mail as the letter you wrote to me?"

He handed to the baroness the letter that he had received from Arsène Lupin. She exclaimed, in amazement:

"Arsène Lupin! How could he know?"

"Did you tell anyone that you had written to me?"

"No one," replied the baron. "The idea occurred to us the other evening at the dinner-table."

"Before the servants?"

"No, only our two children. Oh, no . . . Sophie and Henriette had left the table, hadn't they, Suzanne?"

Madame d'Imblevalle, after a moment's reflection, replied:

"Yes, they had gone to Mademoiselle."

"Mademoiselle?" queried Sholmes.

"The governess, Mademoiselle Alice Demun."

"Does she take her meals with you?"

"No. Her meals are served in her room."

Wilson had an idea. He said:

"The letter written to my friend Herlock Sholmes was posted?"

"Of course."

"Who posted it?"

"Dominique, who has been my valet for twenty years," replied the baron. "Any search in that direction would be a waste of time."

"One never wastes his time when engaged in a search," said Wilson, sententiously.

This preliminary investigation now ended, and Sholmes asked permission to retire.

At dinner, an hour later, he saw Sophie and Henriette, the two children of the family. One was six and the other eight years of age. There was very little conversation at the table. Sholmes responded to the friendly advances of his hosts in such a curt manner that they were soon reduced to silence. When the coffee was served, Sholmes swallowed the contents of his cup, and rose to take his leave.

At that moment, a servant entered with a telephone message addressed to Sholmes. He opened it, and read:

"You have my enthusiastic admiration. The results attained by you in so short a time are simply marvellous. I am dismayed.

"ARSÈNE LUPIN."

Sholmes made a gesture of indignation and handed the message to the baron, saying:

"What do you think now, monsieur? Are the walls of your house furnished with eyes and ears?"

"I don't understand it," said the baron, in amazement.

"Nor do I; but I do understand that Lupin has knowledge of everything that occurs in this house. He knows every movement, every word. There is no doubt of it. But how does he get his information? That is the first mystery I have to solve, and when I know that I will know everything."

ᕰ

That night, Wilson retired with the clear conscience of a man who has performed his whole duty and thus acquired an undoubted right to sleep and repose. So he fell asleep very quickly, and was soon enjoying the most delightful dreams in which he pursued Lupin and captured him single-handed; and the sensation was so vivid and exciting that it woke him from his sleep. Someone was standing at his bedside. He seized his revolver, and cried:

"Don't move, Lupin, or I'll fire."

"The deuce! Wilson, what do you mean?"

"Oh! it is you, Sholmes. Do you want me?"

"I want to show you something. Get up."

Sholmes led him to the window, and said:

"Look! . . . on the other side of the fence. . . ."

"In the park?"

"Yes. What do you see?"

"I don't see anything."

"Yes, you do see something."

"Ah! of course, a shadow . . . two of them."

"Yes, close to the fence. See, they are moving. Come, quick!"

Quickly they descended the stairs, and reached a room which opened into the garden. Through the glass door they could see the two shadowy forms in the same place.

"It is very strange," said Sholmes, "but it seems to me I can hear a noise inside the house."

"Inside the house? Impossible! Everybody is asleep."

"Well, listen—"

At that moment a low whistle came from the other side of the fence, and they perceived a dim light which appeared to come from the house.

"The baron must have turned on the light in his room. It is just above us."

"That must have been the noise you heard," said Wilson. "Perhaps they are watching the fence also."

Then there was a second whistle, softer than before.

"I don't understand it; I don't understand," said Sholmes, irritably.

"No more do I," confessed Wilson.

Sholmes turned the key, drew the bolt, and quietly opened the door. A third whistle, louder than before, and modulated to another form. And the noise above their heads became more pronounced. Sholmes said:

"It seems to be on the balcony outside the boudoir window."

He put his head through the half-opened door, but immediately recoiled, with a stifled oath. Then Wilson looked. Quite close to them there was a ladder, the upper end of which was resting on the balcony.

"The deuce!" said Sholmes, "there is someone in the boudoir. That is what we heard. Quick, let us remove the ladder."

But at that instant a man slid down the ladder and ran toward the spot where his accomplices were waiting for him outside the fence. He carried the ladder with him. Sholmes and Wilson pursued the man and overtook him just as he was placing the ladder against the fence. From the other side of the fence two shots were fired.

"Wounded?" cried Sholmes.

"No," replied Wilson.

Wilson seized the man by the body and tried to hold him, but the man turned and plunged a knife into Wilson's breast. He uttered a groan, staggered and fell.

"Damnation!" muttered Sholmes, "if they have killed him I will kill them."

He laid Wilson on the grass and rushed toward the ladder. Too late—the man had climbed the fence and, accompanied by his confederates, had fled through the bushes.

"Wilson, Wilson, it is not serious, eh? Merely a scratch."

The house door opened, and Monsieur d'Imblevalle appeared, followed by the servants, carrying candles.

"What's the matter?" asked the baron. "Is Monsieur Wilson wounded?"

"Oh! it's nothing—a mere scratch," repeated Sholmes, trying to deceive himself.

The blood was flowing profusely, and Wilson's face was livid. Twenty minutes later the doctor ascertained that the point of the knife had penetrated to within an inch and a half of the heart.

"An inch and a half of the heart! Wilson always was lucky!" said Sholmes, in an envious tone.

"Lucky . . . lucky. . . ." muttered the doctor.

"Of course! Why, with his robust constitution he will soon be out again."

"Six weeks in bed and two months of convalescence."

"Not more?"

"No, unless complications set in."

"Oh! the devil! What does he want complications for?"

Fully reassured, Sholmes joined the baron in the boudoir. This time the mysterious visitor had not exercised the same restraint. Ruthlessly, he had laid his vicious hand upon the diamond snuff-box, upon the opal necklace, and, in a general way, upon everything that could find a place in the greedy pockets of an enterprising burglar.

The window was still open; one of the window-panes had been neatly cut; and, in the morning, a summary investigation showed that the ladder belonged to the house then in course of construction.

"Now, you can see," said M. d'Imblevalle, with a touch of irony, "it is an exact repetition of the affair of the Jewish lamp."

"Yes, if we accept the first theory adopted by the police."

"Haven't you adopted it yet? Doesn't this second theft shatter your theory in regard to the first?"

"It only confirms it, monsieur."

"That is incredible! You have positive evidence that last night's theft was committed by an outsider, and yet you adhere to your theory that the Jewish lamp was stolen by someone in the house."

"Yes, I am sure of it."

"How do you explain it?"

"I do not explain anything, monsieur; I have established two facts which do not appear to have any relation to each other, and yet I am seeking the missing link that connects them."

His conviction seemed to be so earnest and positive that the baron submitted to it, and said:

"Very well, we will notify the police—"

"Not at all!" exclaimed the Englishman, quickly, "not at all! I intend to ask for their assistance when I need it—but not before."

"But the attack on your friend?"

"That's of no consequence. He is only wounded. Secure the license of the doctor. I shall be responsible for the legal side of the affair."

ↄ

The next two days proved uneventful. Yet Sholmes was investigating the case with a minute care, and with a sense of wounded pride resulting from that audacious theft, committed under his nose, in spite of his presence and beyond his power to prevent it. He made a thorough investigation of the house and garden, interviewed the servants, and paid lengthy visits to the kitchen and stables. And, although his efforts were fruitless, he did not despair.

"I will succeed," he thought, "and the solution must be sought within the walls of this house. This affair is quite different from that of the blonde Lady, where I had to work in the dark, on unknown ground. This time I am on the battlefield itself. The enemy is not the elusive and invisible Lupin, but the accomplice, in flesh and blood, who lives and moves within the confines of this house. Let me secure the slightest clue and the game is mine!"

That clue was furnished to him by accident.

On the afternoon of the third day, when he entered a room located above the boudoir, which served as a study for the children, he found Henriette, the younger of the two sisters. She was looking for her scissors.

"You know," she said to Sholmes, "I make papers like that you received the other evening."

"The other evening?"

"Yes, just as dinner was over, you received a paper with marks on it . . . you know, a telegram. . . . Well, I make them, too."

She left the room. To anyone else these words would seem to be nothing more than the insignificant remark of a child, and Sholmes himself listened to them with a distracted air and continued his investigation. But, suddenly, he ran after the child, and overtook her at the head of the stairs. He said to her:

"So you paste stamps and marks on papers?"

Henriette, very proudly, replied:

"Yes, I cut them out and paste them on."

"Who taught you that little game?"

"Mademoiselle . . . my governess . . . I have seen her do it often. She takes words out of the newspapers and pastes them—"

"What does she make out of them?"

"Telegrams and letters that she sends away."

Herlock Sholmes returned to the study, greatly puzzled by the information and seeking to draw from it a logical deduction. There was a pile of newspapers

THE JEWISH LAMP | 281

on the mantel. He opened them and found that many words and, in some places, entire lines had been cut out. But, after reading a few of the word's which preceded or followed, he decided that the missing words had been cut out at random—probably by the child. It was possible that one of the newspapers had been cut by mademoiselle; but how could he assure himself that such was the case?

Mechanically, Sholmes turned over the school-books on the table; then others which were lying on the shelf of a bookcase. Suddenly he uttered a cry of joy. In a corner of the bookcase, under a pile of old exercise books, he found a child's alphabet-book, in which the letters were ornamented with pictures, and on one of the pages of that book he discovered a place where a word had been removed. He examined it. It was a list of the days of the week. Monday, Tuesday, Wednesday, etc. The word "Saturday" was missing. Now, the theft of the Jewish lamp had occurred on a Saturday night.

Sholmes experienced that slight fluttering of the heart which always announced to him, in the clearest manner, that he had discovered the road which leads to victory. That ray of truth, that feeling of certainty, never deceived him.

With nervous fingers he hastened to examine the balance of the book. Very soon he made another discovery. It was a page composed of capital letters, followed by a line of figures. Nine of those letters and three of those figures had been carefully cut out. Sholmes made a list of the missing letters and figures in his memorandum book, in alphabetical and numerical order, and obtained the following result:

CDEHNOPEZ—237.

"Well! at first sight, it is a rather formidable puzzle," he murmured, "but, by transposing the letters and using all of them, is it possible to form one, two or three complete words?"

Sholmes tried it, in vain.

Only one solution seemed possible; it constantly appeared before him, no matter which way he tried to juggle the letters, until, at length, he was satisfied it was the true solution, since it harmonized with the logic of the facts and the general circumstances of the case.

As that page of the book did not contain any duplicate letters it was probable, in fact quite certain, that the words he could form from those letters would be incomplete, and that the original words had been completed with letters taken from other pages. Under those conditions he obtained the following solution, errors and omissions excepted:

REPOND Z—CH—237.

The first word was quite clear: *répondez* [reply], a letter E is missing because it occurs twice in the word, and the book furnished only one letter of each kind.

As to the second incomplete word, no doubt it formed, with the aid of the number 237, an address to which the reply was to be sent. They appointed Saturday as the time, and requested a reply to be sent to the address CH. 237.

Or, perhaps, CH. 237 was an address for a letter to be sent to the "general delivery" of some post office, or, again, they might form a part of some incomplete word. Sholmes searched the book once more, but did not discover that any other letters had been removed. Therefore, until further orders, he decided to adhere to the foregoing interpretation.

Henriette returned and observed what he was doing.

"Amusing, isn't it?"

"Yes, very amusing," he replied. "But, have you any other papers? . . . Or, rather, words already cut out that I can paste?"

"Papers? . . . No. . . . And Mademoiselle wouldn't like it."

"Mademoiselle?"

"Yes, she has scolded me already."

"Why?"

"Because I have told you some things . . . and she says that a person should never tell things about those they love."

"You are quite right."

Henriette was delighted to receive his approbation, in fact so highly pleased that she took from a little silk bag that was pinned to her dress some scraps of cloth, three buttons, two cubes of sugar and, lastly, a piece of paper which she handed to Sholmes.

"See, I give it to you just the same."

It was the number of a cab—8,279.

"Where did this number come from?"

"It fell out of her pocketbook."

"When?"

"Sunday, at mass, when she was taking out some *sous** for the collection."

"Exactly! And now I shall tell you how to keep from being scolded again. Do not tell Mademoiselle that you saw me."

---

* A small coin worth five *centimes,* or 0.05 Francs.

Sholmes then went to M. d'Imblevalle and questioned him in regard to Mademoiselle. The baron replied, indignantly:

"Alice Demun! How can you imagine such a thing? It is utterly impossible!"

"How long has she been in your service?"

"Only a year, but there is no one in the house in whom I have greater confidence."

"Why have I not seen her yet?"

"She has been away for a few days."

"But she is here now."

"Yes; since her return she has been watching at the bedside of your friend. She has all the qualities of a nurse . . . gentle . . . thoughtful . . . Monsieur Wilson seems much pleased. . . ."

"Ah!" said Sholmes, who had completely neglected to inquire about his friend. After a moment's reflection he asked:

"Did she go out on Sunday morning?"

"The day after the theft?"

"Yes."

The baron called his wife and asked her. She replied:

"Mademoiselle went to the eleven o'clock mass with the children, as usual."

"But before that?"

"Before that? No. . . . Let me see! . . . I was so upset by the theft . . . but I remember now that, on the evening before, she asked permission to go out on Sunday morning . . . to see a cousin who was passing through Paris, I think. But, surely, you don't suspect her?"

"Of course not . . . but I would like to see her."

He went to Wilson's room. A woman dressed in a gray cloth dress, as in the hospitals, was bending over the invalid, giving him a drink. When she turned her face Sholmes recognized her as the young girl who had accosted him at the railway station.

Alice Demun smiled sweetly; her great serious, innocent eyes showed no sign of embarrassment. The Englishman tried to speak, muttered a few syllables, and stopped. Then she resumed her work, acting quite naturally under Sholmes' astonished gaze, moved the bottles, unrolled and rolled cotton bandages, and again regarded Sholmes with her charming smile of pure innocence.

He turned on his heels, descended the stairs, noticed M. d'Imblevalle's automobile in the courtyard, jumped into it, and went to Levallois, to the office of the cab company whose address was printed on the paper he had received from Henriette. The man who had driven carriage number 8,279 on Sunday morning not being there, Sholmes dismissed the automobile and waited for the man's return. He told Sholmes that he had picked up a woman in the vicinity of the Parc Monceau, a young woman dressed in black, wearing a heavy veil, and, apparently, quite nervous.

"Did she have a package?"

"Yes, quite a long package."

"Where did you take her?"

"Avenue des Ternes, corner of the Place Saint-Ferdinand. She remained there about ten minutes, and then returned to the Parc Monceau."

"Could you recognize the house in the Avenue des Ternes?"

"*Parbleu!* Shall I take you there?"

"Presently. First take me to 36 Quai des Orfèvres."

At the police office he saw Detective Ganimard.

"Monsieur Ganimard, are you at liberty?"

"If it has anything to do with Lupin—no!"

"It has something to do with Lupin."

"Then I do not go."

"What! you surrender—"

"I bow to the inevitable. I am tired of the unequal struggle, in which we are sure to be defeated. Lupin is stronger than I am—stronger than the two of us; therefore, we must surrender."

"I will not surrender."

"He will make you, as he has all others."

"And you would be pleased to see it—eh, Ganimard?"

"At all events, it is true," said Ganimard, frankly. "And since you are determined to pursue the game, I will go with you."

Together they entered the carriage and were driven to the Avenue des Ternes. Upon their order the carriage stopped on the other side of the street, at some distance from the house, in front of a little café, on the terrace of which the two men took seats amongst the shrubbery. It was commencing to grow dark.

"Waiter," said Sholmes, "some writing material."

He wrote a note, recalled the waiter and gave him the letter with instructions to deliver it to the concierge of the house which he pointed out.

In a few minutes the concierge stood before them. Sholmes asked him if, on the Sunday morning, he had seen a young woman dressed in black.

"In black! Yes, about nine o'clock. She went to the second floor."

"Have you seen her often?"

"No, but for some time—well, during the last few weeks, I have seen her almost every day."

"And since Sunday?"

"Only once . . . until to-day."

"What! Did she come to-day?"

"She is here now."

"Here now?"

"Yes, she came about ten minutes ago. Her carriage is standing in the Place Saint-Ferdinand, as usual. I met her at the door."

"Who is the occupant of the second floor?"

"There are two: a *modiste*,* Mademoiselle Langeais, and a gentleman who rented two furnished rooms a month ago under the name of Bresson."

"Why do you say 'under the name'?"

"Because I have an idea that it is an assumed name. My wife takes care of his rooms, and . . . well, there are not two shirts there with the same initials."

"Is he there much of the time?"

"No; he is nearly always out. He has not been here for three days."

"Was he here on Saturday night?"

"Saturday night? . . . Let me think. . . . Yes, Saturday night, he came in and stayed all night."

"What sort of a man is he?"

"Well, I can scarcely answer that. He is so changeable. He is, by turns, big, little, fat, thin . . . dark and light. I do not always recognize him."

Ganimard and Sholmes exchanged looks.

"That is he, all right," said Ganimard.

"Ah!" said the concierge, "there is the girl now."

Mademoiselle had just emerged from the house and was walking toward her carriage in the Place Saint-Ferdinand.

"And there is Monsieur Bresson."

"Monsieur Bresson? Which is he?"

"The man with the parcel under his arm."

"But he is not looking after the girl. She is going to her carriage alone."

"Yes, I have never seen them together."

---

* Dressmaker.

The two detectives had arisen. By the light of the street-lamps they recognized the form of Arsène Lupin, who had started off in a direction opposite to that taken by the girl.

"Which will you follow?" asked Ganimard.

"I will follow him, of course. He's the biggest game."

"Then I will follow the girl," proposed Ganimard.

"No, no," said Sholmes, quickly, who did not wish to disclose the girl's identity to Ganimard, "I know where to find her. Come with me."

They followed Lupin at a safe distance, taking care to conceal themselves as well as possible amongst the moving throng and behind the newspaper kiosks. They found the pursuit an easy one, as he walked steadily forward without turning to the right or left, but with a slight limp in the right leg, so slight as to require the keen eye of a professional observer to detect it. Ganimard observed it, and said:

"He is pretending to be lame. Ah! if we could only collect two or three policemen and pounce on our man! We run a chance to lose him."

But they did not meet any policemen before they reached the Porte des Ternes, and, having passed the fortifications, there was no prospect of receiving any assistance.

"We had better separate," said Sholmes, "as there are so few people on the street."

They were now on the Boulevard Victor-Hugo. They walked one on each side of the street, and kept well in the shadow of the trees. They continued thus for twenty minutes, when Lupin turned to the left and followed the Seine. Very soon they saw him descend to the edge of the river. He remained there only a few seconds, but they could not observe his movements. Then Lupin retraced his steps. His pursuers concealed themselves in the shadow of a gateway. Lupin passed in front of them. His parcel had disappeared. And as he walked away another man emerged from the shelter of a house and glided amongst the trees.

"He seems to be following him also," said Sholmes, in a low voice.

The pursuit continued, but was now embarrassed by the presence of the third man. Lupin returned the same way, passed through the Porte des Ternes, and re-entered the house in the Avenue des Ternes.

The concierge was closing the house for the night when Ganimard presented himself.

"Did you see him?"

"Yes," replied the concierge, "I was putting out the gas on the landing when he closed and bolted his door."

"Is there any person with him?"

"No; he has no servant. He never eats here."

"Is there a servants' stairway?"

"No."

Ganimard said to Sholmes:

"I had better stand at the door of his room while you go for the commissary of police in the Rue Demours."

"And if he should escape during that time?" said Sholmes.

"While I am here! He can't escape."

"One to one, with Lupin, is not an even chance for you."

"Well, I can't force the door. I have no right to do that, especially at night."

Sholmes shrugged his shoulders and said:

"When you arrest Lupin no one will question the methods by which you made the arrest. However, let us go up and ring, and see what happens then."

They ascended to the second floor. There was a double door at the left of the landing. Ganimard rang the bell. No reply. He rang again. Still no reply.

"Let us go in," said Sholmes.

"All right, come on," replied Ganimard.

Yet, they stood still, irresolute. Like people who hesitate when they ought to accomplish a decisive action they feared to move, and it seemed to them impossible that Arsène Lupin was there, so close to them, on the other side of that fragile door that could be broken down by one blow of the fist. But they knew Lupin too well to suppose that he would allow himself to be trapped in that stupid manner. No, no—a thousand times, no—Lupin was no longer there. Through the adjoining houses, over the roofs, by some conveniently prepared exit, he must have already made his escape, and, once more, it would only be Lupin's shadow that they would seize.

They shuddered as a slight noise, coming from the other side of the door, reached their ears. Then they had the impression, amounting almost to a certainty, that he was there, separated from them by that frail wooden door, and that he was listening to them, that he could hear them.

What was to be done? The situation was a serious one. In spite of their vast experience as detectives, they were so nervous and excited that they thought they could hear the beating of their own hearts. Ganimard questioned Sholmes by a look. Then he struck the door a violent blow with his fist. Immediately they heard the sound of footsteps, concerning which there was no attempt at concealment.

Ganimard shook the door. Then he and Sholmes, uniting their efforts, rushed at the door, and burst it open with their shoulders. Then they stood still, in surprise. A shot had been fired in the adjoining room. Another shot, and the sound of a falling body.

When they entered they saw the man lying on the floor with his face toward the marble mantel. His revolver had fallen from his hand. Ganimard stooped and turned the man's head. The face was covered with blood, which was flowing from two wounds, one in the cheek, the other in the temple.

"You can't recognize him for blood."

"No matter!" said Sholmes. "It is not Lupin."

"How do you know? You haven't even looked at him."

"Do you think that Arsène Lupin is the kind of a man that would kill himself?" asked Sholmes, with a sneer.

"But we thought we recognized him outside."

"We thought so, because the wish was father to the thought. That man has us bewitched."

"Then it must be one of his accomplices."

"The accomplices of Arsène Lupin do not kill themselves."

"Well, then, who is it?"

They searched the corpse. In one pocket Herlock Sholmes found an empty pocketbook; in another Ganimard found several *louis*.* There were no marks of identification on any part of his clothing. In a trunk and two valises they found nothing but wearing apparel. On the mantel there was a pile of newspapers. Ganimard opened them. All of them contained articles referring to the theft of the Jewish lamp.

An hour later, when Ganimard and Sholmes left the house, they had acquired no further knowledge of the strange individual who had been driven to suicide by their untimely visit.

Who was he! Why had he killed himself? What was his connection with the affair of the Jewish lamp? Who had followed him on his return from the river? The situation involved many complex questions—many mysteries—

ᘥ

Herlock Sholmes went to bed in a very bad humor. Early next morning he received the following telephonic message:

"Arsène Lupin has the honor to inform you of his tragic death in the person of Monsieur Bresson, and requests the honor of your presence at the funeral service and burial, which will be held at the public expense on Thursday, 25 June."

---

* Gold coins with a value of 20 Francs.

THE MAN WITH
THE NAILED SHOES

by R. Austin Freeman

1909

Richard Austin Freeman trained as an apothecary and studied medicine at Middlesex Hospital, qualifying in 1887. He entered the Colonial Service, but was forced to return from Africa after contracting blackwater fever. Unable to find a permanent medical position, he turned to writing fiction, while continuing to practice medicine as opportunity permitted.

Doctor John Evelyn Thorndyke first appeared in "The Red Thumb Mark" in 1907, and demonstrates Freeman's mastery of obscure scientific knowledge. While Holmes was similarly well-versed in such matters, it can be argued that Thorndyke is less of a descendant of the great detective, and more a precursor of the forensic investigators of television shows such as *CSI*: a doctor who re-trained in the law, he describes himself as a "medical jurispractitioner."

Thorndyke is further distinguished from Holmes in that many of his exploits are told as "inverted" detective stories. In this sub-genre, which Freeman claimed to have invented, the identity of the criminal is known from the start and the story's interest lies not in the mystery itself, but in the means by which the detective unravels it.

Doctor Thorndyke appeared in twenty-two novels and forty short stories, published between 1907 and 1942. His legacy is a troubled one, and not free from controversy. He was a vocal supporter of eugenics, a social science of the time which was to inspire Nazi policies of racial purity, and expressed a number of other views which would be regarded as offensive today. Raymond Chandler, who had little good to say about the classical detective story, described Freeman as "a wonderful performer" with "no equal in his genre." Some years later, though, British crime writer Julian Symons wrote that "reading a Freeman story is very much like chewing dry straw."

Readers must decide for themselves. "The Man with the Nailed Shoes" is a tidy little mystery, which first appeared in the collection *John Thorndyke's Cases*, published in the United States as *Dr. Thorndyke's Cases*. Freeman's invention of the inverted detective story is still three years in the future, and this case, along with Thorndyke's solution, would not look out of place in a Holmes collection: it even features a doctor as the narrator.

There are, I suppose, few places even on the East Coast of England more lonely and remote than the village of Little Sundersley and the country that surrounds it. Far from any railway, and some miles distant from any considerable town, it remains an outpost of civilization, in which primitive manners and customs and old-world tradition linger on into an age that has elsewhere forgotten them. In the summer, it is true, a small contingent of visitors, adventurous in spirit, though mostly of sedate and solitary habits, make their appearance to swell its meagre population, and impart to the wide stretches of smooth sand that fringe its shores a fleeting air of life and sober gaiety; but in late September—the season of the year in which I made its acquaintance—its pasture-lands lie desolate, the rugged paths along the cliffs are seldom trodden by human foot, and the sands are a desert waste on which, for days together, no footprint appears save that left by some passing sea-bird.

I had been assured by my medical agent, Mr. Turcival, that I should find the practice of which I was now taking charge "an exceedingly soft billet, and suitable for a studious man;" and certainly he had not misled me, for the patients were, in fact, so few that I was quite concerned for my principal, and rather dull for want of work. Hence, when my friend John Thorndyke, the well-known medico-legal expert, proposed to come down and stay with me for a weekend and perhaps a few days beyond, I hailed the proposal with delight, and welcomed him with open arms.

"You certainly don't seem to be overworked, Jervis," he remarked, as we turned out of the gate after tea, on the day of his arrival, for a stroll on the shore. "Is this a new practice, or an old one in a state of senile decay?"

"Why, the fact is," I answered, "there is virtually no practice. Cooper—my principal—has been here about six years, and as he has private means he has never made any serious effort to build one up; and the other man, Dr. Burrows, being uncommonly keen, and the people very conservative, Cooper has never really got his foot in. However, it doesn't seem to trouble him."

"Well, if he is satisfied, I suppose you are," said Thorndyke, with a smile. "You are getting a seaside holiday, and being paid for it. But I didn't know you were as near to the sea as this."

We were entering, as he spoke, an artificial gap-way cut through the low cliff, forming a steep cart-track down to the shore. It was locally known as Sundersley Gap, and was used principally, when used at all, by the farmers' carts which came down to gather seaweed after a gale.

"What a magnificent stretch of sand!" continued Thorndyke, as we reached the bottom, and stood looking out seaward across the deserted beach. "There is something very majestic and solemn in a great expanse of sandy shore when the tide is out, and I know of nothing which is capable of conveying the impression of solitude so completely. The smooth, unbroken surface not only displays itself untenanted for the moment, but it offers convincing testimony that it has lain thus undisturbed through a considerable lapse of time. Here, for instance, we have clear evidence that for several days only two pairs of feet besides our own have trodden this gap."

"How do you arrive at the 'several days?'" I asked.

"In the simplest manner possible," he replied. "The moon is now in the third quarter, and the tides are consequently neap-tides. You can see quite plainly the two lines of seaweed and jetsam which indicate the high-water marks of the spring-tides and the neap-tides respectively. The strip of comparatively dry sand between them, over which the water has not risen for several days, is, as you see, marked by only two sets of footprints, and those footprints will not be completely obliterated by the sea until the next spring-tide—nearly a week from to-day."

"Yes, I see now, and the thing appears obvious enough when one has heard the explanation. But it is really rather odd that no one should have passed through this gap for days, and then that four persons should have come here within quite a short interval of one another."

"What makes you think they have done so?" Thorndyke asked.

"Well," I replied, "both of these sets of footprints appear to be quite fresh, and to have been made about the same time."

"Not at the same time, Jervis," rejoined Thorndyke. "There is certainly an interval of several hours between them, though precisely how many hours we cannot judge, since there has been so little wind lately to disturb them; but the fisherman unquestionably passed here not more than three hours ago, and I should say probably within an hour; whereas the other man—who seems to have come up from a boat to fetch something of considerable weight—returned through the gap certainly not less, and probably more, than four hours ago."

I gazed at my friend in blank astonishment, for these events befell in the days before I had joined him as his assistant, and his special knowledge and powers of inference were not then fully appreciated by me.

"It is clear, Thorndyke," I said, "that footprints have a very different meaning to you from what they have for me. I don't see in the least how you have reached any of these conclusions."

"I suppose not," was the reply; "but, you see, special knowledge of this kind is the stock-in-trade of the medical jurist, and has to be acquired by special study, though the present example is one of the greatest simplicity. But let us consider it point by point; and first we will take this set of footprints which I have inferred to be a fisherman's. Note their enormous size. They should be the footprints of a giant. But the length of the stride shows that they were made by a rather short man. Then observe the massiveness of the soles, and the fact that there are no nails in them. Note also the peculiar clumsy tread—the deep toe and heel marks, as if the walker had wooden legs, or fixed ankles and knees. From that character we can safely infer high boots of thick, rigid leather, so that we can diagnose high boots, massive and stiff, with nailless soles, and many sizes too large for the wearer. But the only boot that answers this description is the fisherman's thigh-boot—made of enormous size to enable him to wear in the winter two or three pairs of thick knitted stockings, one over the other. Now look at the other footprints; there is a double track, you see, one set coming from the sea and one going towards it. As the man (who was bow-legged and turned his toes in) has trodden in his own footprints, it is obvious that he came from the sea, and returned to it. But observe the difference in the two sets of prints; the returning ones are much deeper than the others, and the stride much shorter. Evidently he was carrying something when he returned, and that something was very heavy. Moreover, we can see, by the greater depth of the toe impressions, that he was stooping forward as he walked, and so probably carried the weight on his back. Is that quite clear?"

"Perfectly," I replied. "But how do you arrive at the interval of time between the visits of the two men?"

"That also is quite simple. The tide is now about halfway out; it is thus about three hours since high water. Now, the fisherman walked just about the neap-tide, high-water mark, sometimes above it and sometimes below. But none of his footprints have been obliterated; therefore he passed after high water—that is, less than three hours ago; and since his footprints are all equally distinct, he could not have passed when the sand was very wet. Therefore he probably passed less than an hour ago. The other man's footprints, on the other hand, reach only to the neap-tide, high-water mark, where they end abruptly. The sea has washed over the remainder of the tracks and obliterated them. Therefore he passed not less than three hours and not more than four days ago—probably within twenty-four hours."

As Thorndyke concluded his demonstration the sound of voices was borne to us from above, mingled with the tramping of feet, and immediately afterwards a very singular party appeared at the head of the gap descending towards the shore. First came a short burly fisherman clad in oilskins and sou'-wester, clumping along awkwardly in his great sea-boots, then the local police-sergeant in company with my professional rival Dr. Burrows, while the rear of the procession was brought up by two constables carrying a stretcher. As he reached the bottom of the gap the fisherman, who was evidently acting as guide, turned along the shore, retracing his own tracks, and the procession followed in his wake.

"A surgeon, a stretcher, two constables, and a police-sergeant," observed Thorndyke. "What does that suggest to your mind, Jervis?"

"A fall from the cliff," I replied, "or a body washed up on the shore."

"Probably," he rejoined; "but we may as well walk in that direction."

We turned to follow the retreating procession, and as we strode along the smooth surface left by the retiring tide Thorndyke resumed:

"The subject of footprints has always interested me deeply for two reasons. First, the evidence furnished by footprints is constantly being brought forward, and is often of cardinal importance; and, secondly, the whole subject is capable of really systematic and scientific treatment. In the main the data are anatomical, but age, sex, occupation, health, and disease all give their various indications. Clearly, for instance, the footprints of an old man will differ from those of a young man of the same height, and I need not point out to you that those of a person suffering from *locomotor ataxia** or *paralysis agitans*† would be quite unmistakable."

"Yes, I see that plainly enough," I said.

"Here, now," he continued, "is a case in point." He halted to point with his stick at a row of footprints that appeared suddenly above high-water mark, and

---

* An affliction that impairs control over bodily movements.

† Parkinson's disease.

having proceeded a short distance, crossed the line again, and vanished where the waves had washed over them. They were easily distinguished from any of the others by the clear impressions of circular rubber heels.

"Do you see anything remarkable about them?" he asked.

"I notice that they are considerably deeper than our own," I answered.

"Yes, and the boots are about the same size as ours, whereas the stride is considerably shorter—quite a short stride, in fact. Now there is a pretty constant ratio between the length of the foot and the length of the leg, between the length of leg and the height of the person, and between the stature and the length of stride. A long foot means a long leg, a tall man, and a long stride. But here we have a long foot and a short stride. What do you make of that?" He laid down his stick—a smooth partridge cane, one side of which was marked by small lines into inches and feet—beside the footprints to demonstrate the discrepancy.

"The depth of the footprints shows that he was a much heavier man than either of us," I suggested; "perhaps he was unusually fat."

"Yes," said Thorndyke, "that seems to be the explanation. The carrying of a dead weight shortens the stride, and fat is practically a dead weight. The conclusion is that he was about five feet ten inches high, and excessively fat." He picked up his cane, and we resumed our walk, keeping an eye on the procession ahead until it had disappeared round a curve in the coast-line, when we mended our pace somewhat. Presently we reached a small headland, and, turning the shoulder of cliff, came full upon the party which had preceded us. The men had halted in a narrow bay, and now stood looking down at a prostrate figure beside which the surgeon was kneeling.

"We were wrong, you see," observed Thorndyke. "He has not fallen over the cliff, nor has he been washed up by the sea. He is lying above high-water mark, and those footprints that we have been examining appear to be his."

As we approached, the sergeant turned and held up his hand.

"I'll ask you not to walk round the body just now, gentlemen," he said. "There seems to have been foul play here, and I want to be clear about the tracks before anyone crosses them."

Acknowledging this caution, we advanced to where the constables were standing, and looked down with some curiosity at the dead man. He was a tall, frail-looking man, thin to the point of emaciation, and appeared to be about thirty-five years of age. He lay in an easy posture, with half-closed eyes and a placid expression that contrasted strangely enough with the tragic circumstances of his death.

"It is a clear case of murder," said Dr. Burrows, dusting the sand from his knees as he stood up. "There is a deep knife-wound above the heart, which must have caused death almost instantaneously."

"How long should you say he has been dead, Doctor?" asked the sergeant.

"Twelve hours at least," was the reply. "He is quite cold and stiff."

"Twelve hours, eh?" repeated the officer. "That would bring it to about six o'clock this morning."

"I won't commit myself to a definite time," said Dr. Burrows hastily. "I only say not *less* than twelve hours. It might have been considerably more."

"Ah!" said the sergeant. "Well, he made a pretty good fight for his life, to all appearances." He nodded at the sand, which for some feet around the body bore the deeply indented marks of feet, as though a furious struggle had taken place. "It's a mighty queer affair," pursued the sergeant, addressing Dr. Burrows. "There seems to have been only one man in it—there is only one set of footprints besides those of the deceased—and we've got to find out who he is; and I reckon there won't be much trouble about that, seeing the kind of trade-marks he has left behind him."

"No," agreed the surgeon; "there ought not to be much trouble in identifying those boots. He would seem to be a labourer, judging by the hob-nails."

"No, sir; not a labourer," dissented the sergeant. "The foot is too small, for one thing; and then the nails are not regular hob-nails. They're a good deal smaller; and a labourer's boots would have the nails all round the edges, and there would be iron tips on the heels, and probably on the toes too. Now these have got no tips, and the nails are arranged in a pattern on the soles and heels. They are probably shooting-boots or sporting shoes of some kind." He strode to and fro with his notebook in his hand, writing down hasty memoranda, and stooping to scrutinize the impressions in the sand. The surgeon also busied himself in noting down the facts concerning which he would have to give evidence, while Thorndyke regarded in silence and with an air of intense preoccupation the footprints around the body which remained to testify to the circumstances of the crime.

"It is pretty clear, up to a certain point," the sergeant observed, as he concluded his investigations, "how the affair happened, and it is pretty clear, too, that the murder was premeditated. You see, Doctor, the deceased gentleman, Mr. Hearn, was apparently walking home from Port Marston; we saw his footprints along the shore—those rubber heels make them easy to identify—and he didn't go down Sundersley Gap. He probably meant to climb up the cliff by that little track that you see there, which the people about here call the Shepherd's Path. Now the murderer must have known that he was coming, and waited upon the cliff to keep a lookout. When he saw Mr. Hearn enter the bay, he came down the path and attacked him, and, after a tough struggle, succeeded in stabbing him. Then he turned and went back up the path. You can see the double track between the path and the place where the struggle took place, and the footprints going to the path are on top of those coming from it."

"If you follow the tracks," said Dr. Burrows, "you ought to be able to see where the murderer went to."

"I'm afraid not," replied the sergeant. "There are no marks on the path itself—the rock is too hard, and so is the ground above, I fear. But I'll go over it carefully all the same."

The investigations being so far concluded, the body was lifted on to the stretcher, and the cortege, consisting of the bearers, the Doctor, and the fisherman, moved off towards the Gap, while the sergeant, having civilly wished us "Good-evening," scrambled up the Shepherd's Path, and vanished above.

"A very smart officer that," said Thorndyke. "I should like to know what he wrote in his notebook."

"His account of the circumstances of the murder seemed a very reasonable one," I said.

"Very. He noted the plain and essential facts, and drew the natural conclusions from them. But there are some very singular features in this case; so singular that I am disposed to make a few notes for my own information."

He stooped over the place where the body had lain, and having narrowly examined the sand there and in the place where the dead man's feet had rested, drew out his notebook and made a memorandum. He next made a rapid sketch-plan of the bay, marking the position of the body and the various impressions in the sand, and then, following the double track leading from and to the Shepherd's Path, scrutinized the footprints with the deepest attention, making copious notes and sketches in his book.

"We may as well go up by the Shepherd's Path," said Thorndyke. "I think we are equal to the climb, and there may be visible traces of the murderer after all. The rock is only a sandstone, and not a very hard one either."

We approached the foot of the little rugged track which zigzagged up the face of the cliff, and, stooping down among the stiff, dry herbage, examined the surface. Here, at the bottom of the path, where the rock was softened by the weather, there were several distinct impressions on the crumbling surface of the murderer's nailed boots, though they were somewhat confused by the tracks of the sergeant, whose boots were heavily nailed. But as we ascended the marks became rather less distinct, and at quite a short distance from the foot of the cliff we lost them altogether, though we had no difficulty in following the more recent traces of the sergeant's passage up the path.

When we reached the top of the cliff we paused to scan the path that ran along its edge, but here, too, although the sergeant's heavy boots had left quite visible impressions on the ground, there were no signs of any other feet. At a little distance the sagacious officer himself was pursuing his investigations, walking backwards and forwards with his body bent double, and his eyes fixed on the ground.

"Not a trace of him anywhere," said he, straightening himself up as we approached. "I was afraid there wouldn't be after all this dry weather. I shall have to try a different tack. This is a small place, and if those boots belong to anyone living here they'll be sure to be known."

"The deceased gentleman—Mr. Hearn, I think you called him," said Thorndyke as we turned towards the village—"is he a native of the locality?"

"Oh no, sir," replied the officer. "He is almost a stranger. He has only been here about three weeks; but, you know, in a little place like this a man soon gets to be known—and his business, too, for that matter," he added, with a smile.

"What was his business, then?" asked Thorndyke.

"Pleasure, I believe. He was down here for a holiday, though it's a good way past the season; but, then, he had a friend living here, and that makes a difference. Mr. Draper up at the Poplars was an old friend of his, I understand. I am going to call on him now."

We walked on along the footpath that led towards the village, but had only proceeded two or three hundred yards when a loud hail drew our attention to a man running across a field towards us from the direction of the cliff.

"Why, here is Mr. Draper himself," exclaimed the sergeant, stopping short and waving his hand. "I expect he has heard the news already."

Thorndyke and I also halted, and with some curiosity watched the approach of this new party to the tragedy. As the stranger drew near we saw that he was a tall, athletic-looking man of about forty, dressed in a Norfolk knickerbocker suit, and having the appearance of an ordinary country gentleman, excepting that he carried in his hand, in place of a walking-stick, the staff of a butterfly-net, the folding ring and bag of which partly projected from his pocket.

"Is it true, Sergeant?" he exclaimed as he came up to us, panting from his exertions. "About Mr. Hearn, I mean. There is a rumour that he has been found dead on the beach."

298 | R. AUSTIN FREEMAN

"It's quite true, sir, I am sorry to say; and, what is worse, he has been murdered."

"My God! you don't say so!"

He turned towards us a face that must ordinarily have been jovial enough, but was now white and scared and, after a brief pause, he exclaimed:

"Murdered! Good God! Poor old Hearn! How did it happen, Sergeant? and when? and is there any clue to the murderer?"

"We can't say for certain when it happened," replied the sergeant, "and as to the question of clues, I was just coming up to call on you."

"On me!" exclaimed Draper, with a startled glance at the officer. "What for?"

"Well, we should like to know something about Mr. Hearn—who he was, and whether he had any enemies, and so forth; anything, in fact, that would give as a hint where to look for the murderer. And you are the only person in the place who knew him at all intimately."

Mr. Draper's pallid face turned a shade paler, and he glanced about him with an obviously embarrassed air.

"I'm afraid." he began in a hesitating manner, "I'm afraid I shan't be able to help you much. I didn't know much about his affairs. You see he was—well—only a casual acquaintance—"

"Well," interrupted the sergeant, "you can tell us who and what he was, and where he lived, and so forth. We'll find out the rest if you give us the start."

"I see," said Draper. "Yes, I expect you will." His eyes glanced restlessly to and fro, and he added presently: "You must come up to-morrow, and have a talk with me about him, and I'll see what I can remember."

"I'd rather come this evening," said the sergeant firmly.

"Not this evening," pleaded Draper. "I'm feeling rather—this affair, you know, has upset me. I couldn't give proper attention—"

His sentence petered out into a hesitating mumble, and the officer looked at him in evident surprise at his nervous, embarrassed manner. His own attitude, however, was perfectly firm, though polite.

"I don't like pressing you, sir," said he, "but time is precious—we'll have to go single file here; this pond is a public nuisance. They ought to bank it up at this end. After you, sir."

The pond to which the sergeant alluded had evidently extended at one time right across the path, but now, thanks to the dry weather, a narrow isthmus of half-dried mud traversed the morass, and along this Mr. Draper proceeded to pick his way. The sergeant was about to follow, when suddenly he stopped short with his eyes riveted upon the muddy track. A single glance showed me the cause of his surprise, for on the stiff, putty-like surface, standing out with the sharp distinctness of a wax mould, were the fresh footprints of the man who had just passed, each footprint displaying on its sole the impression of stud-nails arranged in a diamond-shaped pattern, and on its heel a group of similar nails arranged in a cross.

The sergeant hesitated for only a moment, in which he turned a quick startled glance upon us; then he followed, walking gingerly along the edge of the path as if to avoid treading in his predecessor's footprints. Instinctively we did the same, following closely, and anxiously awaiting the next development of the tragedy. For a minute or two we all proceeded in silence, the sergeant being evidently at a loss how to act, and Mr. Draper busy with his own thoughts. At length the former spoke.

"You think, Mr. Draper, you would rather that I looked in on you to-morrow about this affair?"

"Much rather, if you wouldn't mind," was the eager reply.

"Then, in that case," said the sergeant, looking at his watch, "as I've got a good deal to see to this evening, I'll leave you here, and make my way to the station."

With a farewell flourish of his hand he climbed over a stile, and when, a few moments later, I caught a glimpse of him through an opening in the hedge, he was running across the meadow like a hare.

The departure of the police-officer was apparently a great relief to Mr. Draper, who at once fell back and began to talk with us.

"You are Dr. Jervis, I think," said he. "I saw you coming out of Dr. Cooper's house yesterday. We know everything that is happening in the village, you see." He laughed nervously, and added: "But I don't know your friend."

I introduced Thorndyke, at the mention of whose name our new acquaintance knitted his brows, and glanced inquisitively at my friend.

"Thorndyke," he repeated; "the name seems familiar to me. Are you in the Law, sir?"

Thorndyke admitted the impeachment, and our companion, having again bestowed on him a look full of curiosity, continued: "This horrible affair will interest you, no doubt, from a professional point of view. You were present when my poor friend's body was found, I think?"

"No," replied Thorndyke; "we came up afterwards, when they were removing it."

Our companion then proceeded to question us about the murder, but received from Thorndyke only the most general and ambiguous replies. Nor was there time to go into the matter at length, for the footpath presently emerged on to the road close to Mr. Draper's house.

"You will excuse my not asking you in to-night," said he, "but you will understand that I am not in much form for visitors just now."

We assured him that we fully understood, and, having wished him "Good-evening," pursued our way towards the village.

"The sergeant is off to get a warrant, I suppose," I observed.

"Yes; and mighty anxious lest his man should be off before he can execute it. But he is fishing in deeper waters than he thinks, Jervis. This is a very singular and complicated case; one of the strangest, in fact, that I have ever met. I shall follow its development with deep interest."

"The sergeant seems pretty cocksure, all the same," I said.

"He is not to blame for that," replied Thorndyke. "He is acting on the obvious appearances, which is the proper thing to do in the first place. Perhaps his note-book contains more than I think it does. But we shall see."

When we entered the village I stopped to settle some business with the chemist, who acted as Dr. Cooper's dispenser, suggesting to Thorndyke that he should walk on to the house; but when I emerged from the shop some ten minutes later he was waiting outside, with a smallish brown-paper parcel under each arm. Of one of these parcels I insisted on relieving him, in spite of his protests, but when he at length handed it to me its weight completely took me by surprise.

"I should have let them send this home on a barrow," I remarked.

"So I should have done," he replied, "only I did not wish to draw attention to my purchase, or give my address."

Accepting this hint I refrained from making any inquiries as to the nature of the contents (although I must confess to considerable curiosity on the subject), and on arriving home I assisted him to deposit the two mysterious parcels in his room.

When I came downstairs a disagreeable surprise awaited me. Hitherto the long evenings had been spent by me in solitary and undisturbed enjoyment of Dr. Cooper's excellent library, but to-night a perverse fate decreed that I must wander abroad, because, forsooth, a preposterous farmer, who resided in a hamlet five miles distant, had chosen the evening of my guest's arrival to dislocate his bucolic elbow. I half hoped that Thorndyke would offer to accompany me, but he made no such suggestion, and in fact seemed by no means afflicted at the prospect of my absence.

"I have plenty to occupy me while you are away," he said cheerfully; and with this assurance to comfort me I mounted my bicycle and rode off somewhat sulkily along the dark road.

My visit occupied in all a trifle under two hours, and when I reached home, ravenously hungry and heated by my ride, half-past nine had struck, and the village had begun to settle down for the night.

"Sergeant Payne is a-waiting in the surgery, sir," the housemaid announced as I entered the hall.

"Confound Sergeant Payne!" I exclaimed. "Is Dr. Thorndyke with him?"

"No, sir," replied the grinning damsel. "Dr. Thorndyke is hout."

"Hout!" I repeated (my surprise leading to unintentional mimicry).

"Yes, sir. He went hout soon after you, sir, on his bicycle. He had a basket strapped on to it—leastways a hamper—and he borrowed a basin and a kitchen-spoon from the cook."

I stared at the girl in astonishment. The ways of John Thorndyke were, indeed, beyond all understanding.

"Well, let me have some dinner or supper at once," I said, "and I will see what the sergeant wants."

The officer rose as I entered the surgery, and, laying his helmet on the table, approached me with an air of secrecy and importance.

"Well, sir," said he, "the fat's in the fire. I've arrested Mr. Draper, and I've got him locked up in the court-house. But I wish it had been someone else."

"So does he, I expect," I remarked.

"You see, sir," continued the sergeant, "we all like Mr. Draper. He's been among us a matter of seven years, and he's like one of ourselves. However, what I've come about is this; it seems the gentleman who was with you this evening is Dr. Thorndyke, the great expert. Now Mr. Draper seems to have heard about him, as most of us have, and he is very anxious for him to take up the defence. Do you think he would consent?"

"I expect so," I answered, remembering Thorndyke's keen interest in the case; "but I will ask him when he comes in."

"Thank you, sir," said the sergeant. "And perhaps you wouldn't mind stepping round to the court-house presently yourself. He looks uncommon queer, does Mr. Draper, and no wonder, so I'd like you to take a look at him, and if you could bring Dr. Thorndyke with you, he'd like it, and so should I, for, I assure you, sir, that although a conviction would mean a step up the ladder for me, I'd be glad enough to find that I'd made a mistake."

I was just showing my visitor out when a bicycle swept in through the open gate, and Thorndyke dismounted at the door, revealing a square hamper—evidently abstracted from the surgery—strapped on to a carrier at the back. I conveyed the sergeant's request to him at once, and asked if he was willing to take up the case.

"As to taking up the defence," he replied, "I will consider the matter; but in any case I will come up and see the prisoner."

With this the sergeant departed, and Thorndyke, having unstrapped the hamper with as much care as if it contained a collection of priceless porcelain, bore it tenderly up to his bedroom; whence he appeared, after a considerable interval, smilingly apologetic for the delay.

"I thought you were dressing for dinner," I grumbled as he took his seat at the table.

"No," he replied. "I have been considering this murder. Really it is a most singular case, and promises to be uncommonly complicated, too."

"Then I assume that you will undertake the defence?"

"I shall if Draper gives a reasonably straightforward account of himself."

It appeared that this condition was likely to be fulfilled, for when we arrived at the court-house (where the prisoner was accommodated in a spare office, under rather free-and-easy conditions considering the nature of the charge) we found Mr. Draper in an eminently communicative frame of mind.

"I want you, Dr. Thorndyke, to undertake my defence in this terrible affair, because I feel confident that you will be able to clear me. And I promise you that there shall be no reservation or concealment on my part of anything that you ought to know."

"Very well," said Thorndyke. "By the way, I see you have changed your shoes."

"Yes, the sergeant took possession of those I was wearing. He said something about comparing them with some footprints, but there can't be any footprints like those shoes here in Sundersley. The nails are fixed in the soles in quite a peculiar pattern. I had them made in Edinburgh."

"Have you more than one pair?"

"No. I have no other nailed boots."

"That is important," said Thorndyke. "And now I judge that you have something to tell us that bears on this crime. Am I right?"

"Yes. There is something that I am afraid it is necessary for you to know, although it is very painful to me to revive memories of my past that I had hoped were buried for ever. But perhaps, after all, it may not be necessary for these confidences to be revealed to anyone but yourself."

"I hope not," said Thorndyke; "and if it is not necessary you may rely upon me not to allow any of your secrets to leak out. But you are wise to tell me everything that may in any way bear upon the case."

At this juncture, seeing that confidential matters were about to be discussed, I rose and prepared to withdraw; but Draper waved me back into my chair.

"You need not go away, Dr. Jervis," he said. "It is through you that I have the benefit of Dr. Thorndyke's help, and I know that you doctors can be trusted to keep your own counsel and your clients' secrets. And now for some confessions of mine. In the first place, it is my painful duty to tell you that I am a discharged convict—an 'old lag,' as the cant phrase has it."

He coloured a dusky red as he made this statement, and glanced furtively at Thorndyke to observe its effect. But he might as well have looked at a wooden figure-head or a stone mask as at my friend's immovable visage; and when his communication had been acknowledged by a slight nod, he proceeded:

"The history of my wrong-doing is the history of hundreds of others. I was a clerk in a bank, and getting on as well as I could expect in that not very progressive avocation, when I had the misfortune to make four very undesirable acquaintances. They were all young men, though rather older than myself, and were close friends, forming a sort of little community or club. They were not what is usually described as 'fast.' They were quite sober and decently-behaved young fellows, but they were very decidedly addicted to gambling in a small way, and they soon infected me. Before long I was the keenest gambler of them all. Cards, billiards, pool, and various forms of betting began to be the chief pleasures of my life, and not only was the bulk of my scanty salary often consumed in the inevitable losses, but presently I found myself considerably in debt, without any visible means of discharging my liabilities. It is true that my four friends were my chief—in fact, almost my only—creditors, but still, the debts existed, and had to be paid.

"Now these four friends of mine—named respectively Leach, Pitford, Hearn, and Jezzard—were uncommonly clever men, though the full extent of their cleverness was not appreciated by me until too late. And I, too, was clever in my way, and a most undesirable way it was, for I possessed the fatal gift of imitating handwriting and signatures with the most remarkable accuracy. So perfect were my copies that the writers themselves were frequently unable to distinguish their own signatures from my imitations, and many a time was my skill invoked by some of my companions to play off practical jokes upon the others. But these jests were strictly confined to our own little set, for my four friends were most careful and anxious that my dangerous accomplishment should not become known to outsiders.

"And now follows the consequence which you have no doubt foreseen. My debts, though small, were accumulating, and I saw no prospect of being able to pay them. Then, one night, Jezzard made a proposition. We had been playing bridge at his rooms, and once more my ill luck had caused me to increase my debt. I scribbled out an IOU, and pushed it across the table to Jezzard, who picked it up with a very wry face, and pocketed it.

"'Look here, Ted,' he said presently, 'this paper is all very well, but, you know, I can't pay my debts with it. My creditors demand hard cash.'

"'I'm very sorry,' I replied, 'but I can't help it.'

"'Yes, you can,' said he, 'and I'll tell you how.' He then propounded a scheme which I at first rejected with indignation, but which, when the others backed him up, I at last allowed myself to be talked into, and actually put into execution. I contrived, by taking advantage of the carelessness of some of my superiors at the bank, to get possession of some blank cheque forms, which I filled up with small amounts—not more than two or three pounds—and signed with careful imitations of the signatures of some of our clients. Jezzard got some stamps made for stamping on the account numbers, and when this had been done I handed over to him the whole collection of forged cheques in settlement of my debts to all of my four companions.

"The cheques were duly presented—by whom I do not know; and although, to my dismay, the modest sums for which I had drawn them had been skilfully altered into quite considerable amounts, they were all paid without demur excepting one. That one, which had been altered from three pounds to thirty-nine, was drawn upon an account which was already slightly overdrawn. The cashier became suspicious; the cheque was impounded, and the client communicated with. Then, of course, the mine exploded. Not only was this particular forgery detected, but inquiries were set afoot which soon brought to light the others. Presently circumstances, which I need not describe, threw some suspicion on me. I at once lost my nerve, and finally made a full confession.

"The inevitable prosecution followed. It was not conducted vindictively. Still, I had actually committed the forgeries, and though I endeavoured to cast a part of the blame on to the shoulders of my treacherous confederates, I did not succeed. Jezzard, it is true, was arrested, but was discharged for lack of evidence, and, consequently, the whole burden of the forgery fell upon me. The jury, of course, convicted me, and I was sentenced to seven years' penal servitude.

"During the time that I was in prison an uncle of mine died in Canada, and by the provisions of his will I inherited the whole of his very considerable property, so that when the time arrived for my release, I came out of prison, not only free, but comparatively rich. I at once dropped my own name, and, assuming that of

Alfred Draper, began to look about for some quiet spot in which I might spend the rest of my days in peace, and with little chance of my identity being discovered. Such a place I found in Sundersley, and here I have lived for the last seven years, liked and respected, I think, by my neighbours, who have little suspected that they were harbouring in their midst a convicted felon.

"All this time I had neither seen nor heard anything of my four confederates, and I hoped and believed that they had passed completely out of my life. But they had not. Only a month ago I met them once more, to my sorrow, and from the day of that meeting all the peace and security of my quiet existence at Sundersley have vanished. Like evil spirits they have stolen into my life, changing my happiness into bitter misery, filling my days with dark forebodings and my nights with terror."

Here Mr. Draper paused, and seemed to sink into a gloomy reverie.

"Under what circumstances did you meet these men?" Thorndyke asked.

"Ah!" exclaimed Draper, arousing with sudden excitement, "the circumstances were very singular and suspicious. I had gone over to Eastwich for the day to do some shopping. About eleven o'clock in the forenoon I was making some purchases in a shop when I noticed two men looking in the window, or rather pretending to do so, whilst they conversed earnestly. They were smartly dressed, in a horsy fashion, and looked like well-to-do farmers, as they might very naturally have been since it was market-day. But it seemed to me that their faces were familiar to me. I looked at them more attentively, and then it suddenly dawned upon me, most unpleasantly, that they resembled Leach and Jezzard. And yet they were not quite like. The resemblance was there, but the differences were greater than the lapse of time would account for. Moreover, the man who resembled Jezzard had a rather large mole on the left cheek just under the eye, while the other man had an eyeglass stuck in one eye, and wore a waxed moustache, whereas Leach had always been clean-shaven, and had never used an eyeglass.

"As I was speculating upon the resemblance they looked up, and caught my intent and inquisitive eye, whereupon they moved away from the window; and when, having completed my purchases, I came out into the street, they were nowhere to be seen.

"That evening, as I was walking by the river outside the town before returning to the station, I overtook a yacht which was being towed down-stream. Three men were walking ahead on the bank with a long tow-line, and one man stood in the cockpit steering. As I approached, and was reading the name *Otter* on the stern, the man at the helm looked round, and with a start of surprise I recognized my old acquaintance Hearn. The recognition, however, was not mutual, for I had grown a beard in the interval, and I passed on without appearing to notice him; but when I overtook the other three men, and recognized, as I had feared, the other three members of the gang, I must have looked rather hard at Jezzard, for he suddenly halted, and exclaimed: 'Why, it's our old friend Ted! Our long-lost and lamented brother!' He held out his hand with effusive cordiality, and began to make inquiries as to my welfare; but I cut him short with the remark that I was not proposing to renew the acquaintance, and, turning off on to a footpath that led away from the river, strode off without looking back.

"Naturally this meeting exercised my mind a good deal, and when I thought of the two men whom I had seen in the town, I could hardly believe that their likeness to my *quondam** friends was a mere coincidence. And yet when I had met Leach and Jezzard by the river, I had found them little altered, and had particularly noticed that Jezzard had no mole on his face, and that Leach was clean-shaven as of old.

"But a day or two later all my doubts were resolved by a paragraph in the local paper. It appeared that on the day of my visit to Eastwich a number of forged cheques had been cashed at the three banks. They had been presented by three well-dressed, horsy-looking men who looked like well-to-do farmers. One of them had a mole on the left cheek, another was distinguished by a waxed moustache and a single eyeglass, while the description of the third I did not recognize. None of the cheques had been drawn for large amounts, though the total sum obtained by the forgers was nearly four hundred pounds; but the most interesting point was that the cheque-forms had been manufactured by photographic process, and the water-mark skilfully, though not quite perfectly, imitated. Evidently the swindlers were clever and careful men, and willing to take a good deal of trouble for the sake of security, and the result of their precautions was that the police could make no guess as to their identity.

"The very next day, happening to walk over to Port Marston, I came upon the *Otter* lying moored alongside the quay in the harbour. As soon as I recognized the yacht, I turned quickly and walked away, but a minute later I ran into Leach and Jezzard, who were returning to their craft. Jezzard greeted me with an air of surprise. 'What! Still hanging about here, Ted?' he exclaimed. 'That is not discreet of you, dear boy. I should earnestly advise you to clear out.'

"'What do you mean?' I asked.

---

* Latin: "former."

"'Tut, tut!' said he. 'We read the papers like other people, and we know now what business took you to Eastwich. But it's foolish of you to hang about the neighbourhood where you might be spotted at any moment.'

"The implied accusation took me aback so completely that I stood staring at him in speechless astonishment, and at that unlucky moment a tradesman, from whom I had ordered some house-linen, passed along the quay. Seeing me, he stopped and touched his hat.

"'Beg pardon, Mr. Draper,' said he, 'but I shall be sending my cart up to Sundersley to-morrow morning if that will do for you.'

"I said that it would, and as the man turned away, Jezzard's face broke out into a cunning smile.

"So you are Mr. Draper, of Sundersley, now, are you?' said he. 'Well, I hope you won't be too proud to come and look in on your old friends. We shall be staying here for some time.'

"That same night Hearn made his appearance at my house. He had come as an emissary from the gang, to ask me to do some work for them—to execute some forgeries, in fact. Of course I refused, and pretty bluntly, too, whereupon Hearn began to throw out vague hints as to what might happen if I made enemies of the gang, and to utter veiled, but quite intelligible, threats. You will say that I was an idiot not to send him packing, and threaten to hand over the whole gang to the police; but I was never a man of strong nerve, and I don't mind admitting that I was mortally afraid of that cunning devil, Jezzard.

"The next thing that happened was that Hearn came and took lodgings in Sundersley, and, in spite of my efforts to avoid him, he haunted me continually. The yacht, too, had evidently settled down for some time at a berth in the harbour, for I heard that a local smack-boy had been engaged as a deck-hand; and I frequently encountered Jezzard and the other members of the gang, who all professed to believe that I had committed the Eastwich forgeries. One day I was foolish enough to allow myself to be lured on to the yacht for a few minutes, and when I would have gone ashore, I found that the shore ropes had been cast off, and that the vessel was already moving out of the harbour. At first I was furious, but the three scoundrels were so jovial and good-natured, and so delighted with the joke of taking me for a sail against my will, that I presently cooled down, and having changed into a pair of rubber-soled shoes (so that I should not make dents in the smooth deck with my hobnails), bore a hand at sailing the yacht, and spent quite a pleasant day.

"From that time I found myself gradually drifting back into a state of intimacy with these agreeable scoundrels, and daily becoming more and more afraid of them. In a moment of imbecility I mentioned what I had seen from the shop-window at Eastwich, and, though they passed the matter off with a joke, I could see that they were mightily disturbed by it. Their efforts to induce me to join them were redoubled, and Hearn took to calling almost daily at my house—usually with documents and signatures which he tried to persuade me to copy.

"A few evenings ago he made a new and startling proposition. We were walking in my garden, and he had been urging me once more to rejoin the gang—unsuccessfully, I need not say. Presently he sat down on a seat against a yew-hedge at the bottom of the garden, and, after an interval of silence, said suddenly:

"'Then you absolutely refuse to go in with us?'

"'Of course I do,' I replied. 'Why should I mix myself up with a gang of crooks when I have ample means and a decent position?'

"'Of course,' he agreed, 'you'd be a fool if you did. But, you see, you know all about this Eastwich job, to say nothing of our other little exploits, and you gave us away once before. Consequently, you can take it from me that, now Jezzard has run you to earth, he won't leave you in peace until you have given us some kind of a hold on you. You know too much, you see, and as long as you have a clean sheet you are a standing menace to us. That is the position. You know it, and Jezzard knows it, and he is a desperate man, and as cunning as the devil.'

"'I know that,' I said gloomily.

"'Very well,' continued Hearn. 'Now I'm going to make you an offer. Promise me a small annuity—you can easily afford it—or pay me a substantial sum down, and I will set you free for ever from Jezzard and the others.'

"'How will you do that?' I asked.

"'Very simply,' he replied. 'I am sick of them all, and sick of this risky, uncertain mode of life. Now I am ready to clean off my own slate and set you free at the same time; but I must have some means of livelihood in view.'

"'You mean that you will turn King's evidence?' I asked.

"'Yes, if you will pay me a couple of hundred a year, or, say, two thousand down on the conviction of the gang.'

"I was so taken aback that for some time I made no reply, and as I sat considering this amazing proposition, the silence was suddenly broken by a suppressed sneeze from the other side of the hedge.

"Hearn and I started to our feet. Immediately hurried footsteps were heard in the lane outside the hedge. We raced up the garden to the gate and out through a side alley, but when we reached the lane there was not a soul in sight. We made a brief and fruitless search in the immediate neighbourhood, and then turned back to the house. Hearn was deathly pale and very agitated, and I must confess that I was a good deal upset by the incident.

"'This is devilish awkward,' said Hearn.

"'It is rather,' I admitted; 'but I expect it was only some inquisitive yokel.'

"'I don't feel so sure of that,' said he. 'At any rate, we were stark lunatics to sit up against a hedge to talk secrets.'

"He paced the garden with me for some time in gloomy silence, and presently, after a brief request that I would think over his proposal, took himself off.

"I did not see him again until I met him last night on the yacht. Pitford called on me in the morning, and invited me to come and dine with them. I at first declined, for my housekeeper was going to spend the evening with her sister at Eastwich, and stay there for the night, and I did not much like leaving the house empty. However, I agreed eventually, stipulating that I should be allowed to come home early, and I accordingly went. Hearn and Pitford were waiting in the boat by the steps—for the yacht had been moved out to a buoy—and we went on board and spent a very pleasant and lively evening. Pitford put me ashore at ten o'clock, and I walked straight home, and went to bed. Hearn would have come with me, but the others insisted on his remaining, saying that they had some matters of business to discuss."

"Which way did you walk home?" asked Thorndyke.

"I came through the town, and along the main road."

"And that is all you know about this affair?"

"Absolutely all," replied Draper. "I have now admitted you to secrets of my past life that I had hoped never to have to reveal to any human creature, and I still have some faint hope that it may not be necessary for you to divulge what I have told you."

"Your secrets shall not be revealed unless it is absolutely indispensable that they should be," said Thorndyke; "but you are placing your life in my hands, and you must leave me perfectly free to act as I think best."

With this he gathered his notes together, and we took our departure.

"A very singular history, this, Jervis," he said, when, having wished the sergeant "Good-night," we stepped out on to the dark road. "What do you think of it?"

"I hardly know what to think," I answered, "but, on the whole, it seems rather against Draper than otherwise. He admits that he is an old criminal, and it appears that he was being persecuted and blackmailed by the man Hearn. It is true that he represents Jezzard as being the leading spirit and prime mover in the persecution, but we have only his word for that. Hearn was in lodgings near him, and was undoubtedly taking the most active part in the business, and it is quite possible, and indeed probable, that Hearn was the actual *deus ex machina.*"

Thorndyke nodded. "Yes," he said, "that is certainly the line the prosecution will take if we allow the story to become known. Ha! what is this? We are going to have some rain."

"Yes, and wind too. We are in for an autumn gale, I think."

"And that," said Thorndyke, "may turn out to be an important factor in our case."

"How can the weather affect your case?" I asked in some surprise. But, as the rain suddenly descended in a pelting shower, my companion broke into a run, leaving my question unanswered.

On the following morning, which was fair and sunny after the stormy night, Dr. Burrows called for my friend. He was on his way to the extemporized mortuary to make the *post-mortem* examination of the murdered man's body. Thorndyke, having notified the coroner that he was watching the case on behalf of the accused, had been authorized to be present at the autopsy; but the authorization did not include me, and, as Dr. Burrows did not issue any invitation, I was not able to be present. I met them, however, as they were returning, and it seemed to me that Dr. Burrows appeared a little huffy.

"Your friend," said he, in a rather injured tone, "is really the most outrageous stickler for forms and ceremonies that I have ever met."

Thorndyke looked at him with an amused twinkle, and chuckled indulgently.

"Here was a body," Dr. Burrows continued irritably, "found under circumstances clearly indicative of murder, and bearing a knife-wound that nearly divided the arch of the aorta; in spite of which, I assure you that Dr. Thorndyke insisted on weighing the body, and examining every organ—lungs, liver, stomach, and brain—yes, actually the brain!—as if there had been no clue whatever to the cause of death. And then, as a climax, he insisted on sending the contents of the stomach in a jar, sealed with our respective seals, in charge of a special messenger, to Professor Copland, for analysis and report. I thought he was going to demand an examination for the tubercle bacillus, but he didn't; which," concluded Dr. Burrows, suddenly becoming sourly facetious, "was an oversight, for, after all, the fellow may have died of consumption."

Thorndyke chuckled again, and I murmured that the precautions appeared to have been somewhat excessive.

"Not at all," was the smiling response. "You are losing sight of our function. We are the expert and impartial umpires, and it is our business to ascertain, with scientific accuracy, the cause of death. The *prima facie** appearances in this case suggest that the deceased was murdered by Draper, and that is the hypothesis advanced. But that is no concern of ours. It is not our function to confirm an hypothesis suggested by outside circumstances, but rather, on the contrary, to make certain that no other explanation is possible. And that is my invariable practice. No matter how glaringly obvious the appearances may be, I refuse to take anything for granted."

Dr. Burrows received this statement with a grunt of dissent, but the arrival of his dog-cart put a stop to further discussion.

Thorndyke was not subpoenaed for the inquest. Dr. Burrows and the sergeant having been present immediately after the finding of the body, his evidence was not considered necessary, and, moreover, he was known to be watching the case in the interests of the accused. Like myself, therefore, he was present as a spectator, but as a highly interested one, for he took very complete shorthand notes of the whole of the evidence and the coroner's comments.

I shall not describe the proceedings in detail. The jury, having been taken to view the body, trooped into the room on tiptoe, looking pale and awe-stricken, and took their seats; and thereafter, from time to time, directed glances of furtive curiosity at Draper as he stood, pallid and haggard, confronting the court, with a burly rural constable on either side.

The medical evidence was taken first. Dr. Burrows, having been sworn, began, with sarcastic emphasis, to describe the condition of the lungs and liver, until he was interrupted by the coroner.

"Is all this necessary?" the latter inquired. "I mean, is it material to the subject of the inquiry?"

"I should say not," replied Dr. Burrows. "It appears to me to be quite irrelevant, but Dr. Thorndyke, who is watching the case for the defence, thought it necessary."

"I think," said the coroner, "you had better give us only the facts that are material. The jury want you to tell them what you consider to have been the cause of death. They don't want a lecture on pathology."

"The cause of death," said Dr. Burrows, "was a penetrating wound of the chest, apparently inflicted with a large knife. The weapon entered between the second and third ribs on the left side close to the sternum or breast-bone. It wounded the left lung, and partially divided both the pulmonary artery and the aorta—the two principal arteries of the body."

---

* Latin: "on the first face." A legal term.

312 | R. AUSTIN FREEMAN

"Was this injury alone sufficient to cause death?" the coroner asked.

"Yes," was the reply; "and death from injury to these great vessels would be practically instantaneous."

"Could the injury have been self-inflicted?"

"So far as the position and nature of the wound are concerned," replied the witness, "self-infliction would be quite possible. But since death would follow in a few seconds at the most, the weapon would be found either in the wound, or grasped in the hand, or, at least, quite close to the body. But in this case no weapon was found at all, and the wound must therefore certainly have been homicidal."

"Did you see the body before it was moved?"

"Yes. It was lying on its back, with the arms extended and the legs nearly straight; and the sand in the neighbourhood of the body was trampled as if a furious struggle had taken place."

"Did you notice anything remarkable about the footprints in the sand?"

"I did," replied Dr. Burrows. "They were the footprints of two persons only. One of these was evidently the deceased, whose footmarks could be easily identified by the circular rubber heels. The other footprints were those of a person—apparently a man—who wore shoes, or boots, the soles of which were studded with nails; and these nails were arranged in a very peculiar and unusual manner, for those on the soles formed a lozenge or diamond shape, and those on the heel were set out in the form of a cross."

"Have you ever seen shoes or boots with the nails arranged in this manner?"

"Yes. I have seen a pair of shoes which I am informed belong to the accused; the nails in them are arranged as I have described."

"Would you say that the footprints of which you have spoken were made by those shoes?"

"No; I could not say that. I can only say that, to the best of my belief, the pattern on the shoes is similar to that in the footprints."

This was the sum of Dr. Burrows' evidence, and to all of it Thorndyke listened with an immovable countenance, though with the closest attention. Equally attentive was the accused man, though not equally impassive; indeed, so great was his agitation that presently one of the constables asked permission to get him a chair.

The next witness was Arthur Jezzard. He testified that he had viewed the body, and identified it as that of Charles Hearn; that he had been acquainted with deceased for some years, but knew practically nothing of his affairs. At the time of his death deceased was lodging in the village.

"Why did he leave the yacht?" the coroner inquired. "Was there any kind of disagreement?"

"Not in the least," replied Jezzard. "He grew tired of the confinement of the yacht, and came to live ashore for a change. But we were the best of friends, and he intended to come with us when we sailed."

"When did you see him last?"

"On the night before the body was found—that is, last Monday. He had been dining on the yacht, and we put him ashore about midnight. He said as we were rowing him ashore that he intended to walk home along the sands as the tide was out. He went up the stone steps by the watch-house, and turned at the top to wish us good-night. That was the last time I saw him alive."

"Do you know anything of the relations between the accused and the deceased?" the coroner asked.

"Very little," replied Jezzard. "Mr. Draper was introduced to us by the deceased about a month ago. I believe they had been acquainted some years, and they appeared to be on excellent terms. There was no indication of any quarrel or disagreement between them."

"What time did the accused leave the yacht on the night of the murder?"

"About ten o'clock. He said that he wanted to get home early, as his house-keeper was away and he did not like the house to be left with no one in it."

This was the whole of Jezzard's evidence, and was confirmed by that of Leach and Pitford. Then, when the fisherman had deposed to the discovery of the body, the sergeant was called, and stepped forward, grasping a carpet-bag, and looking as uncomfortable as if he had been the accused instead of a witness. He described the circumstances under which he saw the body, giving the exact time and place with official precision.

"You have heard Dr. Burrows' description of the footprints?" the coroner inquired.

"Yes. There were two sets. One set were evidently made by deceased. They showed that he entered St. Bridget's Bay from the direction of Port Marston. He had been walking along the shore just about high-water mark, sometimes above and sometimes below. Where he had walked below high-water mark the footprints had of course been washed away by the sea."

"How far back did you trace the footprints of deceased?"

"About two-thirds of the way to Sundersley Gap. Then they disappeared below high-water mark. Later in the evening I walked from the Gap into Port Marston, but could not find any further traces of deceased. He must have walked between the tide-marks all the way from Port Marston to beyond Sundersley. When these footprints entered St. Bridget's Bay they became mixed up with the footprints of another man, and the shore was trampled for a space of a dozen yards as if a furious struggle had taken place. The strange man's tracks came down from the Shepherd's Path, and went up it again; but, owing to the hardness of the ground from the dry weather, the tracks disappeared a short distance up the path, and I could not find them again."

"What were these strange footprints like?" inquired the coroner.

"They were very peculiar," replied the sergeant. "They were made by shoes armed with smallish hob-nails, which were arranged in a diamond-shaped pattern on the soles and in a cross on the heels. I measured the footprints carefully, and made a drawing of each foot at the time." Here the sergeant produced a long notebook of funereal aspect, and, having opened it at a marked place, handed it to the coroner, who examined it attentively, and then passed it on to the jury. From the jury it was presently transferred to Thorndyke, and, looking over his shoulder, I saw a very workmanlike sketch of a pair of footprints with the principal dimensions inserted.

Thorndyke surveyed the drawing critically, jotted down a few brief notes, and returned the sergeant's notebook to the coroner, who, as he took it, turned once more to the officer.

"Have you any clue, sergeant, to the person who made these footprints?" he asked.

By way of reply the sergeant opened his carpet-bag, and, extracting therefrom a pair of smart but stoutly made shoes, laid them on the table.

"These shoes," he said, "are the property of the accused; he was wearing them when I arrested him. They appear to correspond exactly to the footprints of the murderer. The measurements are the same, and the nails with which they are studded are arranged in a similar pattern."

"Would you swear that the footprints were made with these shoes?" asked the coroner.

"No, sir, I would not," was the decided answer. "I would only swear to the similarity of size and pattern."

"Had you ever seen these shoes before you made the drawing?"

"No, sir," replied the sergeant; and he then related the incident of the footprints in the soft earth by the pond which led him to make the arrest.

The coroner gazed reflectively at the shoes which he held in his hand, and from them to the drawing; then, passing them to the foreman of the jury, he remarked:

"Well, gentlemen, it is not for me to tell you whether these shoes answer to the description given by Dr. Burrows and the sergeant, or whether they resemble the drawing which, as you have heard, was made by the officer on the spot and before he had seen the shoes; that is a matter for you to decide. Meanwhile, there is another question that we must consider." He turned to the sergeant and asked: "Have you made any inquiries as to the movements of the accused on the night of the murder?"

"I have," replied the sergeant, "and I find that, on that night, the accused was alone in the house, his housekeeper having gone over to Eastwich. Two men saw him in the town about ten o'clock, apparently walking in the direction of Sundersley."

This concluded the sergeant's evidence, and when one or two more witnesses had been examined without eliciting any fresh facts, the coroner briefly recapitulated the evidence, and requested the jury to consider their verdict. Thereupon a solemn hush fell upon the court, broken only by the whispers of the jurymen, as they consulted together; and the spectators gazed in awed expectancy from the accused to the whispering jury. I glanced at Draper, sitting huddled in his chair, his clammy face as pale as that of the corpse in the mortuary hard by, his hands tremulous and restless; and, scoundrel as I believed him to be, I could not but pity the abject misery that was written large all over him, from his damp hair to his incessantly shifting feet.

The jury took but a short time to consider their verdict. At the end of five minutes the foreman announced that they were agreed, and, in answer to the coroner's formal inquiry, stood up and replied:

"We find that the deceased met his death by being stabbed in the chest by the accused man, Alfred Draper."

"That is a verdict of wilful murder," said the coroner, and he entered it accordingly in his notes. The Court now rose. The spectators reluctantly trooped out, the jurymen stood up and stretched themselves, and the two constables, under the guidance of the sergeant, carried the wretched Draper in a fainting condition to a closed fly* that was waiting outside.

"I was not greatly impressed by the activity of the defence," I remarked maliciously as we walked home.

Thorndyke smiled. "You surely did not expect me to cast my pearls of forensic learning before a coroner's jury," said he.

---

* A light, horse-drawn carriage.

"I expected that you would have something to say on behalf of your client," I replied. "As it was, his accusers had it all their own way."

"And why not?" he asked. "Of what concern to us is the verdict of the coroner's jury?"

"It would have seemed more decent to make some sort of defence," I replied.

"My dear Jervis," he rejoined, "you do not seem to appreciate the great virtue of what Lord Beaconsfield so felicitously called 'a policy of masterly inactivity'; and yet that is one of the great lessons that a medical training impresses on the student."

"That may be so," said I. "But the result, up to the present, of your masterly policy is that a verdict of wilful murder stands against your client, and I don't see what other verdict the jury could have found."

"Neither do I," said Thorndyke.

I had written to my principal, Dr. Cooper, describing the stirring events that were taking place in the village, and had received a reply from him instructing me to place the house at Thorndyke's disposal, and to give him every facility for his work. In accordance with which edict my colleague took possession of a well-lighted, disused stable-loft, and announced his intention of moving his things into it. Now, as these "things" included the mysterious contents of the hamper that the housemaid had seen, I was possessed with a consuming desire to be present at the "flitting," and I do not mind confessing that I purposely lurked about the stairs in the hopes of thus picking up a few crumbs of information.

But Thorndyke was one too many for me. A misbegotten infant in the village having been seized with inopportune convulsions, I was compelled, most reluctantly, to hasten to its relief; and I returned only in time to find Thorndyke in the act of locking the door of the loft.

"A nice light, roomy place to work in," he remarked, as he descended the steps, slipping the key into his pocket.

"Yes," I replied, and added boldly: "What do you intend to do up there?"

"Work up the case for the defence," he replied, "and, as I have now heard all that the prosecution has to say, I shall be able to forge ahead."

This was vague enough, but I consoled myself with the reflection that in a very few days I should, in common with the rest of the world, be in possession of the results of his mysterious proceedings. For, in view of the approaching assizes, preparations were being made to push the case through the magistrate's court as quickly as possible in order to obtain a committal in time for the ensuing sessions. Draper had, of course, been already charged before a justice of the peace and evidence of arrest taken, and it was expected that the adjourned hearing would commence before the local magistrates on the fifth day after the inquest.

The events of these five days kept me in a positive ferment of curiosity. In the first place an inspector of the Criminal Investigation Department came down and browsed about the place in company with the sergeant. Then Mr. Bashfield, who was to conduct the prosecution, came and took up his abode at the "Cat and Chicken." But the most surprising visitor was Thorndyke's laboratory assistant, Polton, who appeared one evening with a large trunk and a sailor's hammock, and announced that he was going to take up his quarters in the loft.

As to Thorndyke himself, his proceedings were beyond speculation. From time to time he made mysterious appearances at the windows of the loft, usually arrayed in what looked suspiciously like a nightshirt. Sometimes I would see him holding a negative up to the light, at others manipulating a photographic printing-frame; and once I observed him with a paintbrush and a large gallipot; on which I turned away in despair, and nearly collided with the inspector.

"Dr. Thorndyke is staying with you, I hear," said the latter, gazing earnestly at my colleague's back, which was presented for his inspection at the window.

"Yes," I answered. "Those are his temporary premises."

"That is where he does his bedevilments, I suppose?" the officer suggested.

"He conducts his experiments there," I corrected haughtily.

"That's what I mean," said the inspector; and, as Thorndyke at this moment turned and opened the window, our visitor began to ascend the steps.

"I've just called to ask if I could have a few words with you, Doctor," said the inspector, as he reached the door.

"Certainly," Thorndyke replied blandly. "If you will go down and wait with Dr. Jervis, I will be with you in five minutes."

The officer came down the steps grinning, and I thought I heard him murmur "Sold!" But this may have been an illusion. However, Thorndyke presently emerged, and he and the officer strode away into the shrubbery. What the inspector's business was, or whether he had any business at all, I never learned; but the incident seemed to throw some light on the presence of Polton and the sailor's hammock. And this reference to Polton reminds me of a very singular change that took place about this time in the habits of this usually staid and sedate little man; who, abandoning the somewhat clerical style of dress that he ordinarily affected, broke out into a semi-nautical costume, in which he would sally forth every morning in the direction of Port Marston. And there, on more than one occasion, I saw him leaning against a post by the harbour, or lounging outside a waterside tavern in earnest and amicable conversation with sundry nautical characters.

On the afternoon of the day before the opening of the proceedings we had two new visitors. One of them, a grey-haired spectacled man, was a stranger to me, and for some reason I failed to recall his name, Copland, though I was sure I had heard it before. The other was Anstey, the barrister who usually worked with Thorndyke in cases that went into Court. I saw very little of either of them, however, for they retired almost immediately to the loft, where, with short intervals for meals, they remained for the rest of the day, and, I believe, far into the night. Thorndyke requested me not to mention the names of his visitors to anyone, and at the same time apologized for the secrecy of his proceedings.

"But you are a doctor, Jervis," he concluded, "and you know what professional confidences are; and you will understand how greatly it is in our favour that we know exactly what the prosecution can do, while they are absolutely in the dark as to our line of defence."

I assured him that I fully understood his position, and with this assurance he retired, evidently relieved, to the council chamber.

The proceedings, which opened on the following day, and at which I was present throughout, need not be described in detail. The evidence for the prosecution was, of course, mainly a repetition of that given at the inquest. Mr. Bashfield's opening statement, however, I shall give at length, inasmuch as it summarized very clearly the whole of the case against the prisoner.

"The case that is now before the Court," said the counsel, "involves a charge of wilful murder against the prisoner Alfred Draper, and the facts, in so far as they are known, are briefly these: On the night of Monday, the 27th of September, the deceased, Charles Hearn, dined with some friends on board the yacht *Otter*. About midnight he came ashore, and proceeded to walk towards Sundersley along the beach. As he entered St. Bridget's Bay, a man, who appears to have been lying in wait, and who came down the Shepherd's Path, met him, and a deadly struggle seems to have taken place. The deceased received a wound of a kind calculated to cause almost instantaneous death, and apparently fell down dead.

"And now, what was the motive of this terrible crime? It was not robbery, for nothing appears to have been taken from the corpse. Money and valuables were found, as far as is known, intact. Nor, clearly, was it a case of a casual affray. We are, consequently, driven to the conclusion that the motive was a personal one, a motive of interest or revenge, and with this view the time, the place, and the evident deliberateness of the murder are in full agreement.

"So much for the motive. The next question is, Who was the perpetrator of this shocking crime? And the answer to that question is given in a very singular and dramatic circumstance, a circumstance that illustrates once more the amazing lack of precaution shown by persons who commit such crimes. The murderer was wearing a very remarkable pair of shoes, and those shoes left very remarkable footprints in the smooth sand, and those footprints were seen and examined by a very acute and painstaking police-officer, Sergeant Payne, whose evidence you will hear presently. The sergeant not only examined the footprints, he made careful drawings of them on the spot—on the spot, mind you, not from memory—and he made very exact measurements of them, which he duly noted down. And from those drawings and those measurements, those tell-tale shoes have been identified, and are here for your inspection.

"And now, who is the owner of those very singular, those almost unique shoes? I have said that the motive of this murder must have been a personal one, and, behold! the owner of those shoes happens to be the one person in the whole of this district who could have had a motive for compassing the murdered man's death. Those shoes belong to, and were taken from the foot of, the prisoner, Alfred Draper, and the prisoner, Alfred Draper, is the only person living in this neighbourhood who was acquainted with the deceased.

"It has been stated in evidence at the inquest that the relations of these two men, the prisoner and the deceased, were entirely friendly; but I shall prove to you that they were not so friendly as has been supposed. I shall prove to you, by the evidence of the prisoner's housekeeper, that the deceased was often an unwelcome visitor at the house, that the prisoner often denied himself when he was really at home and disengaged, and, in short, that he appeared constantly to shun and avoid the deceased.

"One more question and I have finished. Where was the prisoner on the night of the murder? The answer is that he was in a house little more than half a mile from the scene of the crime. And who was with him in that house? Who was there to observe and testify to his going forth and his coming home? No one. He was alone in the house. On that night, of all nights, he was alone. Not a soul was there to rouse at the creak of a door or the tread of a shoe—to tell as whether he slept or whether he stole forth in the dead of the night.

"Such are the facts of this case. I believe that they are not disputed, and I assert that, taken together, they are susceptible of only one explanation, which is that the prisoner, Alfred Draper, is the man who murdered the deceased, Charles Hearn."

Immediately on the conclusion of this address, the witnesses were called, and the evidence given was identical with that at the inquest. The only new witness for the prosecution was Draper's housekeeper, and her evidence fully bore out Mr. Bashfield's statement. The sergeant's account of the footprints was listened to with breathless interest, and at its conclusion the presiding magistrate—a retired solicitor, once well known in criminal practice—put a question which interested me as showing how clearly Thorndyke had foreseen the course of events, recalling, as it did, his remark on the night when we were caught in the rain.

"Did you," the magistrate asked, "take these shoes down to the beach and compare them with the actual footprints?"

"I obtained the shoes at night," replied the sergeant, "and I took them down to the shore at daybreak the next morning. But, unfortunately, there had been a storm in the night, and the footprints were almost obliterated by the wind and rain."

When the sergeant had stepped down, Mr. Bashfield announced that that was the case for the prosecution. He then resumed his seat, turning an inquisitive eye on Anstey and Thorndyke.

The former immediately rose and opened the case for the defence with a brief statement.

"The learned counsel for the prosecution," said he, "has told us that the facts now in the possession of the Court admit of but one explanation—that of the guilt of the accused. That may or may not be; but I shall now proceed to lay before the Court certain fresh facts—facts, I may say, of the most singular and startling character, which will, I think, lead to a very different conclusion. I shall say no more, but call the witnesses forthwith, and let the evidence speak for itself."

The first witness for the defence was Thorndyke; and as he entered the box I observed Polton take up a position close behind him with a large wicker trunk. Having been sworn, and requested by Anstey to tell the Court what he knew about the case, he commenced without preamble:

"About half-past four in the afternoon of the 28th of September I walked down Sundersley Gap with Dr. Jervis. Our attention was attracted by certain footprints in the sand, particularly those of a man who had landed from a boat, had walked up the Gap, and presently returned, apparently to the boat.

"As we were standing there Sergeant Payne and Dr. Burrows passed down the Gap with two constables carrying a stretcher. We followed at a distance, and as we walked along the shore we encountered another set of footprints—those which the sergeant has described as the footprints of the deceased. We examined these carefully, and endeavoured to frame a description of the person by whom they had been made."

"And did your description agree with the character of the deceased?" the magistrate asked.

"Not in the least," replied Thorndyke, whereupon the magistrate, the inspector, and Mr. Bashfield laughed long and heartily.

"When we turned into St. Bridget's Bay, I saw the body of deceased lying on the sand close to the cliff. The sand all round was covered with footprints, as if a prolonged, fierce struggle had taken place. There were two sets of footprints, one set being apparently those of the deceased and the other those of a man with nailed shoes of a very peculiar and conspicuous pattern. The incredible folly that the wearing of such shoes indicated caused me to look more closely at the footprints, and then I made the surprising discovery that there had in reality been no struggle; that, in fact, the two sets of footprints had been made at different times."

"At different times!" the magistrate exclaimed in astonishment.

"Yes. The interval between them may have been one of hours or one only of seconds, but the undoubted fact is that the two sets of footprints were made, not simultaneously, but in succession."

"But how did you arrive at that fact?" the magistrate asked.

"It was very obvious when one looked," said Thorndyke. "The marks of the deceased man's shoes showed that he repeatedly trod in his own footprints; but never in a single instance did he tread in the footprints of the other man, although they covered the same area. The man with the nailed shoes, on the contrary, not only trod in his own footprints, but with equal frequency in those of the deceased. Moreover, when the body was removed, I observed that the footprints in the sand on which it was lying were exclusively those of the deceased. There was not a sign of any nail-marked footprint under the corpse, although there were many close around it. It was evident, therefore, that the footprints of the deceased were made first and those of the nailed shoes afterwards."

As Thorndyke paused the magistrate rubbed his nose thoughtfully, and the inspector gazed at the witness with a puzzled frown.

"The singularity of this fact," my colleague resumed, "made me look at the footprints yet more critically, and then I made another discovery. There was a double track of the nailed shoes, leading apparently from and back to the Shepherd's Path. But on examining these tracks more closely, I was astonished to find that the man who had made them had been walking backwards; that, in fact, he had walked backwards from the body to the Shepherd's Path, had ascended it for a short distance, had turned round, and returned, still walking backwards, to the face of the cliff near the corpse, and there the tracks vanished altogether. On the sand at this spot were some small, inconspicuous marks which might have been made by the end of a rope, and there were also a few small fragments which had fallen from the cliff above. Observing these, I examined the surface of the cliff, and at one spot, about six feet above the beach, I found a freshly rubbed spot on which were parallel scratches such as might have been made by the nailed sole of a boot. I then ascended the Shepherd's Path, and examined the cliff from above, and here I found on the extreme edge a rather deep indentation, such as would be made by a taut rope, and, on lying down and looking over, I could see, some five feet from the top, another rubbed spot with very distinct parallel scratches."

"You appear to infer," said the chairman, "that this man performed these astonishing evolutions and was then hauled up the cliff?"

"That is what the appearances suggested," replied Thorndyke.

The chairman pursed up his lips, raised his eyebrows, and glanced doubtfully at his brother magistrates. Then, with a resigned air, he bowed to the witness to indicate that he was listening.

"That same night," Thorndyke resumed, "I cycled down to the shore, through the Gap, with a supply of plaster of Paris, and proceeded to take plaster moulds of the more important of the footprints." (Here the magistrates, the inspector, and Mr. Bashfield with one accord sat up at attention; Sergeant Payne swore quite audibly; and I experienced a sudden illumination respecting a certain basin and kitchen spoon which had so puzzled me on the night of Thorndyke's arrival.) "As I thought that liquid plaster might confuse or even obliterate the prints in sand, I filled up the respective footprints with dry plaster, pressed it down lightly, and then cautiously poured water on to it. The moulds, which are excellent impressions, of course show the appearance of the boots which made the footprints, and from these moulds I have prepared casts which reproduce the footprints themselves.

"The first mould that I made was that of one of the tracks from the boat up to the Gap, and of this I shall speak presently. I next made a mould of one of the footprints which have been described as those of the deceased."

"Have been described!" exclaimed the chairman. "The deceased was certainly there, and there were no other footprints, so, if they were not his, he must have flown to where he was found."

"I will call them the footprints of the deceased," replied Thorndyke imperturbably. "I took a mould of one of them, and with it, on the same mould, one of my own footprints. Here is the mould, and here is a cast from it." (He turned and took them from the triumphant Polton, who had tenderly lifted them out of the trunk in readiness.) "On looking at the cast, it will be seen that the appearances are not such as would be expected. The deceased was five feet nine inches high, but was very thin and light, weighing only nine stone six pounds,* as I ascertained by weighing the body, whereas I am five feet eleven and weigh nearly thirteen stone.† But yet the footprint of the deceased is nearly twice as deep as mine—that is to say, the lighter man has sunk into the sand nearly twice as deeply as the heavier man."

The magistrates were now deeply attentive. They were no longer simply listening to the despised utterances of a mere scientific expert. The cast lay before them with the two footprints side by side; the evidence appealed to their own senses and was proportionately convincing.

"This is very singular," said the chairman; "but perhaps you can explain the discrepancy?"

"I think I can," replied Thorndyke; "but I should prefer to place all the facts before you first."

"Undoubtedly that would be better," the chairman agreed. "Pray proceed."

"There was another remarkable peculiarity about these footprints," Thorndyke continued, "and that was their distance apart—the length of the stride, in fact. I measured the steps carefully from heel to heel, and found them only nineteen and a half inches. But a man of Hearn's height would have an ordinary stride of about thirty-six inches—more if he was walking fast. Walking with a stride of nineteen and a half inches he would look as if his legs were tied together.

"I next proceeded to the Bay, and took two moulds from the footprints of the man with the nailed shoes, a right and a left. Here is a cast from the mould, and it shows very clearly that the man was walking backwards."

"How does it show that?" asked the magistrate.

"There are several distinctive points. For instance, the absence of the usual 'kick off' at the toe, the slight drag behind the heel, showing the direction in which the foot was lifted, and the undisturbed impression of the sole."

"You have spoken of moulds and casts. What is the difference between them?"

"A mould is a direct, and therefore reversed, impression. A cast is the impression of a mould, and therefore a facsimile of the object. If I pour liquid plaster

---

*   132 pounds.

†   182 pounds.

on a coin, when it sets I have a mould, a sunk impression, of the coin. If I pour melted wax into the mould I obtain a cast, a facsimile of the coin. A footprint is a mould of the foot. A mould of the footprint is a cast of the foot, and a cast from the mould reproduces the footprint."

"Thank you," said the magistrate. "Then your moulds from these two footprints are really facsimiles of the murderer's shoes, and can be compared with these shoes which have been put in evidence?"

"Yes, and when we compare them they demonstrate a very important fact."

"What is that?"

"It is that the prisoner's shoes were not the shoes that made those footprints." A buzz of astonishment ran through the court, but Thorndyke continued stolidly: "The prisoner's shoes were not in my possession, so I went on to Barker's pond, on the clay margin of which I had seen footprints actually made by the prisoner. I took moulds of those footprints, and compared them with these from the sand. There are several important differences, which you will see if you compare them. To facilitate the comparison I have made transparent photographs of both sets of moulds to the same scale. Now, if we put the photograph of the mould of the prisoner's right shoe over that of the murderer's right shoe, and hold the two superposed photographs up to the light, we cannot make the two pictures coincide. They are exactly of the same length, but the shoes are of different shape. Moreover, if we put one of the nails in one photograph over the corresponding nail in the other photograph, we cannot make the rest of the nails coincide. But the most conclusive fact of all—from which there is no possible escape—is that the number of nails in the two shoes is not the same. In the sole of the prisoner's right shoe there are forty nails; in that of the murderer there are forty-one. The murderer has one nail too many."

There was a deathly silence in the court as the magistrates and Mr. Bashfield pored over the moulds and the prisoner's shoes, and examined the photographs against the light. Then the chairman asked: "Are these all the facts, or have you something more to tell us?" He was evidently anxious to get the key to this riddle.

"There is more evidence, your Worship," said Anstey. "The witness examined the body of deceased." Then, turning to Thorndyke, he asked:

"You were present at the *post-mortem* examination?"

"I was."

"Did you form any opinion as to the cause of death?"

"Yes. I came to the conclusion that death was occasioned by an overdose of morphia."

A universal gasp of amazement greeted this statement. Then the presiding magistrate protested breathlessly:

"But there was a wound, which we have been told was capable of causing instantaneous death. Was that not the case?"

"There was undoubtedly such a wound," replied Thorndyke. "But when that wound was inflicted the deceased had already been dead from a quarter to half an hour."

"This is incredible!" exclaimed the magistrate. "But, no doubt, you can give us your reasons for this amazing conclusion?"

"My opinion," said Thorndyke, "was based on several facts. In the first place, a wound inflicted on a living body gapes rather widely, owing to the retraction of the living skin. The skin of a dead body does not retract, and the wound, consequently, does not gape. This wound gaped very slightly, showing that death was recent, I should say, within half an hour. Then a wound on the living body becomes filled with blood, and blood is shed freely on the clothing. But the wound on the deceased contained only a little blood-clot. There was hardly any blood on the clothing, and I had already noticed that there was none on the sand where the body had lain."

"And you consider this quite conclusive?" the magistrate asked doubtfully.

"I do," answered Thorndyke. "But there was other evidence which was beyond all question. The weapon had partially divided both the aorta and the pulmonary artery—the main arteries of the body. Now, during life, these great vessels are full of blood at a high internal pressure, whereas after death they become almost empty. It follows that, if this wound had been inflicted during life, the cavity in which those vessels lie would have become filled with blood. As a matter of fact, it contained practically no blood, only the merest oozing from some small veins, so that it is certain that the wound was inflicted after death. The presence and nature of the poison I ascertained by analyzing certain secretions from the body, and the analysis enabled me to judge that the quantity of the poison was large; but the contents of the stomach were sent to Professor Copland for more exact examination."

"Is the result of Professor Copland's analysis known?" the magistrate asked Anstey.

"The professor is here, your Worship," replied Anstey, "and is prepared to swear to having obtained over one grain of morphia from the contents of the stomach; and as this, which is in itself a poisonous dose, is only the unabsorbed residue of what was actually swallowed, the total quantity taken must have been very large indeed."

"Thank you," said the magistrate. "And now, Dr. Thorndyke, if you have given us all the facts, perhaps you will tell us what conclusions you have drawn from them."

"The facts which I have stated," said Thorndyke, "appear to me to indicate the following sequence of events. The deceased died about midnight on September 27, from the effects of a poisonous dose of morphia, how or by whom administered I offer no opinion. I think that his body was conveyed in a boat to Sundersley Gap. The boat probably contained three men, of whom one remained in charge of it, one walked up the Gap and along the cliff towards St. Bridget's Bay, and the third, having put on the shoes of the deceased, carried the body along the shore to the Bay. This would account for the great depth and short stride of the tracks that have been spoken of as those of the deceased. Having reached the Bay, I believe that this man laid the corpse down on his tracks, and then trampled the sand in the neighbourhood. He next took off the deceased's shoes and put them on the corpse; then he put on a pair of boots or shoes which he had been carrying—perhaps hung round his neck—and which had been prepared with nails to imitate Draper's shoes. In these shoes he again trampled over the area near the corpse. Then he walked backwards to the Shepherd's Path, and from it again, still backwards, to the face of the cliff. Here his accomplice had lowered a rope, by which he climbed up to the top. At the top he took off the nailed shoes, and the two men walked back to the Gap, where the man who had carried the rope took his confederate on his back, and carried him down to the boat to avoid leaving the tracks of stockinged feet. The tracks that I saw at the Gap certainly indicated that the man was carrying something very heavy when he returned to the boat."

"But why should the man have climbed a rope up the cliff when he could have walked up the Shepherd's Path?" the magistrate asked.

"Because," replied Thorndyke, "there would then have been a set of tracks leading out of the Bay without a corresponding set leading into it; and this would have instantly suggested to a smart police-officer—such as Sergeant Payne—a landing from a boat."

"Your explanation is highly ingenious," said the magistrate, "and appears to cover all the very remarkable facts. Have you anything more to tell us?"

"No, your Worship," was the reply, "excepting" (here he took from Polton the last pair of moulds and passed them up to the magistrate) "that you will probably find these moulds of importance presently."

As Thorndyke stepped from the box—for there was no cross-examination—the magistrates scrutinized the moulds with an air of perplexity; but they were too discreet to make any remark.

When the evidence of Professor Copland (which showed that an unquestionably lethal dose of morphia must have been swallowed) had been taken, the clerk called out the—to me—unfamiliar name of Jacob Gummer. Thereupon an enormous pair of brown dreadnought* trousers, from the upper end of which a smack-boy's† head and shoulders protruded, walked into the witness-box.

Jacob admitted at the outset that he was a smack-master's apprentice, and that he had been "hired out" by his master to one Mr. Jezzard as deck-hand and cabin-boy of the yacht *Otter*.

"Now, Gummer," said Anstey, "do you remember the prisoner coming on board the yacht?"

"Yes. He has been on board twice. The first time was about a month ago. He went for a sail with us then. The second time was on the night when Mr. Hearn was murdered."

"Do you remember what sort of boots the prisoner was wearing the first time he came?"

"Yes. They were shoes with a lot of nails in the soles. I remember them because Mr. Jezzard made him take them off and put on a canvas pair."

"What was done with the nailed shoes?"

"Mr. Jezzard took 'em below to the cabin."

"And did Mr. Jezzard come up on deck again directly?"

"No. He stayed down in the cabin about ten minutes."

"Do you remember a parcel being delivered on board from a London boot-maker?"

"Yes. The postman brought it about four or five days after Mr. Draper had been on board. It was labelled 'Walker Bros., Boot and Shoe Makers, London.' Mr. Jezzard took a pair of shoes from it, for I saw them on the locker in the cabin the same day."

"Did you ever see him wear them?"

"No. I never see 'em again."

"Have you ever heard sounds of hammering on the yacht?"

"Yes. The night after the parcel came I was on the quay alongside, and I heard someone a-hammering in the cabin."

"What did the hammering sound like?"

"It sounded like a cobbler a-hammering in nails."

---

* Heavy-duty.

† A smack is a type of fishing vessel.

"Have you ever seen any boot-nails on the yacht?"

"Yes. When I was a-clearin' up the cabin the next mornin', I found a hobnail on the floor in a corner by the locker."

"Were you on board on the night when Mr. Hearn died?"

"Yes. I'd been ashore, but I came aboard about half-past nine."

"Did you see Mr. Hearn go ashore?"

"I see him leave the yacht. I had turned into my bunk and gone to sleep, when Mr. Jezzard calls down to me: 'We're putting Mr. Hearn ashore,' says he; 'and then,' he says, 'we're a-going for an hour's fishing. You needn't sit up,' he says, and with that he shuts the scuttle. Then I got up and slid back the scuttle and put my head out, and I see Mr. Jezzard and Mr. Leach a-helpin' Mr. Hearn acrost the deck. Mr. Hearn he looked as if he was drunk. They got him into the boat—and a rare job they had—and Mr. Pitford, what was in the boat already, he pushed off. And then I popped my head in again, 'cause I didn't want them to see me."

"Did they row to the steps?"

"No. I put my head out again when they were gone, and I heard 'em row round the yacht, and then pull out towards the mouth of the harbour. I couldn't see the boat, 'cause it was a very dark night."

"Very well. Now I am going to ask you about another matter. Do you know anyone of the name of Polton?"

"Yes," replied Gummer, turning a dusky red. "I've just found out his real name. I thought he was called Simmons."

"Tell us what you know about him," said Anstey, with a mischievous smile.

"Well," said the boy, with a ferocious scowl at the bland and smiling Polton, "one day he come down to the yacht when the gentlemen had gone ashore. I believe he'd seen 'em go. And he offers me ten shillin'* to let him see all the boots and shoes we'd got on board. I didn't see no harm, so I turns out the whole lot in the cabin for him to look at. While he was lookin' at 'em he asks me to fetch a pair of mine from the fo'c'sle, so I fetches 'em. When I come back he was pitchin' the boots and shoes back into the locker. Then, presently, he nips off, and when he was gone I looked over the shoes, and then I found there was a pair missing. They was an old pair of Mr. Jezzard's, and what made him nick 'em is more than I can understand."

"Would you know those shoes if you saw them?"

"Yes, I should," replied the lad.

---

* Worth £58.33 (US $78.15) in 2018, according to online sources.

"Are these the pair?" Anstey handed the boy a pair of dilapidated canvas shoes, which he seized eagerly.

"Yes, these is the ones what he stole!" he exclaimed.

Anstey took them back from the boy's reluctant hands, and passed them up to the magistrate's desk. "I think," said he, "that if your Worship will compare these shoes with the last pair of moulds, you will have no doubt that these are the shoes which made the footprints from the sea to Sundersley Gap and back again."

The magistrates together compared the shoes and the moulds amidst a breathless silence. At length the chairman laid them down on the desk.

"It is impossible to doubt it," said he. "The broken heel and the tear in the rubber sole, with the remains of the chequered pattern, make the identity practically certain."

As the chairman made this statement I involuntarily glanced round to the place where Jezzard was sitting. But he was not there; neither he, nor Pitford, nor Leach. Taking advantage of the preoccupation of the Court, they had quietly slipped out of the door. But I was not the only person who had noted their absence. The inspector and the sergeant were already in earnest consultation, and a minute later they, too, hurriedly departed.

The proceedings now speedily came to an end. After a brief discussion with his brother-magistrates, the chairman addressed the Court.

"The remarkable and I may say startling evidence, which has been heard in this court to-day, if it has not fixed the guilt of this crime on any individual, has, at any rate, made it clear to our satisfaction that the prisoner is not the guilty person, and he is accordingly discharged. Mr. Draper, I have great pleasure in informing you that you are at liberty to leave the court, and that you do so entirely clear of all suspicion; and I congratulate you very heartily on the skill and ingenuity of your legal advisers, but for which the decision of the Court would, I am afraid, have been very different."

That evening, lawyers, witnesses, and the jubilant and grateful client gathered round a truly festive board to dine, and fight over again the battle of the day. But we were scarcely halfway through our meal when, to the indignation of the servants, Sergeant Payne burst breathlessly into the room.

"They've gone, sir!" he exclaimed, addressing Thorndyke. "They've given us the slip for good."

"Why, how can that be?" asked Thorndyke.

"They're dead, sir! All three of them!"

"Dead!" we all exclaimed.

"Yes. They made a burst for the yacht when they left the court, and they got on board and put out to sea at once, hoping, no doubt, to get clear as the light was just failing. But they were in such a hurry that they did not see a steam trawler that was entering, and was hidden by the pier. Then, just at the entrance, as the yacht was creeping out, the trawler hit her amidships, and fairly cut her in two. The three men were in the water in an instant, and were swept away in the eddy behind the north pier; and before any boat could put out to them they had all gone under. Jezzard's body came up on the beach just as I was coming away."

We were all silent and a little awed, but if any of us felt regret at the catastrophe, it was at the thought that three such cold-blooded villains should have made so easy an exit; and to one of us, at least, the news came as a blessed relief.

THE NINESCORE MYSTERY

by Baroness Orczy

1910

Baroness Emma Magdolna Rozália Mária Jozefa Borbála Orczy de Orci—known to her intimates by the more manageable "Emmuska"—was born in Hungary in 1865. Fearing a peasant revolution, her family left the country three years later and traveled across Europe before settling in London when Emma was fourteen. Initially she studied art, and she married a young illustrator named Montague MacLean Barstow in 1894. Their marriage was a long and happy one, but at first she turned to writing as a means to supplement his modest wages.

She is best known today, of course, as the creator of Sir Percy Blakeney, the dashing hero of the French Revolution whose exploits went on to fill eleven novels and two collections of short stories. Her other works include translations of old Hungarian fairytales, plays—including the 1903 stage version of *The Scarlet Pimpernel*—and a staggering number of historical and contemporary novels published over a span of almost fifty years.

Among this remarkable output, she created two detective characters: an unnamed armchair detective known only as The Old Man in the Corner and Lady Molly of Scotland Yard, whose "Female Department" at Scotland Yard anticipated the acceptance of female officers by a decade. The Women's Police Service, founded in 1914, was staffed by volunteers, and the first woman police constable in England was appointed in August 1915, in the provincial town of Grantham. London had to wait another four years.

Although she is officially attached to Scotland Yard, Lady Molly has more in common with Miss Marple and the other female detectives of the Golden Age. Her defining ability is a knack for seeing and understanding small details that a male detective would over-look or discount: Orczy is careful not to invoke such an imprecise concept as "feminine intuition," but maintains that the two sexes experience the world in such different ways that women are naturally more attuned to certain details than men can ever be.

Baroness Orczy wrote twelve Lady Molly stories, all published in the 1910 collection *Lady Molly of Scotland Yard*.

1

Well, you know, some say she is the daughter of a duke, others that she was born in the gutter, and that the handle has been soldered on to her name in order to give her style and influence.

I could say a lot, of course, but "my lips are sealed," as the poets say. All through her successful career at the Yard she honoured me with her friendship and confidence, but when she took me in partnership, as it were, she made me promise that I would never breathe a word of her private life, and this I swore on my Bible oath—"wish I may die," and all the rest of it.

Yes, we always called her "my lady," from the moment that she was put at the head of our section; and the chief called her "Lady Molly" in our presence. We of the Female Department are dreadfully snubbed by the men, though don't tell me that women have not ten times as much intuition as the blundering and sterner sex; my firm belief is that we shouldn't have half so many undetected crimes if some of the so-called mysteries were put to the test of feminine investigation.

Do you suppose for a moment, for instance, that the truth about that extraor-dinary case at Ninescore would ever have come to light if the men alone had had the handling of it? Would any man have taken so bold a risk as Lady Molly did when— But I am anticipating.

Let me go back to that memorable morning when she came into my room in a wild state of agitation.

"The chief says I may go down to Ninescore if I like, Mary," she said, in a voice all a-quiver with excitement.

"You!" I ejaculated. "What for?"

"What for—what for?" she repeated eagerly. "Mary, don't you understand? It is the chance I have been waiting for—the chance of a lifetime? They are all desperate about the case up at the Yard; the public is furious, and columns of sarcastic letters appear in the daily press. None of our men know what to do; they are at their wits' end, and so this morning I went to the chief—"

"Yes?" I queried eagerly, for she had suddenly ceased speaking.

"Well, never mind now how I did it—I will tell you all about it on the way, for we have just got time to catch the 11 A.M. down to Canterbury. The chief says I may go, and that I may take whom I like with me. He suggested one of the men, but somehow I feel that this is woman's work, and I'd rather have you, Mary, than anyone. We will go over the preliminaries of the case together in the train, as I don't suppose that you have got them at your fingers' ends yet, and you have only just got time to put a few things together and meet me at Charing Cross booking-office in time for that 11.00 sharp."

She was off before I could ask her any more questions, and anyhow, I was too flabbergasted to say much. A murder case in the hands of the Female Department! Such a thing had been unheard of until now. But I was all excitement, too, and you may be sure I was at the station in good time.

Fortunately, Lady Molly and I had a carriage to ourselves. It was a non-stop run to Canterbury, so we had plenty of time before us, and I was longing to know all about this case, you bet, since I was to have the honour of helping Lady Molly in it.

The murder of Mary Nicholls had actually been committed at Ash Court, a fine old mansion which stands in the village of Ninescore. The Court is surrounded by magnificently timbered grounds, the most fascinating portion of which is an island in the midst of a small pond, which is spanned by a tiny rustic bridge. The island is called "The Wilderness," and is at the furthermost end of the grounds, out of sight and earshot of the mansion itself. It was in this charming spot, on the edge of the pond, that the body of a girl was found on the 5th of February last.

I will spare you the horrible details of this gruesome discovery. Suffice it to say for the present that the unfortunate woman was lying on her face, with the lower portion of her body on the small, grass-covered embankment, and her head, arms, and shoulders sunk in the slime of the stagnant water just below.

It was Timothy Coleman, one of the under-gardeners at Ash Court, who first made this appalling discovery. He had crossed the rustic bridge and traversed the little island in its entirety, when he noticed something blue lying half in and half out of the water beyond. Timothy is a stolid, unemotional kind of yokel, and, once having ascertained that the object was a woman's body in a blue dress with white facings, he quietly stooped and tried to lift it out of the mud.

But here even his stolidity gave way at the terrible sight which was revealed before him. That the woman—whoever she might be—had been brutally murdered was obvious, her dress in front being stained with blood; but what was so awful that it even turned old Timothy sick with horror, was that, owing to the head, arms and shoulders having apparently been in the slime for some time, they were in an advanced state of decomposition.

Well, whatever was necessary was immediately done, of course. Coleman went to get assistance from the lodge, and soon the police were on the scene and had removed the unfortunate victim's remains to the small local police-station.

Ninescore is a sleepy, out-of-the-way village, situated some seven miles from Canterbury and four from Sandwich. Soon everyone in the place had heard that a terrible murder had been committed in the village, and all the details were already freely discussed at the Green Man.

To begin with, everyone said that though the body itself might be practically unrecognizable, the bright blue serge dress with the white facings was unmistakable, as were the pearl and ruby ring and the red leather purse found by Inspector Meisures close to the murdered woman's hand.

Within two hours of Timothy Coleman's gruesome find the identity of the unfortunate victim was firmly established as that of Mary Nicholls, who lived with her sister Susan at 2, Elm Cottages, in Ninescore Lane, almost opposite Ash Court. It was also known that when the police called at that address they found the place locked and apparently uninhabited.

Mrs. Hooker, who lived at No. 1 next door, explained to Inspector Meisures that Susan and Mary Nicholls had left home about a fortnight ago, and that she had not seen them since.

"It'll be a fortnight to-morrow," she said. "I was just inside my own front door a-calling to the cat to come in. It was past seven o'clock, and as dark a night as ever you did see. You could hardly see your 'and afore your eyes, and there was a nasty damp drizzle comin' from everywhere. Susan and Mary come out of their cottage; I couldn't rightly see Susan, but I 'eard Mary's voice quite distinck. She says: 'We'll have to 'urry,' says she. I, thinkin' they might be goin' to do some shoppin' in the village, calls out to them that I'd just 'eard the church clock strike seven, and that bein' Thursday, and early closin', they'd find all the shops shut at Ninescore. But they took no notice, and walked off towards the village, and that's the last I ever seed o' them two."

Further questioning among the village folk brought forth many curious details. It seems that Mary Nicholls was a very flighty young woman, about whom there had already been quite a good deal of scandal, whilst Susan, on the other hand—who was very sober and steady in her conduct—had chafed considerably under her younger sister's questionable reputation, and, according to Mrs. Hooker, many were the bitter quarrels which occurred between the two girls. These quarrels, it seems, had been especially violent within the last year whenever Mr. Lionel Lydgate called at the cottage. He was a London gentleman, it appears—a young man about town, it afterwards transpired—but he frequently stayed at Canterbury, where he had some friends, and on those occasions he would come over to Ninescore in his smart dogcart and take Mary out for drives.

Mr. Lydgate is brother to Lord Edbrooke, the multi-millionaire, who was the recipient of birthday honours* last year. His lordship resides at Edbrooke Castle, but he and his brother Lionel had rented Ash Court once or twice, as both were keen golfers and Sandwich Links are very close by. Lord Edbrooke, I may add, is a married man. Mr. Lionel Lydgate, on the other hand, is just engaged to Miss Marbury, daughter of one of the canons of Canterbury.

No wonder, therefore, that Susan Nicholls strongly objected to her sister's name being still coupled with that of a young man far above her in station, who, moreover, was about to marry a young lady in his own rank of life.

But Mary seemed not to care. She was a young woman who only liked fun and pleasure, and she shrugged her shoulders at public opinion, even though there were ugly rumours anent† the parentage of a little baby girl whom she herself had placed under the care of Mrs. Williams, a widow who lived in a somewhat isolated cottage on the Canterbury road. Mary had told Mrs. Williams that the father of the child, who was her own brother, had died very suddenly, leaving the little one on her and Susan's hands; and, as they couldn't look after it properly, they wished Mrs. Williams to have charge of it. To this the latter readily agreed.

The sum for the keep of the infant was decided upon, and thereafter Mary Nicholls had come every week to see the little girl, and always brought the money with her.

Inspector Meisures called on Mrs. Williams, and certainly the worthy widow had a very startling sequel to relate to the above story.

"A fortnight to-morrow," explained Mrs. Williams to the inspector, "a little after seven o'clock, Mary Nicholls come runnin' into my cottage. It was an awful night, pitch dark and a nasty drizzle. Mary says to me she's in a great hurry; she

---

*   The British monarch's official birthday is a traditional time for awarding titles and honours.

†   About (archaic).

is goin' up to London by a train from Canterbury and wants to say good-bye to
the child. She seemed terribly excited, and her clothes were very wet. I brings
baby to her, and she kisses it rather wild-like and says to me: 'You'll take great
care of her, Mrs. Williams,' she says; 'I may be gone some time.' Then she puts
baby down and gives me £2, the child's keep for eight weeks."

After which, it appears, Mary once more said "good-bye" and ran out of the
cottage, Mrs. Williams going as far as the front door with her. The night was
very dark, and she couldn't see if Mary was alone or not, until presently she heard
her voice saying tearfully:

"I had to kiss baby—" then the voice died out in the distance "on the way to
Canterbury," Mrs. Williams said, most emphatically.

So far, you see, Inspector Meisures was able to fix the departure of the two
sisters Nicholls from Ninescore on the night of January 23rd. Obviously they left
their cottage about seven, went to Mrs. Williams, where Susan remained outside
while Mary went in to say good-bye to the child.

After that all traces of them seem to have vanished. Whether they did go to
Canterbury, and caught the last up train, at what station they alighted, or when
poor Mary came back, could not at present be discovered.

According to the medical officer, the unfortunate girl must have been dead
twelve or thirteen days at the very least, as, though the stagnant water may have
accelerated decomposition, the head could not have got into such an advanced
state much under a fortnight.

At Canterbury station neither the booking-clerk nor the porters could throw any
light upon the subject. Canterbury West is a busy station, and scores of passengers
buy tickets and go through the barriers every day. It was impossible, therefore, to
give any positive information about two young women who may or may not have
travelled by the last up train on January 23rd—that is, a fortnight before.

One thing only was certain—whether Susan went to Canterbury and travelled
by that up train or not, alone or with her sister—Mary had undoubtedly come
back to Ninescore either the same night or the following day, since Timothy
Coleman found her half-decomposed remains in the grounds of Ash Court a
fortnight later.

Had she come back to meet her lover, or what? And where was Susan now?

From the first, therefore, you see, there was a great element of mystery about
the whole case, and it was only natural that the local police should feel that,
unless something more definite came out at the inquest, they would like to have
the assistance of some of the fellows at the Yard.

So the preliminary notes were sent up to London, and some of them drifted into our hands. Lady Molly was deeply interested in it from the first, and my firm belief is that she simply worried the chief into allowing her to go down to Ninescore and see what she could do.

2

At first it was understood that Lady Molly should only go down to Canterbury after the inquest, if the local police still felt that they were in want of assistance from London. But nothing was farther from my lady's intentions than to wait until then.

"I was not going to miss the first act of a romantic drama," she said to me just as our train steamed into Canterbury Station. "Pick up your bag, Mary. We're going to tramp it to Ninescore—two lady artists on a sketching tour, remember—and we'll find lodging in the village, I dare say."

We had some lunch in Canterbury, and then we started to walk the six and a half miles to Ninescore, carrying our bags. We put up at one of the cottages, where the legend "Apartments for single, respectable lady or gentleman" had hospitably invited us to enter, and at eight o'clock the next morning we found our way to the local police-station, where the inquest was to take place. Such a funny little place, you know—just a cottage converted for official use—and the small room packed to its utmost holding capacity. The entire able-bodied population of the neighbourhood had, I verily believe, congregated in these ten cubic yards of stuffy atmosphere.

Inspector Meisures, apprized by the chief of our arrival, had reserved two good places for us well in sight of witnesses, coroner and jury. The room was insupportably close, but I assure you that neither Lady Molly nor I thought much about our comfort then. We were terribly interested.

From the outset the case seemed, as it were, to wrap itself more and more in its mantle of impenetrable mystery. There was precious little in the way of clues, only that awful intuition, that dark, unspoken suspicion with regard to one particular man's guilt, which one could feel hovering in the minds of all those present.

Neither the police nor Timothy Coleman had anything to add to what was already known. The ring and purse were produced, also the dress worn by the murdered woman. All were sworn to by several of the witnesses as having been the property of Mary Nicholls. Timothy, on being closely questioned, said that, in his opinion, the girl's body had been pushed into the mud, as the head was absolutely embedded in it, and he didn't see how she could have fallen like that.

Medical evidence was repeated; it was as uncertain—as vague—as before. Owing to the state of the head and neck it was impossible to ascertain by what means the death blow had been dealt. The doctor repeated his statement that the unfortunate girl must have been dead quite a fortnight. The body was discovered on February 5th—a fortnight before that would have been on or about January 23rd.

The caretaker who lived at the lodge at Ash Court could also throw but little light on the mysterious event. Neither he nor any member of his family had seen or heard anything to arouse their suspicions. Against that he explained that "The Wilderness," where the murder was committed, is situated some 200 yards from the lodge, with the mansion and flower garden lying between. Replying to a question put to him by a juryman, he said that that portion of the grounds is only divided off from Ninescore Lane by a low brick wall, which has a door in it, opening into the lane almost opposite Elm Cottages. He added that the mansion had been empty for over a year, and that he succeeded the last man, who died, about twelve months ago. Mr. Lydgate had not been down for golf since the witness had been in charge.

It would be useless to recapitulate all that the various witnesses had already told the police, and were now prepared to swear to. The private life of the two sisters Nicholls was gone into at full length, as much, at least, as was publicly known. But you know what village folk are; except when there is a bit of scandal and gossip, they know precious little of one another's inner lives.

The two girls appeared to be very comfortably off. Mary was always smartly dressed; and the baby girl, whom she had placed in Mrs. Williams's charge, had plenty of good and expensive clothes, whilst her keep, 5s. a week, was paid with unfailing regularity. What seemed certain, however, was that they did not get on well together, that Susan violently objected to Mary's association with Mr. Lydgate, and that recently she had spoken to the vicar asking him to try to persuade her sister to go away from Ninescore altogether, so as to break entirely with the past. The Reverend Octavius Ludlow, Vicar of Ninescore, seems thereupon to have had a little talk with Mary on the subject, suggesting that she should accept a good situation in London.

"But," continued the reverend gentleman, "I didn't make much impression on her. All she replied to me was that she certainly need never go into service, as she had a good income of her own, and could obtain £5,000* or more quite easily at any time if she chose."

"Did you mention Mr. Lydgate's name to her at all?" asked the coroner.

"Yes, I did," said the vicar, after a slight hesitation.

"Well, what was her attitude then?"

"I am afraid she laughed," replied the Reverend Octavius, primly, "and said very picturesquely, if somewhat ungrammatically, that 'some folks didn't know what they was talkin' about.'"

All very indefinite, you see. Nothing to get hold of, no motive suggested—beyond a very vague suspicion, perhaps, of blackmail—to account for a brutal crime. I must not, however, forget to tell you the two other facts which came to light in the course of this extraordinary inquest. Though, at the time, these facts seemed of wonderful moment for the elucidation of the mystery, they only helped ultimately to plunge the whole case into darkness still more impenetrable than before.

I am alluding, firstly, to the deposition of James Franklin, a carter in the employ of one of the local farmers. This man stated that about half-past six on that same night, January 23rd, he was walking along Ninescore Lane leading his horse and cart, as the night was indeed pitch dark. Just as he came somewhere near Elm Cottages he heard a man's voice saying, in a kind of hoarse whisper:

"Open the door, can't you? It's as dark as blazes!"

Then a pause, after which the same voice added:

"Mary, where the dickens are you?" Whereupon a girl's voice replied: "All right, I'm coming."

James Franklin heard nothing more after that, nor did he see anyone in the gloom.

With the stolidity peculiar to the Kentish peasantry, he thought no more of this until the day when he heard that Mary Nicholls had been murdered; then he voluntarily came forward and told his story to the police. Now, when he was closely questioned, he was quite unable to say whether these voices proceeded from that side of the lane where stand Elm Cottages, or from the other side, which is edged by the low brick wall.

Finally, Inspector Meisures, who really showed an extraordinary sense of what was dramatic, here produced a document which he had reserved for the last. This was a piece of paper which he had found in the red leather purse already

---

* £571,141.40 (US $ 765,433.23) in 2018, according to online sources.

mentioned, and which at first had not been thought very important, as the writing was identified by several people as that of the deceased, and consisted merely of a series of dates and hours scribbled in pencil on a scrap of notepaper. But suddenly these dates had assumed a weird and terrible significance: two of them, at least—December 26th and January 1st followed by "10 A.M."—were days on which Mr. Lydgate came over to Ninescore and took Mary for drives. One or two witnesses swore to this positively. Both dates had been local meets of the harriers,* to which other folk from the village had gone, and Mary had openly said afterwards how much she had enjoyed these.

The other dates (there were six altogether) were more or less vague. One Mrs. Hooker remembered as being coincident with a day Mary Nicholls had spent away from home; but the last date, scribbled in the same handwriting, was January 23rd, and below it the hour—6 P.M.

The coroner now adjourned the inquest. An explanation from Mr. Lionel Lydgate had become imperative.

3

Public excitement had by now reached a very high pitch; it was no longer a case of mere local interest. The country inns all round the immediate neighbourhood were packed with visitors from London, artists, journalists, dramatists, and actor-managers, whilst the hotels and fly-proprietors of Canterbury were doing a roaring trade.

Certain facts and one vivid picture stood out clearly before the thoughtful mind in the midst of a chaos of conflicting and irrelevant evidence: the picture was that of the two women tramping in the wet and pitch dark night towards Canterbury. Beyond that everything was a blur.

When did Mary Nicholls come back to Ninescore, and why?

To keep an appointment made with Lionel Lydgate, it was openly whispered; but that appointment—if the rough notes were interpreted rightly—was for the very day on which she and her sister went away from home. A man's voice called to her at half-past six certainly, and she replied to it. Franklin, the carter, heard her; but half an hour afterwards Mrs. Hooker heard her voice when she left home with her sister, and she visited Mrs. Williams after that.

---

* Local cross-country races.

The only theory compatible with all this was, of course, that Mary merely accompanied Susan part of the way to Canterbury, then went back to meet her lover, who enticed her into the deserted grounds of Ash Court, and there murdered her.

The motive was not far to seek. Mr. Lionel Lydgate, about to marry, wished to silence for ever a voice that threatened to be unpleasantly persistent in its demands for money and in its threats of scandal.

But there was one great argument against that theory—the disappearance of Susan Nicholls. She had been extensively advertised for. The murder of her sister was published broadcast in every newspaper in the United Kingdom—she could not be ignorant of it. And, above all, she hated Mr. Lydgate. Why did she not come and add the weight of her testimony against him if, indeed, he was guilty?

And if Mr. Lydgate was innocent, then where was the criminal? And why had Susan Nicholls disappeared?

Why? why? why?

Well, the next day would show. Mr. Lionel Lydgate had been cited by the police to give evidence at the adjourned inquest.

Good-looking, very athletic, and obviously frightfully upset and nervous, he entered the little court-room, accompanied by his solicitor, just before the coroner and jury took their seats.

He looked keenly at Lady Molly as he sat down, and from the expression of his face I guessed that he was much puzzled to know who she was.

He was the first witness called. Manfully and clearly he gave a concise account of his association with the deceased.

"She was pretty and amusing," he said. "I liked to take her out when I was in the neighbourhood; it was no trouble to me. There was no harm in her, whatever the village gossips might say. I know she had been in trouble, as they say, but that had nothing to do with me. It wasn't for me to be hard on a girl, and I fancy that she has been very badly treated by some scoundrel."

Here he was hard pressed by the coroner, who wished him to explain what he meant. But Mr. Lydgate turned obstinate, and to every leading question he replied stolidly and very emphatically:

"I don't know who it was. It had nothing to do with me, but I was sorry for the girl because of everyone turning against her, including her sister, and I tried to give her a little pleasure when I could."

That was all right. Very sympathetically told. The public quite liked this pleasing specimen of English cricket, golf and football-loving manhood.

Subsequently Mr. Lydgate admitted meeting Mary on December 26th and January 1st, but he swore most emphatically that that was the last he ever saw of her.

"But the 23rd of January," here insinuated the coroner; "you made an appointment with the deceased then?"

"Certainly not," he replied.

"But you met her on that day?"

"Most emphatically no," he replied, quietly. "I went down to Edbrooke Castle, my brother's place in Lincolnshire, on the 20th of last month, and only got back to town about three days ago."

"You swear to that, Mr. Lydgate?" asked the coroner.

"I do, indeed, and there are a score of witnesses to bear me out. The family, the house-party, the servants."

He tried to dominate his own excitement. I suppose, poor man, he had only just realized that certain horrible suspicions had been resting upon him. His solicitor pacified him, and presently he sat down, whilst I must say that everyone there present was relieved at the thought that the handsome young athlete was not a murderer, after all. To look at him it certainly seemed preposterous.

But then, of course, there was the deadlock, and as there were no more witnesses to be heard, no new facts to elucidate, the jury returned the usual verdict against some person or persons unknown; and we, the keenly interested spectators, were left to face the problem—Who murdered Mary Nicholls, and where was her sister, Susan?

4

After the verdict we found our way back to our lodgings. Lady Molly tramped along silently, with that deep furrow between her brows which I knew meant that she was deep in thought.

"Now we'll have some tea," I said, with a sigh of relief, as soon as we entered the cottage door.

"No, you won't," replied my lady, dryly. "I am going to write out a telegram, and we'll go straight on to Canterbury and send it from there."

"To Canterbury!" I gasped. "Two hours' walk at least, for I don't suppose we can get a trap, and it is past three o'clock. Why not send your telegram from Ninescore?"

"Mary, you are stupid," was all the reply I got. She wrote out two telegrams—one of which was at least three dozen words long—and, once more calling to me to come along, we set out for Canterbury.

I was tea-less, cross, and puzzled. Lady Molly was alert, cheerful, and irritatingly active.

We reached the first telegraph office a little before five. My lady sent the telegram without condescending to tell me anything of its destination or contents; then she took me to the Castle Hotel and graciously offered me tea.

"May I be allowed to inquire whether you propose tramping back to Ninescore to-night?" I asked, with a slight touch of sarcasm, as I really felt put out.

"No, Mary," she replied, quietly munching a bit of Sally Lunn;* "I have engaged a couple of rooms at this hotel and wired the chief that any message will find us here to-morrow morning."

After that there was nothing for it but quietude, patience, and finally supper and bed.

The next morning my lady walked into my room before I had finished dressing. She had a newspaper in her hand, and threw it down on the bed as she said, calmly:—

"It was in the evening paper all right last night; I think we shall be in time."

No use asking her what "it" meant. It was easier to pick up the paper, which I did. It was a late edition of one of the leading London evening shockers, and at once the front page, with its startling headline, attracted my attention:—

THE NINESCORE MYSTERY
MARY NICHOLLS'S BABY DYING

Then, below that, a short paragraph:—

"We regret to learn that the little baby daughter of the unfortunate girl who was murdered recently at Ash Court, Ninescore, Kent, under such terrible and mysterious circumstances, is very seriously ill at the cottage of Mrs. Williams, in whose charge she is. The local doctor who visited her to-day declares that she cannot last more than a few hours. At the time of going to press the nature of the child's complaint was not known to our special representative at Ninescore."

---

* A kind of large, sweet bun or teacake.

"What does this mean?" I gasped.

But before she could reply there was a knock at the door.

"A telegram for Miss Granard," said the voice of the hall porter.

"Quick, Mary," said Lady Molly eagerly. "I told the chief and also Meisures to wire here and to you."

The telegram turned out to have come from Ninescore, and was signed "Meisures." Lady Molly read it out aloud:—

"Mary Nicholls arrived here this morning. Detained her at station. Come at once."

"Mary Nicholls! I don't understand," was all I could contrive to say.

But she only replied:

"I knew it! I knew it! Oh, Mary, what a wonderful thing is human nature, and how I thank Heaven that gave me a knowledge of it!"

She made me get dressed all in a hurry, and then we swallowed some breakfast hastily whilst a fly was being got for us. I had perforce to satisfy my curiosity from my own inner consciousness. Lady Molly was too absorbed to take any notice of me. Evidently the chief knew what she had done and approved of it; the telegram from Meisures pointed to that.

My lady had suddenly become a personality. Dressed very quietly, and in a smart close-fitting hat, she looked years older than her age, owing also to the seriousness of her mien.

The fly took us to Ninescore fairly quickly. At the little police station we found Meisures awaiting us. He had Elliott and Pegram from the Yard with him. They had obviously got their orders, for all three of them were mighty deferential.

"The woman is Mary Nicholls right enough," said Meisures, as Lady Molly brushed quickly past him, "the woman who was supposed to have been murdered. It's that silly bogus paragraph about the infant brought her out of her hiding-place. I wonder how it got in," he added, blandly; "the child is well enough."

"I wonder," said Lady Molly, whilst a smile—the first I had seen that morning—lit up her pretty face.

"I suppose the other sister will turn up, too, presently," rejoined Elliott. "Pretty lot of trouble we shall have now. If Mary Nicholls is alive and kickin', who was murdered at Ash Court, say I?"

"I wonder," said Lady Molly, with the same charming smile.

Then she went in to see Mary Nicholls.

The Reverend Octavius Ludlow was sitting beside the girl, who seemed in great distress, for she was crying bitterly.

Lady Molly asked Elliott and the others to remain in the passage whilst she herself went into the room, I following behind her.

When the door was shut she went up to Mary Nicholls, and assuming a hard and severe manner, she said:—

"Well, you have at last made up your mind, have you, Nicholls? I suppose you know that we have applied for a warrant for your arrest?"

The woman gave a shriek which unmistakably was one of fear.

"My arrest?" she gasped. "What for?"

"The murder of your sister Susan."

"'Twasn't me!" she said, quickly.

"Then Susan *is* dead?" retorted Lady Molly, quietly.

Mary saw that she had betrayed herself. She gave Lady Molly a look of agonized horror, then turned as white as a sheet and would have fallen had not the Reverend Octavius Ludlow gently led her to a chair.

"It wasn't me," she repeated, with a heartbroken sob.

"That will be for you to prove," said Lady Molly dryly. "The child cannot now, of course, remain with Mrs. Williams; she will be removed to the workhouse, and—"

"No, that she shan't be," said the mother excitedly. "She shan't be, I tell you. The workhouse, indeed," she added, in a paroxysm of hysterical tears, "and her father a lord!"

The reverend gentleman and I gasped in astonishment; but Lady Molly had worked up to this climax so ingeniously that it was obvious she had guessed it all along, and had merely led Mary Nicholls on in order to get this admission from her.

How well she had known human nature in pitting the child against the sweetheart! Mary Nicholls was ready enough to hide herself, to part from her child even for a while, in order to save the man she had once loved from the consequences of his crime; but when she heard that her child was dying she no longer could bear to leave it among strangers, and when Lady Molly taunted her with the workhouse she exclaimed, in her maternal pride:

"The workhouse! And her father a lord!"

Driven into a corner, she confessed the whole truth.

Lord Edbrooke, then Mr. Lydgate, was the father of her child. Knowing this, her sister Susan had for over a year now, systematically blackmailed the unfortunate man—not altogether, it seems, without Mary's connivance. In January last she got him to come down to Ninescore under the distinct promise that Mary would meet him and hand over to him the letters she had received from him, as well as the ring he had given her, in exchange for the sum of £5,000.

The meeting-place was arranged, but at the last moment Mary was afraid to go in the dark. Susan, nothing daunted, but anxious about her own reputation in case she should be seen talking to a man so late at night, put on Mary's dress, took the ring and the letters, also her sister's purse, and went to meet Lord Edbrooke.

What happened at that interview no one will ever know. It ended with the murder of the blackmailer. I suppose the fact that Susan had, in a measure, begun by impersonating her sister, gave the murderer the first thought of confusing the identity of his victim by the horrible device of burying the body in the slimy mud. Anyway, he almost did succeed in hoodwinking the police, and would have done so entirely but for Lady Molly's strange intuition in the matter.

After his crime he ran instinctively to Mary's cottage. He had to make a clean breast of it to her, as, without her help, he was a doomed man.

So he persuaded her to go away from home and to leave no clue or trace of herself or her sister in Ninescore. With the help of money which he would give her she could begin life anew somewhere else, and no doubt he deluded the unfortunate girl with promises that her child would be restored to her very soon.

Thus he enticed Mary Nicholls away, who would have been the great and all-important witness against him the moment his crime was discovered. A girl of Mary's type and class instinctively obeys the man she has once loved, the man who is the father of her child. She consented to disappear and to allow all the world to believe that she had been murdered by some unknown miscreant.

Then the murderer quietly returned to his luxurious home at Edbrooke Castle unsuspected. No one had thought of mentioning his name in connexion with that of Mary Nicholls. In the days when he used to come down to Ash Court he was Mr. Lydgate, and, when he became a peer, sleepy, out-of-the-way Ninescore ceased to think of him.

Perhaps Mr. Lionel Lydgate knew all about his brother's association with the village girl. From his attitude at the inquest I should say he did, but of course he would not betray his own brother unless forced to do so. Now, of course, the whole aspect of the case was changed; the veil of mystery had been torn asunder owing to the insight, the marvellous intuition, of a woman who, in my opinion, is the most wonderful psychologist of her time.

You know the sequel. Our fellows at the Yard, aided by the local police, took their lead from Lady Molly, and began their investigations of Lord Edbrooke's movements on or about the 23rd of January.

Even their preliminary inquiries revealed the fact that his lordship had left Edbrooke Castle on the 21st. He went up to town, saying to his wife and household that he was called away on business, and not even taking his valet with him. He put up at the Langham Hotel.

But here police investigations came to an abrupt ending. Lord Edbrooke evidently got wind of them. Anyway, the day after Lady Molly so cleverly enticed Mary Nicholls out of her hiding-place, and surprised her into an admission of the truth, the unfortunate man threw himself in front of the express train at Grantham railway station, and was instantly killed. Human justice cannot reach him now!

But don't tell me that a man would have thought of that bogus paragraph, or of the taunt which stung the motherly pride of the village girl to the quick, and thus wrung from her an admission which no amount of male ingenuity would ever have obtained.

THE SCIENTIFIC CRACKSMAN

by Arthur B. Reeve

1910

While Holmes is an amateur scientist and a professional detective, Professor Craig Kennedy—one of many claimants to the title of "the American Sherlock Holmes"—is an amateur detective and a professional scientist. Based at Columbia University, he applies his extensive knowledge of chemistry and psychology to the mysteries that come his way, and he can also call upon an array of cutting-edge devices such as lie detectors and portable seismographs. Like Augustus S. F. X. van Dusen, who appeared earlier in this collection, he has a resourceful journalist sidekick in the Watson role, although like van Dusen, his exploits are recounted in the omniscient third person rather than Watson's first-person accounts of Holmes.

"The Scientific Cracksman" was first published as "The Case of Helen Bond" in the December 1910 issue of *Cosmopolitan*—then a literary magazine. Its title was changed in the 1912 collection *The Silent Bullet.* Kennedy made eighty-two appearances in *Cosmopolitan*, the last in August 1918. Numerous collections and novels were published, and fresh stories were printed in a number of other magazines.

As the 1920s gave way to the 1930s, Kennedy morphed into a more typical pulp detective, but these later tales seem to have been ghost-written; like Holmes, Kennedy became a brand and moved beyond his creator's control. The character appeared in movie serials in 1919 and 1936, and starred in a television series, *Craig Kennedy, Criminologist,* which ran for twenty-six episodes from 1951 to 1953.

Kennedy's creator, Arthur B. Reeve, graduated from Princeton and attended New York Law School, working as an editor and journalist until 1911, when Craig Kennedy made his name. He also wrote screenplays, including three episodes of a serial starring Harry Houdini, but he stayed in the east rather than going to Hollywood and his film career petered out. He also covered high-profile criminal cases for several newspapers, including the still-unsolved murder of Hollywood director William Desmond Taylor and the trial of the Lindbergh baby kidnapper, Bruno Hauptmann.

I'm willing to wager you a box of cigars that you don't know the most fascinating story in your own paper to-night," remarked Kennedy, as I came in one evening with the four or five newspapers I was in the habit of reading to see whether they had beaten the Star in getting any news of importance.

"I'll bet I do," I said, "or I was one of about a dozen who worked it up. It's the Shaw murder trial. There isn't another that's even a bad second."

"I am afraid the cigars will be on you, Walter. Crowded over on the second page by a lot of stale sensation that everyone has read for the fiftieth time, now, you will find what promises to be a real sensation, a curious half-column account of the sudden death of John G. Fletcher."

I laughed. "Craig," I said, "when you put up a simple death from apoplexy against a murder trial, and such a murder trial; well, you disappoint me—that's all."

"Is it a simple case of apoplexy?" he asked, pacing up and down the room, while I wondered why he should grow excited over what seemed a very ordinary news item, after all. Then he picked up the paper and read the account slowly aloud.

JOHN G. FLETCHER, STEEL MAGNATE, DIES SUDDENLY
SAFE OPEN BUT LARGE SUM OF CASH UNTOUCHED

John Graham Fletcher, the aged philanthropist and steelmaker, was found dead in his library this morning at his home at Fletcherwood, Great Neck, Long Island. Strangely, the safe in the library in which he kept his papers and a large sum of cash was found opened, but as far as could be learned nothing is missing.

It had always been Mr. Fletcher's custom to rise at seven o'clock. This morning his housekeeper became alarmed when he had not appeared by nine o'clock. Listening at the door, she heard no sound. It was not locked, and on entering she found the former steel-magnate lying lifeless on the floor between his bedroom and the library adjoining. His personal physician, Dr. W. C. Bryant, was immediately notified.

Close examination of the body revealed that his face was slightly discoloured, and the cause of death was given by the physician as apoplexy. He had evidently been dead about eight or nine hours when discovered.

Mr. Fletcher is survived by a nephew, John G. Fletcher, II., who is the Blake professor of bacteriology at the University, and by a grandniece, Miss Helen Bond. Professor Fletcher was informed of the sad occurrence shortly after leaving a class this morning and hurried out to Fletcherwood. He would make no statement other than that he was inexpressibly shocked. Miss Bond, who has for several years resided with relatives, Mr. and Mrs. Francis Greene of Little Neck, is prostrated by the shock.

"Walter," added Kennedy, as he laid down the paper and, without any more sparring, came directly to the point, "there was something missing from that safe."

I had no need to express the interest I now really felt, and Kennedy hastened to take advantage of it.

"Just before you came in," he continued, "Jack Fletcher called me up from Great Neck. You probably don't know it, but it has been privately reported in the inner circle of the University that old Fletcher was to leave the bulk of his fortune to found a great school of preventive medicine, and that the only proviso was that his nephew should be dean of the school. The professor told me over the wire that the will was missing from the safe, and that it was the only thing missing. From his excitement I judge that there is more to the story than he cared to tell over the 'phone. He said his car was on the way to the city, and he asked if I wouldn't come and help him—he wouldn't say how. Now, I know him pretty well, and I'm going to ask you to come along, Walter, for the express purpose of keeping this thing out of the newspapers, understand?—until we get to the bottom of it."

A few minutes later the telephone rang and the hall-boy announced that the car was waiting. We hurried down to it; the chauffeur lounged down carelessly into his seat and we were off across the city and river and out on the road to Great Neck with amazing speed.

Already I began to feel something of Kennedy's zest for the adventure. I found myself half a dozen times on the point of hazarding a suspicion, only to relapse again into silence at the inscrutable look on Kennedy's face. What was the mystery that awaited us in the great lonely house on Long Island?

We found Fletcherwood a splendid estate directly on the bay, with a long driveway leading up to the door. Professor Fletcher met us at the *porte cochere*,* and I was glad to note that, far from taking me as an intruder, he seemed rather relieved that someone who understood the ways of the newspapers could stand between him and any reporters who might possibly drop in.

He ushered us directly into the library and closed the door. It seemed as if he could scarcely wait to tell his story.

"Kennedy," he began, almost trembling with excitement, "look at that safe door."

We looked. It had been drilled through in such a way as to break the combination. It was a heavy door, closely fitting, and it was the best kind of small safe that the state of the art had produced. Yet clearly it had been tampered with, and successfully. Who was this scientific cracksman who had apparently accomplished the impossible? It was no ordinary hand and brain which had executed this "job."

Fletcher swung the door wide, and pointed to a little compartment inside, whose steel door had been jimmied open. Then out of it he carefully lifted a steel box and deposited it on the library table.

"I suppose everybody has been handling that box?" asked Craig quickly.

A smile flitted across Fletcher's features. "I thought of that, Kennedy," he said. "I remembered what you once told me about finger-prints. Only myself has touched it, and I was careful to take hold of it only on the sides. The will was placed in this box, and the key to the box was usually in the lock. Well, the will is gone. That's all; nothing else was touched. But for the life of me I can't find a mark on the box, not a finger-mark. Now on a hot and humid summer night like last night I should say it was pretty likely that anyone touching this metal box would have left finger-marks. Shouldn't you think so, Kennedy?"

Kennedy nodded and continued to examine the place where the compartment had been jimmied. A low whistle aroused us: coming over to the table, Craig tore a white sheet of paper off a pad lying there and deposited a couple of small particles on it.

"I found them sticking on the jagged edges of the steel where it had been forced," he said. Then he whipped out a pocket magnifying-glass. "Not from a rubber glove," he commented half to himself. "By Jove, one side of them shows lines that look as if they were the lines on a person's fingers, and the other side

---

* A covered porch, built to protect arriving and departing cars and carriages from the weather.

is perfectly smooth. There's not a chance of using them as a clue, except—well, I didn't know criminals in America knew that stunt."

"What stunt?"

"Why, you know how keen the new detectives are on the finger-print system?* Well, the first thing some of the up-to-date criminals in Europe did was to wear rubber gloves so that they would leave no prints. But you can't work very well with rubber gloves. Last fall in Paris I heard of a fellow who had given the police a lot of trouble. He never left a mark, or at least it was no good if he did. He painted his hands lightly with a liquid rubber which he had invented himself. It did all that rubber gloves would do and yet left him the free use of his fingers with practically the same keenness of touch. Fletcher, whatever is at the bottom of this affair, I feel sure right now that you have to deal with no ordinary criminal."

"Do you suppose there are any relatives besides those we know of?" I asked Kennedy when Fletcher had left to summon the servants.

"No," he replied, "I think not. Fletcher and Helen Bond, his second cousin, to whom he is engaged, are the only two."

Kennedy continued to study the library. He walked in and out of the doors and examined the windows and viewed the safe from all angles.

"The old gentleman's bedroom is here," he said, indicating a door. "Now a good smart noise or perhaps even a light shining through the transom from the library might arouse him. Suppose he woke up suddenly and entered by this door. He would see the thief at work on the safe. Yes, that part of reconstructing the story is simple. But who was the intruder?"

Just then Fletcher returned with the servants. The questioning was long and tedious, and developed nothing except that the butler admitted that he was uncertain whether the windows in the library were locked. The gardener was very obtuse, but finally contributed one possibly important fact. He had noted in the morning that the back gate, leading into a disused road closer to the bay than the main highway in front of the house, was open. It was rarely used, and was kept closed only by an ordinary hook. Whoever had opened it had evidently forgotten to hook it. He had thought it strange that it was unhooked, and in closing it he had noticed in the mud of the roadway marks that seemed to indicate that an automobile had stood there.

---

* Argentinian police adopted fingerprints as an investigative tool in the 1890s. The Fingerprint Branch at Scotland Yard was created in 1901; the New York State Prison system began fingerprinting prisoners in 1903.

After the servants had gone, Fletcher asked us to excuse him for a while, as he wished to run over to the Greenes, who lived across the bay. Miss Bond was completely prostrated by the death of her uncle, he said, and was in an extremely nervous condition. Meanwhile if we found any need of a machine we might use his uncle's, or in fact anything around the place.

"Walter," said Craig, when Fletcher had gone, "I want to run back to town to-night, and I have something I'd like to have you do, too."

We were soon speeding back along the splendid road to Long Island City, while he laid out our programme.

"You go down to the *Star* office," he said, "and look through all the clippings on the whole Fletcher family. Get a complete story of the life of Helen Bond, too—what she has done in society, with whom she has been seen mostly, whether she has made any trips abroad, and whether she has ever been engaged—you know, anything likely to be significant. I'm going up to the apartment to get my camera and then to the laboratory to get some rather bulky paraphernalia I want to take out to Fletcherwood. Meet me at the Columbus Circle station at, say half-past-ten."

So we separated. My search revealed the fact that Miss Bond had always been intimate with the ultra-fashionable set, had spent last summer in Europe, a good part of the time in Switzerland and Paris with the Greenes. As far as I could find out she had never been reported engaged, but plenty of fortunes as well as foreign titles had been flitting about the ward of the steel-magnate.

Craig and I met at the appointed time. He had a lot of paraphernalia with him, and it did not add to our comfort as we sped back, but it wasn't much over half an hour before we again found ourselves nearing Great Neck.

Instead of going directly back to Fletcherwood, however, Craig had told the chauffeur to stop at the plant of the local electric light and power company, where he asked if he might see the record of the amount of current used the night before.

The curve sprawled across the ruled surface of the sheet by the automatic registering-needle was irregular, showing the ups and downs of the current, rising sharply from sundown and gradually declining after nine o'clock, as the lights went out. Somewhere between eleven and twelve o'clock, however, the irregular fall of the curve was broken by a quite noticeable upward twist.

Craig asked the men if that usually happened. They were quite sure that the curve as a rule went gradually down until twelve o'clock, when the power was shut off. But they did not see anything remarkable in it. "Oh, I suppose some of the big houses had guests," volunteered the foreman, "and just to show off the place perhaps they turned on all the lights. I don't know, sir, what it was, but it couldn't have been a heavy drain, or we would have noticed it at the time, and the lights would all have been dim."

"Well," said Craig, "just watch and see if it occurs again to-night about the same time."

"All right, sir."

"And when you close down the plant for the night, will you bring the record card up to Fletcherwood?" asked Craig, slipping a bill into the pocket of the foreman's shirt.

"I will, and thank you, sir."

It was nearly half-past eleven when Craig had got his apparatus set up in the library at Fletcherwood. Then he unscrewed all the bulbs from the chandelier in the library and attached in their places connections with the usual green silk-covered flexible wire rope. These were then joined up to a little instrument which to me looked like a drill. Next he muffed the drill with a wad of felt and applied it to the safe door.

I could hear the dull *tat-tat* of the drill. Going into the bedroom and closing the door, I found that it was still audible to me, but an old man, inclined to deafness and asleep, would scarcely have been awakened by it. In about ten minutes Craig displayed a neat little hole in the safe door opposite the one made by the cracksman in the combination.

"I'm glad you're honest," I said, "or else we might be afraid of you—perhaps even make you prove an alibi for last night's job!"

He ignored my bantering and said in a tone such as he might have used before a class of students in the gentle art of scientific safe-cracking: "Now if the power company's curve is just the same to-night as last night, that will show how the thing was done. I wanted to be sure of it, so I thought I'd try this apparatus which I smuggled in from Paris last year. I believe the old man happened to be wakeful and heard it."

Then he pried off the door of the interior compartment which had been jimmied open. "Perhaps we may learn something by looking at this door and studying the marks left by the jimmy, by means of this new instrument of mine," he said.

On the library table he fastened an arrangement with two upright posts supporting a dial which he called a "dynamometer." The uprights were braced in the back, and the whole thing reminded me of a miniature guillotine.

"This is my mechanical detective," said Craig proudly. "It was devised by Bertillon* himself, and he personally gave me permission to copy his own machine. You see, it is devised to measure pressure. Now let's take an ordinary jimmy and see just how much pressure it takes to duplicate those marks on this door."

Craig laid the piece of steel on the dynamometer in the position it had occupied in the safe, and braced it tightly. Then he took a jimmy and pressed on it with all his strength. The steel door was connected with the indicator, and the needle spun around until it indicated a pressure such as only a strong man could have exerted. Comparing the marks made in the steel in the experiment and by the safe-cracker, it was evident that no such pressure had been necessary. Apparently the lock on the door was only a trifling affair, and the steel itself was not very tough. The safe-makers had relied on the first line of defence to repel attack.

Craig tried again and again, each time using less force. At last he got a mark just about similar to the original marks on the steel.

"Well, well, what do you think of that?" he exclaimed reflectively. "A child could have done that part of the job."

Just then the lights went off for the night. Craig lighted the oil-lamp, and sat in silence until the electric light plant foreman appeared with the card-record, which showed a curve practically identical with that of the night before.

A few moments later Professor Fletcher's machine came up the driveway, and he joined us with a worried and preoccupied look on his face that he could not conceal. "She's terribly broken up by the suddenness of it all," he murmured as he sank into an armchair. "The shock has been too much for her. In fact, I hadn't the heart to tell her anything about the robbery, poor girl." Then in a moment he asked, "Any more clues yet, Kennedy?"

"Well, nothing of first importance. I have only been trying to reconstruct the story of the robbery so that I can reason out a motive and a few details; then when the real clues come along we won't have so much ground to cover. The cracksman was certainly clever. He used an electric drill to break the combination and ran it by the electric light current."

"Whew!" exclaimed the professor, "is that so? He must have been above the average. That's interesting."

"By the way, Fletcher," said Kennedy, "I wish you would introduce me to your fiancée to-morrow. I would like to know her."

---

* Alphonse Bertillon (1853–1914) was a pioneering forensic scientist.

"Gladly," Fletcher replied, "only you must be careful what you talk about. Remember, the death of uncle has been quite a shock to her—he was her only relative besides myself."

"I will," promised Kennedy, "and by the way, she may think it strange that I'm out here at a time like this. Perhaps you had better tell her I'm a nerve specialist or something of that sort—anything not to connect me with the robbery, which you say you haven't told her about."

The next morning found Kennedy out bright and early, for he had not had a very good chance to do anything during the night except reconstruct the details. He was now down by the back gate with his camera, where I found him turning it end-down and photographing the road. Together we made a thorough search of the woods and the road about the gate, but could discover absolutely nothing.

After breakfast I improvised a dark room and developed the films, while Craig went down the back lane along the shore "looking for clues," as he said briefly. Toward noon he returned, and I could see that he was in a brown study. So I said nothing, but handed him the photographs of the road. He took them and laid them down in a long line on the library floor. They seemed to consist of little ridges of dirt on either side of a series of regular round spots, some of the spots very clear and distinct on the sides, others quite obscure in the centre. Now and then where you would expect to see one of the spots, just for the symmetry of the thing, it was missing. As I looked at the line of photographs on the floor I saw that they were a photograph of the track made by the tire of an automobile, and I suddenly recalled what the gardener had said.

Next Craig produced the results of his morning's work, which consisted of several dozen sheets of white paper, carefully separated into three bundles. These he also laid down in long lines on the floor, each package in a separate line. Then I began to realise what he was doing, and became fascinated in watching him on his hands and knees eagerly scanning the papers and comparing them with the photographs. At last he gathered up two of the sets of papers very decisively and threw them away. Then he shifted the third set a bit, and laid it closely parallel to the photographs.

"Look at these, Walter," he said. "Now take this deep and sharp indentation. Well, there's a corresponding one in the photograph. So you can pick them out one for another. Now here's one missing altogether on the paper. So it is in the photograph."

Almost like a schoolboy in his glee, he was comparing the little round circles made by the metal insertions in an "anti-skid" automobile tire. Time and again I had seen imprints like that left in the dust and grease of an asphalted street or the mud of a road. It had never occurred to me that they might be used in any way. Yet here Craig was, calmly tracing out the similarity before my very eyes, identifying the marks made in the photograph with the prints left on the bits of paper.

As I followed him, I had a most curious feeling of admiration for his genius. "Craig," I cried, "that's the thumb-print of an automobile."

"There speaks the yellow journalist,"* he answered merrily. "'Thumb Print System Applied to Motor Cars'—I can see the Sunday feature story you have in your mind with that headline already. Yes, Walter, that's precisely what this is. The Berlin police have used it a number of times with the most startling results."

"But, Craig," I exclaimed suddenly, "the paper prints, where did you get them? What machine is it?"

"It's one not very far from here," he answered sententiously, and I saw he would say nothing more that might fix a false suspicion on anyone. Still, my curiosity was so great that if there had been an opportunity I certainly should have tried out his plan on all the cars in the Fletcher garage.

Kennedy would say nothing more, and we ate our luncheon in silence. Fletcher, who had decided to lunch with the Greenes, called Kennedy up on the telephone to tell him it would be all right for him to call on Miss Bond later in the afternoon.

"And I may bring over the apparatus I once described to you to determine just what her nervous condition is?" he asked. Apparently the answer was yes, for Kennedy hung up the receiver with a satisfied, "Good-bye."

"Walter, I want you to come along with me this afternoon as my assistant. Remember I'm now Dr. Kennedy, the nerve specialist, and you are Dr. Jameson, my colleague, and we are to be in consultation on a most important case."

"Do you think that's fair?" I asked hotly, "to take that girl off her guard, to insinuate yourself into her confidence as a medical adviser, and worm out of her some kind of fact incriminating someone? I suppose that's your plan, and I don't like the ethics, or rather the lack of ethics, of the thing."

"Now think a minute, Walter. Perhaps I am wrong; I don't know. Certainly I feel that the end will justify the means. I have an idea that I can get from Miss Bond the only clue that I need, one that will lead straight to the criminal. Who knows? I have a suspicion that the thing I'm going to do is the highest form of your so-called ethics. If what Fletcher tells us is true that girl is going insane over this thing. Why should she be so shocked over the death of an uncle she did not

---

* "Yellow journalism" was a term applied to newspapers that relied on sensation to sell papers, neglecting proper research and ethics.

live with? I tell you she knows something about this case that it is necessary for us to know, too. If she doesn't tell someone, it will eat her mind out. I'll add a dinner to the box of cigars we have already bet on this case that what I'm going to do is for the best—for her best."

Again I yielded, for I was coming to have more and more faith in the old Kennedy I had seen made over into a first-class detective, and together we started for the Greenes', Craig carrying something in one of those long black handbags which physicians use.

Fletcher met us on the driveway. He seemed to be very much affected, for his face was drawn, and he shifted from one position to another nervously, from which we inferred that Miss Bond was feeling worse. It was late afternoon, almost verging on twilight, as he led us through the reception-hall and thence onto a long porch overlooking the bay and redolent with honeysuckle.

Miss Bond was half reclining in a wicker chair as we entered. She started to rise to greet us, but Fletcher gently restrained her, saying, as he introduced us, that he guessed the doctors would pardon any informality from an invalid.

Fletcher was a pretty fine fellow, and I had come to like him; but I soon found myself wondering what he had ever done to deserve winning such a girl as Helen Bond. She was what I should describe as the ideal type of "new" woman,—tall and athletic, yet without any affectation of mannishness. The very first thought that struck me was the incongruousness of a girl of her type suffering from an attack of "nerves," and I felt sure it must be as Craig had said, that she was concealing a secret that was having a terrible effect on her. A casual glance might not have betrayed the true state of her feelings, for her dark hair and large brown eyes and the tan of many suns on her face and arms betokened anything but the neurasthenic.* One felt instinctively that she was, with all her athletic grace, primarily a womanly woman.

The sun sinking toward the hills across the bay softened the brown of her skin and, as I observed by watching her closely, served partially to conceal the nervousness which was wholly unnatural in a girl of such poise. When she smiled there was a false note in it; it was forced and it was sufficiently evident to me that she was going through a mental hell of conflicting emotions that would have killed a woman of less self-control.

I felt that I would like to be in Fletcher's shoes—doubly so when, at Kennedy's request, he withdrew, leaving me to witness the torture of a woman of such fine sensibilities, already hunted remorselessly by her own thoughts.

---

* Neurasthenia was a medical term, now obsolete, for "weak nerves."

Still, I will give Kennedy credit for a tactfulness that I didn't know the old fellow possessed. He carried through the preliminary questions very well for a pseudo-doctor, appealing to me as his assistant on inconsequential things that enabled me to "save my face" perfectly. When he came to the critical moment of opening the black bag, he made a very appropriate and easy remark about not having brought any sharp shiny instruments or nasty black drugs.

"All I wish to do, Miss Bond, is to make a few, simple little tests of your nervous condition. One of them we specialists call reaction time, and another is a test of heart action. Neither is of any seriousness at all, so I beg of you not to become excited, for the chief value consists in having the patient perfectly quiet and normal. After they are over I think I'll know whether to prescribe absolute rest or a visit to Newport."

She smiled languidly, as he adjusted a long, tightly fitting rubber glove on her shapely forearm and then encased it in a larger, absolutely inflexible covering of leather. Between the rubber glove and the leather covering was a liquid communicating by a glass tube with a sort of dial. Craig had often explained to me how the pressure of the blood was registered most minutely on the dial, showing the varied emotions as keenly as if you had taken a peep into the very mind of the subject. I think the experimental psychologists called the thing a "plethysmograph."[*]

Then he had an apparatus which measured association time. The essential part of this instrument was the operation of a very delicate stop-watch, and this duty was given to me. It was nothing more nor less than measuring the time that elapsed between his questions to her and her answers, while he recorded the actual questions and answers and noted the results which I worked out. Neither of us was unfamiliar with the process, for when we were in college these instruments were just coming into use in America. Kennedy had never let his particular branch of science narrow him, but had made a practice of keeping abreast of all the important discoveries and methods in other fields. Besides, I had read articles about the chronoscope,[†] the plethysmograph, the sphygmograph,[‡] and others of the new psychological instruments. Craig carried it off, however, as if he did that sort of thing as an every-day employment.

"Now, Miss Bond," he said, and his voice was so reassuring and persuasive that I could see she was not made even a shade more nervous by our simple

---

[*] An instrument for recording and measuring variation in the volume of a part of the body, especially as caused by changes in blood pressure.

[†] A highly accurate stopwatch.

[‡] An instrument to measure blood pressure.

preparations, "the game—it is just like a children's parlour game—is just this:
I will say a word—take 'dog,' for instance. You are to answer back immediately
the first word that comes into your mind suggested by it—say 'cat.' I will say
'chain,' for example, and probably you will answer 'collar,' and so on. Do you
catch my meaning? It may seem ridiculous, no doubt, but before we are through
I feel sure you'll see how valuable such a test is, particularly in a simple case of
nervousness such as yours."

I don't think she found any sinister interpretation in his words, but I did, and
if ever I wanted to protest it was then, but my voice seemed to stick in my throat.

He was beginning. It was clearly up to me to give in and not interfere. As closely
as I was able I kept my eyes riveted on the watch and other apparatus, while my
ears and heart followed with mingled emotions the low, musical voice of the girl.

I will not give all the test, for there was much of it, particularly at the start,
that was in reality valueless, since it was merely leading up to the "surprise tests."
From the colourless questions Kennedy suddenly changed. It was done in an
instant, when Miss Bond had been completely disarmed and put off her guard.

"Night," said Kennedy. "Day," came back the reply from Miss Bond.

"Automobile." "Horse."

"Bay." "Beach."

"Road." "Forest."

"Gate." "Fence."

"Path." "Shrubs."

"Porch." "House."

Did I detect or imagine a faint hesitation?

"Window." "Curtain."

Yes, it was plain that time. But the words followed one another in quick
succession. There was no rest. She had no chance to collect herself. I noted the
marked difference in the reaction time and, in my sympathy, damned this cold,
scientific third degree.

"Paris." "France."

"Quartier Latin." "Students."

"Apaches." Craig gave it its Gallicised pronunciation, *"Apash."* "Really, Dr. Kennedy," she said, "there is nothing I can associate with them—well, yes, *les vaches,* I
believe. You had better count that question out. I've wasted a good many seconds."

"Very well, let us try again," he replied with a forced unconcern, though
the answer seemed to interest him, for *"les vaches"* meant "the cows," otherwise
known as the police.

No lawyer could have revelled in an opportunity for putting leading questions more ruthlessly than did Kennedy. He snapped out his words sharply and unexpectedly.

"Chandelier." "Light."

"Electric light," he emphasised. "Broadway," she answered, endeavouring to force a new association of ideas to replace one which she strove to conceal.

"Safe." "Vaults." Out of the corner of my eye I could see that the indicator showed a tremendously increased heart action. As for the reaction time, I noted that it was growing longer and more significant. Remorselessly he pressed his words home. Mentally I cursed him.

"Rubber." "Tire."

"Steel." "Pittsburg," she cried at random.

"Strong-box," No answer.

"Lock." Again no answer. He hurried his words. I was leaning forward, tense with excitement and sympathy.

"Key." Silence and a fluttering of the blood pressure indicator.

"Will."

As the last word was uttered her air of frightened defiance was swept away. With a cry of anguish, she swayed to her feet. "No, no, doctor, you must not, you must not," she cried with outstretched arms. "Why do you pick out those words of all others? Can it be—" If I had not caught her I believe she would have fainted.

The indicator showed a heart alternately throbbing with feverish excitement and almost stopping with fear. What would Kennedy do next, I wondered, determined to shut him off as soon as I possibly could. From the moment I had seen her I had been under her spell. Mine should have been Fletcher's place, I knew, though I cannot but say that I felt a certain grim pleasure in supporting even momentarily such a woman in her time of need.

"Can it be that you have guessed what no one in the world, no, not even dear old Jack, dreams? Oh, I shall go mad, mad, mad!"

Kennedy was on his feet in an instant, advancing toward her. The look in his eyes was answer enough for her. She knew that he knew, and she paled and shuddered, shrinking away from him.

"Miss Bond," he said in a voice that forced attention—it was low and vibrating with feeling—"Miss Bond, have you ever told a lie to shield a friend?"

"Yes," she said, her eyes meeting his.

"So can I," came back the same tense voice, "when I know the truth about that friend."

Then for the first time tears came in a storm. Her breath was quick and feverish. "No one will ever believe, no one will understand. They will say that I killed him, that I murdered him."

Through it all I stood almost speechless, puzzled. What did it all mean?

"No," said Kennedy, "no, for they will never know of it."

"Never know?"

"Never—if in the end justice is done. Have you the will? Or did you destroy it?"

It was a bold stroke.

"Yes. No. Here it is. How could I destroy it, even though it was burning out my very soul?"

She literally tore the paper from the bosom of her dress and cast it from her in horror and terror.

Kennedy picked it up, opened it, and glanced hurriedly through it. "Miss Bond," he said, "Jack shall never know a word of this. I shall tell him that the will has been found unexpectedly in John Fletcher's desk among some other papers. Walter, swear on your honour as a gentleman that this will was found in old Fletcher's desk."

"Dr. Kennedy, how can I ever thank you?" she exclaimed, sinking wearily down into a chair and pressing her hands to her throbbing forehead.

"By telling me just how you came by this will, so that when you and Fletcher are married I may be as good a friend, without suspicion, to you as I am to him. I think a full confession would do you good, Miss Bond. Would you prefer to have Dr. Jameson not hear it?"

"No, he may stay."

"This much I know, Miss Bond. Last summer in Paris with the Greenes you must have chanced to hear, of Pillard, the Apache, one of the most noted cracksmen the world has ever produced. You sought him out. He taught you how to paint your fingers with a rubber composition, how to use an electric drill, how to use the old-fashioned jimmy. You went down to Fletcherwood by the back road about a quarter after eleven the night of the robbery in the Greenes' little electric runabout.* You entered the library by an unlocked window, you coupled your drill to the electric light connections of the chandelier. You had to work quickly, for the power would go off at midnight, yet you could not do the job later, when they were sleeping more soundly, for the very same reason."

---

* Electric cars were popular in the early twentieth century; gasoline-powered vehicles did not become predominant until the early 1920s.

It was uncanny as Kennedy rushed along in his reconstruction of the scene, almost unbelievable. The girl watched him, fascinated.

"John Fletcher was wakeful that night. Somehow or other he heard you at work. He entered the library and, by the light streaming from his bedroom, he saw who it was. In anger he must have addressed you, and his passion got the better of his age—he fell suddenly on the floor with a stroke of apoplexy. As you bent over him he died. But why did you ever attempt so foolish an undertaking? Didn't you know that other people knew of the will and its terms, that you were sure to be traced out in the end, if not by friends, by foes? How did you suppose you could profit by destroying the will, of which others knew the provisions?"

Any other woman than Helen Bond would have been hysterical long before Kennedy had finished pressing home remorselessly one fact after another of her story. But, with her, the relief now after the tension of many hours of concealment seemed to nerve her to go to the end and tell the truth.

What was it? Had she some secret lover for whom she had dared all to secure the family fortune? Or was she shielding someone dearer to her than her own reputation? Why had Kennedy made Fletcher withdraw?

Her eyes dropped and her breast rose and fell with suppressed emotion. Yet I was hardly prepared for her reply when at last she slowly raised her head and looked us calmly in the face.

"I did it because I loved Jack."

Neither of us spoke. I, at least, had fallen completely under the spell of this masterful woman. Right or wrong, I could not restrain a feeling of admiration and amazement.

"Yes," she said as her voice thrilled with emotion, "strange as it may sound to you, it was not love of self that made me do it. I was, I am madly in love with Jack. No other man has ever inspired such respect and love as he has. His work in the university I have fairly gloated over. And yet—and yet, Dr. Kennedy, can you not see that I am different from Jack? What would I do with the income of the wife of even the dean of the new school? The annuity provided for me in that will is paltry. I need millions. From the tiniest baby I have been reared that way. I have always expected this fortune. I have been given everything I wanted. But it is different when one is married—you must have your own money. I need a fortune, for then I could have the town house, the country house, the yacht, the motors, the clothes, the servants that I need—they are as much a part of my life as your profession is of yours. I must have them.

"And now it was all to slip from my hands. True, it was to go in such a way by this last will as to make Jack happy in his new school. I could have let that go, if that was all. There are other fortunes that have been laid at my feet. But I wanted Jack, and I knew Jack wanted me. Dear boy, he never could realise how utterly unhappy intellectual poverty would have made me and how my unhappiness would have reacted on him in the end. In reality this great and beneficent philanthropy was finally to blight both our love and our lives.

"What was I to do? Stand by and see my life and my love ruined or refuse Jack for the fortune of a man I did not love? Helen Bond is not that kind of a woman, I said to myself. I consulted the greatest lawyer I knew. I put a hypothetical case to him, and asked his opinion in such a way as to make him believe he was advising me how to make an unbreakable will. He told me of provisions and clauses to avoid, particularly in making benefactions. That was what I wanted to know. I would put one of those clauses in my uncle's will. I practised uncle's writing till I was as good a forger of that clause as anyone could have become. I had picked out the very words in his own handwriting to practise from.

"Then I went to Paris and, as you have guessed, learned how to get things out of a safe like that of uncle's. Before God, all I planned to do was to get that will, change it, replace it, and trust that uncle would never notice the change. Then when he was gone, I would have contested the will. I would have got my full share either by court proceedings or by settlement out of court. You see, I had planned it all out. The school would have been founded—I, we would have founded it. What difference, I said, did thirty millions or fifty millions make to an impersonal school, a school not yet even in existence? The twenty million dollars or so difference, or even half of it, meant life and love to me.

"I had planned to steal the cash in the safe, anything to divert attention from the will and make it look like a plain robbery. I would have done the altering of the will that night and have returned it to the safe before morning. But it was not to be. I had almost opened the safe when my uncle entered the room. His anger completely unnerved me, and from the moment I saw him on the floor to this I haven't had a sane thought. I forgot to take the cash, I forgot everything but that will. My only thought was that I must get it and destroy it. I doubt if I could have altered it with my nerves so upset. There, now you have my whole story. I am at your mercy."

"No," said Kennedy, "believe me, there is a mental statute of limitations that as far as Jameson and myself are concerned has already erased this affair. Walter, will you find Fletcher?"

I found the professor pacing up and down the gravel walk impatiently.

"Fletcher," said Kennedy, "a night's rest is all Miss Bond really needs. It is simply a case of overwrought nerves, and it will pass off of itself. Still, I would advise a change of scene as soon as possible. Good afternoon, Miss Bond, and my best wishes for your health."

"Good afternoon, Dr. Kennedy. Good afternoon, Dr. Jameson."

I for one was glad to make my escape.

A half-hour later, Kennedy, with well-simulated excitement, was racing me in the car up to the Greenes' again. We literally burst unannounced into the *tête-à-tête* on the porch.

"Fletcher, Fletcher," cried Kennedy, "look what Walter and I have just discovered in a tin strong-box poked off in the back of your uncle's desk!"

Fletcher seized the will and by the dim light that shone through from the hall read it hastily. "Thank God," he cried; "the school is provided for as I thought."

"Isn't it glorious!" murmured Helen.

True to my instinct I muttered, "Another good newspaper yarn killed."

THE COIN OF DIONYSIUS

by Ernest Bramah

1910

In his day, Ernest Bramah was compared to Jerome K. Jerome for his humorous writing, to H. G. Wells for his politically-tinged science fiction, and to Conan Doyle for his detective stories.

Born Ernest Brammah Smith, he dropped out of the Manchester Grammar School aged sixteen and went into farming with the support of his father. He began to contribute small items to a local newspaper, and when his farming enterprise failed he obtained a position as secretary to the popular humorous writer Jerome K. Jerome, eventually becoming editor of one of his magazines.

Bramah's first success as a writer was the creation of the itinerant Chinese storyteller Kai Lung, who appeared in three novels and two story collections published between 1900 and 1940. Max Carrados, the blind detective, first appeared in 1913, and his adventures appeared in the *News of the World, Pearson's Magazine,* and *The Strand.* Despite the widespread claim that Carrados stories appeared in *The Strand* alongside the adventures of Sherlock Holmes and often received higher billing, only one, "The Bunch of Violets," ever seems to have been published in that magazine, in July 1924. While Conan Doyle did contribute to the same issue, it was not with a Holmes story, but rather with the ninth installment of his ten-part memoir, "Memories and Adventures."

"The Coin of Dionysius" is the first Carrados story. Published in *The News of the World* on August 17, 1913 as "The Master Coiner Unmasked," its title was changed in the 1914 collection *Max Carrados.* Blinded in a riding accident, Carrados has refined his other senses to

a level that most sighted people never achieve—so much so that his blindness is not immediately apparent. His manservant Parkinson acts as his eyes when necessary, and is possessed of faculties of observation that rival those of Holmes himself. Interestingly, Carrados
is not presented as a detective, in this story at least. Instead, he is consulted as an expert
in numismatics, by a private investigator who will go on to become a regular companion.

I t was eight o'clock at night and raining, scarcely a time when a business so
limited in its clientele as that of a coin dealer could hope to attract any customer, but a light was still showing in the small shop that bore over its window
the name of Baxter, and in the even smaller office at the back the proprietor
himself sat reading the latest *Pall Mall*. His enterprise seemed to be justified,
for presently the door bell gave its announcement, and throwing down his paper
Mr. Baxter went forward.

As a matter of fact the dealer had been expecting someone and his manner as
he passed into the shop was unmistakably suggestive of a caller of importance.
But at the first glance towards his visitor the excess of deference melted out of
his bearing, leaving the urbane, self-possessed shopman in the presence of the
casual customer.

"Mr. Baxter, I think?" said the latter. He had laid aside his dripping umbrella
and was unbuttoning overcoat and coat to reach an inner pocket. "You hardly
remember me, I suppose? Mr. Carlyle—two years ago I took up a case for you—"

"To be sure. Mr. Carlyle, the private detective—"

"Inquiry agent," corrected Mr. Carlyle precisely.

"Well," smiled Mr. Baxter, "for that matter I am a coin dealer and not an anti-
quarian or a numismatist. Is there anything in that way that I can do for you?"

"Yes," replied his visitor; "it is my turn to consult you." He had taken a small
wash-leather bag from the inner pocket and now turned something carefully out
upon the counter. "What can you tell me about that?"

The dealer gave the coin a moment's scrutiny.

"There is no question about this," he replied. "It is a Sicilian tetradrachm of
Dionysius."

"Yes, I know that—I have it on the label out of the cabinet. I can tell you
further that it's supposed to be one that Lord Seastoke gave two hundred and
fifty pounds for at the Brice sale in '94."

"It seems to me that you can tell me more about it than I can tell you," remarked Mr. Baxter. "What is it that you really want to know?"

"I want to know," replied Mr. Carlyle, "whether it is genuine or not."

"Has any doubt been cast upon it?"

"Certain circumstances raised a suspicion—that is all."

The dealer took another look at the tetradrachm through his magnifying glass, holding it by the edge with the careful touch of an expert. Then he shook his head slowly in a confession of ignorance.

"Of course I could make a guess—"

"No, don't," interrupted Mr. Carlyle hastily. "An arrest hangs on it and nothing short of certainty is any good to me."

"Is that so, Mr. Carlyle?" said Mr. Baxter, with increased interest. "Well, to be quite candid, the thing is out of my line. Now if it was a rare Saxon penny or a doubtful noble I'd stake my reputation on my opinion, but I do very little in the classical series."

Mr. Carlyle did not attempt to conceal his disappointment as he returned the coin to the bag and replaced the bag in the inner pocket.

"I had been relying on you," he grumbled reproachfully. "Where on earth am I to go now?"

"There is always the British Museum."

"Ah, to be sure, thanks. But will anyone who can tell me be there now?"

"Now? No fear!" replied Mr. Baxter. "Go round in the morning—"

"But I must know to-night," explained the visitor, reduced to despair again. "To-morrow will be too late for the purpose."

Mr. Baxter did not hold out much encouragement in the circumstances.

"You can scarcely expect to find anyone at business now," he remarked. "I should have been gone these two hours myself only I happened to have an appointment with an American millionaire who fixed his own time." Something indistinguishable from a wink slid off Mr. Baxter's right eye. "Offmunson he's called, and a bright young pedigree-hunter has traced his descent from Offa, King of Mercia. So he—quite naturally—wants a set of Offas as a sort of collateral proof."

"Very interesting," murmured Mr. Carlyle, fidgeting with his watch. "I should love an hour's chat with you about your millionaire customers—some other time. Just now—look here, Baxter, can't you give me a line of introduction to some dealer in this sort of thing who happens to live in town? You must know dozens of experts."

"Why, bless my soul, Mr. Carlyle, I don't know a man of them away from his business," said Mr. Baxter, staring. "They may live in Park Lane or they may live in Petticoat Lane for all I know. Besides, there aren't so many experts as you seem to imagine. And the two best will very likely quarrel over it. You've had to do with 'expert witnesses,' I suppose?"

"I don't want a witness; there will be no need to give evidence. All I want is an absolutely authoritative pronouncement that I can act on. Is there no one who can really say whether the thing is genuine or not?"

Mr. Baxter's meaning silence became cynical in its implication as he continued to look at his visitor across the counter. Then he relaxed.

"Stay a bit; there is a man—an amateur—I remember hearing wonderful things about some time ago. They say he really does know."

"There you are," exclaimed Mr. Carlyle, much relieved. "There always is someone. Who is he?"

"Funny name," replied Baxter. "Something Wynn or Wynn something." He craned his neck to catch sight of an important motor car that was drawing to the kerb before his window. "Wynn Carrados! You'll excuse me now, Mr. Carlyle, won't you? This looks like Mr. Offmunson."

Mr. Carlyle hastily scribbled the name down on his cuff.

"Wynn Carrados, right. Where does he live?"

"Haven't the remotest idea," replied Baxter, referring the arrangement of his tie to the judgment of the wall mirror. "I have never seen the man myself. Now, Mr. Carlyle, I'm sorry I can't do any more for you. You won't mind, will you?"

Mr. Carlyle could not pretend to misunderstand. He enjoyed the distinction of holding open the door for the transatlantic representative of the line of Offa as he went out, and then made his way through the muddy streets back to his office. There was only one way of tracing a private individual at such short notice—through the pages of the directories, and the gentleman did not flatter himself by a very high estimate of his chances.

Fortune favoured him, however. He very soon discovered a Wynn Carrados living at Richmond, and, better still, further search failed to unearth another. There was, apparently, only one householder at all events of that name in the neighbourhood of London. He jotted down the address and set out for Richmond.

The house was some distance from the station, Mr. Carlyle learned. He took a taxicab and drove, dismissing the vehicle at the gate. He prided himself on his power of observation and the accuracy of the deductions which resulted from it—a detail of his business. "It's nothing more than using one's eyes and putting two and two together," he would modestly declare, when he wished to be deprecatory rather than impressive, and by the time he had reached the front door of "The Turrets" he had formed some opinion of the position and tastes of the man who lived there.

A man-servant admitted Mr. Carlyle and took in his card—his private card with the bare request for an interview that would not detain Mr. Carrados for ten minutes. Luck still favoured him; Mr. Carrados was at home and would see him at once. The servant, the hall through which they passed, and the room into which he was shown, all contributed something to the deductions which the quietly observant gentleman was half unconsciously recording.

"Mr. Carlyle," announced the servant.

The room was a library or study. The only occupant, a man of about Carlyle's own age, had been using a typewriter up to the moment of his visitor's entrance. He now turned and stood up with an expression of formal courtesy.

"It's very good of you to see me at this hour," apologized the caller.

The conventional expression of Mr. Carrados's face changed a little.

"Surely my man has got your name wrong?" he exclaimed. "Isn't it Louis Calling?"

The visitor stopped short and his agreeable smile gave place to a sudden flash of anger or annoyance.

"No, sir," he replied stiffly. "My name is on the card which you have before you."

"I beg your pardon," said Mr. Carrados, with perfect good-humour. "I hadn't seen it. But I used to know a Calling some years ago—at St Michael's."

"St Michael's!" Mr. Carlyle's features underwent another change, no less instant and sweeping than before. "St Michael's! Wynn Carrados? Good heavens! it isn't Max Wynn—old 'Winning' Wynn?"

"A little older and a little fatter—yes," replied Carrados. "I *have* changed my name, you see."

"Extraordinary thing meeting like this," said his visitor, dropping into a chair and staring hard at Mr. Carrados. "I have changed more than my name. How did you recognize me?"

"The voice," replied Carrados. "It took me back to that little smoke-dried attic den of yours where we—"

"My God!" exclaimed Carlyle bitterly, "don't remind me of what we were going to do in those days." He looked round the well-furnished, handsome room and recalled the other signs of wealth that he had noticed. "At all events, you seem fairly comfortable, Wynn."

"I am alternately envied and pitied," replied Carrados, with a placid tolerance of circumstance that seemed characteristic of him. "Still, as you say, I am fairly comfortable."

"Envied, I can understand. But why are you pitied?"

"Because I am blind," was the tranquil reply.

"Blind!" exclaimed Mr. Carlyle, using his own eyes superlatively. "Do you mean—literally blind?"

"Literally. . . . I was riding along a bridle-path through a wood about a dozen years ago with a friend. He was in front. At one point a twig sprang back—you know how easily a thing like that happens. It just flicked my eye—nothing to think twice about."

"And that blinded you?"

"Yes, ultimately. It's called amaurosis."

"I can scarcely believe it. You seem so sure and self-reliant. Your eyes are full of expression—only a little quieter than they used to be. I believe you were typing when I came. . . . Aren't you having me?"

"You miss the dog and the stick?" smiled Carrados. "No; it's a fact."

"What an awful infliction for you, Max. You were always such an impulsive, reckless sort of fellow—never quiet. You must miss such a fearful lot."

"Has anyone else recognized you?" asked Carrados quietly.

"Ah, that was the voice, you said," replied Carlyle.

"Yes; but other people heard the voice as well. Only I had no blundering, self-confident eyes to be hoodwinked."

"That's a rum way of putting it," said Carlyle. "Are your ears never hood-winked, may I ask?"

"Not now. Nor my fingers. Nor any of my other senses that have to look out for themselves."

"Well, well," murmured Mr. Carlyle, cut short in his sympathetic emo-tions. "I'm glad you take it so well. Of course, if you find it an advantage to be blind, old man—" He stopped and reddened. "I beg your pardon," he concluded stiffly.

"Not an advantage perhaps," replied the other thoughtfully. "Still it has com-pensations that one might not think of. A new world to explore, new experiences, new powers awakening; strange new perceptions; life in the fourth dimension. But why do you beg my pardon, Louis?"

"I am an ex-solicitor, struck off in connexion with the falsifying of a trust account, Mr. Carrados," replied Carlyle, rising.

"Sit down, Louis," said Carrados suavely. His face, even his incredibly living eyes, beamed placid good-nature. "The chair on which you will sit, the roof above you, all the comfortable surroundings to which you have so amiably alluded, are the direct result of falsifying a trust account. But do I call you 'Mr. Carlyle' in consequence? Certainly not, Louis."

"I did not falsify the account," cried Carlyle hotly. He sat down, however, and added more quietly: "But why do I tell you all this? I have never spoken of it before."

"Blindness invites confidence," replied Carrados. "We are out of the running—human rivalry ceases to exist. Besides, why shouldn't you? In my case the account *was* falsified."

"Of course that's all bunkum, Max," commented Carlyle. "Still, I appreciate your motive."

"Practically everything I possess was left to me by an American cousin, on the condition that I took the name of Carrados. He made his fortune by an ingenious conspiracy of doctoring the crop reports and unloading favourably in consequence. And I need hardly remind you that the receiver is equally guilty with the thief."

"But twice as safe. I know something of that, Max. . . . Have you any idea what my business is?"

"You shall tell me," replied Carrados.

"I run a private inquiry agency. When I lost my profession I had to do something for a living. This occurred. I dropped my name, changed my appearance and opened an office. I knew the legal side down to the ground and I got a retired Scotland Yard man to organize the outside work."

"Excellent!" cried Carrados. "Do you unearth many murders?"

"No," admitted Mr. Carlyle; "our business lies mostly on the conventional lines among divorce and defalcation."*

"That's a pity," remarked Carrados. "Do you know, Louis, I always had a secret ambition to be a detective myself. I have even thought lately that I might still be able to do something at it if the chance came my way. That makes you smile?"

"Well, certainly, the idea—"

"Yes, the idea of a blind detective—the blind tracking the alert—"

"Of course, as you say, certain faculties are no doubt quickened," Mr. Carlyle hastened to add considerately, "but, seriously, with the exception of an artist, I don't suppose there is any man who is more utterly dependent on his eyes."

---

* Misappropriation of funds.

Whatever opinion Carrados might have held privately, his genial exterior did not betray a shadow of dissent. For a full minute he continued to smoke as though he derived an actual visual enjoyment from the blue sprays that travelled and dispersed across the room. He had already placed before his visitor a box containing cigars of a brand which that gentleman keenly appreciated but generally regarded as unattainable, and the matter-of-fact ease and certainty with which the blind man had brought the box and put it before him had sent a questioning flicker through Carlyle's mind.

"You used to be rather fond of art yourself, Louis," he remarked presently. "Give me your opinion of my latest purchase—the bronze lion on the cabinet there." Then, as Carlyle's gaze went about the room, he added quickly: "No, not that cabinet—the one on your left."

Carlyle shot a sharp glance at his host as he got up, but Carrados's expression was merely benignly complacent. Then he strolled across to the figure.

"Very nice," he admitted. "Late Flemish, isn't it?"

"No. It is a copy of Vidal's 'Roaring lion.'"

"Vidal?"

"A French artist." The voice became indescribably flat. "He, also, had the misfortune to be blind, by the way."

"You old humbug, Max!" shrieked Carlyle, "you've been thinking that out for the last five minutes." Then the unfortunate man bit his lip and turned his back towards his host.

"Do you remember how we used to pile it up on that obtuse ass Sanders and then roast him?" asked Carrados, ignoring the half-smothered exclamation with which the other man had recalled himself.

"Yes," replied Carlyle quietly. "This is very good," he continued, addressing himself to the bronze again. "How ever did he do it?"

"With his hands."

"Naturally. But, I mean, how did he study his model?"

"Also with his hands. He called it 'seeing near.'"

"Even with a lion—handled it?"

"In such cases he required the services of a keeper, who brought the animal to bay while Vidal exercised his own particular gifts. . . . You don't feel inclined to put me on the track of a mystery, Louis?"

Unable to regard this request as anything but one of old Max's unquenchable pleasantries, Mr. Carlyle was on the point of making a suitable reply when a sudden thought caused him to smile knowingly. Up to that point he had,

374 | ERNEST BRAMAH

indeed, completely forgotten the object of his visit. Now that he remembered the doubtful Dionysius and Mr. Baxter's recommendation he immediately assumed that some mistake had been made. Either Max was not the Wynn Carrados he had been seeking or else the dealer had been misinformed; for although his host was wonderfully expert in the face of his misfortune, it was inconceivable that he could decide the genuineness of a coin without seeing it. The opportunity seemed a good one of getting even with Carrados by taking him at his word.

"Yes," he accordingly replied, with crisp deliberation, as he recrossed the room; "yes, I will, Max. Here is the clue to what seems to be a rather remarkable fraud." He put the tetradrachm into his host's hand. "What do you make of it?"

For a few seconds Carrados handled the piece with the delicate manipulation of his finger-tips while Carlyle looked on with a self-appreciative grin. Then with equal gravity the blind man weighed the coin in the balance of his hand. Finally he touched it with his tongue.

"Well?" demanded the other.

"Of course I have not much to go on, and if I was more fully in your confidence I might come to another conclusion—"

"Yes, yes," interposed Carlyle, with amused encouragement.

"Then I should advise you to arrest the parlourmaid, Nina Brun, communicate with the police authorities of Padua for particulars of the career of Helene Brunesi, and suggest to Lord Seastoke that he should return to London to see what further depredations have been made in his cabinet."

Mr. Carlyle's groping hand sought and found a chair, on to which he dropped blankly. His eyes were unable to detach themselves for a single moment from the very ordinary spectacle of Mr. Carrados's mildly benevolent face, while the sterilized ghost of his now forgotten amusement still lingered about his features.

"Good heavens!" he managed to articulate, "how do you know?"

"Isn't that what you wanted of me?" asked Carrados suavely.

"Don't humbug, Max," said Carlyle severely. "This is no joke." An undefined mistrust of his own powers suddenly possessed him in the presence of this mystery. "How do you come to know of Nina Brun and Lord Seastoke?"

"You are a detective, Louis," replied Carrados. "How does one know these things? By using one's eyes and putting two and two together."

Carlyle groaned and flung out an arm petulantly.

"Is it all bunkum, Max? Do you really see all the time—though that doesn't go very far towards explaining it."

"Like Vidal, I see very well—at close quarters," replied Carrados, lightly running a forefinger along the inscription on the tetradrachm. "For longer range I keep another pair of eyes. Would you like to test them?"

Mr. Carlyle's assent was not very gracious; it was, in fact, faintly sulky. He was suffering the annoyance of feeling distinctly unimpressive in his own department; but he was also curious.

"The bell is just behind you, if you don't mind," said his host. "Parkinson will appear. You might take note of him while he is in."

The man who had admitted Mr. Carlyle proved to be Parkinson.

"This gentleman is Mr. Carlyle, Parkinson," explained Carrados the moment the man entered. "You will remember him for the future?"

Parkinson's apologetic eye swept the visitor from head to foot, but so lightly and swiftly that it conveyed to that gentleman the comparison of being very deftly dusted.

"I will endeavour to do so, sir," replied Parkinson; turning again to his master.

"I shall be at home to Mr. Carlyle whenever he calls. That is all."

"Very well, sir."

"Now, Louis," remarked Mr. Carrados briskly, when the door had closed again, "you have had a good opportunity of studying Parkinson. What is he like?"

"In what way?"

"I mean as a matter of description. I am a blind man—I haven't seen my servant for twelve years—what idea can you give me of him? I asked you to notice."

"I know you did, but your Parkinson is the sort of man who has very little about him to describe. He is the embodiment of the ordinary. His height is about average—"

"Five feet nine," murmured Carrados. "Slightly above the mean."

"Scarcely noticeably so. Clean-shaven. Medium brown hair. No particularly marked features. Dark eyes. Good teeth."

"False," interposed Carrados. "The teeth—not the statement."

"Possibly," admitted Mr. Carlyle. "I am not a dental expert and I had no opportunity of examining Mr. Parkinson's mouth in detail. But what is the drift of all this?"

"His clothes?"

"Oh, just the ordinary evening dress of a valet. There is not much room for variety in that."

"You noticed, in fact, nothing special by which Parkinson could be identified?"

"Well, he wore an unusually broad gold ring on the little finger of the left hand."

"But that is removable. And yet Parkinson has an ineradicable mole—a small one, I admit—on his chin. And you a human sleuth-hound. Oh, Louis!"

"At all events," retorted Carlyle, writhing a little under this good-humoured satire, although it was easy enough to see in it Carrados's affectionate intention—"at all events, I dare say I can give as good a description of Parkinson as he can give of me."

"That is what we are going to test. Ring the bell again."

"Seriously?"

"Quite. I am trying my eyes against yours. If I can't give you fifty out of a hundred I'll renounce my private detectorial ambition for ever."

"It isn't quite the same," objected Carlyle, but he rang the bell.

"Come in and close the door, Parkinson," said Carrados when the man appeared. "Don't look at Mr. Carlyle again—in fact, you had better stand with your back towards him, he won't mind. Now describe to me his appearance as you observed it."

Parkinson tendered his respectful apologies to Mr. Carlyle for the liberty he was compelled to take, by the deferential quality of his voice.

"Mr. Carlyle, sir, wears patent leather boots of about size seven and very little used. There are five buttons, but on the left boot one button—the third up—is missing, leaving loose threads and not the more usual metal fastener. Mr. Carlyle's trousers, sir, are of a dark material, a dark grey line of about a quarter of an inch width on a darker ground. The bottoms are turned permanently up and are, just now, a little muddy, if I may say so."

"Very muddy," interposed Mr. Carlyle generously. "It is a wet night, Parkinson."

"Yes, sir; very unpleasant weather. If you will allow me, sir, I will brush you in the hall. The mud is dry now, I notice. Then, sir," continued Parkinson, reverting to the business in hand, "there are dark green cashmere hose. A curb-pattern key-chain passes into the left-hand trouser pocket."

From the visitor's nether garments the photographic-eyed Parkinson proceeded to higher ground, and with increasing wonder Mr. Carlyle listened to the faithful catalogue of his possessions. His fetter-and-link albert of gold and platinum was minutely described. His spotted blue ascot, with its gentlemanly pearl scarf pin, was set forth, and the fact that the buttonhole in the left lapel of his morning coat showed signs of use was duly noted. What Parkinson saw he recorded but he made no deductions. A handkerchief carried in the cuff of the right sleeve was simply that to him and not an indication that Mr. Carlyle was, indeed, left-handed.

But a more delicate part of Parkinson's undertaking remained. He approached it with a double cough.

"As regards Mr. Carlyle's personal appearance; sir—"

"No, enough!" cried the gentleman concerned hastily. "I am more than satisfied. You are a keen observer, Parkinson."

"I have trained myself to suit my master's requirements, sir," replied the man. He looked towards Mr. Carrados, received a nod and withdrew.

Mr. Carlyle was the first to speak.

"That man of yours would be worth five pounds a week to me, Max," he remarked thoughtfully. "But, of course—"

"I don't think that he would take it," replied Carrados, in a voice of equally detached speculation. "He suits me very well. But you have the chance of using his services—indirectly."

"You still mean that—seriously?"

"I notice in you a chronic disinclination to take me seriously, Louis. It is really—to an Englishman—almost painful. Is there something inherently comic about me or the atmosphere of The Turrets?"

"No, my friend," replied Mr. Carlyle, "but there is something essentially prosperous. That is what points to the improbable. Now what is it?"

"It might be merely a whim, but it is more than that," replied Carrados. "It is, well, partly vanity, partly *ennui*, partly"—certainly there was something more nearly tragic in his voice than comic now—"partly hope."

Mr. Carlyle was too tactful to pursue the subject.

"Those are three tolerable motives," he acquiesced. "I'll do anything you want, Max, on one condition."

"Agreed. And it is?"

"That you tell me how you knew so much of this affair." He tapped the silver coin which lay on the table near them. "I am not easily flabbergasted," he added.

"You won't believe that there is nothing to explain—that it was purely second-sight?"

"No," replied Carlyle tersely; "I won't."

"You are quite right. And yet the thing is very simple."

"They always are—when you know," soliloquized the other. "That's what makes them so confoundedly difficult when you don't."

"Here is this one then. In Padua, which seems to be regaining its old reputation as the birthplace of spurious antiques, by the way, there lives an ingenious craftsman named Pietro Stelli. This simple soul, who possesses a talent not inferior to that of Cavino at his best, has for many years turned his hand to the not unprofitable occupation of forging rare Greek and Roman coins. As a collector and student of certain Greek colonials and a specialist in forgeries I have been familiar with Stelli's workmanship for years. Latterly he seems to have come under the influence of an international crook called—at the moment—Dompierre, who soon saw a way of utilizing Stelli's genius on a royal scale. Helene Brunesi, who in private life is—and really is, I believe—Madame Dompierre, readily lent her services to the enterprise."

"Quite so," nodded Mr. Carlyle, as his host paused.

"You see the whole sequence, of course?"

"Not exactly—not in detail," confessed Mr. Carlyle.

"Dompierre's idea was to gain access to some of the most celebrated cabinets of Europe and substitute Stelli's fabrications for the genuine coins. The princely collection of rarities that he would thus amass might be difficult to dispose of safely but I have no doubt that he had matured his plans. Helene, in the person of Nina Brun, an Anglicised French parlourmaid—a part which she fills to perfection—was to obtain wax impressions of the most valuable pieces and to make the exchange when the counterfeits reached her. In this way it was obviously hoped that the fraud would not come to light until long after the real coins had been sold, and I gather that she has already done her work successfully in several houses. Then, impressed by her excellent references and capable manner, my housekeeper engaged her, and for a few weeks she went about her duties here. It was fatal to this detail of the scheme, however, that I have the misfortune to be blind. I am told that Helene has so innocently angelic a face as to disarm suspicion, but I was incapable of being impressed and that good material was thrown away. But one morning my material fingers—which, of course, knew nothing of Helene's angelic face—discovered an unfamiliar touch about the surface of my favourite Euclideas, and, although there was doubtless nothing to be seen, my critical sense of smell reported that wax had been recently pressed against it. I began to make discreet inquiries and in the meantime my cabinets went to the local bank for safety. Helene countered by receiving a telegram from Angiers, calling her to the death-bed of her aged mother. The aged mother succumbed; duty compelled Helene to remain at the side of her stricken patriarchal father, and doubtless The Turrets was written off the syndicate's operations as a bad debt."

"Very interesting," admitted Mr. Carlyle; "but at the risk of seeming obtuse"—his manner had become delicately chastened—"I must say that I fail to trace the inevitable connexion between Nina Brun and this particular forgery—assuming that it is a forgery."

"Set your mind at rest about that, Louis," replied Carrados. "It is a forgery, and it is a forgery that none but Pietro Stelli could have achieved. That is the essential connexion. Of course, there are accessories. A private detective coming urgently to see me with a notable tetradrachm in his pocket, which he announces to be the clue to a remarkable fraud—well, really, Louis, one scarcely needs to be blind to see through that."

"And Lord Seastoke? I suppose you happened to discover that Nina Brun had gone there?"

"No, I cannot claim to have discovered that, or I should certainly have warned him at once when I found out—only recently—about the gang. As a matter of fact, the last information I had of Lord Seastoke was a line in yesterday's *Morning Post* to the effect that he was still at Cairo. But many of these pieces—" He brushed his finger almost lovingly across the vivid chariot race that embellished the reverse of the coin, and broke off to remark: "You really ought to take up the subject, Louis. You have no idea how useful it might prove to you some day."

"I really think I must," replied Carlyle grimly. "Two hundred and fifty pounds the original of this cost, I believe."

"Cheap, too; it would make five hundred pounds in New York to-day. As I was saying, many are literally unique. This gem by Kimon is—here is his signature, you see; Peter is particularly good at lettering—and as I handled the genuine tetradrachm about two years ago, when Lord Seastoke exhibited it at a meeting of our society in Albemarle Street, there is nothing at all wonderful in my being able to fix the locale of your mystery. Indeed, I feel that I ought to apologize for it all being so simple."

"I think," remarked Mr. Carlyle, critically examining the loose threads on his left boot, "that the apology on that head would be more appropriate from me."

ACKNOWLEDGMENTS

I would like to thank the following people, without whom this book would never have been possible:

Lawrence Ellsworth's *Big Book of Swashbuckling Adventure* was the inspiration behind this and my other anthologies. He generously introduced me to Philip Turner, my agent, who taught me how to create a solid book proposal. I am indebted to both.

William Claiborne Hancock and the rest of the staff at Pegasus Books have, as always, been a pleasure to work with. My particular gratitude goes to Daniel O'Connor and Maria Fernandez for editing and production, and Bowen Dunnan and Katie McGuire for promotion and publicity.

Thanks, too, to Linda Biagi of Biagi Literary Management for helping to bring my books to foreign audiences, and to Meg Sherman at W. W. Norton for making sure I always have books to sign at book signings!

I am pleased and honored that Leslie S. Klinger agreed to provide a preface for this book, and gratified by his kind comments on an early draft. Anything bearing his name is highly recommended to readers interested in learning more about Holmes and his era in the history of detective fiction.

Thanks are also due to:

Jamie Paige Davis, my wife, my love, my friend, and my fellow author, who somehow manages to keep putting up with me;

Basil Rathbone, Jeremy Brett, and all the other great actors who have played Holmes on screen, sparking my interest in the character, detective fiction, and the period;

British television in general for its tireless commitment to quality detective stories from all periods of history, featuring too many great actors and great characters to name;

Pete Knifton, renowned fantasy artist and erudite Holmesian, for decades of conversation on genre fiction and much besides, first over after-work beers in Nottingham and now online;

And, of course, the writers and their detectives, from the original to the derivative, from the earnest to the pastiche, and from all parts of the world, who attended the birth of detective fiction as a genre.